Addicted

A Falcon Pointe Novel

Jennifer Harrison

Visit www.jenniferharrisonwrites.com

Cover Design: Hayling Bookstorm Ltd Services

Amazon:

Goodreads: https://www.goodreads.com/jenniferharrison
Instagram: https://www.instagram.com/jennifer.harrison.writes/

Facebook: https://www.facebook.com/jennifer.harrison.writes

TikTok: https://www.tiktok.com/@jennifer..harrison

Author's Note

Addicted addresses sensitive and potentially triggering topics that may be distressing for some readers. These include:

- **Childhood Abuse** (Sexual, Physical, Emotional – referenced, not shown on page)

- **Sexual Assault** (referenced, not shown on page)

- **Addiction and Substance Abuse**

- **Self-Harm**

- **Emotional Abuse and Manipulation**

- **Trauma and PTSD**

- **Religious Trauma**

Please take care when reading and remember that you are not alone. If you feel overwhelmed or need help, it is okay to take breaks, pause, or seek support. Your emotional well-being comes first.

Resources & Support

If you or someone you know is struggling with issues related to the topics discussed in this book, there are resources available. Please don't hesitate to reach out for support.

National Domestic Violence Hotline

Call: 1-800-799-SAFE (1-800-799-7233)

Text: "START" to 88788

Website: https://www.thehotline.org

RAINN - Rape, Abuse & Incest National Network

Call: 1-800-656-HOPE (1-800-656-4673)

Website: https://www.rainn.org

National Suicide Prevention Lifeline

Call: 1-800-273-TALK (1-800-273-8255)

Website: https://suicidepreventionlifeline.org

Self-Injury Support

Website: https://www.selfinjury.com

Helpline: 1-800-DONT-CUT (1-800-366-8288)

Substance Abuse and Mental Health Services Administration (SAMHSA)

National Helpline: 1-800-662-HELP (1-800-662-4357)

Website: https://www.samhsa.gov

Crisis Text Line

Text HOME to 741741 for free, 24/7 confidential support

Website: https://www.crisistextline.org

Soundtrack

1. A Thousand Miles - Vanessa Carlton

2. Pillowtalk - Zayn

3. Weatherman - Zach Hood

4. Man! I Feel Like a Woman - Shania Twain

5. Daphne Blue - The Band CAMINO

6. Change For You - Friday Pilots Club

7. Dopamine - Zach Hood

8. I'll Be Damned - Gavn!

9. Troubled Waters - Alex Warren

10. Sugar Sweet - Benson Boone

11. Espresso - Sabrina Carpenter

12. Holding On - Bailey Zimmerman

13. Cold - Jessie Murph

14. Thinking out Loud - Ed Sheeran

For the quiet ones and the wild ones. For the ones who burned too brightly and the ones who loved them anyway.

Whitney

I've always lived for the rush - the thrill of the unknown, the freedom to chase whatever adventure comes next. But when my reckless life caught up with me, I found myself in Falcon Pointe, standing face-to-face with my estranged brother and the demons I've spent years running from. What I didn't expect was Grady.

Grady's my brother's best friend - quiet, steady, and the complete opposite of everything I am. He's a man who doesn't take risks, who plays it safe. So, when he's forced to babysit me, I can't help but feel the pull. His calmness, his kindness, the way he listens... It's like I'm finally able to breathe. But the more I get to know him, the harder it is to keep my distance. I can't stop wanting him. I've always kept people at arm's length, but Grady... he makes me want to lean in.

Grady

I like my life predictable. Quiet. Safe. So, when Jackson's little sister shows up in town, I'm stuck with her. She's trouble. Wild, fearless, and a million miles from my comfort zone. But the more I'm around her, the more I realize there's something about Whitney that pulls me in.

She's everything I'm not. She's chaos where I'm calm. She's fiery, and I'm... well, I'm not. But I can't seem to help myself. Every time I try to push her away, she gets under my skin, and before I know it, I'm doing things I never thought I would. I'm starting to feel something I didn't expect, something I'm not sure I know how to handle. The worst part? I'm falling for her, and that's the last thing I need.

Prologue

Whitney

Age 16

I swallowed thickly, and adjusted my backpack over my shoulder as I passed Mr. Robbins' truck in the driveway. A chill ran down my spine; *what was he doing home?*

Home. That was a joke. This place wasn't my home. My real home was long gone, buried beneath a pile of rubble, or whatever was left of it after tornadoes ripped through and killed our parents. Jackson and I were lucky to be alive. Or at least that's what people always said.

Thinking about Jackson made my chest ache. I hadn't spoken to him since they split us up, five years ago. Apparently the only available foster homes at the time could take one, but not both of us. I kind of thought he'd come for me when he turned eighteen, but that was four years ago. Four years and three foster homes. *Did he even think about me anymore?*

I shoved thoughts of my brother aside as I crept up to the house. Something had to be wrong if Mr. Robbins was home. He was a long-haul trucker, home one weekend a month. And this wasn't it.

I cracked the front door just enough to peek inside before pushing it all the way open. The house appeared to be empty. I breathed out a sigh of relief and stepped lightly down the hall until I reached my room. I dropped my backpack, then froze.

Mr. Robbins was already there, sitting on my bed, legs spread, his eyes like black ice.

"M-Mr. Robbins," I stammered. "W-what are you doing here?"

"Shut the door, girl."

"I-I don't think that's a g-good idea."

He stood, his hands dropping to his belt. "Don't sass me. Shut the damn door. Now!"

My heart slammed in my chest as I obeyed. His fingers slipped the cracked leather through his belt loops. I wanted to run, but where would I go? I'd tried that before. They always caught me, and every home got worse after that.

"Get on the bed," his tongue darted out to lick his lips as his gaze dragged down my body.

"Mr. Robbins, I-I don't think..."

"You're not here to think, girl!" his hand swung out, striking me across the face.

"Ah!" I cried out, one hand flying to my cheek as blood trickled from the corner of my mouth.

"On the bed," he growled. He yanked at my shirt collar, tearing the fabric and shoving me backward.

I didn't fight. I knew what that got me - broken bones. Or worse. I stripped, laid back and closed my eyes, and sang "A Thousand Miles" by Vanessa Carlton in my head, waiting for it to be over.

"How was school?" Mrs. Robbins asked at dinner.

Myles, their actual son, shrugged, and Mike, my foster brother, muttered under his breath, the words too low to make out.

"Excuse me?" Mr. Robbins snapped, "speak up, boy."

He'd lost his job a week ago, and had been snapping at everyone since.

Mike cleared his throat. "It was good."

Mr. Robbins turned to me. "How about you, Whitney? Still need help with that extra credit assignment?"

I flinched. That "extra credit" assignment was his excuse for slipping into my room at night. "No, sir."

"We'll see about that," he said with a wink.

"May I be excused?" I pushed away from the table, not bothering to wait for a response.

I rinsed my plate in the sink, then bolted to my room, yanking out my phone as I went. I fired off a quick text to my boyfriend, Eric.

> **Me:** I can't stay here anymore. I don't know what to do

Eric responded almost immediately.

> **Eric:** You're stronger than you give yourself credit for, baby

> **Me:** You don't understand. There's something I haven't told you

Eric: You can tell me anything

Me: Can I come stay with you

Eric: What about school?

Me: I don't care about school. I need to get out of here. I want to be with you

Eric: Pack a bag, baby. I'll be right there

Me: Park down the street. Text me when you're close. They can't know I'm leaving. He'd never let me go

Eric: Okay. But we're talking later

Me: Okay

I dumped out my backpack, replacing my school books with clothes and anything I could call mine. It wasn't much.

I pressed my ear to the door and listened carefully. I could still hear faint chatter coming from the dining room. I wedged my desk chair under the door knob and crossed the room to the window and slid it open.

I had been sneaking out for a few months now, so the screen was loose and easy to remove. I popped it out and dropped my backpack on the ground, just outside. With one last look, I grabbed my stuffed bunny, the only thing I had left from my life before, and climbed through the window. The second I got the text from Eric that he was close, I went into my phone settings, initiated a full system restore, and tossed the phone back through the window. I mentally high-fived myself when it landed on the bed.

I pulled the window shut the best I could from outside and replaced the screen.

It took less than two minutes to reach Eric. He sat idling on his red 2014 Kawasaki Ninja, and held out a helmet as I approached. "Hey, baby."

I took the helmet from his outstretched hand. "Thanks for picking me up." I leaned in and pressed a kiss to his cheek.

"Of course. Where to?" he asked, eyeing my backpack as I pulled the helmet on.

"Can we just go home?"

His eyebrow arched, "You're sure about this?"

"One hundred percent. I'm done with this, with them." I climbed on and wrapped my arms around his waist. "I just want to be with you."

"Let's go home." He squeezed my thigh reassuringly and took off down the street, easily doing double the speed limit.

My heart thundered. The wind whipped against my face.

Halfway to the highway, I let go of his waist and threw my arms into the air.

"WOOOO!"

He laughed, body vibrating against mine.

I was finally free.

Chapter 1

Whitney

Present

I wedged my phone between my shoulder and ear, fumbling through my purse for my keys.

Our apartment wasn't in the greatest neighborhood, but it was cheap. Cheap enough to be manageable, when we could pay the rent. And when we couldn't... I shook the thought off. I wasn't doing that anymore. Not for anyone.

"Relax, Eric," I said, finally closing my hands around the keys. "I already took care of it."

"No, baby, please tell me you didn't."

My stomach clenched. His voice wasn't just worried, it was scared.

"Why? What's going on?"

"Where are you right now?" His voice dropped, tense and urgent.

Something was off. The hallway was quiet, too quiet. The scent of burnt coffee and mildew usually clung to the air like a bad habit, but today it smelled... different.

"I'm just getting home," I said, more to reassure myself than him.

"Whit... don't go inside. Get back in the car. I..."

The door to our apartment swung open before I could even insert the key.

A man filled the frame. Tall, built like a linebacker with close-cropped hair and dark eyes that didn't blink.

"Welcome home," he said, a slow smile spreading across his face.

My breath caught in my throat and I carefully maneuvered my keys between my fingers like I learned in middle school self defense. "Who are you?"

Eric's voice screamed through the phone now. "Run, Whit! Get out of there!" But before I could react, a hand shot out, fast as a snake, and snatched the phone from my ear

"Eric," he said smoothly, lifting the phone to his own ear. "You were warned."

He glanced over his shoulder into the apartment before turning back to me. "I'll give you twenty-four hours. You don't pay, we collect... from her."

He stepped back inside.

I took a step back, then another.

But I didn't see the second man until I slammed into him.

"Going somewhere, sweetheart?"

I tried to twist away, but he grabbed my wrist and wrenched it. A sickening pop rang in my ears, followed by a wave of pain that exploded through my arm, radiating down to my fingers like fire, making it impossible to focus on anything but the agony.

"Aaah!"

The first guy peeked back through the door. "Bring her in."

"No... please..."

The second man dragged me over the threshold like I weighed nothing. I kicked at him, but he only laughed and shoved me to the floor.

I curled around my broken wrist, nausea thick in my throat. The carpet scratched against my cheek. I couldn't breathe, couldn't think.

The man crouched next to me, holding up the phone, now on speaker, like a trophy.

"Twenty-four hours, loverboy," he said. "Tell your girl goodbye."

Eric's voice cracked on the other end. "Don't you touch her! Whitney, baby. I'm coming! I'm coming for you!"

The man hung up and hurled the phone into the wall.

"You're being awful quiet," he sneered, leaning closer, "for someone about to get fucked. Your boyfriend sell you often?"

I turned my head, eyes burning. "You don't know anything."

He chuckled. "I know enough. Your boyfriend owes Marco money, and you're the collateral."

I lunged toward the door.

A third man stormed in. He yanked me backward by the hair, then forced me onto my knees.

"Get off me!" I dug my nails into his face - hard - dragging them down his cheek until I felt warm, wet blood.

"You bitch!" he roared, slapping me so hard my ears rang. But I saw the damage. Four angry red lines down his jaw. He'd remember me.

Another voice, cruel and calm, spoke above me. "On your knees."

"No."

Pain burst through me as my legs were kicked out from under me. I hit the floor, hard. Then hands were on me - tearing, grabbing, pressing.

I squeezed my eyes shut and went still.

And like every time before, I went away.

"A Thousand Miles."

My mom's favorite song.

The wind tugged at her dress as she twirled barefoot in the soft grass, arms outstretched toward the old boom box on the car trunk. The sun dappled her face, her laughter like music in the air, and I could almost feel the joy radiating from her like warmth. I felt safe there. I was whole.

"This is the greatest song ever," she said, her eyes dancing.

Jackson laid on the picnic blanket, arms crossed behind his head, pretending to be annoyed. But I saw the smile twitching at his lips.

I was safe there.

I was whole.

I stayed in that memory until the screaming stopped, and the silence came back for me.

Chapter 2

Grady

"I'm telling you, Coach Prime is taking us all the way this year."

I rinsed a glass and shot Jackson a look over the bar. "You said that last year."

"Yeah, and I wasn't wrong. He flipped the whole damn culture. Sold out Folsom. Got ESPN cameras crawling over Boulder like it's Bama."

"They still went 4-8," I said, setting the glass on the drying rack. "And that O-line couldn't block a sneeze."

Jackson folded his arms. "Jeez, Grady, could you be any more negative?"

"I'm not negative. I'm realistic."

"You think rebuilding CU happens overnight?"

"No. But you don't win games with flash and Instagram reels."

"It's not just flash. Prime's bringing in real talent. Top transfers. Kids who want to play for him."

I leaned back and gave him a look. "And yet they're still getting smoked by teams with less hype and twice the discipline."

That shut him up, for a second. But I saw the shift in his expression. The tightness in his jaw.

"You know it means more to you than the scoreboard," I said.

Jackson stared at the floor. "I was supposed to go pro. Junior year at CU, I was peaking. The scouts were looking at me, I could taste it. Then that fucking hit." He exhaled through his nose. "ACL snapped like a twig. One second I'm living the high life, the next I'm out."

I nodded, tossing the towel over my shoulder. "They screwed you."

"It is what it is." His voice dropped, low and serious. "So yeah, I believe in Prime. Because he's giving those kids something I never got. A shot to come back from the bottom."

The bar phone rang. Jackson turned, already halfway across the room. "Hold that thought," he muttered.

I went back to wiping the bar, but my eyes stayed on him.

"What hospital?" His voice sharpened. "You're sure? Is she going to be okay?"

I froze.

"Don't let her leave," he said quickly. "And don't let anyone into her room. I'm on my way."

He hung up and turned around, face pale.

"What the hell happened?"

"It's Whitney," he said. "She's in the hospital."

I hadn't seen him look like that in years. Pale. Gutted. Like his insides had gone hollow.

My stomach dropped. "I thought you hadn't talked to her?"

"Not really. We spoke once after she got arrested last year, but... I didn't know where she was until now."

"You going to get her?"

"Yeah. I have to."

"Where is she?"

"Utah. Salt Lake. LDS Hospital or something."

I nodded. "You need anything from me?"

"Yeah." He looked around the empty room, then back at me. "I need you to watch the bar. Just until I get back."

"Done."

He clapped me on the shoulder. "Thanks, man."

A cool burst of air swept through the open door just before it thudded shut.

Of course. Emily.

"Who was arrested?" she asked, sliding onto a stool like she hadn't just interrupted something important.

Jackson stiffened beside me. "None of your business."

Her eyes flicked between us. "Okay, jeez. Just asking."

Jackson turned to me. "I need to hit the road."

"You bringing her back here?" I asked.

"Yeah," he said without hesitation. "She needs a place to go. And I'm not letting her stay with that asshole boyfriend."

"Who's staying here?" Emily asked, already pouting.

"His sister," I said carefully.

Her eyebrows shot up. "Wait - you have a sister?"

"Don't start," Jackson said, his tone flat and unamused.

"I'm just surprised. You never mentioned her."

"Because it's none of your goddamn business," he snapped.

"Jesus, hostile much?" She turned to me. "Why's he always like this with me?"

I sighed. "Can we not do this right now?"

"I'm serious," she said, crossing her arms and pushing her chest out. "I'm trying to be part of your life, Grady. That includes your friends, family or not."

Jackson scoffed. "You don't give a damn about my life. If you did, you wouldn't treat Grady like he's disposable."

"Excuse me?" she blinked, leaning over the bar, her blouse strategically unbuttoned, eyes wide and fake-sweet. She knew exactly how to look harmless, right before she tore you apart.

Jackson didn't flinch. He never did.

He'd always had that quarterback presence - broad shoulders, tall, lean, the kind of build that looked like it belonged under stadium lights. But it wasn't his size that made people take a step back. It was the weight behind his words when he was done being polite.

"You heard me. You walk in here like you didn't cheat on him - what, twice? Three times? And still expect him to jump when you snap your fingers?"

"That was a long time ago," she said, looking at me for backup. "We've moved past that, haven't we, Grady? Or are you still holding on to the past?"

I looked down at the towel in my hands.

Jackson stepped closer. "No, *you* moved past it. Grady just doesn't know how to leave."

Her expression hardened. "Wow. You really think I'm the villain here?"

"You're not the villain," I muttered, still not meeting her eyes. "But you're not helping either."

"Unbelievable," she said, pushing off the stool. "You know what? I'm not doing this tonight."

"Good," Jackson said. "Get out."

"Grady, are you seriously going to let him talk to me like that?"

I scratched at the scruff along my jaw and pushed my hair back from my face. Too long again. Emily liked it this way, said it made me look like a brooding rockstar. But it mostly just got in the way.

I looked at her.

And for once, I didn't feel anything. No heat. No guilt. Just a dull ache in my chest.

"He's not wrong."

Emily froze, stunned.

"Call me later," she said finally, before storming out.

The door slammed.

The silence after Emily left felt heavier than I expected. I wasn't sure if I was relieved or just... empty. I should've kicked her out long ago, but somehow, it always felt easier to keep letting her stay.

Jackson didn't speak for a moment. Then he exhaled hard. "You okay?"

I nodded slowly. "Yeah."

"You don't have to keep doing that, man. Letting her tear you down to feel tall."

"I know," I said. And I did. But knowing didn't make it easier to walk away.

"Bringing her back here is going to complicate things."

"Good," he said. "Maybe it's time for a little complication."

Chapter 3

Whitney

"*A* Thousand Miles."

My mom's favorite song.

The old boom box sat on the trunk of the car, tinny speakers just loud enough to fill the warm spring air. She danced barefoot in the grass, twirling like she didn't care who saw.

"This is the greatest song ever written," she said, grinning. "I don't care what anyone says."

Jackson lay on the picnic blanket, arms crossed behind his head, pretending to be annoyed. We all knew he would rather be with Abby, but he humored us anyway.

I was eleven.

The grass tickled my legs. My mom's dress billowed. My brother laughed.

The world was good.

I hold onto that day like it's stitched into my skin, because it was the last time we were all together. The last time everything felt untouched.

And then the wind shifted.

The sky, still blue, suddenly felt *wrong*.

A low, hollow hum began to rise - not the music, not the breeze. Something deeper. More primal.

Jackson sat up, squinting toward the horizon. "Is that a...?"

My mom stopped mid-spin. Her face changed.

Then came the sirens.

She reached for me. "Time to go, baby. Now."

"But I want to..."

"Now."

I didn't want to. I remember that. I wanted to stay, to keep the moment from ending.

But it ended anyway.

The music warped. The colors smeared. The dream fractured.

The siren grew louder. Closer...

Until it wasn't a siren at all. It was a beeping.

I jolted awake.

Everything was too bright.

A white ceiling. Harsh lights. The sour scent of antiseptic.

Hospital.

I was on my back, stiff and heavy like I'd been filled with wet cement. My wrist was wrapped tight in a cast. My lips were cracked. Every breath scraped down my throat.

I turned my head, slowly, and winced. A nurse stood near the monitors, writing something on a chart like it was just another day.

I blinked again, hoping I could fall back asleep, crawl back into the grass and sunlight and music.

But the pain was still there.

I couldn't breathe. My chest felt tight, like I was being squeezed in a vice, each shallow breath like dragging a needle through my lungs

I stared at the sterile white ceiling and felt the weight of the years, the distance from that sunny day with my mom and dad and Jackson. It felt like a different lifetime now. I was so far from that little girl, from that safety, that it was hard to remember what it felt like to trust anyone again. "You're safe now."

I hadn't realized I was crying until I felt a hand on mine. Gentle. Gloved.

The nurse. She had kind eyes and a voice like gravel.

"You're in LDS Hospital. You've been here two days."

I opened my mouth, but the words didn't come. Only a rasp.

"Don't strain yourself. You've been through..." Her mouth tightened. "You're lucky to be alive."

I closed my eyes. I didn't feel lucky.

"There's someone here to see you," she said after a pause. "Detective Madsen. He's with the Salt Lake Police Department. He wants to ask you some questions. About what happened at your apartment."

My chest tightened.

The apartment.

The man in the doorway. The one I scratched. The phone flying against the wall. The attack.

"Do I have to?" My voice sounded small. Raw.

"Not right now," she said gently. "But he's waiting outside. He's going to ask eventually." She patted my shoulder, "You don't have to talk to him alone if you don't want to. I can ask someone from victim services to sit in."

"Who called the cops?" I whispered.

"Anonymous tip," she said. "Whoever it was hung up without a name."

"Tell the detective..." I started, but the words jammed in my throat.

What could I tell him? That I didn't remember all of it? That I let it happen? That I knew I should've run... but I didn't?

"Tell him to give me a few minutes."

I stared down at my hands, folded in my lap the best I could. Not only was my left wrist broken and stuck in an ugly blue cast, but my right eye was nearly swollen shut. My head was pounding, my arm was throbbing, and don't even get me started on my leg. That big-ass mother fucker broke my leg. All I wanted was some vicodin, some percocet, or really, some oxy... I could seriously go for oxy.

Too bad I gave up drugs when we moved to Salt Lake. Six months sober didn't seem like that long, but the idea of having to start all over again was enough to make me bite my tongue.

No one claps for you when you stay clean. They just wait for you to mess up again.

I didn't notice the man until he cleared his throat. A suit, badge, notebook. Typical.

"Miss Taylor," he said, "I'm Detective Madsen. Salt Lake PD. I know this is a lot, but I need to ask you a few questions."

I looked up into the exasperated face of one of Salt Lake's finest. "I'm sorry, officer, what did you say?"

He sighed, "I know it's hard, but can you remember anything about them? Maybe something in the way they spoke, or the way they moved?"

I started to shake my head, then stopped when a sharp pain pierced my temple. "No. I-I was hit from behind. I didn't see anything."

I'd gotten good at lying to cops. I didn't even flinch anymore.

But somewhere deep down, I hated how easy it was.

"What about sound? Did they say anything?"

"Not that I recall." I inhaled slowly and looked back down at my hands, my left was swollen where it peeked out of the cast, bits of purple just visible around my thumb. "Can I go home now?"

"I'm afraid not. Your apartment is still an active crime scene. We contacted your brother..."

I jerked my head up at that. "My brother?" I haven't spoken to Jackson since he bailed me out of jail last year. God, I was such an idiot back then, and he told me he didn't want to talk to me again until I cleaned my act up. I swallowed thickly. I was clean, but this didn't look good. Not to him. "Wha-what did he say?"

"He *said* what the hell happened, Whit?" A deep voice rumbled from the doorway.

I twisted in the bed, wincing as pain burst from my ribs and my vision blurred at the edges. "Jackson?"

I stared at the man in the doorway, my brother, a practical stranger. I hadn't seen him in over twelve years, yet he somehow looked the same despite his size. He was huge, his sandy brown hair was darker, and his once bright eyes weary. "I got here as soon as I could." His shoulders were wider than I remembered, but he still walked like a quarterback - chest up, eyes steady, like nothing could rattle him. "What happened?"

I started to shrug, then stopped when the pain hit me. "I got jumped, it's no big deal."

"Miss Taylor..." The officer started at the same time Jackson said, "Not a big deal?"

"I'm fine, Jackson!"

"Who did this to you?" Jackson asked, reaching out and gently cupping my cheek as he assessed the damage.

I sighed and closed my eyes. "I don't know who they were."

"They? So there was more than one?" The cop cut in and I cursed myself for saying too much. I wasn't a rat, and I wasn't about to get Eric into more trouble by opening my big mouth.

"When can I go home? I just want to go home."

"Like I said before, your apartment is still an active crime scene..."

"This happened at your apartment?" Jackson interrupted, taking a step back.

"It's not that big of a deal," I insisted. "It's not the greatest neighborhood. We'll get some better locks, it'll be fine."

Jackson shook his head. "No. Not happening. You're coming home with me."

My head whipped up to look at him, and I bit the inside of my cheek as pain roared through me. *Don't let them see your weakness.* "No, I need to go home. I have a job, people who rely on me. I can't just take off. Besides, I don't even know where you live."

"Miss Taylor, I don't believe this was some random attack. It might not be a bad idea..."

"Can I have a minute with my brother," I snapped. "Alone."

The cop blew out a heavy breath and got to his feet. "Sure. I'll check back with you soon."

"Whitney, come on. You know you can't stay here." Jackson started before the cop was even out of the room.

"I can't just leave."

He sat down on the edge of my bed and lightly ran his hand over the ugly cast that covered my right leg. "Just for a little while, until you're back on your feet. We can talk to your work. Give the police some time to find these guys..."

I inhaled deeply and blew it out slowly. "What about Eric?"

"What about him?" Jackson practically growled. "Why are you even with him?"

"That's none of your fucking business," I snapped.

Jackson rolled his eyes, "It is my fucking business when my sister is going to jail or winds up beaten and bloody in a hospital!"

I crossed my arms over my chest, wincing as pain speared through me with the movement. "It's not his fault," I argued, though if I were being honest, it was, at least a little. Especially in this case. Eric promised me he was done gambling after the last time. He didn't mean to get caught up in shit, things just got away from him sometimes.

"Look, I don't want to fight with you. I'm just worried. I don't want anything to happen to you."

I huffed and rolled my eyes. Jackson was good at putting on the big brother act, first last year, after I was arrested for prostitution - which was a complete bullshit charge, and now after all of this. But where was he when I was being abused in the foster system? Where was he when I needed him?

"Can I borrow your phone?"

He studied my face for a moment before sighing and pulling his phone from his pocket and handing it over. I took it and shooed him away. "A little privacy?"

"You've got five minutes."

I waited for the door to snick closed before looking at the phone in my hand. The bastard didn't even bother to unlock it. I stared at the lock screen, and only one password came to mind. 1104, Abby's birthday. It's the code he always used when we were kids, and though I doubt he's seen her since the day we were ripped away from the only home we ever knew, something told me to try it.

"Gotcha!" I cheered when it worked. I quickly dialed Eric's number from memory.

"Hello?"

"Eric, it's me."

"Whit? Baby? Where are you? Are you okay? The apartment is swarming with police, I can't go back there."

If they found him, he'd be arrested. Again. And I'd be alone.

"Shh, I know, it's okay. I'm at the hospital. I'm trying to get out of here, but the cops keep asking me questions."

"Don't answer them. Please baby. Make something up. Lie if you have to. But please... If they find out..."

"I didn't tell them anything, but look. Jackson is here."

"Your brother?"

"Yeah. The cops called him." I sighed, looking up at the closed door. "He wants to take me home with him."

"Shit, baby. As much as I hate to say it, that might not be a bad idea. Get away from here, at least until I can get Marco off my back."

"Eric, what did you do?"

"Don't worry about it, Whit. I'll take care of it."

"I don't want to leave you, Eric."

"I know, baby. But it's temporary. Your brother still live in Colorado?"

I sighed, "I don't know. I think so. But..."

"Please, Whit. Do this. For me? I can't stand the idea of anyone hurting you."

A knock on the door interrupted my train of thought and I found myself giving in. "Promise you'll come for me?"

"I promise. I love you, Whit."

"I love you too. I gotta go."

Jackson shook his head as he crossed the room and held his hand out for his phone. I hung up and gave it back. "When do we leave?"

"How does right now sound?"

Chapter 4

Grady

Few things in life felt better than a woman's body, pressed up against me, her breath warm on my neck, skin soft under my fingers...

But even as my hands slid under Emily's shirt, that familiar voice echoed in the back of my head.

Sinner.

I clenched my jaw, forcing the thoughts away. Not now.

"Grady," Emily gasped, grinding her hips down against me. "Don't stop. Get out of your head."

I froze.

I hated that she always knew when my thoughts wandered. Hated even more that she was usually right.

"I need music," I muttered, desperate for something to drown out the noise in my head.

She stretched over the couch to grab her phone, the shift of her body pulling her shirt tighter across her chest. A moment later, Zayn's "Pillowtalk" filled the room.

Not my first choice, but the beat helped.

I focused on the rhythm as I pulled her top off and let it fall to the floor. Her bra followed. She straddled me and kissed me hard, like she was trying to make me forget.

I almost did.

Then...

"Nice tits."

Emily shrieked and scrambled to cover herself, while I reached for her top and pulled it back down, "Jesus, Jackson!"

My heart was still hammering as I looked up to see him standing in the doorway, arms crossed, scowling like the grim reaper. "You're back earlier than I expected."

Jackson didn't miss a beat. "How many times I gotta tell you. No fucking on the couch?"

"Like that's stopped you before," I chuckled, thinking back to last week when I walked in on him balls deep in a skinny redhead.

"Yeah, but at least I'm not fucking *that*," he snapped, jerking his chin toward Emily.

Before Emily could launch into one of her tirades, another voice piped up behind him.

"God, *Zayn*? Really? This is what you were getting hot and heavy to?"

My eyes darted toward the hallway.

There, half-hidden behind Jackson's broad shoulders, was a woman. No - *her*.

Whitney.

She stepped fully into the room, leaning on crutches, wearing a pair of oversized sweats and a stretched-out T-shirt that had seen better days. Her arm and leg were both casted, and her face was bruised, swollen at the eye. But her presence was anything but weak.

She swept her gaze across the room, Emily's disheveled hair, my flushed face, Jackson's simmering fury, and smirked.

"Zayn? Really? And yet, here we are…"

Emily gaped. "Who the hell are you?"

Her resemblance to Jackson was uncanny as she smiled brightly. "I'm welcome here, unlike you…"

Jackson sighed, pinching the bridge of his nose, clearly sensing a cat fight, and it didn't look like Whitney would survive another hit. "Emily, this is my sister Whitney. Whitney, this raging cunt is the local whore."

Whitney gave a small, mocking wave with her good hand, her smirk wide and unapologetic. "Hey. Don't worry, I don't like you either."

Emily's eyes narrowed. "Excuse me?"

"I mean, 'Pillowtalk'?" Whitney said, grinning. "It's like someone dumped glitter on a breakup and called it sexy."

I couldn't help it, I laughed.

Jackson looked like he was holding back a grin too, which only made Emily more furious.

"Jackson…" she started.

"No," he snapped. "Just no. Get your shit and get out."

She turned to me. "Grady, seriously? You're just going to stand there and let him talk to me like I'm trash?"

"Jackson…" I warned.

He held his hands up. "Emily, would you be so kind as to get the fuck out. We have family business to attend to, and you'll never be family if I have anything to say about it."

I looked at her. No heat. No guilt. Just a dull ache in my chest. "He's not wrong."

Emily whipped around, grabbed her purse, and turned to me with a fake pout. "Call me later?"

I didn't answer. She kissed my cheek anyway, uninvited, and flounced out, slamming the door behind her like it would leave a dent in our lives.

Jackson flicked the lock into place. "Swear to God, man. I'm close to staging an intervention. Or an exorcism."

I scrubbed a hand over my face. "I don't wanna talk about it." It should feel like freedom. But all I could think about was the way she kissed me, uninvited, as if it mattered. Like it was supposed to make everything okay. But it never did.

He crossed the room and yanked me into a rough hug, clapping my back. "Then don't. Just please don't knock her up."

I chuckled, "Yeah, you have nothing to worry about there."

"Sorry to interrupt your little bromance, but I'm tired. Where's my room?" Whitney grumbled.

Jackson sighed, "Whitney, this is my brother Grady. Grady, this is my sister, Whitney."

I reached out my hand to shake hers and she just stared at it, her expression unimpressed. "Nice to finally meet you," I said, dropping my hand.

"Come on, Whit, be nice."

"I'm tired, and I don't want to be here. Let's not pretend we're some happy family. Now where do you want me?"

Jackson shook his head and lifted her bag over his shoulder. "Come on, you can take my room. I'll sleep on the couch."

She blinked. "Wait. The same couch you were bitching about them defiling? That's your new bed?"

He gave her a look. "Don't test me."

She grinned, hobbling past me toward the hall. "Cool, cool. Just remember to disinfect the throw pillows."

I flushed again and avoided eye contact. Whitney had known me for five minutes and had already managed to embarrass me twice.

I waited until they were out of sight before dropping down onto the couch and breathing a sigh of relief. Jackson was finally home and things could go back to normal. I wasn't completely co-dependent; I was capable of living life on my own, but everything just *worked* better when he was around. The voices in my head were quieter, and Emily didn't push me as much.

I picked up my guitar from the coffee table and began strumming a few soft chords. The notes of Zach Hood's "Weatherman" floated through the room, soft and slow.

Jackson reappeared a few minutes later and dropped into the seat beside me.

"When are you going to play your own stuff?" he asked, voice low.

I stilled my fingers and shook my head. "I'm just foolin' around."

"Bullshit. You're better than that."

I started playing again, changing chords, letting the moment hang. "How is she?"

He ran a hand through his hair. "Rough. She's banged up pretty bad. But it's more than that. It's like something inside her just... shut off. Like she's locked the world out."

I didn't say anything, just let the music fill the space between us.

"She's not talking about what happened," he said eventually. "I think she's covering for someone, probably that asshole boyfriend of hers."

My fingers froze. "Seriously?"

He kicked at the coffee table. "I don't know what to do. She's mad at me and won't say why. And I'm trying to help, but... I don't know, man. It's like she built a wall, and I'm the one who put it there"

"Anything I can do?"

"Nah. I'll figure it out."

He looked at me, and something in his expression softened. "Just... be here. Be you."

I nodded, then went back to strumming. The notes were softer now, and heavier.

I didn't know Whitney. Not really. But the way Jackson looked at her, like he was afraid she'd vanish if he blinked, told me enough.

She was more than just his sister.

She was the piece of him he thought he'd lost forever. Or at least one of them.

Chapter 5

Whitney

Something was wrong. The bed was too soft, the air too cool. I reached out and found the space beside me empty. Deep blue walls greeted me when I opened my eyes and I sat up, far too quickly. Pain seared through my ribs and I had to grit my teeth to keep from screaming. That's when I remembered where I was.

"Jackson?" I called out. "Jackson!"

There was a knock on the door a moment before it cracked open and a face I recognized from last night peeked in. Chin-length sandy blonde hair framed one of the most handsome faces I had ever seen. His tan skin was flecked with stubble, his eyes looked worried.

"Hey, Whit. Jackson ran to the bar; he said to give him a call when you're up."

"Grady, right?"

He nodded and pushed the door open a little wider, revealing the body of an athlete. Tall, at least six feet, and muscular beneath the red flannel shirt and blue jeans he wore.

"Can I get you anything?"

God, he was beautiful. reminded that this man was neither my friend nor my family, despite what Jackson said. I hated how attractive he was. It made me feel off balance.

"Yeah. You can get the fuck out."

My words seemed to hit their mark as he stumbled a step back and promptly closed the door without another word. I almost called him back. But I didn't. Couldn't.

I swung my legs over the side of the bed and looked around. I had crutches, but they were a pain to use, considering my broken wrist. Part of me wished I'd listened to Jackson and gotten the scooter thing. *Why did I have to be so stubborn?*

I hobbled around the bed, pulling on the oversized sweatpants I wore from the hospital. I wanted to go back to my apartment and grab some things, but officer dipshit wouldn't allow it, and Jackson promised he'd take me shopping.

I stumbled down the hall, managing with just one crutch, and eyed the couch when I got to the living room. There was no way I was sitting on that. Especially after what we saw last night. It's not like I'm a prude, I've had my fair share of sex. Hell, I've had a lot of sex, with a lot of different people, some at the same time. But seeing Jackson's *brother* getting down and dirty with that snob... I hate to think what they left behind.

"Hey! You got a phone I can use?" I called out.

Grady appeared in the doorway a second later, as if he was waiting for me. *This could be convenient.*

"You hungry?"

I shook my head. "Just the phone, please."

He pulled his cell from his back pocket and unlocked it before handing it over. I hit Jackson's contact, which was interestingly the most recent call in his call log, and waited for him to answer.

"Hey, man. Whit up yet?"

"I don't need a babysitter." I snapped.

"Hey, Whitney, how'd you sleep?" I could hear the exhaustion in his voice. *Good.*

"I've had better nights. When are you gonna take me to the store?"

"Something came up at the bar and it's gonna take me a couple of hours. Can you wait? Or can Grady take you?"

I scoffed. "I'd rather not."

"I'll be back as soon as I can. I promise."

I rolled my eyes. "Your promises don't mean much." I hung up, and when I realized Grady wasn't in the room, I decided to snoop a little. I opened his text messages and frowned. He didn't talk to many people...

I opened the messages between him and my brother. I scrolled down the page, these weren't texts. The guy wrote freaking novels. I chuckled as I read the texts he sent last night before we got home.

> **Grady:** Hey, man. How's Whitney? I'm sorry to bother you, but when are you coming home? She's back and I can't make it stop. Emily is coming over and I'm scared. I need you

> **Jackson:** Be home soon. Stay strong

What the hell is he afraid of? Seemed to me he had things well in hand. Literally. But something about the words got under my skin. I didn't know what "make it stop" meant, but it lodged somewhere deep, because I knew what it was to need someone that badly.

I opened his texts to Emily. She was needy as fuck.

Emily: Baby! When are you coming over?

Emily: I'm so horny

Emily: Come on, I don't care if you can't get it up. There's other ways you can make me come.

Grady: I can't tonight

Emily: You promised

Grady: I'm sorry. Something came up. I'll make it up to you tomorrow

For Grady's sake, I hoped tomorrow never came. If a woman had to beg you for it, clearly you weren't interested. And if he couldn't even get it up... I shuddered.

The only other texts he had were from Mrs. Bryant. If I remembered correctly, that's the name of the foster family they ended up with.

Mrs. Bryant: Don't forget Sunday dinner

Grady: I wouldn't miss it

"Find anything interesting?"

I jumped at the sound of Grady's voice.

"You're not very popular." I responded, covering my embarrassment at getting caught with snark.

"I like my circle small."

"Yeah, okay," I mocked, though really, I was more curious than anything. I handed him his phone back and hobbled over to the kitchen table. "What's for breakfast?"

Grady just stared at me, his mouth slack. "Uh…"

"What's the matter? Cat got your tongue?" I laughed. "Come on, I'm hungry and Jackson said you'd take care of me."

"Uh, yeah, okay. It's just…"

I rolled my eyes. Could this guy be any more pathetic? But the guilt nipped at me again. Maybe I was being too hard on him. He didn't do anything wrong, other than keeping my brother away from me when I needed him most. "Come on, big guy. It's just breakfast."

He raised his hand to the back of his neck, squeezing it like he was trying to eliminate the tension. "Yeah, it's just… Things have been a little hectic. I haven't been shopping."

I sighed. "Then I guess you're taking me shopping."

Grady refused to look at me as I perused rack after rack of lingerie. I picked up a red, lacy thong and held it up, "What do you think of this one?"

"Whatever you like," he said, not even looking up from his phone. His fingers gripped the phone so tight I thought it might snap in half.

"You can look, you know. It's just underwear."

I shrugged, sucking in a sharp breath as pain flared through my ribs when he didn't respond and returned it to the rack. If I was honest, I was used to the bargain bin at Walmart. When I told Grady I wanted to go to Victoria's Secret, I expected him to tell me no. Instead, he helped me into his truck and drove forty minutes to a strip mall. He's been glued to his phone ever since.

Eric loved lingerie; my best pieces were all gifts from him. And though we never had much money, he always enjoyed shopping with me. So what was wrong with Grady?

I grabbed a couple of pairs of simple, sexy panties and matching bras and held them out. "Okay, let's get out of here."

Grady glanced up at me then, and his face went white as a sheet as he took in the skimpy underwear. His mouth opened slightly, like he wanted to say something, but no words came.

"You have to pay, I don't have any money," I said when he took a step away from me.

He swallowed visibly and nodded, but refused to take the garments. I followed him as best I could using only one crutch, and set the underwear on the counter for the clerk to ring up.

Grady kept his eyes trained on the cashier's face and held out his credit card to pay. Bag in hand, I hobbled out of the store and back out to his truck.

"Where to now?" He asked, once we were settled.

"We can just go to Walmart or something."

I didn't know why his awkwardness made me so angry. It wasn't like I expected him to drop everything and be my knight in shining armor. But something about him shutting me down without a word made me feel small, like I was asking for too much.

He nodded and started the engine, his eyes fixed on the road, his jaw tight with something I couldn't place.

The remainder of our shopping trip was just as uneventful, though he didn't seem to have a problem looking at jeans and t-shirts.

Interesting.

Chapter 6

Grady

I ran my rag over the bar top again, even though it was already clean. I just needed to keep myself busy. I couldn't get the image of Whitney and those lacy black panties out of my head. If whoever beat the hell out of her wanted to mar her good looks, they didn't do a very good job. Even with the black eye, she was a knockout.

And completely off-limits.

My best friend's little sister. Young. Hurt. Traumatized.

And *fuck*, I should not be thinking about her like that.

Then there was Emily, who was still pissed I blew her off.

I adjusted myself behind the bar, biting back a groan as I imagined how her skin might feel beneath my hands. How her voice might sound in my ear if she said my name like she meant it.

Disgust twisted in my gut. What the hell was wrong with me? I muttered a curse and looked at the clock. Almost closing time.

"Last call!"

I mixed two more drinks before finally locking up for the night. The cold air hit me like a slap, sharp and cleansing. A reminder summer was ending, and with it, another year I'd failed to ask Emily to marry me.

The thought hit hard.

Would it fix anything? Maybe. Maybe not. The guilt, the expectations, the pain... maybe it would all finally settle if I gave her what she wanted, what I *needed* to silence the voices once and for all. But then what?

No freedom. No space. No chance of feeling something real.

Emily would love the title of wife more than the actual job. She'd never be faithful. She'd be a terrible mother.

Mother. Jeez. Why was I even thinking about kids?

No. I didn't want kids. Not when I knew what the world did to them, what it did to me. It twisted innocence into guilt. Left you bleeding on the inside with no one to blame but yourself.

I swung my leg over my bike, one of the few things that felt like it was truly mine, and revved the engine, the sound of it vibrating through my chest. The rumble tore through the quiet night. My mother would've called it a sin, a death wish.

Maybe it was.

I took off down the street, wind in my face, the chill biting at my skin. After an afternoon with Whitney, it was the only thing that could clear my head.

I stopped just outside of Emily's apartment, not ready to go home yet. I breathed a sigh of relief seeing her windows were dark. I promised I'd stop by, but I didn't have the energy. Not for that.

I pressed on, the streets blurring past me, headlights streaking against the dark, but it wasn't fast enough. I gunned the throttle harder, letting the engine scream beneath me. Wind ripped through my jacket. Still not enough.

The image of her wouldn't leave.

Whitney, half-smiling, holding out that stupid red thong like it was a joke. Like it meant *nothing*. But it meant everything. The flush in her cheeks. The way her eyes watched me, daring me to look. She didn't even know what she was doing.

Or maybe she did.

God help me.

Sinner.

My mother's voice, sharp and cruel, sliced through the roar of the bike. She had a thousand names for me. Weak. Perverted. Disappointment.

I could almost feel her hand on my shoulder the night I asked her why my dick got hard. "Your soul is rotting, Grady. This is how hell starts." The guilt gnawed at me, but it didn't stop the way my body reacted. It never did.

I leaned into a curve too fast, tires screeching, almost hoping I'd go down. Almost hoping I'd feel something worse than guilt.

Emily never made me feel this way. With her, everything was physical. Transactional. A performance I was supposed to enjoy. But Whitney... *she* made it dangerous. Not because of her body, but because she made me want something *real*.

And I couldn't go there.

Back at the house, I pulled into the garage and sat there, listening to the engine tick as it cooled. The adrenaline was fading, but the guilt remained.

When I finally went inside, Jackson was on the couch, gripping my helmet like it was the only thing keeping him from falling apart. His face was pale, eyes wide.

"Thank fucking God," he said, standing and throwing his arms around me.

I blinked. "I'm sorry."

"Are you okay?" His voice cracked as he stepped back, wiping his face. "You didn't answer your phone. I thought..."

I let out a slow breath. "Yeah. I just... needed to think."

"Don't scare me like that, okay? I..." He stopped and shook his head. "Never mind."

"I know you're not crying over me. What happened? Is Whitney...?"

"No, she's fine." He smiled suddenly, wide and boyish. "I found her."

It took a second for the words to register.

"Her?" I said. "You mean Abby?"

He nodded. "She's in Kansas. I have her number. Her address."

"Holy shit. That's... that's incredible."

"Have you spoken to her? Does she know you've been looking for her?"

He scratched the back of his neck nervously. "I want to go out there, see her in person."

"And you're sure it's her?"

He nodded, "Yeah. I got a picture."

He pulled out his phone and opened a picture. The woman looked just how he described, only older, and a little curvier.

"So, what the hell are you still doing here?"

He collapsed onto the couch. "I can't. Not with Whitney here. The bar, everything..."

I sat on the coffee table, elbows on my knees. "You have to go. I can take care of the bar. And Whitney," I sighed, not wanting to put myself in this position, but it was the least I could do, "I'll take care of your sister. You can trust me."

"I know I can trust you, it's just..." He looked at me, eyes full of conflict. "She's still mad at me, Grady. She thinks I left her. That I didn't come for her. And now I'm just going to walk away again?"

I could see the struggle in Jackson's eyes. He had spent years trying to make up for the time he'd lost with her. I could tell he was terrified of making that same mistake again, of walking away when she needed him most.

"Does she know why you didn't?"

He shook his head. "Not yet."

"Then tell her. But don't let this stop you. You've been chasing Abby for how long?"

He ran a hand over his face. "Eleven years."

I looked toward the hallway. Whitney's light was still on, a thin sliver glowing beneath the door.

"Talk to her," I said. "Tell her the truth. Then go find your girl."

He nodded slowly. "You sure?"

I didn't want to be in charge of taking care of Whitney, but the thought of her being alone in this, stuck with the ghosts of her past, made something inside me ache. She wasn't my responsibility, but damn it, she felt like it.

I clapped his shoulder. "I've got you, man. Always."

Chapter 7

Whitney

I couldn't sleep. Nervous energy thrummed beneath my skin like static. I needed to move, to do something, anything, but I was stuck in a house that didn't belong to me, in a broken body I barely recognized. At least back home, Eric would've known how to make the noise stop. He always made sure the demons stayed away.

I'd thought maybe being here, with Jackson, would help. Maybe we fix this rift that's grown between us. We were always so close as kids. He used to be my safe place. I never wanted to believe that he could forget about me so easily. Yet, since I'd gotten here, I'd seen more of his "brother" than Jackson himself. When he was home, he barely looked up from his phone.

I groaned, rolling onto my side as pain exploded through my ribs, sharp and searing like fire. I clenched my teeth to keep from crying out. God, I could really go for some weed, something to calm my mind, but I couldn't even bring myself to ask. I didn't know if my employer would look at weed if it showed up on my drug test at work. If I even still have a job when I get back.

The silence was unbearable. I reached over and flicked on the bedside lamp. The low hum of electricity filled the void, but it wasn't enough. I needed something to drown out the noise in my head. I needed to go home where it wasn't unusual to hear police sirens or screaming at all hours of the night. Without that, memories had free reign...

I stared at the shadows on the ceiling until they warped into something else. Cold linoleum. Gray walls. The smell of antiseptic.

Pain shot through my arm, but I knew better than to cry out. Mrs. Jeppsen had no patience for crybabies, even if it was her sharp nails digging into my arm causing the pain. "You don't say a word, do you hear me?" she said, her voice tight and furious.

"Yes ma'am," I whispered.

The clinic was cold and unwelcoming. The gray walls and checkered floors made me think of the old hospitals in the horror games Jackson used to play. I hated the way my sneakers squeaked against the linoleum.

"Whitney?"

A nurse called my name, and I looked to Mrs. Jeppsen for permission to stand. She nodded and took my hand, the picture of maternal care. I learned quickly that appearances were everything to her. What people didn't see, didn't matter, and they never saw my bruises.

The nurse led us down a long, fluorescent-lit hallway and into a cold, sterile room.

"Why don't you hop up on up," she said gently, patting the exam table.

I obeyed, grateful to put some distance between myself and my foster mother.

"How old are you, sweetie?"

"Twelve."

She blinked, eyebrows shooting up. "Um. When was your last period?"

I swallowed hard. I never paid attention to that stuff. It was Mrs. Jeppsen who noticed I hadn't been using the pads she bought.

"I-I think January."

The nurse nodded slowly. "And you took a pregnancy test?"

"Yes," Mrs. Jeppsen said. "I gave her one last night. It was positive."

"Do you know who the father is?"

I clenched my fists, my chest tightening with frustration... "No."

But I did. I always knew.

A soft knock on the door followed by the turning knob startled me back to the present.

"Come in," I called, my voice rough.

Jackson poked his head through the door. "Hey, you busy?"

I rolled my eyes. "So busy. I have so much to do here, I don't know how I'll ever get it done."

He laughed nervously before stepping all the way into the room. "How are you feeling?"

I shrugged, "As good as can be expected. What's up? I thought you were going to bed."

"I..." He cleared his throat and looked down at his phone, clenched in his hand. "I have to leave town for a while."

"What?" I snapped, before I could stop myself.

Jackson's face dropped and he rubbed the back of his neck nervously. "It's kind of a long story, but something came up and I have to handle it."

My chest tightened. "What about me? You dragged me all the way out here, and now you're going to bail?"

I sucked in a deep breath, feeling that familiar ache of abandonment all over again. Of course he was leaving. They always left. Just when I thought I could count on someone...

"I know the timing sucks, but..."

I shook my head. "It's fine. I've never been a priority to you, why start now."

"Come on, Whit, that's not fair..."

"No. You don't get to do that. Not now, not ever." I took a deep breath and blew it out slowly, already forming a plan in my head. "When are you leaving?"

Jackson's words felt empty in my ears, like they were rehearsed, meant to placate me. It wasn't enough to fix what had been broken between us. He didn't know what it felt like to be left behind, over and over. He had no idea how much it hurt when someone promised they'd be there and then walked away

His shoulders slumped and he dropped his head. At least he had the decency to look ashamed. "First thing in the morning."

"Great. I'll call Eric. I'm sure he'd be happy to come get me."

"That's not happening."

"Excuse me? You can't tell me what to do, especially if you're leaving." I moved to get up and cursed when my cast got caught in the covers. "Damn it!"

Jackson placed his hand on my arm and stalled my movement. "Stay. Please. I need to know you're safe. I know you hate me right now, but I promise you, if this wasn't important..."

"Why would I stay when you're not?"

"I won't be gone long. A few days, a week max," he started. "Grady will be here."

I shook my head. "In case you didn't notice, Grady's not my family. You are. Eric is."

"Eric's not family," he practically snarled. "That bastard..." He let the words fall off and squeezed his eyes shut. "Give me a chance to make it right."

I sighed, already knowing I was going to give him what he wanted. "What's so important?" I asked quietly. "More important than me? Than us?"

He hesitated.

Then, finally, he smiled. His cheeks flushed red, and I instantly wondered if it was a girl. "I don't want to say, I'm afraid of jinxing it."

"Does Grady know?" I asked, already knowing the answer.

Jackson nodded, "Yeah, but that's because he's been here since the beginning."

A sharp pang twisted in my chest. "You were my brother first." I felt like an insolent child, but part of me didn't really care.

He reached for my hand, squeezing it between his own. "You are my sister, and Grady... he's the best friend I've ever had."

"Even better than Abby?" I arched an eyebrow, remembering their relationship when we were little flooding back. The two were practically attached at the hip. They had their own inside jokes, secret language, stories to share.

Jackson's cheeks flushed, a flicker of something - regret? Hope? - in his eyes.

"It's different."

"Because he's a guy?"

He shook his head. "Because we're brothers."

Chapter 8

Grady

I stumbled out of my room to find Whitney, barely clothed, bent over the kitchen table, her body a perfect curve that I couldn't look away from. My eyes were instantly drawn to the smooth skin of her toned legs, traveling upward until they disappeared under a t-shirt that barely covered her ass. I groaned internally. Why did I have to be drawn to her, and why did she have to look like that?

Jackson left a few hours ago, he woke me up just before he walked out the door. I promised to take care of his sister, but if he only knew the ways my body wanted to take care of her... I licked my lips and pushed my hair away from my face, wishing I had grabbed a hair band to keep it out of my eyes.

If this was going to work, I was going to need to do a better job of keeping myself in check.

"Morning," I mumbled, and she squealed with a little jump, spinning around to face me.

"Jesus! Don't do that!" She winced; one arm wrapped around her middle.

I tried to fight my smile, but knew I failed when she glared at me. "Sorry."

"Damn creeper," she grumbled, turning back to whatever she was doing.

"What's that?" I asked, stepping closer, inhaling the scent of her strawberry shampoo.

She glanced back at me over her shoulder and held up a new phone. "Jackson must've picked it up before he left this morning."

I nodded. I knew a little about what happened in Salt Lake, but didn't have all the details. In all honesty, I was afraid to ask. I stepped around her and reached for the coffee maker, dropping a pod into the machine. I set my mug and waited, thankful when it was finished and I could retreat back to the safety of my room.

"I'm gonna…" I gestured over my shoulder to the hall just as Whitney pressed her new phone to her ear.

With every step I took away from her, a wave of relief washed over me. But it didn't last long. Every time she was near me, my body betrayed me. It was like I couldn't breathe when she was around. My hands twitched, wanting to reach out to her, but I pulled back, every nerve in my body screaming at me to stop. She was Jackson's sister. She was off-limits.

I was halfway to my room when I heard her voice soft, but sharp. "Hey, Eric. Who's there with you?" Her voice grew low, detached somehow. "Jessica? But I thought… No, it's just…"

My stomach twisted. I didn't want to hear more. I ducked into my room and dropped onto the bed, only for my phone to start ringing, Emily's face flashing on the screen.

I sighed and answered. "Hey, babe."

"Why didn't you come over last night?" Emily started, not wasting a second on pleasantries.

"I did, but your lights were out when I got there. I figured you went to bed."

"I did."

I frowned. "Okay, so what's the problem then?"

"I wanted you to spend the night."

I sighed, "Em. We've talked about this."

"I don't understand what the problem is," I could hear her rolling her eyes. Of course she didn't understand. She didn't understand *me*, and that wasn't likely going to change, not after ten years. "We've already had sex. You might as well enjoy it now. It's not like you can go to hell twice."

My stomach roiled. "It's not that simple."

"You're the one making it complicated. You said you'd come over. You promised."

She always did this, twisted things until I was the one who had to apologize. Until I gave in.

"Was there something else, or did you just call to belittle me?" I pushed my hand through my hair in frustration.

"Don't be mad."

I closed my eyes and inhaled, praying for patience. "I'm not mad."

"Then come over. I miss you."

I closed my eyes and took a breath. "Fine. Give me thirty."

I readjusted my position on the couch, if you could even call it that. The small, two-seater was uncomfortable, meant more for appearances than functional use. Sitting on it for extended durations was never ideal, and I swear, Emily had to be going on her third hour of new cheers.

"What did you think of that one?" she asked, stopping the music. I couldn't even begin to tell you what auditory torture she was subjecting me to, only that it sounded like Olivia Rodrigo, if she were a wounded pomeranian.

I rubbed my hand over my face, needing a moment to inject some sort of interest into her latest passion project. "It was…"

"Were you even watching?" Emily pouted, sticking out her bottom lip and pressing her hand to her hip.

"I was. I just…" I sighed. "I thought you were done with cheerleading."

Her shoulders slumped and she plopped down onto the couch beside me. "The new cheer coach down at the high school asked me to help, and I'm really excited about this. I thought you would be too."

"I'm excited you're excited, it's just…"

"Just what?"

I sighed. "High school was ten years ago. Aren't you ready to move on?"

She frowned, the crease between her eyebrows getting more defined the longer I remained silent. "You're gorgeous, Emily, but…" I closed my eyes, unable to say any of this while looking at her. "I want to be with a woman, not someone who's still trying to relive their glory days."

"That's what you think I'm doing?" Her eyebrows shot up. "You think I'm still trying to relive my *glory days*?"

"That's not what I said."

"It's exactly what you said!"

"Come here."

She hesitated, then dropped into my lap. I brushed her hair away from her face and kissed her nose. "You're a beautiful woman. You don't need to shake your ass to get my attention."

"You mean that?"

"I do."

She shifted on my lap, and I cursed myself as my body responded. "Do you think I'm sexy?" she whispered, kissing my ear.

"Emily..." I clenched my fists, fighting the urge to grab her, but when she ground down on my hardening length, I lost the battle. I gripped her ass and squeezed. "We shouldn't."

She nipped at my lobe, hands sliding down my chest. "It's been so long."

Her voice was a siren, drawing me in, even though I knew it was a trap. Her lips felt good. Her hands felt better. I closed my eyes and shut my mind off. I wanted to fight it, but with her, I always caved. It was easier than saying no. Easier than facing the truth. But in that moment, I felt it: I wasn't in love with her anymore. I hadn't been for a long time. I was just too afraid to admit it.

"Will you write me a song?" Emily's fingers trailed across my chest like nothing had happened, like she hadn't just cracked me open and poured guilt straight into the hollow.

I didn't answer right away. My lungs were working overtime; I wasn't even sure I was breathing.

My skin still buzzed with the leftover rush, but my heart was already miles away, hiding behind a wall of disgust and shame. I sat up as my mind kicked into overdrive. *What have I done?*

"Yeah," I muttered, the word tasting like ash. "Sure."

She kept talking, her voice light, too light, like she hadn't noticed I was splintering right there beside her. I was already pulling on my jeans, scanning the room like I could outrun what just happened. My boxers were gone, lost somewhere on the floor. But I didn't care. My heart pounded in my ears, too loud, too fast.

My body had wanted it. *Needed* it, even. But now? Now I just wanted to scrape it off my skin. I wanted to un-feel all of it.

"Grady..."

"I have to go," I said quickly, too quickly. I scanned the room for my shoes, my socks, anything that could get me out the door faster.

"Grady. *Grady!*"

I paused, one hand on the doorknob, staring at the grain in the wood like it held answers. I couldn't turn around. I couldn't see the look on her face - hope, need, maybe even love.

"Yeah?"

"When will I see you again?"

My throat tightened. "I'll call you later," I said, voice rough.

It was the same lie I always told her.

I grabbed my other shoe and practically ran, not even bothering to tie my laces. I just needed air. Cold, biting, punishing air. I slammed the truck door shut and sat there for a second, my fingers trembling on the wheel.

I'd lasted weeks, months, even, fighting it. Trying to be better. Cleaner. Stronger.

But tonight, I gave in. And the worst part?

I didn't even know who I was trying to be anymore.

I ran to the truck, speeding home as my shame burrowed even deeper. Silence met me like a balm the moment I walked into the house.

I paused just outside of Jackson's room. I hadn't heard from him, or Whitney all day. I slowly cracked the door open and peered inside. I could just make out her small frame curled up in the bed, her casted leg hanging out over the edge, soft snores filling the room.

A flutter hit my chest, and I shut the door gently.

In my room, I sat on the edge of the bed and stared at the wall. I owed Jackson everything. When he proposed opening the bar together, I jumped at the idea. Then, when he suggested we buy this house, I didn't hesitate. He got the master bedroom, and I was happy just to be here. A place of my own, with no one looking over my shoulder or judging me.

It couldn't have come at a better time either, Emily had just cheated on me, in our bed, and I couldn't stay there anymore.

At one time, I thought I could have a future with her. I thought she could be the one, especially after I gave her my virginity. Then she showed me her true colors. She would only remain faithful if I gave her everything she wanted and needed, and I already knew I wasn't capable. I was broken.

I scratched at my arms nervously, feeling like ants were crawling under my skin. I grabbed a towel and my shaving kit and crossed the hall to the bathroom.

I turned on the tap, letting the cold water run as I pulled off my shirt and unzipped my shaving kit. In a small pocket near the back, I found what I needed.

The blade glinted in the mirror, its edge catching the light as I turned it over in my fingers, feeling the weight of it like an old friend. It had been a while since I welcomed its sting.

I squeezed my eyes shut and inhaled deeply, blowing it out slowly. I promised Jackson I wouldn't do it again, not after the last time he found me bleeding out on the bathroom floor.

Except he's not here, and I promised him I could handle things.

I took a deep breath and stared at myself in the mirror. My sandy blonde hair was a disheveled mess, giving away what I had spent the afternoon doing.

My hazel eyes looked lifeless, and for a moment I wondered who's eyes I had. Were they my mothers? Or my fathers? What happened to them? Why didn't they want me?

I clenched my jaw and flexed my bicep. I was on my own, as I always have been. My adoptive parents loved me, I was sure of it, until I sinned...

Something I seemed incapable of stopping.

I pressed the blade to my arm, high enough that my t-shirt would cover the evidence, hiding it from everyone, even from myself. The sting grounded me. The pain bled out the guilt, taking with it my dark desires, my sin.

As the blood ran down my arm, my adoptive mothers voice echoed in my head.

"Oh my Jesus! Why did you curse me with this child?" She fell to her knees before me; her hands folded in prayer as she looked to the sky.

"I'm sorry, mother. I didn't mean to!"

"You're just like the rest of them!" she snapped.

"I'm not! I promise! I didn't touch it, just like you said not to!"

What I didn't say was that Miss Becky dragged me into the church office. She kissed me. She touched me. She made it feel good, and my body responded. I didn't know why.

"You did it. That doesn't happen by itself! You're a sinner, Grady. A good for nothing sinner. You're worthless!"

"Mother, please!"

She turned away.

"Mother!"

"NOOO! STOP! DON'T TOUCH ME!"

The scream pierced the memory like a gunshot.

Whitney.

Everything inside me stilled.

Another cry tore through the house - louder, broken, *begging*.

My own pain disappeared. The buzzing in my head went silent. I didn't even register my bare feet hitting the tile as I ran - the bathroom door slammed open behind me, the towel forgotten, the blade abandoned.

Chapter 9

Whitney

*M*r. Hernandez's hand clamped tightly around my wrists, forcing them over my head. Rough fingers stroked my cheek, his lips tipping up into a sinister smile. "I've heard about you."

I shook my head, feeling the weight of those two letters in my chest. 'No. Please, no."

He gripped my face and squeezed, his breath hot and sour as he licked over my lips. "You taste like watermelon. And I love watermelon."

I struggled, and he grinned wider, his yellowing teeth glinting in the moonlight. "Please don't," I cried.

He laughed, letting go of my face, his hand wandering down to my pajama shirt and then lower. "Shhh, this can be our little secret."

I kicked out to no avail. "Nooo! Stop! Don't touch me!"

His hand covered my mouth, cutting off my air...

Warmth enveloped me and I inhaled sharply. The scent was all wrong, Irish Spring soap instead of sweat and grime. My limbs froze, then relaxed all at once as I realized I wasn't there anymore. I was safe. I wasn't safe. But I was... here. And that was the only truth I could hold onto right now.

Big hands brushed my hair away from my face.

"Shh, you're safe," Grady whispered.

I stopped fighting and opened my eyes. Not Jackson. *Grady.*

I wanted to scream at him, after all, *what did he know?* I'm no safer now than I was back in Salt Lake. Safety is an illusion, but who was I to burst his perfect little bubble?

But I swallowed it. He meant well, even if I didn't believe the words.

"What are you doing in here?"

"I heard you screaming," he said, pulling back, and I hated the cold that replaced him.

Then something wet hit my arm. A drop of red.

"Oh my god. You're bleeding!" I scrambled away from him, landing awkwardly on my butt as I tried to stand. The blood on his arm - bright, clean, deliberate - wasn't from an accident.

My mind flashed to Chrissy, my second foster sister, who used to wear long sleeves all summer long and flinch when the shower turned on. She called them "pressure valves." Said sometimes the pain inside needed somewhere to go.

Grady jumped, like he hadn't noticed it until just now, but the trail down his arm told a different story. "It's okay," he muttered. "It's just a scratch." He covered it with his hand, but blood still slipped off his fingertips.

"Let me help you," I rushed into the ensuite bathroom and grabbed a washcloth and soaked it in cold water. I was surprised he was still standing there when I hobbled back into the room and pressed it over his arm.

"What happened?"

He shrugged.

"It looks like…"

"It's fine," he cut me off. He took the cloth and turned away. "Are you okay now?"

"Yeah, I'm good."

If he could lie, so could I.

"I'll be down the hall if you need me," he mumbled as he left the room, closing the door behind him.

I dropped down onto the bed and looked at my damp cast. "Damn it!" No way was I asking Grady for a hairdryer.

I flopped back on the bed, already knowing I wouldn't be going back to sleep. Not while Mr. Hernandez's hands still clawed at the edges of my memory.

My eyes hung heavy, but sleep wouldn't come. I moved to the couch, thinking maybe a change in scenery would shut my mind off, but nothing worked. Or rather, nothing *I* had worked. I needed pills, booze, maybe a little something to smoke.

I needed all the things that would ruin my life.

But I had nowhere to go. My job was waiting for me, but not if I failed a drug test. I couldn't fall off now.

My ears perked at the quiet snick of a door closing. I sat up, my eyes instantly meeting the warm hazel of Grady's weary gaze.

"Morning."

He looked up, eyes tired, hair messy from sleep. "Uh, morning."

I ran my eyes over his strong body, noticing he was wearing a long-sleeve, black Henley and wondered if that had anything to do with the cut I saw on his arm last night.

Was he trying to hide it?

He shuffled down the hall and into the bathroom. As much as I wanted nothing to do with him, I was going stir crazy just sitting around in Jackson's house. And not just that. The nightmares I thought I had gotten rid of, were haunting my every moment.

The second the bathroom door opened, I hopped to my foot, biting back a wince as pressure flared up my leg. My crutch lay abandoned by the couch; I was over it. The damn thing slowed me down more than it helped. "What are you doing today?" I asked the moment Grady stepped into the living room.

"Uh..." He looked past me toward the kitchen, no doubt jonesing for coffee. I knew the feeling. "I gotta open the bar."

"Can I come?"

He paused, halfway to the kitchen. "Uh, there's not really anything there for you to do."

"I'll do anything, I don't care." I hobbled to the counter, the movement sent a jolt of pain up my shin, and I sucked in a breath, gripping the counter to steady myself. I grabbed a mug and dropped a pod into the coffee maker. "I'll wash tables, do dishes. I'll sweep and mop the floors. Just please don't make me stay here."

I handed him the mug, and he took it, eyes closing like he'd just tasted salvation.

"Please, Grady." I hated how my voice cracked, but I couldn't stand one more hour of silence and memories and that damn ceiling fan ticking like a time bomb.

"What about your arm? Your leg?" He asked, eyes flicking to my cast.

"I'll be fine. You don't have to worry about me." I tried to wave him off, but the motion jostled my ribs, and I bit back a groan. "Please. I'm used to being busy. I don't like free time."

He took another long sip, then nodded. "I'm leaving in fifteen. Can you be ready in time?"

"Yes. Yes." I turned too quickly, my casted foot catching on the mat beneath the sink. Pain shot through me again, and I almost went down, only catching myself on the counter with a grunt. "Totally ready."

He didn't say a word, just raised an eyebrow and kept drinking.

Back in my room, I threw on the only clean clothes I had, shorts and a tank top, and scrubbed my teeth. A quick look in the mirror told me my hair was a disaster, but what did it matter? I wasn't looking for attention. Even though Eric was back home sleeping with someone else, didn't mean I wanted to. I was a one-guy kind of girl, and Eric was my guy.

I brushed my unruly locks into a ponytail, added deodorant, grabbed my crutch, and hobbled out just as Grady reached the door.

"Would you have really left without me?"

He glanced over his shoulder and shrugged. "Guess you'll never know."

"Asshole," I grumbled, following him out.

The outside of the bar didn't give me high hopes.

The Hideaway looked like an old saloon, complete with weathered wood siding, a rusted tin roof, and a sign that looked hand-painted and barely hanging on.

I stood behind Grady as he unlocked the door and held it open for me.

I hobbled inside slowly, and everything changed.

The place was beautiful, and not in a flashy, overdone kind of way. It was clean, modern, and warm. I stood frozen, taking everything in as he moved around me, flipping on lights as he went.

Dark walls gave it a sleek edge, offset by rich polished wood floors that clicked quietly under my crutch. The bar stretched out in front of me like a centerpiece where smooth black glass reflected the rows of liquor bottles behind it like a mirror.

It looked expensive.

Sexy.

The tables were tall and made of real wood, with heavy barstools that didn't wobble when you sat down. Booths lined the wall to my left, deep and padded, like little private corners for anyone who didn't want to be seen. Flat screens above the bar were dark at the moment, but I could imagine them airing a football game, my brother chatting up customers as they talked stats.

But the part that really caught my eye was in the back.

A small, raised platform sat off to the side, just waiting for something. Live music, maybe. The lights weren't strung yet and a mic stand leaned against the wall, forgotten for now. But I could already feel it, like the place was *almost* something more. Not just a bar. A scene. A vibe. A place people came to *be*.

I hated how much I liked it.

This wasn't just some dive bar in the middle of nowhere. It was Jackson and Grady's. And for once, I had to admit... they did something right.

"How long have you guys owned this place?"

Grady was making his way around the room, taking chairs down from the tables. He paused and looked over at me, rubbing at the scruff on his chin. "About three years."

"It's nice."

His cheeks went red as he turned away. "Thanks."

I traced my fingers over the bar, surprised by the cleanliness, the detail. Jackson always said he'd be a football star, the next *John Elway*. I could still remember watching him play on Friday nights, back before everything happened; sitting on the bleachers, eating stale popcorn, drinking a cherry Icee that was mostly liquid...

The ringing of a phone pulled me from my thoughts, and I glanced up in time to see Grady slip through a doorway.

I made myself useful, pulling down bar stools from the counter. Thirty minutes later, he was still gone, and people were trickling through the door.

"What'll it be?" I asked an old man as he dropped down into the barstool in front of me, the rest of his friends watching curiously as they filed past, and into a booth on the far side of the room.

"You're new here." It wasn't a question.

I looked him up and down, taking in his carefully styled white hair, and brown bomber jacket. It was still hot outside, considering it was the beginning of August, but based on the patches on his coat, I'd say he was ex-military, and proud of it. "Beer?"

The corner of his lips tipped up into a smile and he gave me a nod. "Make it a pitcher. And four glasses."

"Five!" Someone shouted from the table, where there were, in fact, already four people sitting.

"Get your own, Simmons," the man gruffed with a shake of his head.

I grabbed a pitcher and filled it easily enough, setting it on the counter. I set out four glasses and looked to the register, realizing I didn't know how to use it, or if it even had a till. "Uh..."

"Ray," the old man said, holding out his hand. "Tell Grady to put it on my tab."

I took his hand, his shake was firm, reminding me of my dad. I gave him a small nod. "Yes sir. Is there anything else?"

He shrugged, "I dunno. How long you gonna be around?"

"I, uh…" I stammered. I hadn't really thought about it.

"Ray! Leave the poor girl alone and get your ass over here!"

He chuckled. "Yeah, yeah." He grabbed the glasses and the pitcher and gave me a wink before turning and heading over to his friends.

As soon as he was gone, I hobbled over to the door Grady disappeared through earlier. I cracked it open, just enough for a peek. He was there with his back to me, one hand holding his phone to his ear, the other running through his hair. His words were muffled, but the conversation sounded heated, and I didn't want to interfere. I carefully closed the door and returned to the bar.

I could manage things while he was busy. How hard could it be?

Not very, I quickly found out when a group of guys strolled in a few minutes later, followed by a slow, but steady, trickle of customers from that point on. Another employee, Steven, showed up at some point - Grady was still MIA.

"Is this place always this busy?" I asked, filling a glass from the tap. I handed the beer to the cute guy across the bar with a smirk and turned my attention back to Steven as he handed a cute woman the drink he just finished mixing.

"Yeah, mostly. Jackson and Grady have really done a lot with the place."

I glanced around the once empty room. Not a single table stood vacant, though the dance floor was a different story. I cocked my head to the side, taking in the quiet tones of, "What the hell are we listening to?" I didn't recognize the sultry voice, and while it wasn't bad, it wasn't good either.

"Uh...," Steven shrugged. "I have no idea. One of the guys usually just turns on a playlist and lets it go."

I glanced back toward the office just in time to see Grady walking out, or more accurately, being dragged out. The tiny woman he was with the night I met him.

He didn't look happy as she forced him down on one of the open barstools and put her hands on his shoulders. I rolled my eyes.

"Where's the sound system? The office?"

Steven nodded, "Yeah. Why? What are you thinking?"

I grinned. "This place is hoppin, but it's not hoppin, if you know what I mean."

He shook his head while he mixed another drink, "Don't do anything crazy."

I scoffed as I hobbled backward, "Don't act like you know me." I stole a peek at Grady as I cracked open the office door. His hands were full - literally, gripping Emily's hips as she ground her ass into him. He looked uncomfortable as hell.

Fortunately, he was not my problem.

I shuffled into the office and found the sound system. I pulled my phone from my pocket and quickly synced it to the Bluetooth, then opened my Spotify and found the perfect playlist. I hit play and squealed, a burst of energy shooting through me at the opening to "Man! I Feel Like a Woman," by Shania Twain.

"Hey, Steven! Help a girl out!" I called out over the music, slapping the top of the bar with both hands. "Give me a lift."

Steven raised a brow, "What are you doing?"

"I'm a woman on a mission. Don't stop me now," I couldn't help the smile that spread across my face, the first rush of adrenaline I'd had since getting to this small town.

Steven's hands were strong where they gripped my waist and easily lifted me up onto the bar. My toes barely brushed the surface of the counter when fire shot through my shin, like the bones inside were grinding together. I bit back a scream and turned it into a toss of my hair and a playful groan.

"Okay, maybe not my best idea."

Pain or no pain, I wasn't giving up yet.

"Who's ready to have some fun?" I shouted.

I didn't care that my leg was throbbing, that the pain was making it hard to breathe. All I wanted was to feel something else. To feel like I had control over something, anything, in my life. So, I danced. Not for anyone else, but for me.

I closed my eyes and let myself *feel* the music. My hips swayed, one arm raised over my head. When I finally looked around, I caught the eye of the cute guy from earlier and winked.

Cheers rang out across the room. Energy thrummed through my veins. *Finally*, I felt like I could breathe again. I closed my eyes and with my arms in the air, swayed my hips to the beat, running my hands down my body seductively. I let all the troubles that occupied my mind go and focused on the here and now, the energy in the room, the excitement that filled my bones. I didn't know if people were staring, or if they let go of their own inhibitions and joined in, all I knew was I felt good.

And then his voice... It was so deep and gruff, it sent a shiver of excitement through me. "Whitney, you've got to get down!" Grady wasn't happy with me.

"I think I'll stay."

"Whitney!" He whisper-shouted.

I cracked an eye and looked down at his worried face. "Relax, I'm just dancing."

He reached up to grab me, but quickly pulled his hands back, a look of guilt flashing across his face. "Please. You can't do that here."

I rolled my eyes and lowered to the bar, dropping down on my butt then winced when the landing sent a jolt of pain through my leg. The song was almost over anyway.

I held my arms out for him, and he hesitated like he was afraid to touch me. Finally, he gripped my waist and lifted me as though I weighed nothing. I couldn't help sucking in lungfuls of his intoxicating smell. But it wasn't enough to make me forget he just stole my fun. "What's wrong with dancing?" I asked, once I was solidly on the ground.

He let go of me and quickly took a step back, stuffing his hands in his pockets like they'd betrayed him. "Nothing is wrong with dancing, just not like... that."

I smiled, unable to hide my amusement. "*Like that*, huh?"

His face flushed pink and I immediately had a new goal. See how far I can push Grady.

Chapter 10

Grady

As soon as I parked my truck outside the bar, I knew bringing Whitney was a mistake. She had a history with drugs and alcohol, and the last thing I needed was to contribute to her delinquency. Jackson would kill me. And worse, I'd never forgive myself.

My phone rang, silencing my thoughts. I sighed as I glanced at the screen. Emily.

I rolled my neck from side to side, already dreading the conversation I was about to have. "Hey, babe, now's not…"

"Don't." Emily snapped, her voice sharp as a blade.

I skirted the edge of the bar, heading straight for the office. Steven would be here soon, and could handle opening for me. It wouldn't be the first time.

"You don't get to fuck me and bail like I don't matter."

Bile rose in my throat. My stomach turned with the memory of her skin against mine, her voice in my ear, and the way I gave in. Again. After I swore I wouldn't. I swallowed thickly, my heart pounding as she continued to shout at me. I braced a hand against the wall, "Stop," I managed between panting breaths. "Emily, please, stop."

"No, I will not stop. We've been together for ten years, Grady! When are you going to grow up?"

"I'm sorry," I muttered, dropping into the desk chair, eyes squeezed shut. "Please, just..."

"It's okay, baby.... Let me help you."

Her voice was low, coaxing. Just like Becky's had been. Just like when she told me it was okay to close my eyes and pray afterward.

Sex is a sin; it's of the devil. You're evil Grady! I wish I never adopted you!

My mother's voice. Sharp, cruel, indelible.

Miss Becky's hands. Her mouth. The praise she whispered.

"Are you even listening to me?" Emily snapped again.

"Emily, I..." I shook my head. No, I wasn't.

I closed my eyes, trying to block out the feeling of her hands on me, the way her touch made me feel dirty. Every time she got close, I heard my mother's voice, *"You're just like them, Grady. Just like the rest of them."* The shame curled up inside me, like a snake ready to strike.

"I'm coming over."

The call ended before I could stop her.

I stared at the phone in my hand, then set it down gently, like it might explode. I gripped my upper arm, pressing hard over the fresh cut beneath my sleeve, trying to bring the pain into focus. Just enough to breathe again.

"It's okay, I'm okay," I whispered, even though neither was true.

I could feel myself spiraling. I needed to talk to someone. I needed...

I picked up my phone and opened my texts, guilt washing over me as I looked at the unopened message from a few days ago. I tapped on it.

> **Mrs. Bryant:** Missed you at dinner. Please call me, let me know you're okay.

> **Me:** I'm sorry I missed dinner. Jackson said he talked to you. Can I come over tomorrow?

Her response was almost immediate.

> **Mrs. Bryant:** Of course you can. Lunch?

> **Me:** Yes, thank you.

When Emily showed up, I still wasn't in a good place.

She knew about my past. She knew how hard intimacy was for me, yet she just kept pushing me. Always pushing me.

I stayed with Emily because it was easier than facing the truth. I was afraid of being alone, afraid of facing the same emptiness my mother had condemned me to. It was easier to pretend I didn't feel the walls closing in, that I didn't hear my mother's voice in my head, telling me I was worthless. But the truth was, I couldn't save her, and I couldn't save myself.

Maybe Jackson was right, maybe I needed to let her go.

But honestly, letting her go was never the problem. I think I let her go the first time she cheated on me. I don't know why I took her back. Or the second time. Or the third. I knew then, just like I know now, I can't give her what she wants.

"I can't talk about this right now, Emily. I need..."

She leaned in, lips brushing my ear. "I know what you need."

I shook my head. "Not today. I need to get back out there, I left Whitney alone."

Emily dropped her forehead to my chest with a sigh, "She's fine, I saw her when I came in. She actually looks like she knows what she's doing."

"That's because she's an alcoholic," I muttered. Then, instantly regretting it, I added, "Forget I said that."

Emily smiled like she hadn't heard me, or worse, like she had and didn't care. She slid her hands down my chest, fingers trailing heat, and tugged me toward the door.

As soon as we hit the bar, I saw she was right. Whitney *did* look like she belonged.

She moved like she'd always been there, cast and all, pouring drinks with one hand and keeping pace like it was nothing.

Emily pushed me down into a stool at the end of the counter and draped herself over my shoulders, her hips swaying to whatever bullshit music was playing. I closed my eyes and threw back my head, praying for patience and strength every time her ass ground against me.

I wasn't in the mood.

I rarely was, but especially not now.

Even when she palmed me through my jeans, nothing. Just... nothing.

"Emily," I gritted. "Stop."

To my surprise, she did, but only because the music changed.

A sharp guitar twang filled the bar. Familiar. Playful.

Shania Twain.

"Man! I Feel Like a Woman."

I glanced across the bar and saw Steven looking confused as hell. And there was Whitney, hobbling away from the office with a wicked grin on her face.

Then she did the unthinkable.

Steven's hands wrapped around her waist as he lifted her, cast and all, onto the bar.

She winced as her foot bumped the counter, but she didn't stop. She tossed her hair over her shoulder, posed like a damn rockstar, and lit up.

My body went hot.

Emily grinned beside me, misreading my reaction. She thought it was for her.

But it wasn't.

It was Whitney.

Whitney, who was moving to the beat, swaying her hips like temptation incarnate, running her hands down her body with a confidence that set the whole room buzzing.

And that was the moment I knew I was in real trouble.

This wasn't temptation, it was sabotage. Hers? Mine? I didn't know. I only knew my skin felt too tight and my breath too shallow.

Closing time couldn't come fast enough.

As soon as the last customer walked out, I flipped the lock and let out a breath I hadn't realized I'd been holding all night.

Whitney was still behind the bar, wiping it down with a rag that had seen better days. She didn't say much, didn't have to. She looked content. Energized.

And that scared the hell out of me.

I helped her into the passenger seat of my truck, her cast thudding softly against the running board. She sat with her back pressed to the door, arms crossed under her chest, pushing her breasts up in a way that was absolutely not intentional and absolutely not something I could ignore.

I shifted in my seat and looked straight ahead.

Think about something else.

Anything else.

Her scent, warm and sweet, filled the cab. Not fancy perfume. Just her. And it was wrecking me.

"So…" she said, breaking the silence. "What's the deal with Emily?"

I clenched the steering wheel. "What do you mean?"

"She's your girlfriend, right?"

"Yeah."

Whitney raised a brow. "Jackson doesn't seem to like her much."

I sighed. "It's complicated."

"I've got time."

"I don't want to talk about it."

She rolled her eyes and looked out the window. "She's really pretty."

"Yeah."

Emily was gorgeous, no argument there. That wasn't the problem. The problem was, her beauty only ran skin deep. Under the surface she was manipulative, cold, and vengeful.

And so incredibly selfish.

Most of the time, I didn't even recognize myself when I was with her.

I could feel Whitney watching me. She hadn't said anything in a beat too long, like she was waiting. But what was I supposed to say? That I was stringing along a relationship I'd emotionally checked out of years ago? That guilt and trauma made me stay?

That every time Emily touched me, I felt like I was back in that church basement again, whispering *no* while someone told me it was okay?

No.

Maybe she expected me to follow that up with *but she's not as pretty as you.*

Instead, silence filled the cab.

She turned to the window. "She's really pretty," she said again, quieter this time.

I didn't know what to say, so I kept quiet. And the silence between us grew heavier.

Her jaw tightened. Whatever flicker of playfulness had been there earlier, it was gone now.

Better to say nothing at all.

I pulled into the driveway and killed the engine. I reached for my door handle, already planning to leave, when I heard hers open behind me.

"Whitney. Hold on."

Too late.

She was already out, hopping down from the truck and walking, not hobbling, toward the house like she didn't have a damn cast on her leg.

"Hey!" I called after her. "I don't think you're supposed to be walking on that."

"It's fine. Don't worry about it," she said, not looking back. Her gait was stiff, but she powered through it like she had something to prove.

"I *do* worry." I grabbed her crutch from the back of the truck, frustrated. "You shouldn't be putting weight on it."

The muscles in her jaw were clenched tight, like maybe the pain wasn't as easy to shake off as she wanted me to think. But she wasn't limping, not yet. Just... gritting her teeth through it. Pretending.

"Why? I'm just Jackson's pesky little sister. Barely even that."

I opened the door and held it for her. "Don't be like that."

She didn't thank me. Just tossed a casual, "I'm going to bed," over her shoulder and disappeared down the hall.

"Whitney," I called after her, knowing it was useless.

"Goodnight, Grady," she singsonged, then slammed the door to Jackson's room like punctuation.

I exhaled slowly, frustration building in my chest. Stubborn didn't even begin to describe her. She was like a hurricane, tearing through everything in her path, and I was helpless to stop it.

I stared at the closed door for a beat, then propped her crutch up against the wall just beside it. I couldn't make her use it, but I could at least put it within a reasonable distance.

Back in my room, I collapsed on the bed, phone in hand. I had a few missed calls and several new texts, but only one caught my attention.

Jackson: It's definitely her. She's exactly how I remember.

Jackson: Except she doesn't want to talk to me.

Jackson: I need more time.

Jackson: You okay watching the bar for a little longer?

I didn't even have to think. It was and always would be yes.

Me: Take your time, I've got it handled.

I parked on the street in front of what looked like nothing more than a faded yellow house. Small, simple. The kind of place you'd drive by without a second glance.

But I knew better.

What sat behind that crooked white fence wasn't just a house. It was a home, full of love and more importantly, hope. The Bryant's were a godsend. The foster family I didn't know I needed, until I landed on their doorstep when I was seventeen, an abused and broken boy.

I hadn't even made it to the gate when the front door burst open.

"Grady!" Mrs. Bryant came running barefoot down the sidewalk, arms wide. "I've missed you!"

I smiled despite myself and wrapped her in a hug. Her arms were warm. Solid. Familiar. "Hi Mrs. Bryant."

"You look tired," she said, pulling back to inspect me. "And too skinny. Are you eating?"

"Trying."

She led me inside, her bare feet slapping against the hardwood. The house smelled like cinnamon and lemon cleaner. Laughter echoed from the kitchen. She always had a houseful of kids. Even when they stressed her out, she loved it.

We sat down at the table, and she slid a plate of fresh snickerdoodles in front of me. "Talk. What's going on with you?"

I took a bite and nodded slowly. "These are your best cookies yet."

She smiled, but her eyes narrowed. She wasn't going to let me off the hook, not today. "How's Emily?"

I grimaced. "You know?"

"Of course I know. Jackson told me. He begged me to knock some sense into you."

I shook my head; that sounded like something he would do.

"She's…" I sighed. "I don't know what I'm doing."

Mrs. Bryant got up, poured me a glass of milk, then sat beside me. "Start from the beginning."

"I mean…" I didn't want to say it, but if anyone deserved the truth, it was her. "She cheated on me, repeatedly. She…" I snapped my mouth closed and took a deep breath.

"Out with it. We don't keep secrets in this family. There's nothing you can tell me that will make me think any less or different of you."

I scrubbed my hand over my face. "She's been pressuring me to… to have sex."

"And you don't want to?"

I shook my head, then shrugged. "Yes. No. I don't know. My head's all messed up."

Her voice softened. "You still hear your mom's voice?"

I nodded. That cruel, hateful voice I could never quite silence. *Sex is sin. You're filthy. God will never love you.*

"She's still there," I said quietly.

Mrs. Bryant reached across the table and took my hand. "You know I'm not the most religious person. I believe, don't get me wrong, but I also think that God isn't going to punish you for every little thing. What makes this sin worse than any other?"

I thought about it for a moment, then when I couldn't come up with an answer, I shrugged. "It just is."

"Do you remember what I told you when you were just a boy?"

My lips quirked up into a smile, "You told me lots of things, you'll have to be more specific."

She swatted at me. "I told you that I once heard a pastor compare sin to a broken chain. Do you remember?"

I nodded.

"Each link on that chain connects a person to God. Sin causes a break in the link. Does it matter how big the break is?"

I shook my head. "No."

"A break is a break. And no person is without sin, therefore everyone's chain is broken. So, what do we do?"

Mrs. Bryant reached across the table and took my hand.

I swallowed thickly, trying to remember the words. "We put our faith in Jesus."

She nodded. "That's right. Because no one is perfect, everyone sins and God knows this, that's why he sent his son to save us."

I looked down at our hands. Her fingers were still strong. Still steady. Like they'd never once failed me.

"Now, am I telling you to go have sex with Emily?" she shook her head, "Oh, hell no. I think you should dump that girl and never look back.

I cracked a smile, leave it to Mrs. Bryant to not pull her punches. "I don't think she gets it. She just wants what she wants."

Mrs. Bryant sighed. "Then she's not your person."

"She wants us to get married."

She arched a brow. "And do you want to marry her?"

The answer was immediate. "No."

"Then don't."

"It's not that easy."

"No, it's not. But staying in the wrong place isn't easier. You think loving her out of guilt is going to make you feel better? Or more worthy? You're already worthy. You don't have to earn that."

Her words hit hard. I felt them in my ribs, like something breaking loose inside me.

"I just don't want to hurt her."

"And that's exactly what makes you a good man."

Her words pierced through the fog of my confusion. I hadn't realized how much I needed someone to tell me I wasn't worthless, that I didn't have to earn my worth with every mistake I made. Mrs. Bryant, with her warm smile and open heart, was the mother I never had. And in that moment, I realized how much I'd been starving for her love.

"Tell me about Whitney," she said, like she hadn't just changed my life with one sentence.

I ran a hand through my hair, trying to laugh but failing. There was no humor left in me, just a hollow ache that wouldn't go away. "She's... a handful."

"Pretty?"

"Beautiful." The word slipped out before I could stop it.

Mrs. Bryant grinned like she'd just won a bet. "And what does Jackson think about you crushing on his sister?"

"I'm not..." I stopped, the lie hanging between us.

She nodded, taking a bite of a cookie. "Sure, dear."

I didn't know what I'd say to Whitney when I saw her again. But I already couldn't stop thinking about it.

Chapter 11

Whitney

I kicked my legs back and forth from the edge of the exam table, the crinkly paper crumpling beneath me like my last nerve. Jackson had been gone a week. He said he'd check in regularly but regularly turned out to mean *barely*. Most of the updates I got came second-hand from Grady, who was now apparently responsible for chauffeuring me to follow-up appointments, like I was some fragile porcelain doll.

I didn't *feel* fragile. Just... forgotten. Again.

"This is pointless," I muttered, arms folded tightly across my chest. "We should just go."

Grady didn't even look at me. "You need to get that checked out," he said, voice flat, arms crossed over his own chest like a stubborn mirror of mine.

I glanced down at my cast. It still looked mostly clean, except for the bottom, which had dulled to a dingy gray from the weight I shouldn't have been putting on it. I wasn't *supposed* to be walking on it, sure. But crutches with a broken arm? Sadistic.

My skin itched beneath the cast. I shifted and scratched above the edge, just to get some relief. All it did was make the damn thing feel tighter.

A knock cut through the silence, and the door creaked open.

"Mrs. Taylor?" The doctor stepped in, a tall guy with a long face and nervous energy. His eyes bounced from Grady to me.

"Yes," I answered, just as Grady blurted, "No."

He stood up quickly, as though the very suggestion that we might be a couple was a personal insult. "We're not married. I can wait outside."

"No!" The word escaped before I could stop it. Panic rushed up my throat. "Don't leave me."

He froze. I could see it in his eyes - surprise, maybe something softer - but he nodded and sank back into the chair without another word.

The doctor raised a brow but said nothing. Instead, he flipped through a chart and walked over to examine my leg.

"What happened here?" he asked, his fingers grazing the damaged part of the cast.

Grady chuckled, and I shot him a look that could peel paint. "I, uh..."

"She needs a walking cast," he cut in, his voice flat like he'd been waiting for this moment.

Ninety minutes, two sets of x-rays, and a lot of poking and prodding later, I had a new waterproof cast on my arm and a boot strapped around my leg.

Apparently, the leg break wasn't too bad, but the wet arm cast had basically turned my healing into a slow-motion nightmare. The doctor said something about skin irritation and delayed healing, but I'd stopped listening after "no more crutches."

Grady offered a hand to help me into the truck, and I swatted it away. "I'm fine."

He sighed, but didn't argue. Still, I could feel his eyes on me the whole time I climbed in. Not with judgment, but with something worse.

Concern.

I hated it.

As soon as Grady started the engine, I glanced at the dash. Just after four. Still early. Still time to do *something*. "We heading to the bar?" I asked, already picturing the new drinks I wanted to test. Steven would be there, which helped. He had proven himself best friend worthy, something I desperately needed, especially now that Eric had apparently forgotten how phones worked.

"Not tonight," Grady muttered, eyes on the road.

I slumped in the seat, the excitement draining out of me like someone had pulled a plug. Grady was in one of *those* moods again. Tense, quiet, unreadable. Since Jackson left, the bar had become the only place that made me feel steady. Distracted. Busy. But going back to that quiet house, where everything hurt and nothing happened, made my skin crawl. Too many shadows. Too many chances to think.

"Can we do something else?" I asked, my voice barely hiding the desperation creeping into my chest.

"Like what?" His voice was flat, cautious.

"I dunno. What's around here?"

He shook his head, glancing out his side window. "Not a lot."

I groaned and tilted my head toward him. "What about your motorcycle? I saw it in the garage. It's yours, right?"

"No."

"Why not?"

He scrubbed a hand over his face, his fingers dragging slowly like even *talking* was wearing him down. "Because you can't ride a bike with a broken leg. And Jackson would kill me."

I opened my mouth to argue, but something flashed past my window - bright yellow, big and bold against the sky. "What's that?" I pointed out the glass, sitting up straighter.

Grady followed my gaze, then turned his eyes back to the road. "Adventure Land."

I grinned. "Let's go."

"No."

"Why not?"

"Boot. Cast. Injury. Common sense." He ticked them off, like he hadn't already made his case twenty times today.

I rolled my eyes. "No, seriously. Have you forgotten what it's like to *live*? I'm not dead, Grady, just a little broken."

His jaw twitched. He gripped the wheel tighter, knuckles flexing. For a beat, I thought that was it; that he'd shut me down again with some logical excuse or overprotective grunt. But then he blew out a long breath, low and tired, and flicked on his blinker.

He took the exit.

I blinked at him. "Wait... seriously?"

He didn't look at me. "Might as well let you burn off some steam before you set the couch on fire out of boredom."

But I saw the corner of his mouth tug, just a little. Barely there.

And that tiny smile? Yeah. That was for me.

I could've hugged him right then.

Grady stepped around the truck and nudged my arm, "Come on."

Even though I had to slow down, thanks to the boot and my need to take it all in, Grady didn't rush. He walked at my pace, shoulder brushing mine now and then like it was nothing. But it wasn't. Not to me. Not with the way that contact lit up something warm and stupid inside my chest.

When I veered toward the Go-Karts, already picturing the thrill, the speed and the wind in my hair, Grady's voice cut in.

"Nope."

I turned to him, my jaw clenching in frustration, already bracing for his refusal. "But…"

"They'll never let you drive with that thing," he said, gesturing toward my leg like it was the most obvious thing in the world.

"Ugh," I grumbled. "Well, what can we do?"

"Come on," he said.

I crossed my arms. "Ugh. Okay, smart guy, what *can* we do?"

"Come on," he said again, vague and annoyingly cryptic.

He led us toward a smaller building with a faded red awning and a cartoon golf ball smiling like a serial killer. I stopped cold as soon as I read the banner. "Nope. Nuh-uh. No way."

"Two, please," Grady told the cashier, like I hadn't said anything at all.

I scowled. "I'm not playing some stupid golf game." I could still remember the last time I played. I was ten and Jackson was sixteen. Our parents said it would be fun, but he made fun of me the entire time.

"It's just putt-putt," he said, already handing me a pink ball and one of those sad little pencils like it was some kind of peace offering. "You wanted to do something, remember?"

"I meant something *fun*," I huffed, but I took the ball anyway.

He smirked as he grabbed a club. "This can be fun."

"Says the guy who thinks rules are fun."

I glanced around and lit up as someone zipped past on a line above us, suspended midair with wind in their hair and that perfect, weightless laugh. "Now *that* looks like fun."

"They're not gonna let you zip line or do the ropes course with a boot and a busted arm," he said, nudging me gently toward the first hole. "Try this instead. It'll be as much fun as you let it."

"What's that supposed to mean?"

"It means," he said, passing me the club, "you can be miserable and whine through the whole thing, or you can chill for ten minutes and maybe enjoy yourself."

"Fine," I muttered. "But I'm going first."

I stepped up to the tee and bent over, maybe a little too slow, a little too on purpose. My ass brushed his front. He jerked back like I'd shocked him.

Pretty sure he groaned.

Game on.

Too bad my first six shots were pathetic. The seventh skimmed right over the hole like it was allergic to winning.

"This is stupid," I muttered. "The ball hates me."

Grady laughed, that deep, rough sound that went straight to the part of me that craved comfort and chaos at the same time. "Pretty sure it's not personal."

"Says the guy whose ball went in on the second try!"

"Because it's physics. Not feelings."

I rolled my eyes. "When can we do something fun?"

He just gestured toward my ball like the debate was settled. "Again."

I hobbled over and lined up the club. Determined. Ready. Still wildly uncoordinated.

"Hold on," Grady said, stepping in close behind me.

Heat flared up my spine.

His hands wrapped around mine, gentle, steady, and he angled the club just right. His breath touched my neck, and I forgot my name. Forgot how to breathe.

The ball rolled and dropped into the hole.

I blinked, stunned, then lit up. "I *did it!*" I threw my arms around his neck before I could stop myself.

He chuckled against my hair, low and warm. "Yeah, you did. Now do it again. Hole nine is next."

I groaned. "Seriously?"

"I'll make you a deal. Finish the course, and you pick what we do next."

I turned to him, eyebrows raised. "Anything?" Images of white-water rafting, bungee jumping, and skydiving filled my head.

"Anything," he said. Then, a beat later, "Within reason."

"Whose reason?"

"Jackson's," he said, deadpan. "Ask yourself, 'Would Jackson be okay with this?' If the answer's no, then neither am I."

That hit harder than it should have.

Of course Jackson had rules for me. He always had rules. And Grady had been there for all of them. He knew my brother better than I did. Got the years I lost. Got the protection I never had.

For a second, it felt easy, normal. Like this could be a thing.

But normal wasn't for girls like me. Not anymore.

I looked down at my arm. At the way it didn't straighten all the way. It never would. Not after Mrs. Williams shattered the bones. Not after what she caught me doing, even though it wasn't my choice. It never had been.

I swallowed the memory like poison. Felt it burn all the way down.

"Hey." Grady's hands were suddenly on my cheeks, soft and grounding. He knelt to eye level; concern etched deep into his brow. "Where'd you go?"

He was close. *Too* close. And I could feel the tension between us building. Every time his hand brushed mine, it felt like a spark, something too strong to ignore. But I could see the distance in his eyes, like he was holding back. And maybe I was too.

"Nowhere." I shook him off and forced a smile. "Come on. I'm gonna kick your ass."

"Within reason!" he called after me.

I didn't answer, just laughed, letting the sound distract me as I grabbed my ball and hobbled toward the next hole. He was still annoyingly overprotective, but the way he laughed, like, *actually* laughed, was starting to mess with my head.

Despite my best efforts, I did not kick Grady's ass. I folded my arms over my chest as he maneuvered his truck out of the parking lot and back toward the highway.

"What are you, some kind of putt putt shark?"

"A what?" Grady arched an eyebrow, and if I didn't know any better, I'd say he was trying not to laugh.

"A shark. A hustler. Did you hustle me, Grady?"

He barked out a laugh, full and unexpected, and shook his head. "No. I think I'm just more practiced than you are."

I narrowed my eyes. "Play putt putt often?"

He sighed and scratched at the stubble growing along his jaw. "Not anymore, but when I was little, we went every weekend, my parents and I"

"Oh." I turned to the window, watching the world blur past. I didn't know his full story, only that he ended up in foster care, like Jackson and me. Maybe tragedy hit his family too. Maybe he had ghosts that still whispered in the dark.

"I'm sorry," I said quietly

"It's okay."

I hesitated, then turned back to him. "Do you want to talk about them?"

"My parents?" He snorted, more bitter than amused. "Uh, no. Thanks."

I let my eyes roam from his jaw down to his hands, strong and steady, gripping the wheel like he needed it to anchor him. I knew that feeling.

"It's okay to miss them," I said, softer this time.

Grady exhaled through his nose, then changed lanes like the question hadn't just carved him open. "What do you want to do now?"

The sudden change in topic was jarring, though not unexpected. I didn't blame him, talking about family was like reopening a wound - messy, painful, and pointless.

Suddenly, I didn't feel like being around people either. Not the curious looks or the whispers. Not the pity. "Let's just go home."

"You sure?"

I nodded. "Yeah."

A beat of silence passed before a grin tugged at my lips. "Actually... I believe I saw a guitar in the living room."

Grady side-eyed me. "And?"

"And I want to hear you play."

He scoffed. "How do you know it's not Jackson's?"

I laughed. "My brother? Unless it's shaped like a football or doubles as a weight bench, it's not his."

Grady shook his head, but I could tell, just beneath the stoic exterior, he didn't mind the idea. Not really.

He still held the wheel like it was the only thing keeping him steady. But I'd seen the cracks. And maybe, just maybe, tonight I'd get him to let go, just a little.

Chapter 12

Grady

I considered lying, telling Whitney the guitar wasn't mine, that it belonged to a friend. But my conscience, loud and persistent as ever, shut it down before the words could form. I was already tangled in a deep enough mound of guilt, I didn't need to add lying to the pile.

Still, the idea of playing for her made my stomach twist.

I parked the truck and stepped out, trying to gather the nerve to say something. By the time I rounded the front, Whitney was already halfway to the door, moving faster than she should've been with a cast and a boot.

No way out now.

I unlocked the front door and followed her inside, the familiar weight of the house settling over me like static. The living room was dim and quiet, safe on a normal day, but tonight it felt different. Like the air had shifted, thick with expectation.

Whitney made a beeline for the guitar stand and plucked it up with a grin. "Come on," she said, holding it out to me like an offering. "I wanna hear you play."

I hesitated, staring at the guitar like it might bite. When I took it, the wood was warm beneath my fingers; comforting, familiar, but my chest tightened all the same.

"You sure there isn't something else you'd rather do?" I asked, keeping my voice light, like I wasn't already looking for an exit.

She dropped onto the couch and stuck her boot out like it was some kind of royal decree. "Nope. This is it. Unless you're too scared."

I sighed and rubbed a hand over my jaw. The stubble was getting too long, scratchy. "Not scared," I muttered. "I just..."

"Just what?"

I took a deep breath and blew it out slowly. "I don't play for people."

Her brow arched. "Do you play for Emily?"

The question landed heavier than I expected.

"That's different."

"How?" she asked, folding her arms. "Because you looove her?" She dragged out the word with a smirk.

I groaned. "Because she doesn't give me a choice." I looked down at the guitar in my hands, thumb running absently over the edge. "She wears me down. It's not... it's not like this."

Whitney tilted her head. "Like what?"

"Voluntary."

Her teasing faded just enough for something softer to flicker in her expression. "Then pretend I'm not here."

"It's not that simple."

"Why not?"

Because I want you to hear me.

Because I want to matter.

Because if I let you see this part of me, I don't know how to take it back.

But I didn't say any of that. *Couldn't.*

"Wouldn't you rather do something else?" I asked instead. "Watch a movie? Play a video game?"

She squinted at me. "What kind of video game?"

I glanced at the TV. Jackson's Madden collection was out of the question, but the Switch Mrs. Bryant had gotten us was still an option...

"Mario Kart?"

Her face lit up instantly. That look of bright, unfiltered joy cracked something in me. "Are you serious?"

"Yeah," I said, shrugging like it didn't mean anything. "I have no problem kicking your ass at that too."

She leaned forward, eyes gleaming. "How about this. One song. Then I destroy you."

I slung the guitar strap over my shoulder, already resigned. There was no getting out of it now, not with her looking at me like that. I sat on the coffee table, directly across from her, the guitar resting on my thigh like it belonged there. Like I belonged there. My fingers hovered over the strings, but I still hesitated.

"What do you want to hear?" I asked, stalling more than anything.

Whitney grinned like she'd already won. "Um... shit, I don't know. I doubt you'd know anything I like. Just play whatever you feel."

That was the problem. I *felt* too much.

I leaned my head back, closing my eyes, searching for something familiar, something safe. But the moment my fingers touched the strings, all that noise in my head - Emily, my mom, my own shame - quieted. The music knew where to go even if I didn't.

I kept my voice low, just a quiet hum beneath the chords. I didn't trust it not to crack, not with her watching. When I said I didn't play for people, I meant it. It wasn't about nerves. I knew I was good. I used to sing in the church choir before everything fell apart.

But it was the attention I couldn't stand. The feeling of being watched. Judged. Picked apart. Every time I played for someone, it felt like I was being peeled open. Like they could see too much.

That's why Jackson and I worked. He took the spotlight so I wouldn't have to.

I strummed the final chord and opened my eyes.

Whitney was already watching me, eyes wide, soft, and quiet in a way I hadn't expected. Like she'd just heard something sacred.

She gave a little shake of her head, like she was trying to come back to earth. "Was... was that 'Daphne Blue'?"

Heat crept into my cheeks. She recognized the song without me even singing. "You know The Band CAMINO?" I asked, fingers still moving lightly over the strings, more out of instinct than thought. I needed something to do with my hands, something to anchor me.

Whitney laughed, and it settled something in me I hadn't realized was coiled tight. Her laughter wasn't forced or flirty, it was real, easy. Like we were just two people in a room, not a guy carrying a history he never talks about.

"Do I know them? Please. I'm shocked *you* do. They're not exactly mainstream."

A smile tugged at my mouth before I could stop it. "Mainstream music's overrated anyway. I mean... Beyoncé? Taylor Swift? Linkin Park?"

"Hey," she said, pointing a mock-warning finger at me. "Leave Linkin Park out of this."

I shrugged, the rhythm of our conversation settling into something comfortable. Familiar, almost. "OG Linkin Park was solid. Meteora, Hybrid Theory... classics. But these days I lean more indie. I like music that feels like something real."

When I looked up, Whitney had moved closer, still casual, but there was a quiet intensity in her eyes. Not romantic, just... present. Like she saw me. Like she got it.

The air between us thickened. I could smell her shampoo, feel the warmth radiating from her. Every inch of me screamed to pull away, but my body didn't listen. It wanted more.

"There's just something about indie artists," she said, her voice soft. "They're hungry. Passionate. You can tell it means something to them."

I nodded slowly, her words fitting into thoughts I hadn't said out loud. "It's not just noise," I said. "It's... personal."

"Play me something else?" Whitney asked, breaking the quiet that had wrapped around us like a blanket.

I didn't answer right away. My fingers kept moving over the strings, slow and aimless, not forming any real melody yet. Just sound. Just breath.

Playing for her didn't feel like a performance, it felt like conversation. Like she was listening to more than chords and notes. Like she was hearing *me*.

She wasn't flattering me. She wasn't making this into something more. She wasn't trying, and that was exactly what made it real.

And maybe that's what caught me most off guard.

"Any requests?" I asked, my voice a little hoarse. I cleared my throat and tried again. "I'll play whatever you want."

Her smile was quiet this time, less teasing than before. "Know any Friday Pilots Club?"

I started playing "Change For You" before I could think better of it. The guitar part came easy. My fingers moved on instinct, but when I hit the chorus, the lyrics settled heavy in my chest.

But honey, I can change for you.

I hadn't meant to sing that part. Most of the time, I avoided singing like it was a spotlight I didn't want. But the words slipped out before I could stop them, soft, raw, too close to the truth.

Whitney was already moving, swaying to the beat, her boot thudding softly against the floor with each uncoordinated step. Her arm was still in a cast, and she looked a little ridiculous, off-balance, a little wild.

But she didn't care.

She twirled with her head tipped back and her eyes closed, laughing like the music had poured straight into her bloodstream. No shame. No performance. Just joy.

She was breathtaking.

I kept playing. Kept singing. And for once, I didn't think about how my voice sounded, or whether she was judging me, or if the old voices in my head were whispering about sin and shame.

I just... let go.

She danced like she'd never been told to sit still. Like no one had tried to break her. And something about that, the freedom in it, cracked something open in me.

Maybe I wasn't singing the words *to* her.

But maybe, deep down, I *meant* them.

Maybe I *could* change.

For her.

For me.

For something that didn't hurt to believe in.

She caught me watching her and froze mid-twirl. Her eyes locked on mine - wide, soft, searching. Like she'd seen a ghost but wasn't afraid of it.

Her hair fell in messy waves around her face, a little frizzy from the movement, her cheeks flushed. She didn't look embarrassed. She didn't look like she was second-guessing herself. She just looked... present. With me.

Chapter 13

Whitney

Grady could sing. That's all I could think as his voice, low, raw, beautiful, filled the room, curling around each chord like it was made to live there. A shiver rolled through me. I never would've guessed a man like him - broad, quiet, guarded - would sound like that. It didn't matter how exhausted I was. I had to move. I had to feel it in my body.

He hit the chorus, and I spun slowly, watching him from the corner of my eye. His eyes were closed, his whole body relaxed, like the weight he always carried had finally slipped off. I wondered what other pieces of him were tucked away like this - quiet, powerful, unexpected. Maybe music was his release the way adrenaline was mine. Maybe this was how he survived.

The song ended too soon. I stilled, breath caught, heart thudding as his eyes opened and locked on mine. A flush crept into his cheeks and, without a word, he looked away and started playing again, something softer this time. Something I didn't recognize.

He didn't strike me as someone who shared this part of himself often. And honestly, that was a damn shame. As much as I hated to admit it, he was incredible.

I lost track of time. One song faded into the next, his fingers never missing a beat. The sunlight that once slipped through the curtain seams had vanished, traded for soft streaks of orange, then pink, then deep violet. Now, all that remained were dark skies.

I collapsed onto the couch across from him, every part of me aching, in a good way. The sting of bruised ribs and broken bones was forgotten, replaced by the pleasant burn of used-up muscles and breathless lungs. "Where'd you learn to play like that?" I asked. I needed to know. This man I swore to hate was becoming someone I couldn't ignore. Someone whose soul felt strangely familiar.

There was something different about him. Something I didn't expect. I didn't just feel safe with Grady. I felt seen. And that, more than anything, scared me.

He set the guitar down gently, like it was something sacred, and dragged a hand through his messy curls. "Mrs. Bryant taught me."

"She was your foster mom, right? Yours and Jackson's?"

He nodded, eyes fixed on his hands, folded tightly in his lap. "One of them, yeah. The last one."

That was another reminder that I barely knew him. And if his time in foster care was anything like mine, surviving it was a damn accomplishment. But something told me he didn't come out completely unscathed.

"How many did you have?"

He rubbed the back of his neck, gaze still down. "Three."

Three. That meant he was around twelve or thirteen when it started. Young, just like me. I opened my mouth to ask more, but of course, that's when my phone buzzed sharply in my hand. The music stopped and Grady looked up for just a beat before standing, his shoulders stiff as he left the room.

I didn't want him to go.

But I also couldn't ignore the call. I answered without checking the screen.

"Hello?"

"Hey, babe." Eric's voice slid through the line like a familiar song, gravelly and soft. "What're you up to?"

"I was just listening to music." I glanced at the hall, even though Grady was long gone. "Where've you been? You haven't answered any of my calls."

"I know," he said quickly, and for once, there was no lazy charm in his voice, just something raw. "I've been trying to figure things out. But I miss you, Whit. I think it's time you come home."

Home. The word hit low and deep. I closed my eyes and swallowed the knot in my throat.

"I miss you too," I whispered. "But... is that really a good idea? What about..." I hesitated, still checking for signs of Grady, though he hadn't returned. I lowered my voice. "What about the debt?"

"I've got it handled," he said, too fast. "You don't have to worry about that."

"You always say that."

"Because I mean it." He paused, and the silence felt heavier than his words. "You know I wouldn't ask you to come back if it wasn't important."

That flutter in my chest came again. Familiar. Dangerous. Eric never asked for help. Never admitted weakness. But there it was, in between the lines.

"What's going on?" I asked gently. "Just tell me."

"I can't. Not over the phone." His voice dropped to a whisper. "But I need you, Whit. I need you here."

"I'm not even with Jackson," I said, trying to stall, trying to think. "He left. It's just me and Grady now."

There was a long pause. "Who the hell is Grady?"

I didn't answer right away.

"Is that the guy Jackson used to live with?"

"Yeah," I admitted. "He's... he's been helping."

Eric scoffed, the edge returning. "Helping? I thought Jackson was supposed to look out for you. Now you're with some guy I've never met?"

"He's not just *some guy*," I said quietly, unsure why I felt the need to defend Grady. "He's... different."

"Yeah, that's what worries me," Eric muttered. "You said you were going for a couple of weeks, tops. I let you go because I thought your brother would keep you safe. Not this Grady guy."

I bit down on my tongue, tasting frustration and guilt. "I *am* safe."

"But for how long?" His voice broke, barely, but I heard it. "I don't like this. I don't like not knowing where you are, who you're with, what's going through your head."

"I'm not doing anything wrong."

"I know. But he might be." A long breath, and then, quieter: "I'm scared, Whit. Not just for you. For me. For us. I know I've screwed things up. Hell, I've done more wrong than right, but you've always been my reason. I don't know how to keep going without you."

My heart clenched. Eric didn't talk like that. He didn't let himself unravel. He was the guy who fixed things. Who protected me when no one else did. Who found me after I ran, fed me, gave me a place to sleep, told me I could be something more. He'd been my home when I had nothing. No one.

But now, I wasn't sure if I still belonged in the world we built together, or if I'd simply gotten used to surviving in it.

"I just need a little more time," I said, my voice soft. "Let me talk to Jackson. I'll figure things out."

"Are you saying you're staying longer?"

"I'm saying... I don't know yet."

His silence this time felt wounded. "I'm losing you, aren't I?"

"No." The word slipped out too fast, too loud. I lowered my voice. "No, Eric. You're not."

Another pause. Then, "I don't want to fight with you, Whit. I just want you to come home."

"I know," I whispered. "I'll call Jackson in the morning. I'll figure it out."

"I can come get you..."

"No." My voice cracked. "You still have a warrant. If they catch you, that's it. You go to prison, and I... I can't lose you like that."

His breath stuttered through the line. "Okay. Okay, baby. I'll wait. Just don't forget what we have."

"I haven't," I said, even though part of me wished I could.

"I love you."

"I love you too."

I hung up before he could say anything else, before the guilt twisted deeper.

Then I sat there in the quiet, staring at the dark window, wondering how the hell I was supposed to choose between the life I had and the one I never thought I could have.

I dropped my phone onto the couch beside me and buried my face in my hands. The silence didn't soothe. It suffocated.

I hated him.

No, I didn't.

But sometimes I wanted to.

Eric had broken our rule. *The* rule. The one thing we promised each other no matter how messy life got: honesty first. We agreed that being open only worked if we communicated, if we stayed honest, always. And then while I was away, hiding from his mistake, he slept with someone else and *didn't tell me*.

I found out when I heard her in the background of a phone call. I hadn't been gone a week, and already he was thinking with his dick.

And God, I was furious.

But also, God, I was guilty. Because while he was back there, holding everything together, probably scared out of his mind, I was here... starting to fall for someone else. Someone who didn't know me the way Eric did but somehow made me feel more known than I'd ever been.

I sank back into the cushions, letting the exhaustion pull at my bones, and stared up at the ceiling.

I still remembered that last day at the Robbins' house. I was sixteen and ready to do something incredibly stupid. But he picked me up, let me run away with him. He didn't just give me a place to stay. He gave me purpose. Stability. Someone who'd always be there.

Even if it was messy. Even if he screwed up.

Even if I was still furious.

And now he was scared. He needed me. He never said it, not like that, but I heard it in his voice tonight. The strain. The panic. The way he said, *"I need you here."* Eric never said things like that.

So why did I feel like I couldn't go back?

Why did part of me *not* want to?

Because of Grady.

Because Grady, with his soft voice and haunted eyes, didn't ask anything from me. He didn't need me to fix his world; he just let me

be in it. With Eric, I always had to be strong. With Grady, I could be...
broken. Messy. Me.

And even that felt like a betrayal.

I covered my face again, blinking back tears. This wasn't how it was
supposed to be. I thought it would be clear. Like in books, or movies.
But it wasn't. All I felt was torn.

I loved Eric.

But maybe love wasn't enough anymore.

Maybe love wasn't supposed to *hurt* this much.

I didn't know who I was without him, but maybe I needed to find
out.

And that scared the hell out of me.

*The air felt weird. Wrong. Like when you hold your breath too long and
everything gets too quiet.*

*"They said it was over," I whispered, squinting up at the sky. "They
said it was gone."*

But the clouds didn't listen.

*They hung low and heavy, the color of bruises, blue and green and
gray all smudged together. A gust of wind tugged at the hem of my yellow
dress. I slapped it down, annoyed. I didn't want to go home yet. Not with
Mom and Dad being all kissy and gross. Jackson had already taken off
to see Abby. I just needed a few more minutes.*

Then the wind changed. Fast. Sharp.

*Dust swirled up from the ground, stinging my eyes. I rubbed at them
with my fists, blinking hard. That's when I saw it.*

A thick, twisty rope coming down from the clouds. I stared as it touched the ground, slow, like it was testing the earth. Then everything started moving fast.

It was heading straight for our neighborhood.

I froze. My legs wouldn't work. My brain screamed Run, but I couldn't. I was just... stuck.

That was our house. That was where Mom and Dad were. And I wasn't there. I was supposed to be there. Did they know I wasn't there?

A siren started screaming somewhere far away. I couldn't tell if it was real or just in my head. The tornado was growing, eating everything in its way. It hit the grocery store, the one Mom always dragged me to even though I hated it, and it disappeared like it never existed.

A car zoomed around the corner, too fast, like it didn't know. I tried to wave, to shout, but the wind grabbed the sound right out of my mouth. The car was there, then it wasn't. It flipped and flew and crashed so close I could see the driver's hair through the window. I think I screamed. I don't remember.

I turned to run, finally, but my feet just shuffled backward, slow and clumsy, like I was underwater. The wind pushed against me like it wanted to knock me down. My dress whipped around me, my hair smacking my cheeks.

And still, I watched.

Watched as it hit our house.

Watched as the roof lifted like a toy lid.

Watched as my world came apart.

I wasn't crying. I wasn't screaming. I wasn't moving.

I just... stood there. Frozen. While everything I loved was taken away.

I woke up with a jolt, sitting straight up in bed. My heart thundered against my ribcage like it was trying to escape. Sweat clung to my skin, soaking through my shirt, the sheets twisted and damp beneath me. I shoved the covers away and dragged a hand across my forehead.

It had been years since I dreamed about that night, since I saw that monstrous cloud, that spiraling force, bearing down on my house. I used to have the dream all the time, when the grief was still fresh and the world hadn't dulled the edges. But this time was different.

This time, it lingered.

The way I'd just stood there. Frozen. Helpless. I'd always told myself it was because I was a kid, too young to understand, too scared to move. But what if that wasn't true? What if it had been something else?

What if part of me *wanted* to stand there? To see it? To bear witness to what I was about to lose?

What if, even then, I didn't know how to run?

I curled onto my side and stared at the far wall. The room was quiet, but it didn't feel still. My thoughts spun like the wind in that funnel cloud. Eric's voice still echoed in my head, soft and needy, begging me to come home. And Grady's voice - low, steady, honest - wrapped around my bones like a melody I didn't want to forget.

I didn't run from the tornado.

And now? I didn't know if I was staying with Eric because I loved him... or because I didn't know how to leave.

The truth was uglier than I wanted to admit. I was still that little girl, watching the storm rip everything apart, and doing nothing to stop it.

Somewhere in the quiet, I swore I could still hear the strum of Grady's guitar, faint and fleeting, like a memory I wasn't ready to let go of. It stayed with me as I lay there in the dark, caught between the past I couldn't change... and the future I wasn't sure I deserved.

And all I could do was lay there, staring into the dark, my thoughts as tangled as the sheets around me.

Eventually, exhaustion crept back in, not the peaceful kind, but the heavy, dragging kind that smothers you slowly. I pulled the damp blanket over my chest, even though the heat hadn't left me. I was still shaking. From the dream. From the call. From the ache of being pulled in two.

My eyelids grew heavy, and I let them fall.

I thought maybe, if I could just rest… I'd wake up knowing what to do.

But the dark didn't let go easily.

And somewhere, far off in sleep, the storm found me again.

Chapter 14

Grady

My eyes popped open, heart pounding. A scream tore through the quiet, high and sharp, and even before my brain caught up, I knew it was her.

Whitney.

She cried out in her sleep sometimes; I'd gotten used to the way the house seemed to bend around those late-night sounds. But this one? This one cut deeper. Raw. Ripped from somewhere inside her.

And still, I didn't move.

I wanted to. God, I wanted to. I wanted to run to her room, pull her into my arms, tell her it was just a dream, that she was safe. That I'd never let anything happen to her again.

But I couldn't.

She wasn't mine.

She had *him*.

And I had Emily; complicated, possessive Emily. A mess I didn't know how to untangle myself from.

So I stayed in bed. Eyes on the ceiling. Fists clenched in the sheets. Fighting the pull of something I didn't have a right to want.

Didn't mean her pain didn't speak to mine.

Didn't mean I didn't feel it.

I knew nightmares. I knew what it was like to wake up gasping from dreams full of hands and blame and voices that told you it was *your* fault.

Mine always smelled like perfume and pews and old Bibles.

Whitney's probably smelled like blood.

Another cry echoed through the house. This one softer, choked. I sat up, swinging my legs over the edge of the bed, cursing under my breath.

"Fuck."

I knew I shouldn't. I had no business going to her. But my feet were already moving, my hand already on her door.

I pressed my forehead to the wood, the coolness grounding me for a moment.

Last time I woke her, she looked at me like I was her safe place. Like I mattered.

But that wasn't real. That was fear. She wasn't looking at *me*, she was looking for an anchor. Anyone who wasn't her past.

I closed my eyes, jaw clenched, heart tight.

God, I wanted to be that anchor. Not just for tonight. Not just because she was hurting.

Always.

But wanting wasn't the same as having.

Especially not when she belonged to someone else.

I pressed my ear to the door and held my breath, listening for any sign of distress. Aside from the rustling of blankets, it was quiet now. No more cries. No more whispered pleas. Still, I stood there like an idiot, forehead against the cool wood, wondering what I thought I'd do if she screamed again. Kick down the door? Crawl in beside her?

It wasn't like I hadn't thought about it. About her.

But that wasn't what this was. Not really.

It was about the way her voice cracked when she cried out. The way it echoed in the silence, too close to the sounds I used to make in the dark. It was about how I understood the helplessness of nightmares you couldn't wake up from, because sometimes even when your eyes opened, the fear stayed.

I'd spent years clawing my way out of that same kind of darkness. Jackson found me when I was halfway gone, angry, silent, lashing out at everyone who tried to care. Then Mrs. Bryant helped put me back together in pieces. But it never really left, not completely.

And now I was standing outside a door I had no right to be near, aching to do for Whitney what Jackson and Mrs. Bryant had done for me; just be there. Even if it wasn't enough.

But I wasn't hers. She wasn't mine. She had Eric. And I had Emily, whether I wanted her or not.

I turned away from the door and went back to my room.

Morning came early, and with it, the kind of sleep-deprived fog I hadn't felt in years. I didn't even try to crawl back into bed. Instead, I grabbed my guitar and let my fingers find the chords before my mind could catch up.

The melody came uninvited. Light at first, then slow and aching, like it didn't know where it was going but had to keep moving. There were no lyrics, just sound. But every note felt like something pulled from my chest. A bruise. A scar. A truth I hadn't said out loud.

It was hers. I didn't want to admit it, but the moment the melody formed, I knew. The song was for Whitney.

And that scared the hell out of me.

I sat cross-legged on the floor, guitar balanced against my thigh, my fingers moving over the strings like they had a mind of their own. The melody had started as a whisper in the back of my mind, barely there, but now it was the only thing anchoring me. It wasn't finished. It wasn't even structured. But it was mine.

My thumb plucked at a soft rhythm as I let the chords fall into place. Some days music felt like muscle memory. Other days, like today, it was breath. I didn't need lyrics, just notes, quiet and clear, blooming in the silence of the room.

I closed my eyes and leaned my head back against the couch. For the first time in what felt like days, maybe weeks, the voices were quiet. No Emily. No guilt. No shame hissing through the cracks in my self-control. Just me. Just this. Just the ache I didn't know how to name.

I used to play to disappear. Now it felt like I was trying to be seen.

That realization struck deep.

Maybe that's why I hadn't wanted to stop. Why I kept replaying the same sequence again and again, changing a single chord here, adding a progression there. Because this wasn't just music, it was something I hadn't known I was still capable of. Want. Hope. A future.

My thumb slowed, and I let the final note ring out. It echoed through the quiet house, haunting and hollow.

I hadn't written a song for someone since high school. Not since everything fell apart. I swore I never would again.

But this... this was different.

And I didn't know what scared me more, that the music came so easily... or that it came because of her.

A soft creak pulled me from the moment.

I didn't look up right away. I didn't need to. I felt her before I saw her. That quiet energy she carried with her, like a storm you didn't know you loved until it was already overhead.

Her voice broke the silence, gentle but curious. "What's that? I haven't heard that one before."

I stilled, fingers hovering above the strings, pulse jumping like I'd been caught doing something I shouldn't. My instinct was to hide it, switch to something safer. But I didn't. I let the last chord ring out, let the moment breathe.

"Just something I've been working on," I said, my voice low. Rough.

She stepped further into the room, settling onto the couch like she belonged there. "It's beautiful," she said softly, her gaze steady on me. "Play it again?"

I swallowed hard, caught off guard by how easily she disarmed me. But I didn't say no. I didn't retreat. Instead, I adjusted the guitar in my lap and started again, letting the melody spill out.

This time, I didn't think. I just played.

And she listened.

Not with polite interest. Not with flirtation.

She listened like she *heard* me.

She didn't say anything for a long while. Just sat there, watching me like the song had wrapped itself around her bones.

When I finished, she leaned forward slowly, eyes shining in the dim morning light. "It's sad," she whispered. "But there's something... peaceful about it too. Like it knows what hurt is. But it still hopes."

I swallowed, the words catching in my throat. She got it. Not just the melody, but *me*.

I dropped my gaze to the fretboard, fingers still shifting over the strings, not ready to break the spell. "I didn't write it on purpose. It just... came to me."

"Yeah," she said, her voice softer than I'd ever heard it. "That happens when it's real."

I risked a glance at her. Her eyes weren't teasing. No smirk. No distance. Just quiet honesty. Like she was letting me be someone no one else had seen.

And damn if it didn't make my chest ache.

She scooted a little closer, careful, slow, her knee brushing my arm. "You should play more," she said. "People need to hear that."

I shook my head. "It's not for people."

Her brow furrowed. "Then who's it for?"

I looked at her. Really looked. The firelight in her hair from the morning sun. The faint bruise on her cheek, almost healed. The way she tilted her head, waiting, like she actually cared what I had to say.

"For the parts of me I can't explain," I said quietly. "For the things I can't say out loud."

She nodded, like she understood exactly what I meant. Her hand lifted slightly, like she might reach for me, but she stopped, curling her fingers into her palm instead.

"Same," she said. "I used to get that from climbing. From adrenaline. Now..." She exhaled. "Now it just feels like I'm chasing something I can't catch."

"I know the feeling," I said.

The silence stretched again, but this time it wasn't heavy. It wasn't awkward. It felt like music too. Like a space between verses, holding its breath before something new begins.

She looked down at my guitar, then back up at me with something wistful in her eyes. "Will you teach me?" she asked, her voice softer now. "To play, I mean."

I blinked. "Yeah... sure. If you want."

But instead of smiling, her gaze dropped to her hands. She turned one palm up, staring at it for a second like it wasn't really hers. Then the other. I watched as her fingers curled slightly inward.

"I used to play piano," she said after a beat. "Back before..." She stopped, bit her lip. "There was this old upright in one of the homes. I'd sneak down at night to mess around with it. Just to feel the keys. It was the only thing that ever made me feel... calm. Like I wasn't drowning."

Something shifted in her voice, a crack beneath the words.

"But one night, I guess I stayed up too long. My foster dad didn't like that." She flexed her fingers, wincing slightly. "He took a hammer to my hands."

My throat clenched. "Oh my god, Whitney...."

"They healed," she added quickly, like that made it better. "Sort of. I mean, they work. But they don't move the same anymore. Not for the piano. Not for anything delicate."

She finally looked up at me, and the sadness there hit me like a punch. "So, yeah. I'd love to learn. But I don't think I can."

I didn't know what to say. Her pain was so quiet, so tightly packed behind those words, but it was massive. A whole goddamn ocean she'd been treading water in for years.

I set the guitar aside and leaned forward, elbows on my knees, not reaching for her, just *being there*.

"You don't have to play to be part of the music," I said softly. "You already are."

She blinked like she didn't know what to do with that.

And maybe she didn't.

"I should... uh..." She stood abruptly, brushing her palms on her jeans like she needed to scrub the moment off her skin. "I should change. Grab us some coffee or something."

Her voice was tight, clipped. Not angry. Just... retreating. Like she'd accidentally said too much, felt too much, and now needed space to breathe.

I opened my mouth to say something, anything, but the words lodged in my throat.

"Thanks for the song, Grady." She offered a faint smile that didn't quite reach her eyes. "It was beautiful."

I nodded, watching her disappear down the hall. The ache in my chest sharpened the longer she was gone.

I didn't play for people. I *never* played for people.

But I played for her.

And maybe that was the problem.

She returned a few minutes later, two steaming mugs in hand. She set one down on the coffee table in front of me and perched across from me like the space between us hadn't grown into a canyon.

I took the mug gratefully, its warmth grounding me. But I could already feel the shift in her. Something was coming.

"I, um," she started, wrapping her hands around her cup. "Have you heard from Jackson?"

I nodded, not expecting the question. "He called this morning."

She frowned and pulled her phone from her back pocket, her fingers moving fast. "He hasn't responded to my texts."

"Things aren't going as well as he had hoped," I said, then instantly regretted it. "He just needs more time."

Whitney set her coffee down with more force than necessary and folded her arms across her chest. "Time?" She repeated, voice hard.

"I…" She shook her head, stepping around the coffee table. "What am I even doing here?"

"Recuperating." I said automatically, even though we both knew this was about more than a cast and bruised ribs.

She spun on me. "I could do that at home. I'm an adult, in case you haven't noticed. I only came because… because…"

"Because of Jackson?" I offered when she trailed off.

Her jaw tightened. "Right. Because of Jackson." She shoved a hand through her hair, tying it up into a ponytail. "I have to go."

My chest tightened, I shook my head, struggling to find words. Finally, I whispered, "You can't."

Her eyes flared. "What do you mean, *I can't*. I'm a grown-ass woman, Grady. And if Jackson doesn't care enough about me to stick around and fix our relationship, then I don't know what I'm doing here."

"You're here to heal. To be safe. Until they find the guys who hurt you." My voice rose without meaning to. "Or did you forget about that?"

"They're not going to come after me again."

"You don't know that?"

"Yes, I do. Because I have Eric! He'll protect me, like he always does!"

I laughed bitterly. "Right. Where was your mighty protector when you were being beaten and left for dead? Where was he when your ribs cracked and your wrist was broken?" I shook my head.

She flinched, but I didn't stop. *Couldn't.* "No, Whitney. You're not leaving. I won't let you."

Her hands dropped to her hips. "You won't *let* me?"

"No." I stood. "Jackson trusted me to keep you safe. That's what I'm doing."

She popped her hip and rested her hand on it, "Oh, really?"

"Really. You're important to him, even though it may not feel like it right now. Trust me, you need to stay."

She tilted her head, voice suddenly softer, more dangerous. "And what about you, Grady? What do *you* want?"

My throat closed. What I wanted? I wanted to keep her here. I wanted to keep her safe. I wanted to kiss her until she forgot every man who ever failed her. But I couldn't say any of that. Not with Emily waiting. Not with everything between us hanging by a thread.

I shut my eyes, heart hammering, and gave her the only answer I could live with. "You're family," I said, each word like gravel in my mouth. "And I don't want anything to happen to you."

She stilled. For a second, she looked... crushed. Like I'd just confirmed something she'd been afraid of. She nodded once, sharply, and stepped back.

"Family," she echoed. "Right."

She turned away before I could stop her. And I stood there, fists clenched at my sides, wondering if the truth would've been kinder than the lie.

Chapter 15

Whitney

"**D**amn it!" I closed my eyes and counted to five, there was no way I'd make it to ten. The bar was packed, and I'd just dropped another bottle, this time a top-shelf tequila. Thankfully it hadn't broken. Thankfully it wasn't even open.

"Whoa, there." Steven's hand closed gently around my elbow, guiding me away from the counter with practiced ease. "You good?"

I shook my head, "It's fine, I'm fine. Just got a case of the dropsies tonight."

Steven didn't look convinced. With both hands on my shoulders, he ducked down until we were eye level. "You sure that's it? Because something tells me there's more going on."

Damn him for reading me so easily. In another life, Steven and I could've been best friends. But in this one, I had a decision to make, and running was starting to look like the best option. Because if I stayed, I'd have to decide. Eric or Grady. Safety or something that felt like it could ruin me.

I missed the way Eric always knew what to say, how his touch made me feel like everything would be okay, even when it wasn't. But how could I go back to that when everything between us had changed?

"You ever feel like you're lost? Like you're living your life for everyone else?"

He cocked his head to the side, studying me. "Sure. When I was sixteen and afraid to come out to my parents."

I blinked. "Wait, you're...?"

"Bi? Yep. Now stop deflecting. What's going on? Did something happen with the boss man?"

I arched an eyebrow. "What makes you say that?"

He rolled his eyes. "The way he's been stalking around like a kicked puppy all night. And then there's the sexual tension between the two of you, it's suffocating. Did he finally snap?"

I glanced past him toward the bar, where Grady was busy helping customers, pointedly ignoring us. "There's no tension," I muttered, knowing damn well it was a lie. There was tension, all right. Problem was, it felt entirely one-sided. After all, I was family. Grady's words. Not mine.

Steven snorted. "Lie to yourself all you want. I've known Grady a long time, and I've never seen him like this, like *someone's* gotten under his skin."

"Never?"

He shook his head. "So? Care to tell me what happened?"

I sighed, ducking my head. I couldn't. Not yet. Not when it was still raw and embarrassing. How was I supposed to tell him that the boyfriend I loved wanted me to come home, and all I wanted was for Grady to give me a reason to stay?

Instead, I pivoted, choosing to change the subject, grabbing the first question that had been echoing in my head since this morning. "Why doesn't he play for people?"

Steven blinked, caught off guard, but rolled with the shift. "It's not a great story." He rubbed the back of his neck, suddenly uncomfortable. "Come on. We'll talk later. Right now, we've got a bar full of thirsty people."

He sounded disappointed I wasn't spilling my guts. Truth was, I didn't even know what those guts looked like. I was a mess of frayed wires and second guesses. All I knew for sure was that part of me wanted to go home to Eric, and part of me didn't. And the part that didn't was getting louder.

The crowd thinned around eleven, and sometime after one, *she* showed up.

Emily.

Wearing the world's shortest skirt and a tank top that left nothing to the imagination. I could see the curve of her ass cheeks and not a single flaw on her smooth, perfect skin, except maybe those bruises. Hand-shaped. Deep. My stomach turned.

She didn't even glance my way. Just beelined for Grady, grabbing the collar of his shirt and yanking him down to kiss her. Red lipstick smeared his mouth like a brand.

If I knew anything about Grady, it was that he hated public affection. Hated eyes on him. And yet, he didn't fight her as she tugged him toward the door.

"I'll be back before close!" he called over his shoulder as the door swung shut behind them.

Steven chuckled and shook his head. I swear, my blood pressure spiked just watching her paw at him.

"Relax," he said under his breath. "Put the green-eyed monster away."

"I am not jealous," I snapped, stomping my boot, and immediately regretting it as pain shot up my leg. "I'm not," I repeated, quieter.

"Sure," Steven said dryly. "And I'm not about to down this shot of Jameson. Oh, wait," he did just that, tossing it back without flinching.

I sighed. "Fine. Okay. Whatever. Now that the she-devil's made an appearance and dragged him away, why don't you tell me why Grady doesn't play for people?"

Steven poured another shot, but didn't drink it right away. He looked down at it like maybe it held answers. Then he blew out a long breath before tossing it back. "How much of his story do you actually know?"

"Not much," I admitted. "Just that he was in the system. Like me. Like Jackson."

He nodded and moved to the sink, rinsing glasses with more force than necessary. "I don't know everything. Jackson probably knows the most. But I know enough to tell you Grady's childhood? It was a special kind of hell."

He paused, bracing himself on the edge of the counter. "His parents were religious zealots. The kind who thought guilt was the only path to God. He was sheltered. Shamed for everything - his body, his thoughts, even the sound of his voice. When he got here, he didn't know how to be a person. Didn't like to be looked at. Definitely didn't like to be touched."

I felt something hollow open inside my chest. "That could just be trauma from..."

"Oh, it was," Steven said, cutting me off. "And it got worse before it got better. He was thirteen when he went into the system. Got bounced around, ended up with the Bryant's. That's when he picked up his first guitar."

Steven grabbed another glass. His hands kept moving like if they stopped, the truth might come out too fast.

"He was good. Really good. Music gave him something - control, maybe. Something that was his. Jackson convinced him to try out for the school's talent show. Said it would help people see him for who he really was."

I could already feel the disaster coming.

"He got up there and played his own song. An original. And Jesus, Whitney, it was beautiful. You could hear every cracked piece of him in it. Raw and vulnerable. The kind of thing that sticks with you."

"So, what happened?" I asked. "He choke?"

Steven shook his head. "Worse. People loved it, until they didn't. Someone in the crowd recognized a lyric from the song. It was a line Grady had once said to his abuser, a phrase she used to make him believe what was happening was love, not manipulation. He didn't know any better back then. He was just a kid, trying to survive. But once people made the connection, they turned on him. Laughed. Whispered. Spread rumors. They took something sacred and twisted it into something filthy."

I felt the color drain from my face.

"They turned it into a joke," Steven said quietly. "Mocked him. Called him a pervert. A freak. He shut down after that. Never per-formed in public again."

My throat burned. "Fuck..."

"He was a kid," Steven said. "He didn't even know the rules of the world he'd landed in. Just knew he broke them by trying to speak."

"And Jackson's trying to get him to play again?" I asked, voice brittle.

"Yeah," Steven said. "And maybe someday he will. But it's not about talent. It never was. It's about shame. It's about what people took from him when he dared to let them in."

I nodded, staring down at the towel in my hands, twisting it into knots. I understood that feeling more than I wanted to admit.

"Hey, do you know anything about this secret mission my brother is on?"

Steven let out a heavy sigh. "Not entirely." He turned to face me, drying his hands with a towel. "I probably don't have to tell you, your brother's magnetic. People are drawn to him like moths to a flame."

I nodded. "Yeah, he's always been like that."

"Right. So, when he moved here, it didn't take long. All the ladies, and a few of the guys, wanted a piece of him. Even the queen bitch herself tried to stake her claim."

"Emily?"

Steven nodded with a half-laugh.

"I thought they hated each other."

"Oh, they do. Now. That came later."

"What happened?" I leaned back against the counter, scanning the room. Only a few customers remained, and Grady was nowhere to be seen.

Steven shrugged. "Like I said, everyone wanted Jackson. He's hot, smart, funny, and god, that arm..." He made a mock throwing gesture. "Emily was head cheerleader, so naturally, she assumed the quarterback belonged to her. But he wasn't interested."

"Was she as awful then as she is now?"

Steven winced. "She's worse now, believe it or not. But back then, it wasn't just Emily he turned down. Jackson only had eyes for one girl. Someone nobody around here had ever laid eyes on."

"Abby?" I whispered her name like it was some sort of a secret.

He nodded. "Yeah. He was gone for her. Totally smitten. He talked about her constantly. Texted her, called her, smiled like an idiot anytime her name came up. Then one day - silence."

"What happened? They break up?"

Steven shook his head slowly. "No. It was worse. The football team was traveling to your old stomping grounds for the playoffs. He was over the moon. Abby was finally going to see him play. Grady had moved here by then, and Jackson kept saying how excited he was for us all to meet her. Hell, I even borrowed my mom's car and drove out just to see what kind of girl could so completely steal the heart of Jackson Taylor.

"But when I got there, there was no girl cheering in the stands. No Abby. After the game, Jackson was gone. Grady told me Abby never showed. Her phone was disconnected. Jackson left during halftime, ran straight to her house."

I swallowed hard. "And?"

"Gone. Place was empty. A 'For Sale' sign in the yard. No warning. No goodbye. Just... gone."

I shook my head. "That doesn't sound like her. Abby wasn't the kind of girl to disappear without a word. She used to whisper goodnight to Jackson over the phone every single night. She wouldn't just leave. She wouldn't." But then again, I hadn't seen her since I was eleven. What did I really know anymore?

Steven called last call and mixed a couple drinks before returning to the story. "Jackson was missing for a couple weeks after that. The school got involved and the police were called. The Bryant's almost lost him. And Grady. But Jackson sweet-talked his way out of trouble when he came back. Still, he was different after that."

"How so?"

Steven rubbed the back of his neck, hesitating like he wasn't sure how much to say. Finally, he sighed. "All the people who used to want his attention? They finally got it. We all did." His cheeks flushed.

"You mean...?"

"Your brother would fuck just about anyone. And damn, can that man..."

"Stop. Please." I held up a hand, laughing despite myself. I did *not* want that visual in my head.

Steven chuckled. "Fair enough. For the record, he's not gay or bi, not really. He was just... hurting. Doing whatever it took to stop feeling anything at all."

I nodded slowly. That explained so much. I knew Jackson loved Abby. He would've given her the world if he could. I could still remember the look on his face the day he first kissed her.

Watermelon juice dribbled down my chin and splashed onto the front of my pink cotton dress, leaving behind a sticky, red stain. I knew I'd get in trouble for the mess, but at least I was outside, where it didn't count as much.

Behind me, through the screen door, my parents were fighting again. Loud. Their rare shouting matches had become a little less rare lately. This one sounded worse than usual.

I flinched at the sound of shattering glass. Something had been thrown. I told myself not to worry. They always made up. My dad would bring flowers. My mom would make her famous lemon cake. That's how it went. Still, I kept my back to the house and stared hard at the watermelon slice in my hands, pretending not to hear.

Gravel crunched under tires. I looked up, squinting into the sun just as Mom's car rolled into the drive. Jackson climbed out, grinning like a fool. His whole face lit up, the kind of grin you could see coming from a mile away.

He took one step toward the porch and his smile faltered, just for a second, his eyes cutting toward the house. Then it came back, brighter than before, like he'd decided to ignore whatever he'd just heard.

He nudged my leg with his knee and plopped down beside me on the porch. I scooted over automatically, making room the way I always did. "How long's that been going on?" he asked, nodding toward the door.

I glanced at the pile of rinds stacked on my plate. Three slices down. "Maybe half an hour?"

"What about this time?" he asked, but I just shrugged. I was more interested in him. His eyes were lit up with something bigger than a good day. I narrowed mine suspiciously. "Why are you smiling like that?"

He leaned back, hands laced behind his head, stretching out like he didn't have a care in the world. "I've had the best day, Whit. Even our fighting parents can't ruin it."

I picked up another slice even though my stomach was already full. It gave me something to do while I waited.

"I thought you were just hanging out with Abby," I said casually.

His grin stretched wider. "I was."

He sat up, suddenly serious. "Can I tell you a secret?"

I dropped my watermelon and wiped my hands on the front of my dress. I already knew the answer. "Of course."

I held out my pinkie. He hooked his around it, like always, and together we recited, "From here until eternity, your secret is safe with me."

Jackson leaned in. His voice dropped to a whisper. "I kissed Abby."

My eyes went wide. "You what?" I squeaked, too loud.

"Shhh!" he laughed, putting a finger to his lips. "It's a secret, remember?"

I leaned in, whispering now. "Abby? Really?"

"She's so perfect," he said, with this dreamy look on his face. "She's fun and smart and so pretty. And she smells like orange blossoms. Like... springtime."

"Did she kiss you back?"

He nodded, all proud and bashful at the same time.

"I'm gonna marry her someday," he said, like it was already settled. "Just you wait."

My heart felt heavy as the memory slipped away, like a stone sinking in still water.

"So, what's all that got to do with his secret mission?" I asked.

Steven glanced over my shoulder again, probably checking to see if Grady had returned from his little rendezvous with the she-bitch. "I can't say for sure," he said. "But my guess? He found her."

"Her?" My voice dropped. "As in Abby?"

He nodded. "Your brother's tried everything to move on, but he's never been able to let her go. He buried himself in school, got that full ride to CU Boulder, played like a legend until that stupid sack took out his ACL. He came back here, slept his way through every girl in town, hell, even a few guys, and none of it meant a damn thing. All he wanted was her."

Steven's voice softened. "I answered the phone one night, some PI. A private investigator. He'd hired someone to find her. I think Abby's the only person who could've made him leave. The bar. Grady. *You.*"

"Well, damn it." I turned and kicked the cabinet before I could stop myself. Pain lit up my leg like fireworks. I clenched my jaw, riding the wave.

"What?" Steven asked.

"How am I supposed to stay mad at him now?" I whispered, wincing.

He shrugged. "How about don't?"

"It's not that simple." I stared at the floor, then forced my eyes up. "He left me. Left me in those homes where..." My voice broke. I inhaled deep, then let it all out slow. "Eric wants me to come home," I said, like it was a confession.

Steven blinked. "Are you going to?"

I shook my head slowly. "I don't see how I can now."

Chapter 16

Grady

The house was dark when I got home. Too dark.

When Emily dragged me out of the bar, I'd told myself, told Whitney, I'd be back before close.

I wasn't.

A cold twist settled in my gut. What if she was gone? She'd been talking about leaving, and why wouldn't she? Her life, her friends, her boyfriend, were all back in Salt Lake. The only reason for her to stay was currently five hundred miles east, tangled up in a mess of guilt, craving, and silence.

And God help me, I wanted to be a reason for her to stay.

I turned the key and slipped inside, dropping my shoes by the door with more shame than noise. My steps were quiet as I padded down the hallway. When I pushed Jackson's door open just enough to peer inside, I saw the shape of her, small and curled under the covers.

Her breathing was steady. Peaceful.

Something in my chest cracked wide open.

I closed the door with care and walked to my own room, every inch of me heavy with the weight of everything I hadn't said.

I should've come back. I should've stayed away from Emily.

But it was always Emily. Loud, demanding, relentless. I hated myself for what I'd let her do to me. But I hated her more for making me feel like I had no other choice. I used to think she made me feel seen. Now all she made me feel was used up. Wrong.

My shirt hit the floor, followed by my jeans. I crawled under the covers in just my boxer briefs, the chill of the sheets cutting against the heat still clinging to my skin.

I needed a shower, but I couldn't move. I lay there, face buried in the pillow, trying to smother the trace of her perfume, the sharp, synthetic sweetness of Emily that lingered like a bruise.

And then...

Whitney.

I pictured her there in the dark, not six feet away. I'd seen her that morning, sleepy and barefoot, humming under her breath like she didn't even realize it. I remembered the curve of her smile, the way she tilted her head when she was pretending not to be watching me.

And her scent - fresh, clean, like strawberries and something softer. Something warmer. Like comfort. Like home.

I shifted beneath the covers, aching in a way that wasn't just physical.

It wasn't just want, it was *need*. But not the kind I was used to.

It was the kind that whispered *maybe you're worth something too.*

And that scared the hell out of me.

I told myself I just needed to sleep. To let everything fade; Emily's grip, my guilt, the ache of wanting someone I could never have.

I closed my eyes.

Just for a second.

Let the quiet wrap around me, let the soft rhythm of Whitney's breathing down the hall convince me everything was okay. That she was safe. That *I* was safe.

And then...

A scream tore through the house. Sharp. Raw. Terrified.

"Jackson!"

I was out of bed before I knew I'd moved, tearing down the hall, not even stopping to get dressed. My feet barely touched the floor as I burst through her door.

Whitney sat up in bed, her face in her hands, body wracked with sobs.

I didn't hesitate. I just *moved*. Sat beside her and pulled her into my arms, my heart pounding like I'd just sprinted a mile.

"It's okay," I whispered, brushing her hair back from her damp cheeks. "Shh, it was only a dream."

She clung to me, trembling. Her breath hitched against my chest, and all I could do was hold her tighter. Her pain sat heavy on my chest, an ache I couldn't rub away.

I pressed a kiss to the top of her head. "Wanna talk about it?"

She shook her head, then whispered into the space between us, "Did Jackson really go after Abby?"

My breath stuttered. "How do you know about that?"

She pulled back just enough to look at me. Her honey eyes were glassy, but steady now. The corners of her mouth twitched with something that wasn't quite a smile. "Steven."

I huffed out a humorless breath. "Of course. Should've figured..."

"Tell me."

Her voice was soft, but there was steel in it, like she needed the truth more than comfort.

I smoothed her hair back, fingers lingering. God, she felt so breakable in my arms, and yet she was the only one who ever made me feel like I wasn't.

I didn't want to say anything bad about Steven. he might be the only person here who gave a damn about her besides me, but I also didn't want to lie. Not to her.

"It's just... Steven has this way of knowing things," I said. "He hears everything, puts it all together. Like a sixth sense for secrets. He's not malicious about it, but yeah. If something's going on, odds are, he's the first to find out."

Whitney didn't respond right away. Instead, her fingers brushed over my forearm, slow and unthinking, until they stilled over the raised lines of a scar.

"What are these from?" she asked, touching one of the deeper ones near my wrist.

I opened my mouth, but nothing came out. For a second, I just stared at her hand against my skin, then slowly turned my arm over, tracing the jagged path myself.

I hated this part of me. Hated what it said about who I used to be. And sometimes, still was.

"When I was thirteen, my adoptive parents gave me up," I said quietly. "They didn't want a kid who got... messed up. I landed in a group home, and then got placed with this family that made them look like saints."

Whitney shifted closer, tucking herself tighter against me like she already knew I'd need the warmth.

"They weren't religious, not like my parents had been," I continued. "In fact, they believed in nothing. No God. No soul. Just nature. Survival. Hedonism."

She tilted her head. "That doesn't sound so bad."

"Maybe not," I said. "Unless you've spent your whole life believing the opposite. That every step, every breath, had to glorify God. That your body was a vessel, and wanting anything too much was sin."

The smell of cigar smoke ghosted through my memory and I swallowed hard.

"One night, before dinner, I bowed my head. Didn't even ask them to join me, I just prayed. Quietly. Mr. Wickby lit one of his cigars, told his oldest son to hold me down. Said if I wanted to be holy so badly, he'd mark me as the Lord's chosen."

Whitney's breath hitched. Her fingers curled around mine, gentle but firm. I let her touch my scars, knowing they were more than just marks on my skin. They were a part of me I couldn't forget. And now, somehow, Whitney was making me want to.

"He burned you?" she whispered.

I nodded. "More than once."

She didn't say anything for a long moment. Then, with the softest touch, she brought my wrist to her lips and kissed the scar.

It wasn't sexual. It wasn't pity, either.

It was adoring.

A holy kind of tenderness I didn't think I deserved.

And it broke me.

I sank deeper into the warmth of my bed as the last vestiges of sleep faded. Why is it that you always wake just as you get truly comfortable? I couldn't remember the last time I slept so well.

A faint song played somewhere nearby, tugging me out of sleep.

I rolled onto my side and drew a deep breath, the fresh scent of strawberries filling my lungs, just as my arm brushed smooth, warm skin.

My eyes popped open.

Whitney.

She lay beside me, sound asleep. Only she wasn't a little sister. Not anymore. My gaze drifted across the expanse of her tan legs, the curve of her ass peeking out from beneath a scrap of cloth, her stomach bare where Jackson's old Falcon Pointe Football tee had ridden up.

She was beautiful.

And I was hard as steel.

That song started again. I knew the tune but couldn't quite place it.

Whitney stirred, stretching her arms overhead. She rolled toward me, eyes still half-lidded, her lips curving into a slow, sleepy smile. "Morning."

I couldn't breathe, couldn't focus. Whitney, with her sleep-mussed hair and lazy smile, was too much, and not enough all at once. My body didn't care that I shouldn't want her. It just did. I turned away fast, cheeks burning as I tried to hide the situation happening in my boxers. "Morning." I cleared my throat. "How'd you sleep?"

"Amazing," she said with a breathy laugh. "I can't remember the last time I slept that well. How about you?"

I rubbed the back of my neck, other hand strategically placed under the covers. "I'm sorry. I didn't mean..."

Her fingers wrapped around my arm, gentle. "Don't. It's okay. We just slept."

"I know, but..."

She sat up on her knees and leaned in, hands framing my face. "Grady. Look at me."

I sighed and did as she asked. Her honey-brown eyes met mine, flecked with gold, green, and something fierce and unflinching.

"We didn't do anything wrong," she said. "We talked. We fell asleep. It's okay."

I swallowed hard and nodded. "I'm sorry," I whispered.

Her smile was soft, real. The kind that made my chest ache.

Then the music played again, pulling her attention.

"What is that?" I asked.

"My ringtone."

"*That's* your ringtone?"

She shrugged as the chorus swelled again. "Why not? Everyone loves Shania."

And suddenly, it hit me.

It was the same one she danced to on the bar, a week ago, leg in a cast, and hair flying like she owned the world.

God help me, she still did.

"Man! I feel like a woman!" she sang along as she crawled across the bed, reaching for her phone.

Any calm I'd gained unraveled as her ass shifted in front of me, her legs stretching, her shirt riding higher. My cock definitely didn't notice how perfect she looked; how perfectly she'd fit in my hands.

I adjusted myself quickly just as she popped back up, a frown forming between her brows.

"What is it?" I asked.

"It's Eric."

"Your boyfriend?"

She half-shrugged. "Yeah. It's complicated."

"Wanna talk about it?"

She flopped onto her back, sighing so hard her wild hair puffed into the air. "He wants me to come home."

I brushed a strand of hair from her face. "What do *you* want?"

She threw an arm over her eyes. "I don't know. I mean..." She sat up, bracing herself on her elbows. "I love my life. I really do. But when I first got here, it was rough. I missed my bed. My job. My friends." She chuckled softly. "The pain was almost unbearable. I'd have done just about anything for some oxy. Hell, even a joint."

I tensed, remembering what Jackson had told me. I wanted to reach for her, but I was afraid she'd stop talking.

"Funny thing is," she continued, "the longer I stayed, the less I felt like I needed any of that. Like I could just be me. And that was enough. Even without Jackson."

"He didn't want to leave you."

She lifted her casted arm in exasperation. "I get that now. But why couldn't he just tell me?"

"He thought it might jinx things."

She laughed, light and surprised. "Always so damn superstitious. When we were kids, he carried around..."

"A lucky rabbit's foot," we said in unison.

We both laughed.

"He still has it, you know."

"You're kidding."

I shook my head. "It's looking a little rough, but it's there, on his keys for the bar."

"Damn. I guess some things don't change."

The moment stretched, peaceful, until her phone rang again.

"You gonna get that?" I asked.

She sighed and reached for it. "I'll talk to you later."

I slid out of bed, no longer self-conscious about being in nothing but boxers. Something about her put me at ease in a way no one else did. I crossed the room, pulling the door shut behind me, but I didn't walk away.

I stood there, ear to the door, heart in my throat.

And then I heard her say it.

"I can't come home yet."

My heart clenched at her words. She wasn't staying because of me. But some part of me clung to the hope anyway. Maybe it wasn't just fear keeping her here. Maybe it wasn't just Jackson. Maybe, just maybe, she felt it too.

I backed away from the door, careful not to make a sound. If she caught me listening, it'd all unravel. The quiet between her words stretched, punctuated only by the occasional hum of her voice - low, tired, frayed around the edges.

Chapter 17

Whitney

I held my arm out of the truck window, my hand soaring through the air as we sped down some old back road. Grady said he preferred this way, even if it took longer - less traffic and fewer people.

"Where are we going?" I asked, not for the first time, trying to kick my feet up on the dash and failing. Damn boot.

Grady shook his head, a smile tugging at his lips.

"Don't," I warned, though even I could barely keep a straight face.

He mimed zipping his lips and tossing the key.

I turned back to the window, grinning despite myself. Falcon Pointe was small, but it still stretched across hundreds of square miles. The farther out we drove, the more rural it got. We passed cornfields, cattle ranches, even a field full of horses.

I leaned out the window. "Hi, horsies!"

Grady chuckled. "What are you doing?"

I flopped back into my seat. "Don't judge."

"I wasn't. I'm not."

"Haven't you ever waved at the horses while you drove past?"

"Can't say as I have."

"Well, that's just sad."

He laughed. "Never pegged you for a horse girl."

"Oh, all girls are horse girls at some point. Some of us just never grow out of it."

"Fair."

We rolled into a quiet neighborhood. Grady turned down a side street and stopped in front of a sunny yellow house with white shutters and flowers lining the driveway.

"Where are we?" I asked, just as the front door opened and an older woman stepped onto the porch, two small kids trailing behind her.

Without answering, Grady hopped out, rushing across the lawn. The kids ran to him, clinging to his legs and giggling as they flopped onto his feet. He laughed and wrapped the woman in a hug, saying something I couldn't quite hear.

My heart clenched.

We were either at his old foster home... or his girlfriend's house. And that woman was her mother.

I climbed out of the truck, praying it was the former.

Grady waved me over. I pasted on a smile and crossed the drive, nerves tightening in my chest. I didn't usually care what people thought of me, but something about this place, this woman, felt different.

Or maybe it was the fact that I was pretty sure this was a foster home, and after everything I'd been through, I'd sworn never to step inside one again.

"You must be Whitney," the woman said.

I shoved my hands into my back pockets. "Yes, ma'am."

She grinned and opened her arms. "Come here, sweetie. Let me get a good look at you. I've heard so much."

I shot a glance at Grady. "You have?"

She pulled me into a warm hug, and somehow... it didn't feel strange. It felt... safe.

"Jackson used to talk about you all the time," she said. "His little sister who wasn't afraid of anything. He said you were the bravest person he knew."

"He did?" I asked, cheeks warming.

She smiled and smoothed my hair like I was still a little girl. "He loves you so much. If only I could've taken you both. But the timing wasn't right. And then..."

"Maybe we should take this inside," Grady cut in. One kid was on his hip, the other climbing his back like a jungle gym. He looked... natural. Effortless. A pang hit my chest. He'd make an amazing father one day.

"Good idea. I hope you're hungry, I made Grady's favorite."

The moment we stepped inside, cozy warmth wrapped around me like a blanket fresh from the dryer. The house smelled like something rich and buttery, and it felt nothing like any foster home I'd ever known.

Then, there was a crash.

Something clattered to the floor in the living room, just off the entryway, a ceramic mug, I think, shattering into three clean pieces on the hardwood. One of the little kids stood frozen beside it, eyes wide, lip quivering.

Mrs. Bryant started toward him, but Grady beat her there.

He knelt down slowly, like he didn't want to startle the boy, and offered a small, reassuring smile. "Hey, it's alright, buddy," he said gently. "Stuff breaks. No big deal."

The boy didn't move, just kept staring at the mess like he was bracing for a storm.

Grady reached out and placed a hand on his shoulder. "You okay?"

The boy finally gave him a small, shaky nod.

Grady ruffled his hair. "I'll clean it up," he offered. "Go get dinner on the table."

He was already moving, careful, quiet, and something in the back of my throat burned.

Not because of the broken mug. But because Grady hadn't flinched. Hadn't raised his voice. Hadn't even looked annoyed.

That boy was prepared for a punishment, and all Grady gave him was calm.

I folded my arms tight over my chest. I'd spent too many years walking on eggshells, too many nights listening for footsteps, holding my breath. This wasn't that kind of house, and Grady sure as hell wasn't that kind of man.

Mrs. Bryant linked arms with me and led me down the hall, lined with photos. School portraits, beach vacations, holiday chaos. I stopped at one, Jackson, shirtless in bright yellow swim trunks, his arm slung over a younger Grady's shoulders.

Jackson was grinning. Grady... wasn't. His smile didn't quite reach his eyes.

"Oh, I remember that day," she said, brushing her fingers along the frame. "Dan's boss let us use his cabin at Coyote Ridge. It was shortly after Grady arrived."

She looked wistful, then turned to Grady. "You were so quiet back then."

"I'm still quiet," he muttered.

She hummed. "Yeah, but it's a different kind of quiet now."

"Can we talk about something else?" Grady rubbed the back of his neck.

It struck me then; how little I really knew about Grady. Where he came from. What he'd survived. And yet, I understood. Some stories don't get told unless they had to be.

She winked at me. "Come on, before dinner gets cold."

I took one last look at the photo, Jackson's grin, Grady's discomfort, and followed them to the kitchen.

The dining room opened into the kitchen. Grady pulled out a chair for me, and I sat while the two kids settled at a small table nearby. The Bryant's were obviously good people.

Why couldn't I have ended up here, too?

I shoved the thought down. It didn't help. Some kids had it worse. But that didn't make the ache in my chest go away.

"So," I asked, desperate for distraction, "what was Grady like as a kid?"

Her back was turned as she plated food, but I could hear the smile in her voice. Grady carried two plates over to the kids, then returned with more - pork chops, mashed potatoes, gravy, corn on the cob. My stomach growled.

I hadn't had a meal like this since... before. Before the tornado.

"A lot like he is now," she said, sitting down. "Kind, generous, hardworking. But also so, so talented."

Grady's cheeks turned pink. He focused on the kids' food, clearly hoping to dodge the attention.

I took a bite of pork chop and nearly moaned. "I've heard him play. He's incredible."

"He's played for you?" she asked, clearly surprised.

"And sang. He has an amazing voice."

She paused, fork halfway to her mouth. "He does," she said slowly, giving me a long, assessing look.

Grady dropped into the seat beside her, clearly hoping to melt into it. "It's not a big deal."

She gave his shoulder a pat, letting it go.

"So, Whitney," she said, "tell me about yourself. Jackson hasn't shared much since you two reconnected. How are you getting along out here?"

"I, uh..." I floundered. No one ever asked about me.

"Whitney's been helping down at the bar," Grady offered.

She smiled knowingly. "Is that right?"

I nodded. "Back when Eric and I lived in Denver, I bartended. Apparently, it's like riding a bike, it came right back."

"That's wonderful. I know the boys needed help, especially with Jackson leaving so suddenly."

"I'm happy to help. Especially once I found out Jacks... Ow!"

My eyes flew to Grady, who'd just kicked me under the table and gave the most unconvincing innocent shrug I'd ever seen.

"Sorry," he said with zero remorse. "Foot slipped."

Sure it did.

But I let it go.

For now.

Chapter 18

Grady

"Sorry," I muttered, though I wasn't. I shot her a subtle shake of my head - no. "Foot slipped."

Jackson didn't want Mrs. Bryant to know the real reason he left town. And for good reason.

Whitney narrowed her eyes, but I needed to pivot fast. "I don't think I ever asked, but what do you do for a living out there in Salt Lake?"

The last thing I wanted to do was talk about her home, her other life, especially when she was already debating going back. I knew she told her boyfriend she couldn't come home yet, but that could change at any second.

Her face lit up, something bright and unguarded. "Oh! Right, not even Jackson knows," she laughed and carefully set her fork on the edge of her plate. "I work at this gym, Everest. We host indoor rock climbing lessons and sometimes take groups up on the mountain for guided climbs."

"Rock climbing?" Mrs. Bryant arched a surprised eyebrow. I wasn't far behind her.

Whitney nodded, "Oh yeah. It's mostly kids, after school or on weekends. But sometimes adults come in, wanting to try something new."

"How did you get into that?" Mrs. Bryant asked.

I was glad she did. I couldn't find my voice, too busy trying to imagine Whitney scaling a rock wall.

"Well, when we first moved out there, I didn't know anybody. It was just me and Eric. I, uh..." She picked up her fork and started poking at her food. "I like to keep busy, so one day I checked it out and started taking lessons after work, or on weekends. Before long I was out in nature, climbing actual mountains. I love it. The thrill, the danger. Looking down over a cliff's edge, knowing it's just you and the mountain... It's a rush."

"Doesn't it scare you?"

She shrugged. "Well, yeah. But how else are you gonna feel alive?"

Mrs. Bryant cocked her head to the side, trying to make sense of her. I got it. I understood that need, to feel something sharp and real, just to know you're alive. But my version wasn't as noble. It came in bruises and blood; in scars I didn't let anyone see.

Just when the silence threatened to stretch too far, Mrs. Bryant smiled. "My dear, you are an incredible young woman."

I couldn't agree more. And that was becoming dangerous.

After dinner, I was practically dragged outside by Edward and Edie, the five-year-old twins Mrs. Bryant had taken in about six months ago.

It didn't matter that September evenings had a bite in the air, those two always wanted to be outside.

Thankfully tonight, they settled for the swing set. As long as I was pushing them.

"Higher, Grady!" Edie called out.

I gave her another push and stole a peek over my shoulder. Mrs. Bryant and Whitney were seated on the porch swing, bathed in the gold-pink light of sunset. I could still remember the day Mr. Bryant brought that swing home in his pickup. Jackson and I helped him mount it to the ceiling, and it became Mrs. Bryant's favorite place to sit in the evenings.

Tonight, she looked more relaxed than I'd seen her in ages, especially while Mr. Bryant was out of town on business. And Whitney, damn. She was laughing, head thrown back, hair catching the light like an unguarded flame. That tug in my chest came back strong. The only other times I'd seen her look so free, were when she was stirring up trouble; dancing on the bar, rubbing up against me on the mini-golf course. Or when she was dancing while I played.

I caught Whitney watching me from the porch swing. Her smile was soft, unreadable. And for a second, I let myself pretend she was mine.

Why did she have to be so captivating? She was my best friend's little sister, taken, and had more life experience than I could dream of.

And then there was me, with all my issues. There was no doubt I wanted her. But could someone like her ever want someone like me?

The sun was starting to dip behind the mountains as we pulled away from my teenage home. Instead of turning left toward town, I went right.

"Where are we going?" Whitney asked, looking back toward the road we came in on.

I sucked in a breath and regretted it almost immediately. Her intoxicating scent filled my lungs, strawberries and something I couldn't name. I rolled the window down, trying to focus.

"Home," I said. "Just thought we'd take the scenic route."

"Good idea. It's such a beautiful night."

We rode in silence down the old country back road I'd driven a hundred times to clear my mind. Only tonight, there wasn't much clearing happening.

Whitney shifted in her seat and started to reach for the radio when she abruptly pulled her hand back. "Can I?" she asked.

"Yeah," I said, my voice dry, scratchy. The second the radio came on and I heard the opening notes of the song I'd been trying to learn, my heart stuttered. I forgot it was still set to replay. It looped again, and I scrambled for my phone.

Whitney caught my hand. "What is that?"

I quickly pulled up a safer playlist and tapped on a song I knew she liked. "Nothing. Just something I was working on."

"It's so sad."

She wasn't wrong. Emily had asked for a love song, something tender, something that said forever. But I couldn't write it. I wasn't even sure I loved her anymore. Maybe I did, once. But whatever it was had withered and died somewhere around the third time I caught her cheating.

This song was more honest. About being a placeholder. About never being enough.

Thankfully, she didn't press. Her head started to bob with the beat of the next track, and then she was singing. Not quietly. Bold, effortless, like her soul knew the words before her lips ever moved.

And man... this girl could sing.

Her voice was scratchy and low, a little raspy, and when she laughed between verses or leaned forward to belt the chorus, something inside me cracked open. I didn't even know I'd been guarding it.

One song after another, every lyric flawless, every note full of feeling. I missed my turn, I was so caught up in her voice.

We reached a long stretch of open road that could take us anywhere - into the city, the mountains, out of my damn mind. Whitney knelt on her seat, despite the awkward boot, looking out the window at the violet sky spilling behind the hills.

"Oooh, pull over. Right there." She pointed to the turn off for one of the local trailheads.

I pulled in without hesitation.

She opened her door and called over her shoulder, "Leave it on."

I did, music playing, headlights dim, truck idling, and followed her out.

She was already barefoot, the boot and her sneaker left behind. She stepped onto the gravel with bare feet like it didn't even hurt. The wind caught her hair and whipped it around her face. She laughed as she turned to me, glowing in the golden spill of dusk and the hum of the stereo.

"Dance with me," she said.

She reached for my hands, placed them at her waist. My breath caught in my throat as her arms came around my neck, slow and sure, like this wasn't terrifying. Like this was normal. Like we did this all the time.

"I can't..." I muttered, locked in place.

"It's okay." Her thumb brushed the corner of my mouth, a touch so soft I almost didn't feel it. "It doesn't have to mean anything."

But it did. God, it did.

She leaned her head against my chest, and I didn't think, I just held her. She was warm, soft, real. And I'd never felt more alive or more exposed. My hands settled at her waist, then curved lower to her hips, just enough to feel the shape of her body as we moved.

I swayed with her, clumsy and unsure, but she didn't seem to care.

"Eric isn't much of a dancer," she whispered against my shirt.

I swallowed hard.

She pulled back just enough to look up at me as her fingers slid into the curls at the nape of my neck. "You're different," she said.

I didn't know what that meant, if it was good or bad, but I clung to it anyway. Her chest brushed mine with every breath, and the space between us grew smaller, impossibly smaller. If I just dipped my head...

No.

I couldn't.

So, I closed my eyes and buried my face in her hair instead. Strawberries. Always strawberries. And sunshine. And everything I didn't think I deserved.

She made me feel clean. Not like the boy who got passed around or punished for wanting too much. Not like the sinner my mother said I was. Not like Emily's toy or her doormat.

Whitney made me feel like maybe I was worth holding onto.

The song ended and another began, this time louder, faster. But she didn't let go. Her arms stayed around me. My hands stayed at her waist. And we kept moving, not even trying to find the beat. Just swaying.

"When are you going back home?" I asked, hating myself even as the words left my mouth.

She exhaled slowly, her lips brushing my collarbone. "Sick of me already?"

"No. I..."

She leaned back, eyes searching mine. Then she smiled, soft and sure, and brushed my hair from my face. "I'm just kidding," she whispered. "I think I'd like to stay a little longer. If that's okay with you."

I didn't say a word. I just held her tighter.

Because *God*, yes.

Yes, it was okay with me.

Chapter 19

Whitney

I looked up into the depths of Grady's hazel eyes, their golden flecks catching what little starlight remained. A few errant curls had fallen across his forehead, soft and wild in the night air. I reached up, brushing them aside. My fingertips lingered on his cheek longer than they should've, skimming the rough edge of stubble that had grown in since this morning.

"I'm not sure," I said softly, the words sticking in my throat. "I think I'd like to stay a little longer, if that's okay with you."

The moment hung, suspended between us. I searched his face for anything, a flicker of hesitation, a flash of regret. I was good at reading people. But Grady? He was frustratingly hard to pin down. He felt things deeply, I knew that now, but he rarely let anything slip.

Then a smile curved at the corner of his mouth, soft, like the first warmth of sunrise after a long night.

"Of course," he said. "Steven really likes having you help out at the bar."

My heart sank, the warmth in my chest snuffed out in a heartbeat. I don't know what I expected. Maybe for him to say, "*I* like having you here," but the mention of Steven snapped something fragile in me.

"Oh." I shifted back, already preparing to untangle myself from his arms as heat crept up my neck. I knew this feeling. Being tolerated. Useful. Wanted, but only until I wasn't.

But before I could retreat, Grady's arms tightened around me. I averted my gaze, not ready to see pity in his expression. Then his hand was at my chin, rough fingers coaxing my face back to his.

"I like having you around too."

Something loosened inside me. Just a little. Just enough to let warmth unfurl in my chest like a soft ache.

"You do?" My voice cracked more than I wanted it to.

He nodded and drew me in, until there was no space left between us. My chest pressed to his, and the heat of him seeped into my skin. He lowered his head and kissed the crown of mine. My entire body softened into his hold, but my heart twisted in a way I couldn't ignore.

This wasn't just about attraction anymore. This was something else. Something I hadn't let myself feel in a long time, *wanted* in a way that had nothing to do with sex or survival.

And yet, I couldn't pretend I didn't want *that*, too.

Grady smelled like soap and something uniquely him. He was strong and quiet, gentle in ways that should've made me pull back, but I didn't. My breath caught when I felt the steady rhythm of his heart against my cheek.

God, what was I doing?

My body ached for him, for his mouth, his hands, his weight pinning me to something solid, but the guilt came just as fast. I wasn't free. I hadn't earned this. I didn't even know what *this* was.

Still, I stayed. Wrapped up in the only warmth I'd wanted in weeks.

A flash of guilt scraped at the edges of my chest, sharp and unwanted. I'd been here before; different man, same ache. I told myself this wasn't betrayal, not really. Eric and I had rules. We'd broken them, bent them, twisted them so often they barely resembled boundaries anymore. But even with all of that...

I'd never *felt* this way with someone else.

I sank deeper into Grady's arms, closing my eyes as the breeze caught my hair. Everything about this felt too big, too real. His arms tightened slightly, as if he could sense I was slipping away; not physically, but emotionally. Like he was afraid to let go.

"I shouldn't be here," I whispered into his chest.

He didn't move. Didn't ask me to explain.

"You okay?" he asked, his voice low, the kind of voice you could fall into if you weren't careful.

I wanted to lie. To say *yeah, fine*, and change the subject. But I couldn't. I wasn't okay. I didn't even know what *okay* felt like anymore.

"Mmm hmm," I murmured instead, a sound that meant nothing and everything all at once.

Grady shifted slightly, just enough to brush his lips against my temple. I felt that kiss everywhere. My breath stuttered. I could feel the beat of his heart against mine, and it terrified me how badly I wanted to stay in that moment forever.

"How come I don't believe you?" he asked, his voice rough with concern.

I almost said it. *Because I'm falling for you and I don't know what to do about it.* But the words caught somewhere behind my teeth. Instead, I laughed once, too soft to mean anything. "You shouldn't."

His hand moved up and down my arms, slow and steady. I didn't realize how cold I was until the warmth of his palms made me shiver.

I told myself it was just the weather, but I knew better. I'd been cold for years, even when I was wrapped up in someone else's body.

"We should probably get back," I said, pulling back just enough to look at him. "It's getting dark."

He nodded, his eyes scanning the horizon like he'd only just noticed the setting sun. "Yeah," he said. "And you're cold."

But when he let go, the air between us felt colder than any breeze.

He helped me into the truck, closing the door gently behind me like I was something fragile. He didn't speak as he walked around and climbed into the driver's seat. I reached for the radio, needing something to break the silence in my mind, but he beat me to it. A soft acoustic track played low through the speakers, something I didn't recognize, but it felt right. Like it understood the things I didn't have the words for.

I stared out the window as the trees blurred past, my thoughts spinning. I didn't know what to do with this feeling blooming in my chest. I didn't know if I could trust it, or him, or even myself.

But I knew one thing.

I wasn't ready to leave.

By the time we pulled into the driveway, the stars had taken over the sky, bright and indifferent.

Grady helped me out of the truck, his hand warm and steady beneath mine. He didn't let go right away, not until I steadied myself on the porch. Even then, his fingers lingered against mine, like he was memorizing the shape of my hand.

When we reached the door, I touched his arm. "Thank you."

He turned, brows drawing together. "For what?"

"The dance." My voice was quieter than I meant it to be, but I didn't repeat myself.

Grady's ears flushed, a soft pink creeping across his cheekbones. "Anytime."

He unlocked the door and stepped inside, heading straight for the kitchen. "I'm gonna make some hot chocolate. Want some?"

I hesitated in the doorway, watching the way he moved. Casual. Comfortable. But there was tension under it, like he didn't quite know what to do with himself either.

I smiled. He really was the strangest combination - bad boy aesthetics with a soft, golden heart. "I think I'm just gonna go to bed."

He nodded. "Goodnight."

"'Night."

The bedroom felt colder than it had earlier. I sank down onto Jackson's bed, peeling off my jacket and rubbing my arms to chase away the chill. I stared at my phone for a long time before I unlocked it. The screen was blank, no new messages. No missed calls. Of course not.

Back in Salt Lake, my phone had been a scrapbook of our life. Me and Eric smiling on a summit. Me leading a group of climbers. Sunset shots. Drinks with friends. None of that felt real anymore. It felt like someone else's life. Someone who didn't know what it meant to ache for something more.

I hovered over my contacts and tapped Jackson's name.

It rang twice before his voicemail picked up.

"Hey, this is Jackson. You know what to do."

I closed my eyes. "Hey, big brother. Why didn't you tell me?" My throat tightened. "All these years, I thought you didn't care. And now I know the truth. I could've been there for you. I should've been. But I guess we both did what we had to do to survive."

I swallowed hard. "You deserve this. You deserve to be happy. Call me when you can. I love you."

I hung up and stared at the screen again.

One more call. The one I didn't want to make but had to.

My thumb hovered, then tapped *Eric*.

He answered on the fourth ring. "Hey baby."

I didn't let myself hesitate. "We need to talk."

"You ready to come home?" Eric asked, his voice light, smug, like he already knew the answer.

Laughter burst in the background. High-pitched. Feminine.

My stomach turned. "Who's all there?"

"Oh, you know," he said, like that explained anything. "Just some people."

I sat up straighter. "Who, Eric?"

"It's no one, baby. Just some friends."

The lie was so lazy it almost hurt more than the truth.

"Please," I said. "Just tell me."

There was a pause, then a sigh. "Amanda came over," he admitted. "She brought a friend. It wasn't planned or anything. One thing led to another and..."

"Stop," I cut him off. "Just... stop. I don't want to hear the details."

"Don't be like that."

I bit the inside of my cheek so hard I tasted blood. My fingers were shaking. I told myself to stay calm, to be rational; he always said he loved how level-headed I was. But right now, it felt like being rational was the thing that had been killing me slowly.

We have an arrangement, I reminded myself. Still, there was something I needed to know, because even our arrangement had its limitations.

"How many times?"

He hesitated. "Whitney..."

"How many?" I gritted out through clenched teeth. I wanted the answer, no matter how much it broke me.

He groaned. "A couple."

"A couple as in two?"

"I don't want to lie to you."

"Then don't."

I could hear him moving through the apartment, then the click of a door shutting.

"Come on," I said. "Just tell me."

"I miss you, Whitney."

"I miss you too," I said automatically. But it felt like I was reciting a line from a script I no longer believed in. "What does that have to do with you screwing someone else while I'm gone?"

"You know how it is. We have an arrangement."

That word again. *Arrangement.* Like love was some kind of business deal.

"I know we do. But we're supposed to talk first. That was the whole point. We *agree.*"

"You've been gone for weeks."

"You could've called," I snapped. "You didn't even *try.*"

"When?" he shot back. "When you were in the hospital? When you were playing house with Jackson and *Grady*?"

I flinched. Not because he was wrong, but because he sounded so bitter. Like he resented me for surviving.

"I am literally a phone call away," I said, voice raw now. "You didn't even give me the courtesy of a heads-up before sleeping with someone else."

"It's not like I'm in love with her."

"That's not the point," I whispered. "It was supposed to be *us.* You and me."

"It still is! Besides, you can't tell me you haven't been with someone else, and you don't see me getting upset."

"I haven't been with anyone else!" I shouted. "I would've talked to you first! Like we agreed. Remember?"

The worst part was, I *meant* it. Even after everything, I never once looked at someone else. I didn't *ask* for more. Not until now. Not until a man held me like I was more than a body to be passed around. Not until Grady.

But that only made everything more confusing.

Because this wasn't about rules. This was about how I felt. And I didn't even know what to do with that.

I let out a shaky laugh, but there was nothing funny about any of this. "How many more times, Eric? How many more times do I have to swallow it just to keep the roof over our heads?"

"Don't say it like that."

"How else am I supposed to say it?" My throat burned. "You've given me away to strangers like I'm..." My voice cracked. "Like I'm something you own. But the second I feel something for someone else, you lose your shit."

There was silence on the other end.

Finally, he said, "I don't want you mad at me."

"I'm not mad," I lied. "I'm hurt."

Another pause. Then, softer: "I love you."

I closed my eyes, wishing I didn't still want to believe it. I wiped my face with the back of my hand. "I love you too."

"Call me tomorrow?"

"Yeah," I murmured.

"Goodnight, baby."

"Night."

I set my phone down gently and stared at it, like it might somehow fix everything if I just looked long enough.

But all I saw was the same cycle. Empty apologies. Empty bed.

And I was tired of sleeping alone with nothing but regrets for company.

I didn't want sex. I didn't want revenge.

I just didn't want to feel so *alone*.

So, I stood, feet moving before my brain caught up, and the next thing I knew, I found myself in front of Grady's door, heart pounding, grief and confusion bubbling up beneath my skin.

He opened the door like he'd been waiting.

And there he was. Bare chest, wild curls, and those eyes that saw too much.

"Whitney?"

Chapter 20

Grady

I waited until Whitney disappeared into her room before dumping the hot chocolate down the sink and heading to mine. I couldn't stop thinking about the way her body fit so perfectly against mine. I wanted to pull her closer, but I knew I had to keep my distance. She wasn't mine to keep.

I peeled off my shirt and tossed it toward the hamper and missed, not that I cared. The quiet was a welcome reprieve.

I collapsed onto the bed and grabbed my phone, wincing at the screen.

Emily: When are you coming over?

Emily: You have to see these new leggings I got

Emily: Aren't you home from dinner yet?

Emily: Are you ignoring me?

Emily: *[selfie in bed]*

Emily: Answer the phone!

I barely made it through the flood before the screen lit up again, her name flashing like a warning light.

I swiped to answer. "Hey, Emily."

"Where have you been?"

"It's Sunday."

"I know what day it is. But it's after ten. You're never there this late."

I rubbed the back of my neck, already feeling the tension build. "I took Whitney to meet Mrs. Bryant."

Silence. Then the familiar scoff. "What is it with this girl, huh? Are you fucking her?"

I sat up straighter. "What the hell, Emily? She's Jackson's sister."

"Yeah," she said, voice thick with sarcasm. "And that means what exactly? You think I don't see how you look at her?"

"How do I look at her?" I snapped, already regretting answering her call.

"Like you want to know what she tastes like."

"Damn it, Emily." My voice rose before I could stop it. "Have you forgotten which one of us was the cheater?" I sucked in a breath. "I didn't mean..."

"Yes, you did," she snapped. "I thought we were past that."

I leaned back against the wall and closed my eyes. *Past it.* Like I could ever forget the look on her face as she rode Jimmy Ramsey's cock in the backseat of his car. Or the time I walked in on Frank Sutton plowing into her from behind on our couch. Or the strange man she screwed in our bed. That was the day I packed my shit and walked out.

But she always found her way back in.

"I'm tired," I said finally. "I don't want to fight. I don't have the energy to babysit your insecurities tonight."

There was a pause. "Grady…"

"Goodnight, Emily."

"But we're okay, right?"

Her voice was smaller now. Almost afraid.

I didn't answer.

I hung up, switched my phone to Do Not Disturb, only Jackson and the Bryant's could break through, and set it face down on the nightstand. I barely had time to breathe before I heard it.

A soft knock.

My heart stuttered.

There was only one other person in the house.

I crossed the room, hand already on the doorknob, and opened it.

Whitney stood in the hallway, hair tousled, eyes glassy with unshed tears.

"Whitney?"

"Can I sleep in here tonight?" Whitney's voice was barely above a whisper. "I don't want to be alone."

A lump formed in my throat. I stepped aside and gestured her in. "Yeah. Of course."

She moved past me; arms wrapped around herself like armor. I grabbed a clean t-shirt from the dresser and handed it to her. "Hey, I'm just gonna…" I motioned toward the hallway. "Be right back."

I closed the door behind me, giving her space to change. Then I headed to the bathroom and gripped the edge of the sink like it might hold me together. I turned on the faucet and splashed cold water on my face, trying to clear my head.

Not from Emily, though that mess still churned in my gut, but from Whitney. From the sight of her standing in my doorway with tear-swollen eyes and a voice that broke something open inside me.

What had happened between the drive home and now? She'd been quiet, sure, but not like this. Not cracked open.

Had she overheard my call with Emily?

I stared into the mirror. My reflection didn't offer any answers. Just a guy trying, and failing, not to fall for someone who'd been hurting longer than he could fathom.

The room was dim. Whitney was already in bed, curled on her side, her wild hair fanned over my pillow like it belonged there. I stood for a second just watching her. She looked small. Tired. Wrecked.

I changed into a pair of loose sweats, careful not to make any noise, and slid under the covers, leaving space between us like it was some kind of boundary I had to keep. For both our sakes.

I lay stiff on my back, one arm tucked beneath my head, the other anchored to the edge of the comforter. My chest ached for reasons I couldn't explain. We'd shared a bed before, once, out of necessity, but this felt different. This was deliberate. Fragile.

I glanced over.

Whitney was still. Too still.

"Grady?"

Her voice startled me.

"Yeah?" I said, throat suddenly dry.

She rolled to face me, just a shadow and a whisper. "Will you hold me?"

I hesitated for a beat too long. Not because I didn't want to, but because I did. Too much.

Still, I shifted, rolling onto my side as she scooted back until her spine met my chest. I wrapped my arms around her, slowly, deliberately, like I was afraid she'd break.

She didn't say anything. Just trembled.

Then the sobs started.

Raw. Silent. Real.

I held her tighter.

"Shh," I murmured into her hair. "I've got you. Just let it out." I pressed a kiss to her temple, soft as a prayer.

Her fingers curled around my forearm, clutching me like I was the only thing anchoring her. I didn't move. I barely breathed.

After a few minutes, her breathing slowed, but I knew she wasn't asleep.

"Wanna talk about it?" I asked quietly.

She shook her head. "No. I'm okay. I should go back to my room. I'm sorry."

She started to shift, but I tightened my hold without thinking. "Don't go," I whispered. "Just sleep. That's all."

She hesitated.

"But..."

"No pressure," I said. "Just... don't be alone tonight."

Her body relaxed, inch by inch, until she melted back into me.

I pressed a kiss to the back of her head, just once, and closed my eyes, breathing in her strawberry shampoo and the soft scent that was purely Whitney.

Emily's voice faded.

Everything else faded.

It was just this.

Her.

And for the first time in a long time, I didn't feel empty.

I rolled over, stretching out like I normally do, only something felt off.

A crash of pans from the kitchen jolted me fully awake. My first thought: Jackson's home.

But he couldn't be.

The faint scent of strawberries still clung to my sheets, pulling me back to last night. Whitney.

I scrubbed my hands over my face, memories of her pressed against me flooding in. Innocent, sure, but it didn't feel that way. Not to me. Not with the way her body fit into mine, or how I'd breathed her in like she was oxygen and I'd been holding my breath for years.

I let the memory linger a few seconds too long, then forced myself out of bed and padded toward the noise.

The kitchen looked like it had been hit by a small tornado. Flour dusted the counters. A pan was upside down in the sink. And there in the middle of the chaos was Whitney, barefoot, wearing my shirt, shaking her ass like she didn't have a care in the world.

Her phone played something upbeat, the bass low and thumping. She held a spatula like a microphone, belting out the chorus with just enough attitude to make it sexy as hell.

Good thing her back was to me, because sweatpants did nothing to hide the kind of problem she gave me first thing in the morning.

I leaned against the doorframe, arms crossed, a grin tugging at my mouth.

When the song ended, I clapped.

Whitney jumped a mile, spinning around with wide eyes. A half-cooked pancake went flying, landing on the floor with a wet splat.

"Oh my god, you scared the shit out of me!"

I burst out laughing. "I didn't know you could cook."

She rolled her eyes, cheeks flushed but smiling. "There's a lot about me you don't know."

That much was becoming clearer by the minute.

"Can I help?" I asked, stooping to grab the fallen pancake.

"You can set the table."

I raised a brow at her, but didn't argue. I grabbed what I needed and started laying everything out - plates, silverware, glasses - muscle memory kicking in even though it had been years since anyone used that table for more than sorting mail or playing poker.

"Good boy," she teased with a wink, setting down a plate stacked high with pancakes.

I shook my head, laughing. "You're trouble, you know that?"

She just grinned, looking way too pleased with herself.

I loaded my plate, drowning the pancakes in syrup. One bite and I groaned, actually groaned, without meaning to. "Holy shit. These are incredible."

"Good?" she asked, clearly fishing for the compliment.

I nodded, mouth full. "So good."

She beamed, and something in my chest cracked open. I wanted to see her like that always. Unguarded, happy, home.

"It's my mom's recipe," she said, sitting across from me.

I swallowed and raised an eyebrow. "Did your mom have more than one pancake recipe? Because Jackson swears he uses your mom's too, and his taste like cardboard."

Whitney laughed. "Nope, just the one. But Jackson never paid attention unless it involved football or Abby."

I chuckled, that tracked. But hearing her talk about her mom, even casually, stirred something in me, grief, maybe. Or the ache of wanting something I never had.

"So," she said, twirling her fork. "What's the plan for today?"

I glanced at the clock, surprised to see it was just after ten. I wasn't usually up this early, especially not after skipping a night at the bar. I had to work tonight, which meant our time was limited.

But an idea struck me, something spontaneous, a little reckless, and totally Whitney. Jackson would probably kill me. Hell, I might kill myself.

I grinned. "It's a surprise."

Chapter 21

Whitney

Grady offered to clean up after breakfast, but I quickly shooed him away. The man looked way too good in his white tee and low-slung gray sweatpants, his hair pulled back in a low ponytail like some sort of soft-spoken rockstar who didn't know how dangerous he looked.

I hadn't realized it was that long. Or that he could pull that off.

He disappeared into his room, murmuring into his phone about "logistics" and "timing" while I tried to pretend I wasn't dying of curiosity. I prayed whatever surprise he had brewing, didn't involve Emily. I was not emotionally equipped for that kind of morning.

Cleanup took next to no time, my mom drilled "clean as you go" into us like gospel. I wiped down the counters, hung the towel neatly on the oven handle, and tried not to pace. I debated spying on Grady, just to get a peek or overhear something helpful. But I stopped myself.

This wasn't just anyone. This was *Grady*. He wasn't trying to screw with my head. I could wait. Probably.

Thirty minutes later, we were in his truck, windows down, radio up, the wind teasing my hair as we flew down the highway. He still refused to give me any hint other than to dress comfortably and wear sneakers, quite possibly the most useless guidance ever. That narrowed things down to about ninety percent of the known universe.

But one look at him, one real look, and I let it go. His smile tipped just slightly at the corners, like he was trying not to give himself away. He drove with one hand, relaxed in a way I'd never seen, and he let me take full control of the radio without even pretending to care.

I don't think I'd ever seen him like this. At peace.

Oddly enough, I felt it too. The breeze on my face, his music mixing with mine, the vague hum of not knowing what was next... It felt like I could *breathe*. Like for the first time in years, I could just be *me* without having to fight for it.

When we crossed the Colorado-Wyoming border, my pulse jumped. The guys at work used to talk about a place up in Laramie, some off-the-wall adrenaline spot. No way Grady was taking me there, though. Jackson would probably hunt him down and bury him with his bare hands.

I unstrapped my stupid boot and tucked my feet under me like a kid, like I could maybe spot something on the horizon if I sat just right.

Grady caught the motion and chuckled, shaking his head. His grin spread until I could see just a flash of teeth, and damn it if it didn't make my heart skip.

"How about a hint?" I asked, trying not to sound like I was begging.

He scratched the stubble along his jaw, like he was pretending to think. "It's indoor."

I scoffed. "That's not a hint. That's barely a direction."

He laughed, clearly enjoying himself. "Okay, okay. You'll feel the wind in your hair. And you'll need goggles."

Goggles?

My mind raced with the possibilities. Swimming? No, I hadn't packed a swimsuit. I didn't even *own* one at the moment. So... not water. Not hiking. Not anything that made sense. "Better," I admitted, "but still not good enough."

He threw me another lopsided grin, eyes gleaming. "So, here's the thing," he said, "I've been here before, but not since it opened."

I blinked at him. "Wait, so you've been, but not... been?"

"Exactly."

We shared a look, and I couldn't help but laugh.

The next song on the radio made me stop short. I turned the volume up instinctively. "Troubled Waters." The song. *My* song. The one that made me feel like I could come up for air.

I remembered the first time I'd heard it, how I'd stood on a mountainside, the sun filtering through trees, strangers' voices fading into the background. It wasn't just music. It was a decision. That night, I'd gone home and said no. No to the pills. No to the tequila.

I thought about Ashley, my boss at the gym, who was already pushing her luck letting me guide hikes again. I'd already failed two random drug tests. One more, and I'd lose the only thing that gave me purpose.

But that song made something in me want to try again.

Hearing it now, flying down the road with Grady beside me, made the moment feel whole. Like that choice hadn't just been for then. It was for *now* too.

Grady drove past Laramie. Past Cheyenne. Past everything I thought I knew.

By the time we took the exit for Silverlake, my curiosity was eating me alive. But the smile on his face said he wasn't ready to give it up just yet.

"Are we there yet?" I asked, grinning like a kid.

He looked over, that same calm amusement on his face. "Almost. Five more minutes."

I stared out the window at the blur of little shops and parking lots, until something I spotted something that couldn't be... "Wait a second..."

He just grinned and pulled into a crowded lot, cutting the engine. "Sky High," I read off the storefront.

Butterflies erupted in my stomach. And this time, they had nothing to do with fear.

He nodded, his Adam's apple bobbing as he swallowed. "I know the owner - Jeffrey. He and I had done some time together at one of our foster homes. When he told me he was opening this place, I thought he was crazy. I mean, who goes skydiving in general, let alone indoors?"

I bounced in my seat, my hand in the air. "Me! Me! I do!"

He chuckled, "You remind me of him. He always had to be doing something to quiet the thoughts in his head. Not that you do that, I mean..."

"It's okay," I cut him off. He had me pegged. "The thrill, the adrenaline. It keeps the nightmares at bay."

"For him too." He dropped his gaze to his hands. "Can I ask... are your dreams more about your foster homes, or what happened to your parents?" His voice was low, careful. "Jackson mentioned a little..."

I raised my hand to cut him off, not wanting to think about that day. I closed my eyes as flashes of rolling storm clouds tried to invade my thoughts. I shook it off. "Both, but mostly the foster homes."

He didn't push for more, just took my hand, his calloused fingers rough against my skin. "I understand," he whispered.

Something told me he did, and I hated that for him.

A surge of adrenaline bloomed in my chest as Grady held the door to the indoor skydiving center open for me. Sky High was no longer just a cheesy kids movie. This place was an adrenaline junkie's drug, even more so than the rock-climbing gym I worked at. For years I had dreamed about bungee jumping, paragliding, and yes, skydiving. Eric always said it was too dangerous. He wasn't willing to lose me just so I could get another high. He did, however, take me zip lining, and once we even managed to go parasailing down in Pueblo.

I bounced on the balls of my feet, hardly able to control my excitement. "Do we get to...?" I let my question hang, unable to finish the thought.

"Come on, let me introduce you to Jeffrey."

With his hand on the small of my back, Grady led me past a group of teenagers, all dressed in different colored jumpsuits, and the wind tunnel that stood front and center. It looked like a little kid and probably an instructor, were taking their turn, soaring high, then practicing a slower descent.

We didn't even make it to the counter before we were approached by a rather imposing man. At least six-five, his rich mahogany skin contrasted beautifully with his wide, white smile.

"Grady!" He greeted him with a typical bro-hug, bumping chests, slapping backs.

"Hey, man. Thanks for this," Grady gestured around us.

Before he could introduce me, Jeffrey had already turned. "You must be Whitney."

I held out my hand and he brushed it away, pulling me in for a hug instead. "You better treat him right," he whispered so low only I could hear, then pulled back, that brilliant smile back in place.

"I cannot believe you are here," he laughed, throwing an arm over Grady's shoulder and leading him away, back toward the front desk.

I followed close behind, not quite sure how to feel anymore. His words were a softly spoken warning, but not unkind. Protective, maybe. I didn't know what Grady had told him, but whatever it was, it made him care.

Jeffrey grabbed a couple of clipboards and pens. "First, I'll need you two to fill out these forms."

Grady shook his head. "Oh, no. I'm just here to watch."

"No way, man. You can't come all the way out here and not fly!"

"See, that's the thing," he said, smiling. "I can."

"What are you so afraid of?" Jeffrey teased. "Embarrassing yourself in front of your girlfriend?"

I swear my jaw hit the floor, my cheeks flaring red.

Grady just laughed, still refusing to take the clipboard. "Nah, this just isn't my thing," he said, not denying anything.

Jeffrey rolled his eyes, but let it go. "Yeah, yeah. I had to try."

I eyed them curiously for another minute before turning my attention to the paper in front of me. My heart stuttered in my chest. I was actually going to go skydiving! Well, indoor skydiving... Close enough.

The next hour flew by in a flurry of instructions, getting suited up, then convincing Grady that Jackson wouldn't kill him, even on the rare chance something bad happened to me.

"It's fine, Grady. What's the worst that can happen?"

He blew out a heavy breath and double checked the zipper on my jumpsuit, his fingers grazing my neck. "I know." He gripped my shoulders, his thumbs brushing back and forth, studying my face like he needed to be absolutely sure I wasn't scared. I wasn't. I only felt the heat of his hands and the rush of something I wasn't quite ready to name.

I knew my adrenaline addiction wasn't healthy, but it was so much better than the alternative.

He leaned in and pressed a kiss to my forehead before pulling me into his arms. My heart stuttered in my chest; an unfamiliar feeling raced through my veins all the way to the tips of my fingers. "Just be careful," he whispered.

I relaxed into him, relishing his warmth and the safety of his arms. "I will. Promise."

Grady gave my hand one final squeeze and stepped back, but the way his eyes lingered on me, like I was doing something sacred, left my chest tight. It wasn't fear. It was something else. Something I didn't quite know how to name.

The instructor motioned me toward the tunnel. My heart thundered, not from fear, but from the sheer anticipation of it. Of flying.

I stepped forward, wind rushing in waves through the vertical chamber, tugging at my suit, my hair, my skin. I looked back once, just once, and saw Grady through the glass, arms crossed, watching me like I was the only thing in the room. My chest clenched, and then the instructor gave the signal.

And I flew.

The wind caught me and lifted me effortlessly, like gravity forgot I existed. It ripped at my face, a cold, exhilarating rush that drowned out everything but the beat of my own heart. I felt weightless, as if the world was suspended in that moment, just me and the air around me. I tilted my hands, adjusted my legs, just like the training, and soared higher. It was loud and chaotic, and somehow the most peaceful thing I'd ever known. There was no room for anxiety. No room for memories. No space for the scars or the cravings or the guilt.

It was just me. Weightless. Breathless. Free.

No pill had ever given me this. No high had ever felt this clean.

I tipped into a slow spin, and I caught a flash of Grady again, eyes wide, a hand pressed to the glass. Like he couldn't believe what he was seeing.

For once, neither could I.

When I landed, my legs shook, not from nerves, but from the rush of it. I couldn't stop smiling. Couldn't stop laughing. I tore off my goggles, flung open the door to the tunnel, and ran. Straight into his arms.

Grady caught me mid-laugh, his hands steady on my waist, his chest warm against mine.

"That was amazing!" I gasped. "Can I go again?"

His smile was soft, a little dazed, like he wasn't sure what hit him. "Whatever you want," he said.

And I believed him.

Chapter 22

Grady

Whitney's laughter echoed even after she'd taken off running, her arms out like wings, wild and breathless and alive in a way I hadn't seen from her before. She looked over her shoulder once, her cheeks flushed, her smile stretched wide across her face, and damn if it didn't lodge something sharp right behind my ribs.

Jeffrey nudged my shoulder, a cocky grin already forming. "You good, man?"

I tried to play it cool, rolling out my shoulders and crossing my arms. "What was I thinking, bringing her here?"

"Maybe that you wanted your girl to have a good time." he said, like it was the most obvious thing in the world.

"She's not my girl," I muttered, an unfamiliar ache blossoming in my chest. "She's..."

"Jackson's baby sister, yeah, yeah," he cut in. "You keep saying that like it explains a damn thing, but I'm looking at you, man. And what I see? That's not you being a big brother."

I opened my mouth, but he kept going, ticking off fingers like he was building a case.

"You brought her to Sky High - voluntarily. You've got that tight, quiet look you get when something matters. And you haven't taken your eyes off her since she walked through that door."

I scoffed, but my gaze snagged on Whitney again, mid-spin in the air tunnel, her limbs stretched out like she'd been made to fly. "I'm so screwed."

Jeffrey cracked up, slapping his thigh. "Nah, man. The word you're looking for is *fucked*."

I glared at him from the corner of my eye. I don't know when it happened, or even how, but somewhere over the past few weeks, something in me had shifted. I didn't know what to do with it. I had caught feelings for my best friend's little sister.

"She's so much better than Emily," he added, quieter this time.

My whole body went tense. "Fuck."

Jeffrey turned toward me, all joking gone. "Whoa, whoa, whoa. You're not seriously still with her?"

I lifted one shoulder. "Yeah. I took her back again."

His face darkened. "After everything?"

I didn't answer. I didn't have to.

He stared at me, disappointed but not surprised. "Grady, come on. You're not in this for love, or sex, or... hell, anything good."

"I know."

"You can do better."

I shrugged. "Even if I could, it wouldn't matter."

"Because of Jackson?"

"Because I'm messed up," I said, tapping my temple. "I don't know how to do normal. I don't know how to *be* enough."

Jeffrey's voice dropped. "That's not true."

I didn't reply. I couldn't.

Just then, Whitney pulled off the cleanest dive I'd seen all day, landing like she'd been doing this for years. She beamed through the glass, glowing with a kind of joy that made my chest ache.

"She's okay," Jeffrey said, like he knew what I was thinking.

"She's incredible," I breathed.

He looked at me sidelong. "And so are you. Even if you can't see it yet."

I sighed. "Even if that were true, it doesn't matter. She has a boyfriend."

Whitney slowly landed on the edge of the tunnel, and wasted no time stepping out, the biggest smile on her face. "Oh yeah? And does she look at him the way she looks at you?"

Before I could respond, Whitney burst out of the tunnel, her grin still in place. She sprinted toward us, eyes locked on mine and launched herself into my arms. I caught her without thinking, the weight of her body pressed flush to mine, her laughter tumbling against my throat.

She pressed a quick, impulsive kiss to my lips - just a brush, but it sent my thoughts spinning. Then she was gone again, bouncing on her toes, waiting for her next turn.

I stared after her, stunned.

Jeffrey let out a low whistle. "Boyfriend, huh?"

I didn't answer. I couldn't. Not when every single part of me wanted to call her mine.

Whitney talked the entire drive back. About the wind, the instructor, the rush of lifting off. Her words tumbled over each other, animated and breathless, like the flight hadn't left her body yet. I just listened, stealing glances at her whenever I could.

She glowed.

And I'd done that. I'd given her that.

The weight in my chest was the good kind, the kind that settled in deep and warm, even if it scared the hell out of me.

By the time we pulled into the bar parking lot, I didn't want the night to end. I just wanted to keep driving. Keep her beside me, barefoot in the passenger seat, talking about flying like it saved her.

Inside, she moved through the bar like she'd always been there, like she belonged. She leaned on the counter, laughing with one of the regulars, her boot propped on the rung of a stool, her head thrown back. She didn't notice me watching.

My chest squeezed.

I wanted to stay in that moment, but the buzz of my phone dragged me out of it. Again.

I fished it out of my pocket, hoping for Jackson's name, that anchor I kept reaching for to remind me this wasn't mine to want.

No such luck.

Emily.

The screen lit up with her face and her name and that familiar dread settled into my gut.

I glanced at Whitney, caught her eye, and gave a quick nod toward the office. She gave me a thumbs up, casual, like this was nothing.

But it wasn't nothing.

Once inside, I shut the door behind me and leaned against the desk like it might hold me up.

"Hey, Emily. I'm kinda busy right now."

"Oh no, you don't, Grady Thomas. I've been calling you all day!"

I pinched the bridge of my nose. "Give me a minute."

"No. You've been dodging me. Again."

"I've had things going on."

"Like what?" she snapped. "You forget you have a girlfriend?"

Her voice always had that edge, like sweetness sharpened to a knife. I hated how fast it got under my skin. How fast it made me feel like I owed her something I didn't have in me to give.

"I'm just tired, Emily."

"Tired of what?" Her tone softened like she was switching gears. "Of me?"

I stayed quiet too long.

"I could come over," she offered. "Give you one of those back rubs you like."

I closed my eyes. I didn't want that. I didn't want *her*. But the words wouldn't come.

"I don't think that's a good idea," I said finally.

"Grady, come on," she said, all gentle now. "You need me. What kind of girlfriend would I be if I wasn't there for you?"

I let out a slow breath and let defeat settle in. "I won't be home until close to three."

"That's fine. Gives me time to get ready. See you then."

The line went dead.

Every call with Emily felt like a chain around my ankle, and every second with Whitney felt like a breath of fresh air. But how could I want that? How could I want her?

I stared at the phone for a long beat before I set it down beside me and raked a hand through my hair. I knew what I needed to do. I just needed someone else to say it out loud.

I pulled up Jackson's number and hit call.

Voicemail.

"Hey, this is Jackson. You know what to do."

I exhaled through my nose and tried to hold it together. "Hey, brother. The bar's fine. Whitney's fine. I just really need to talk to you. It's important. Please call me back when you can."

I ended the call and sat there, phone in hand, the weight of everything pressing in from all sides. The bar was quiet. Whitney's laugh filtered through the walls, muffled but unmistakable.

And all I could think was how badly I wanted to be enough - for her, for myself. For once.

But I wasn't.

Not yet.

Not tonight.

Chapter 23

Whitney

The bar lights glowed soft and amber, but inside, I was lit up. My chest felt light. My lungs pulled in air like it mattered, like *I* mattered. For the first time in months, I didn't feel numb or strung out or halfway here. I felt *alive*.

I'd actually slept last night. No nightmares clawing at me, no chasing a high just to shut off my brain. Just real rest. And I went skydiving. Well, indoor skydiving. But still. It was the closest I'd ever come to flying, and it beat anything I'd felt in years. The only thing that could top it might be the real deal. And I doubted Grady would ever let me jump out of an actual plane.

That's okay. Baby steps.

"Well, hello there, little lady. You're looking ravishing tonight."

I turned, grinning. "You're such a charmer."

Ray, Falcon Pointe's resident flirt, winked. He was pushing sixty and had a comeback for everything. "What'll it be tonight?"

He grinned, "Oh, you know. The usual."

"Not ready to spice things up?" I asked, already pouring his Coors.

"Only if you're planning on getting spicy with me," he teased.

I handed him the pint and leaned on the counter. "You're trouble."

He settled onto the stool, eyes twinkling. "So, you gonna tell me what put that glow on your face, or do I gotta go find the boss?"

I froze mid-laugh. "I don't know what you're talking about."

"Mmm hmm. Let's see what Grady has to say about that."

Just hearing his name sent a current through me. "Why would Grady know anything?"

Ray sipped, then wiped his mouth with the back of his hand. "Maybe because he's wearing the same look."

I rolled my eyes. "He is not."

"Don't bullshit a bullshitter."

I shook my head. "It's nothing."

"Then why not just tell old Ray and save yourself the aggravation?"

"Why do you care so much?"

He grinned. "Because whatever put that look on your face? Should happen more often. A woman like you deserves to float on cloud nine."

I raised an eyebrow. "First glowing, now I'm gonna start levitating? What's next, aliens?"

He made a move to wave Grady over, and I nearly leapt across the bar to stop him. "Okay, okay!" I whisper-shouted.

Ray folded his hands under his chin, practically bouncing with anticipation. "I'm all ears, darlin'."

I opened my mouth just as Grady caught my eye. He gestured to his phone, then toward the office. I gave him a thumbs-up. His timing was impeccable. The last thing I wanted was to gush about my day while he was right there listening.

I turned back to Ray. "Grady took me skydiving."

Ray's brows shot up. "Grady? *Our* Grady?"

I nodded.

"Took you *skydiving*?"

"Well... indoor skydiving."

Ray shook his head and tapped the bar. "I think I need a shot of whiskey."

I grabbed a glass and filled it to the brim. "Why is that so shocking?"

He downed it in one go and set the glass down with a thud. "Sweetheart, I've known that man since he first came to Falcon Pointe. Not once have I seen him go looking for a thrill. The guy barely risks jaywalking."

I arched a brow. "He's dating Emily. I'd call *that* risky."

Ray laughed. "Fair point. But skydiving? That's different."

I nodded. Grady was full of contradictions. The quiet brooder with the soul of a storm. All long curls and tightly coiled strength. The kind of man who made you feel both safe... and a little dangerous. "Tell me about him."

"You're the one living with him."

"Exactly. I know the version he lets me see. I want to know more."

Ray slid his glass forward, and I refilled it. He downed the second shot and let out a breath. "Back when I worked with the department, I got called in to help with tough cases. Grady came in after supposedly assaulting a foster brother in another town." He shook his head. "Sixteen, black eye, covered in bruises. Scared out of his damn mind. There's no way he started that fight."

"Poor Grady." I swallowed hard. I knew something about being on the wrong end of abuse - physical, emotional, the kind no one saw coming.

"He barely spoke. But I'll tell you this, I've never seen a kid with such good manners. Please, sir. Thank you, sir. He was broken, but not bitter. That's rare."

It sounded like the Grady I knew.

"So what does any of that have to do with indoor skydiving?"

"You know he played football?"

"Yeah. With Jackson."

"Well, that year was huge. Jackson Taylor, star quarterback... The town's golden boy. It was the first time in a long time that the Bulldogs were winning games every week. Then Grady shows up. Quiet, nervous, jumpy. Jackson took him under his wing. Taught him how to hold his own. Taught him how to push back against fear."

I tilted my head. "Grady rides a motorcycle..."

Ray sighed. "There's a story there, too."

"Let me guess... Jackson made him do it?"

Ray barked a laugh. "That'd be the day. Jackson *hates* bikes."

"Then why..."

"That's a story for another time." He rubbed a hand over his face. "And maybe one Grady should be the one to tell."

The office door slammed, loud and sudden. I jumped.

Grady stormed out, face like thunder. He didn't look at me, didn't speak, just pushed through the main doors and disappeared into the night.

I started to move, instinct kicking in like a reflex, but Ray caught my wrist.

"Give him a minute."

"But..."

"You've got a good heart," Ray said, his voice low. "But that man... he has some demons."

"Don't we all?" I muttered, barely above a whisper.

He looked at me for a long second, then let go of my wrist with a slow shake of his head. "Yeah. Something tells me you know all about that."

I stared at the door Grady had vanished through. I still wanted to go after him. Still wanted to know what had cracked through that calm, steady exterior.

But for once, I didn't.

Not because I didn't care, but because maybe, just maybe, I cared enough to wait.

So I stayed.

Chapter 24

Grady

Relief hit me hard when I saw the empty driveway. No Emily. Not yet. *Maybe she forgot?* No, I wasn't that lucky. *Maybe she fell asleep?*

I clung to that hope as I unlocked the door and held it open for Whitney. She had been quiet ever since I came back. I couldn't blame her. For all I knew, slamming doors was a trigger for her, yet in that moment, it felt like the only way to release the pressure.

That and the walk I took afterward.

"I'm gonna..." Whitney gestured to Jackson's room.

We didn't need to say anything. The way our hands brushed as we passed each other, the way we lingered just a second too long... Those were the moments that spoke louder than words

"Goodnight."

"Thank you. You know, for earlier."

I couldn't help the smile that spread across my face or the warmth that welled in my chest. "It was my pleasure. I'm glad you enjoyed it."

"I did. Very much." She opened the door to Jackson's room, but before she closed it, turned back one last time. "Goodnight, Grady."

I blew out a breath. Today had been one of the best days of my life. Then Emily called.

I looked at my guitar, propped beside the couch. My fingers itched to play, to pour it all out, but I was too tired. I grabbed a glass of water and drained it before heading to my room.

I pulled my shirt off as I stepped inside, exhausted and ready to crash, only to stop dead in my tracks.

"Hey, baby," Emily purred, sprawled across my bed in nothing but a scrap of pink lace. "Welcome home."

My breath caught, more from disbelief than anything else. "What... what are you doing here?"

She stretched like a cat, crawling to the foot of the bed. "I came to make you feel better."

I glanced around the room. No clothes. No bag. "How did you get in? I didn't see your car."

"I took an Uber," she said lightly, like it was the most normal thing in the world. "Used the key under the mat."

Of course she did. I'd told Jackson that was a bad idea.

She ran a hand up my bare chest. "You seemed tense earlier. I thought maybe you needed me."

"I said I was tired." I stepped away and grabbed a clean shirt from the dresser, but her arms slipped around my waist from behind.

"Then let me take care of you," she whispered, fingers ghosting toward my belt.

My stomach turned. She didn't get it. Didn't even try to.

I pulled away and turned to face her. "Emily, I told you..."

But she was already kneeling, working my zipper open. Her hands slid into my boxers.

I flinched. "Em. Stop."

She looked up, confused. "What's wrong?"

"I'm just... I'm tired."

Her expression faltered. "Right." She tried to recover, standing and tossing her hair. "Then come to bed. Let me hold you."

"You didn't answer me. Why are you really here?" I asked, pulling out my phone.

I frowned, there were no missed texts or calls from Jackson, even though I left him a voicemail earlier. Weird. He should've called back by now.

"To be with you." Her eyes darted toward my phone. "You've been ignoring my calls. I thought maybe if I showed up in person..."

She reached toward the phone, brushing it with her fingertips. "You don't need to call anyone right now. Let's just focus on us."

Something cold and instinctual crept into my chest. I set the phone down slowly.

She slipped her arms around my neck again. "Remember how good we used to be?" she breathed. "I know you, every inch of you."

Her lips found my collarbone.

"Emily..." I stepped back. "We need to talk."

She froze, then laughed softly. "Talk? Now?"

"Yes. Now."

I sat on the edge of the bed and looked up at her, practically naked, clinging to a fantasy that didn't exist anymore. "I can't do this. We're not good together. Not anymore."

Her smile wavered. "This isn't about me. This is about her, isn't it? The little runaway in your house?"

I stood, jaw tightening. "This is about me finally doing what I should have done months ago."

"You're making a mistake."

"No. I made the mistake by letting this drag on. By thinking I owed you something because of what we used to be."

"I *love* you, Grady."

I softened my tone. "I believe you *think* you do."

She flinched like I'd slapped her.

"I care about you. I always will," I added. "But it's not the kind of love that builds a life."

Emily blinked rapidly, fighting tears, and failing. "If you do this, don't come crawling back. We're done."

"I know."

She stomped her foot like a toddler. "Grady! Come on, seriously?"

I opened my bedroom door, signaling it was time for her to leave. "Do you need me to order you a car?"

She stared at me like she didn't recognize the person in front of her. Then she turned, storming into the hall.

Whitney's door creaked open just as Emily grabbed her coat. I silently willed her to leave, to just walk out, but of course things are never that easy.

Emily stopped short and turned. "I hope you're happy," she snapped.

Whitney didn't flinch. She smiled, slow and sweet. "I am, actually."

With a final stomp and a slammed door, Emily was gone.

The silence afterward was beautiful.

I exhaled. I could breathe again.

Whitney raised a brow. "What happened to her clothes?"

I raked a hand through my hair. "Your guess is as good as mine."

She started laughing, then crossed the room. "Are you okay?"

I looked at her, hair wild, skin soft under Jackson's old t-shirt. I wanted her. God, I wanted her.

"I'm okay." I reached up and tucked a curl behind her ear.

Whitney tilted her head. "Were those baby pink panties?"

I barked a laugh. "What?"

"I'm serious!"

I locked the door and put the chain in place. "I'm surprised you could see them."

"Wasn't exactly trying," she said. "But it's not every day you see someone try to seduce a guy in baby pink. Like, 'Hey, knock me up so we can see this shade on everything!'"

I grinned. "Baby pink?"

"Yeah. The classic girl color. Why does blue get all the baby glory?"

She brushed past me into my room, pulled back the covers, and slid into my bed like it was hers.

I swallowed hard. My body responded instantly.

"Fair point," I said, climbing in beside her.

She pressed her back to my front. My arms wrapped around her on instinct.

"Just sleep," she whispered.

I kissed the back of her head.

"Just sleep."

Chapter 25

Whitney

Life with Grady felt unexpectedly safe, like I could finally exhale after holding my breath for months. It was like the black cloud that used to hover over him had blown away. Honestly, I think it followed Emily out the door that night.

I hadn't meant to walk in on his epic breakup, but after reading the string of texts from Eric, ranging from sweet and apologetic, to impatient and angry, I was ready to run. It was a side of Eric I rarely saw, but one I knew too well; a side that always drove me to another drink, a smoke, a handful of pills, anything to numb the feelings it elicited.

I'd started searching through Jackson's room, hoping for something, anything, that might take the edge off. The back of the closet, his dresser drawers... But of course, Jackson was basically a grown-up Boy Scout. The only surprises I found were some adult-themed "toys" I doubted he'd want me discovering.

I paused, thinking about what Steven had said. Was Jackson bi? Maybe. I loved him either way. That didn't change anything.

I'd put everything back where I found it and stepped into the hall. It didn't take a genius to know something was about to go down. Grady had been in a foul mood ever since that mystery phone call. Then, when we got home, there was a distinctly feminine coat slung over the armchair. It wasn't mine, and Jackson was still MIA. That only left one person.

A shudder ran through me. I'd expected to hear things I didn't want to hear. Emily was a knockout; long, silky blonde hair, curves in all the right places. Exactly Eric's type. Her lips alone would've earned her his crude label: DSL.

I glanced at Grady on the couch, fingers moving over his guitar like the melody lived inside him. That same haunting tune, over and over, until it felt like it had burrowed into me too. Grady was beautiful, there was no other way to describe him. He was tall, lean, and his hair was the perfect amount of wild. His eyes held a soulful depth, I had to be careful not to stare into them for too long, for fear of getting lost.

I'd imagined his hands on my body more than once. Those fingers, rough in all the right ways. I could still feel them ghosting over my stomach when he thought I was asleep, his breath brushing the back of my neck.

But Grady was more than looks and talent. He was kind. Thoughtful. Gentle in ways that caught me off guard.

For the past week, I'd been sleeping in his bed. And while he didn't hide his reactions, his impressive size pressing against me in the middle of the night, he never made a move. Just held me close. Sometimes, his fingers danced absently across my stomach, like he was playing some silent song meant only for us.

Heat stirred low in my belly, and I squeezed my thighs together. I'd tried to get him to make a move, more than once.

My phone buzzed on the table. I exhaled, expecting another plea or guilt trip from Eric. I was so done with that loop.

But when I saw the name on the screen, everything else disappeared.

"Jackson? Is it really you?"

His warm, familiar voice came through. "Who else?"

Grady stopped playing and stood. He hadn't been able to reach Jackson either.

"Where have you been?" I asked. "Why haven't you answered any of our calls or texts?"

"Things got a little crazy here, but now that you know... I have to tell you. She's amazing, Whit."

"So, you found her?" My heart leapt. "You really found her?"

"I did." His voice softened. "I've got so much to tell you."

I sank into my chair. "I'm all ears."

He laughed. "I figured. But now's not the best time. Soon."

"Promise?"

"I promise. Hey, how's Grady doing? I got a few weird voicemails and texts from him, but I haven't been able to reach him."

I looked up. Grady had crept closer, his expression a mix of worry and hope. "He's right here. Want to talk to him?"

"Please."

I started to pass the phone, but Jackson's voice stopped me.

"Wait!"

"Yeah?"

"I love you, Whitney. Thank you for being there for him. It's the only reason I can stomach being away so long."

"Love you too, big brother."

"Okay," he chuckled. "Now hand him the phone."

I passed the phone to Grady, who took it like it was something fragile. "He's all yours," I said with a wink, then slipped out of the room to give them privacy.

My brother was safe. He'd found the love of his life. And with any luck, he'd be coming home soon, with Abby in tow.

I always loved her when we were kids.

And now, with Grady on the phone and distracted, I had the perfect opportunity to start planning how I was going to get him up on that damn stage.

Chapter 26

Grady

Some days, my guitar felt like an extension of me; a limb more fluent in emotion than I was. The familiar weight, the hum of the strings beneath my fingers, steadied something inside me.

I started the song over again, not needing to think. It was coming together. The first song I'd written in years, born from the kind of inspiration I wasn't supposed to entertain. Whitney Taylor.

I closed my eyes, fingers tracing the melody while my thoughts drifted. I could still feel the warmth of her skin, the way her breath hitched when my fingers grazed her stomach. She was everything. And off-limits.

The buzz of her phone on the table jolted me back to the present. Probably her boyfriend. Again. I tried not to care, but every time it lit up, I wanted to know more. Were they fighting? Were they done? Even if they were, she still wasn't mine.

"Jackson?! Is it really you?"

Whitney's voice pulled me upright. My fingers stilled, muting the strings. I was on my feet before I knew what I was doing, heart hammering. Was it really him?

I crossed the room, adrenaline pushing me forward. He hadn't answered calls, texts, nothing. I knew he was chasing something big, but the silence had gutted me.

Whitney passed me the phone, smiling like she understood exactly how much I needed this.

"Grady?"

Jackson's voice cracked something open. "Yeah. I'm here."

"God, man. It's good to hear your voice."

I sank into the chair Whitney had vacated, rubbing a hand over my face. "You too. Is everything okay?"

"Don't do that," Jackson scolded. "Don't pretend with me. What's going on? I got your messages, your texts and I've been trying to reach you, but you haven't responded or answered. Are you okay?"

I grabbed my phone. No missed calls. No texts.

My brow furrowed. That didn't make sense, but it was a problem for later.

A tight knot formed in my stomach. "No. Yes," I sighed. "I don't know."

"Relax, okay. Walk me through it. What's going on?"

I inhaled slowly, held it, exhaled. "The bar's good."

"I know," he laughed. "I'd never have left if I didn't know it wasn't in the best hands. What else?"

"I, uh... I broke up with Emily."

"Fucking finally!"

I couldn't help it, I laughed.

"I'm proud of you. I know I've been... less than supportive of your relationship. But you can do so much better!"

I thought of Whitney. The quiet way she steadied me. The way she looked in my bed, curled up in one of Jackson's old shirts. Guilt tugged at my chest.

"Actually," I said, voice low. "There's something I need to tell you."

"You found someone?"

"No. Not exactly."

I glanced down the hall. My pulse picked up.

"It's about your sister."

His tone shifted immediately. "Is she okay?"

"She's great. Really great. Smart. Funny. And somehow, she quiets the noise in my head like no one else has."

Silence stretched. Then, "What are you saying?"

"I like her." I swallowed hard. "I didn't mean to. Nothing's happened. She has a boyfriend. But... I've been spending time with her, and if it ever turned into something..."

"Slow down, Grady. Breathe..."

I did as he said. "I'm sorry. If you're mad..."

"Who said I'm mad?"

I blinked. "I thought you would be."

"I want you to take a second and tell me... What do you want?"

I closed my eyes and blew out a heavy breath. "I can't."

"That's okay. It's okay. Let's talk through it, like we used to. Sound good?"

I nodded, "Yeah."

"You have feelings for Whitney."

It wasn't a question, and as much as I wanted to deny it, to save myself the pain of having to shut these feelings down, or lose my best friend, my brother, I couldn't lie to him. "Yes."

"Friendly, or romantic?"

I swallowed thickly, "Both."

"Okay. And what does she think?"

"I don't know..."

He chuckled, and something in me eased. "You haven't told her?"

"No. I couldn't. I can't."

"Why?"

"You know why."

"Yeah, I guess I do. Have you talked to anyone else about this?"

"Jackson, can you just... Stop being my friend for a minute and be the protective big brother? Tell me to stay away?"

"Who's big brother? Hers or yours?"

I closed my eyes and raked my free hand through my hair. "Hers."

"Is that what you really want? Me to tell you to stay away from her?"

"Yes..." I exhaled sharply. "No. I don't know."

"I need you to listen to me, okay?"

I nodded, even though he couldn't see me. "Okay."

"Grady," Jackson said gently. "You are the best man I know. You're my best friend, my brother. I have seen you at your lowest, and I've seen you at your worst. And if I had to choose someone to take care of my sister, to love her... it would be you."

The air rushed out of my lungs like I'd been holding it for weeks. He wasn't angry. He wasn't shutting me out. He was giving me his trust, and his sister.

Unfortunately, his trust didn't change my past, didn't change *me*. "But, what about..."

"I told you before, and I'll tell you again. The right woman will change everything for you."

"She's not like Emily."

"I know," he chuckled. "I may have missed the past ten plus years of her life, but we have the same origin story. The same example of loving parents. And since she was in the system for much longer than I was, I suspect she understands you in ways I never will."

"That's not true."

"It is. Don't think for a second that I don't hear you late at night, when you think I'm asleep."

"You... What?" My hand immediately went to the long scab on my arm where I cut myself most recently. *Did he know about this too?*

"I know there are things you've been through that you haven't told me. Things that you don't talk about. I get it. You don't have to tell me everything for me to understand that you endured some fucked up shit. I got lucky. I know that. But you and my sister? I can't even imagine."

"Jackson..." I had to force myself to swallow around the lump in my throat.

"I love you, man."

"I love you too," I said, voice tight.

"So... what now?"

"Nothing," I said. "She still has a boyfriend."

"Ugh," I could practically hear him rolling his eyes. "She can do so much better than that guy."

I smiled faintly. "She deserves to make her own choice."

"And that is why you're a better man than I am."

I shook my head, but the words stayed with me. I couldn't help but wonder if Eric would always have a hold on her. If the ghost of him would shadow us, no matter how much I wanted to be the one who healed her.

"How's Mrs. B?"

"She's good. Taking full advantage of Mr. Bryant being gone. There's been a lot of strawberry shortcake."

Jackson laughed. "God, I miss her."

"When are you coming back?"

He paused. "I don't know. It's complicated."

"But it's her? Abby?"

"Yeah. It wasn't her choice to leave. There's a lot more, but I can't get into it yet."

"I'm here when you're ready."

"I know." He paused. "And Grady?"

"Yeah?"

"Keep being there for Whitney."

I smiled. "Always."

Chapter 27

Whitney

I drummed my fingers on the bar top, each tap louder than the last. I didn't need to check the clock to know that my perfect window of opportunity was slipping away.

"Relax," Steven murmured, stilling my hand with his own. "He'll be here."

I swatted him away. "When I called Mrs. Bryant to help keep Grady busy so I could pull this together, I didn't expect her to make him late to his own surprise."

Steven rolled his eyes. "What do you think happened? He got lost between the mashed potatoes and her apple cobbler?"

"I don't know, that's why I asked you!"

He chuckled. "Relax, sweet girl." He slid his arm around my shoulders and gently turned me toward the growing crowd. "Take a look. Do you feel that?"

I followed his gaze. The bar glowed under soft, dim lighting. A warm hum of chatter filled the space, glasses clinking and laughter bouncing off the walls. It wasn't anything drastic, but it felt... transformed.

The same brick walls. The same sleek bar. But now, in the back corner, the stage I'd envisioned stood ready. The elevated platform had been cleared and polished, the brick backdrop scrubbed, bringing out its natural beauty. A new sign hung overhead, "The Hideaway Live," its soft glow casting a gentle spotlight. Twinkle lights draped down the walls on either side like strands of stars.

Steven had scored a vintage burgundy Persian rug for the stage and set up a simple, worn leather stool dead center beneath the mic stand. A pair of large speakers were suspended from the ceiling, angled just right. For the first time ever, my short stint as a groupie had paid off. I successfully set everything up myself, no help needed.

All that remained was getting Grady's guitar without him suspecting anything. As it was, I fully expected him to take one look at what I did and turn around and run.

Luckily, I'd managed to sneak it into the back of his truck earlier, and I was far too stubborn to let him leave without at least playing something. He was too talented not to share it with the world, even if that world only consisted of the people in this bar.

Just when I was about to give up hope, the door opened and this time, instead of yet another customer, it was the man I had been waiting for all night.

Grady walked in with a swagger I hadn't seen before. His eyes found mine instantly, and that smile, God, that smile, lit him up from the inside.

"You're late," I teased. "I was starting to think you got kidnapped."

He slipped behind the bar, shaking his head. "The kids insisted I stay for dinner." He lifted a small brown bag. "Mrs. Bryant sent you leftovers."

My stomach growled at the memory of her cooking. "She didn't have to," I said, already taking the bag from his hand.

"She did. Also, she wants you to call her tomorrow. Said she needs an update?"

I nodded. She definitely did.

Grady glanced around. "Looks busier than usual tonight..." His voice trailed off as he spotted the stage.

His whole body stilled.

"What...?"

I leaned in. "What do you think?"

He stared, jaw slack, fists clenching and unclenching like he couldn't decide whether to run or stay. "Jackson?" he asked, glancing toward the office.

"Close," I said with a grin. "But he's still on his top-secret mission."

He turned to me. "You?"

I nodded. "Do you like it?"

Before he could answer, Steven stepped onto the stage, holding Grady's guitar in one hand and the mic in the other.

"Good evening!" Steven's voice boomed across the room, confident and full of showmanship. "Welcome to The Hideaway's first-ever open mic night!"

The crowd erupted into applause and cheers.

"Tonight is a very special night. As you may or may not know, the men behind The Hideaway have always had a vision for its future. A place for friends and family to gather, have a drink... Or two," hands across the room raised their glasses with cheers, "and have a good time. I'd like to think that mission has been successful over the years, especially with all the familiar faces I see every night." He paused as the crowd cheered again, a grin on his face as he soaked up their excitement for what was next.

"Our dear Jackson always wanted to go a step further though. He started with a stage, and now, thanks to a certain determined woman," he winked at me, "that dream's taking its next step."

More cheers. I felt my cheeks flush.

"And tonight," he continued, "what better way to kick things off than with a performance from our very own... Grady Thomas!"

Applause exploded across the bar. Glasses slammed, voices chanted, feet stomped, thunderous. In an instant, the sound doubled in volume, then tripled.

Grady stiffened beside me like he'd been struck. His breathing hitched, shallow and fast. I turned to him just in time to see his eyes widen, his pupils shrinking to pinpricks as the chanting began.

"Grady! Grady! Grady!"

His name might as well have been a gunshot.

"No." His voice was barely a whisper. He shook his head, eyes darting toward the exit like a cornered animal. His fists clenched, and I saw the pulse in his neck hammering against his skin.

He tried to step back, but I caught his arm, and for a heartbeat, I almost let him go. His fear was raw, bone-deep. But then I remembered why this mattered. Why I'd done all of this.

Grady needed to be seen.

He tried to step away, but I tightened my grip, interlacing my fingers with his. "You can do this," I whispered.

He looked at me, but it was like he wasn't really seeing me. Like he wasn't in this room at all.

"They're all looking at me," he muttered.

A fresh wave of panic rolled off him like heat. His chest rose and fell in rapid bursts. Sweat beaded at his hairline. I saw his jaw tighten, his throat bob as he swallowed hard, but it did nothing to clear the tremble in his voice.

"I can't do this," he rasped. "Not again. Not..."

My heart cracked. Something had broken loose inside him, something old and sharp and deeply embedded. I didn't know the whole story, but I didn't have to. I could feel it. In the way his hands trembled. In the way his shoulders curled inward, like he was trying to make himself disappear.

I stepped in front of him, blocking his view of the crowd. "Hey," I whispered, lifting my hands to cup his face. "Look at me. Just me. You're not there anymore. You're here. With me."

I reached up, brushing his hair back, gently cradling his face between my hands. When he opened his eyes, the vulnerability there nearly broke me.

"You have a gift," I said softly. "A real one. Not just for music, but for connection. You quiet the noise. You make people *feel seen*."

He looked down, trying to pull away, but I held him steady.

"Look at everything you've built. You didn't let those assholes from school define you. You've created something beautiful here. And the world deserves to see the man I see."

He opened his mouth to protest, but I cut him off.

"Don't do this for me. Or for Jackson, though yes, he's rooting for you. Do this for *you*. Let them hear you. Let them *see* you."

He took a shaky breath. "But what if I mess up?"

I smiled, brushing my thumb across his cheek. "What if you don't?"

Chapter 28

Grady

"**G**rady! Grady! Grady!"

The crowd's chant slammed into me like a wave, stealing the air from my lungs. My vision narrowed. The lights above the stage blurred into starbursts, and all I could hear was the pounding of my heart, thudding in my ears like a war drum.

I wiped my palms on my jeans again. My fingers were trembling. My knees wanted to buckle. Everything in me screamed to turn and run.

I swore I'd never do this again. Never get on a stage. Never put myself back in front of a crowd who might laugh, or worse, remember.

Whitney stood in front of me, her hand curled tightly around mine. She didn't flinch. She didn't let go. Her eyes met mine with unwavering calm, and she leaned in close, voice low and steady.

"I'm scared," I admitted. My voice was barely audible, but I knew she heard.

"It's okay to be scared," she said gently. "The key is to not let it stop you."

I wanted nothing more than to run. To disappear. To rewind the night and stay behind with Edie and Edward, reading bedtime stories in a warm house where the only audience was a pair of sleepy kids. But there was a part of me, a stubborn, desperate part, that wanted this. Wanted to play. To be seen.

Whitney reached for my hand and gave it a light squeeze. "Just one song. Okay?"

I nodded, not because I was ready, but because her voice was the only thing cutting through the chaos in my head.

She tugged gently. I followed.

Step by step across the bar floor, the crowd parting like the Red Sea. I could feel their eyes. Feel the weight of them. And yet somehow, Whitney's grip grounded me. Her presence was a tether keeping me from spinning off into fear.

The second my foot touched the edge of the stage, the air shifted. My body knew before I did, this was the point of no return. Two more steps, then I was there. Center stage.

Steven handed me my guitar, and the moment my fingers wrapped around the neck, a sliver of calm settled in my chest. I clutched it like a life vest, the smooth wood familiar beneath my fingers. I eased onto the stool. My legs shook so bad I thought it might collapse beneath me.

He clapped a hand to my shoulder. "You got this, man," he said, squeezing hard before stepping away.

Whitney moved in close and kissed my cheek, her breath warm and steady. "You'll do amazing," she whispered, then disappeared into the crowd.

I closed my eyes and took a breath.

Just one song, I told myself. One song, and then I could disappear.

I let my fingers drift over the strings, coaxing out a slow, deliberate chord. The crowd hushed. Conversation died. Phones lowered. Every eye turned toward me, but not in mockery. Not in malice. They were waiting. Listening.

I could almost pretend I was at home, on the couch, playing for Whitney alone.

I took another breath, deeper this time, and let the music take the lead.

The first notes of Benson Boone's "Sugar Sweet" poured out of me, tentative at first, then stronger, steadier. My voice wavered as I sang the first line, but no one laughed. No one jeered. And when I reached the chorus, something happened.

They started singing with me.

It wasn't loud. Just a few voices at first. But the sound grew. Scattered voices weaving into harmony with mine, until the entire room felt like it was singing with me, not at me. *With* me.

My chest cracked open.

I opened my eyes, and there she was.

Whitney, sitting on the bar, swaying to the rhythm, arms raised like she was at a concert. Her smile was electric, her joy undeniable. I didn't know if I was the one performing or if I was just caught in her orbit. Either way, I couldn't stop smiling. Not even if I tried.

The second verse came easier. I didn't have to think anymore. My fingers moved on instinct, the chords flowing like water. The fear was still there, but it had nowhere to go. It got swallowed up in the sound, reshaped into adrenaline. Into joy.

I had forgotten how good this felt.

To sing. To *feel*. To be seen - not for my scars, but for the music I carried inside me. For something that was mine.

The final chorus soared, and I let my voice rise with it. Strong. Clear. Unafraid.

The moment the last note faded into silence, the room erupted.

Applause. Whooping. Whistles. Laughter. Cheers so loud they rattled the bottles on the shelves behind the bar. It was like I'd cracked something open, not just in them, but in me.

People stood.

They clapped and shouted my name, and someone called out *Encore!*

Another voice echoed them. Then another. And another.

"Encore! Encore! Encore!"

I didn't hesitate. Not for a second. My fingers found a new progression, something upbeat, something exciting, and I dove back in - no fear, no second-guessing.

For the first time in my life, I felt it.

The high. The freedom. The thrill of doing something I loved with nothing holding me back.

I was *alive*.

And I never wanted to come down.

Energy like I'd never felt before coursed through my veins. My body buzzed, not just with adrenaline, but with something deeper - pride, maybe. Relief. Joy. The room was still vibrating from the last chord when I stepped off stage, guitar in hand, heart still hammering in my chest.

"That was amazing," came a voice at my ear, low and silky. Casey, one of Emily's best friends, all too familiar and suddenly far too close. "I didn't realize you were so good with your hands."

She let the words linger, her breath brushing my skin. A blush rose up my neck. I was still flying from the performance, and the last thing I wanted was to land here.

"Can I get you a drink?" I asked, already ducking behind the bar.

Casey slid onto a stool like she owned the place, elbows up, cleavage on display. "Sure," she said with a purr. "Surprise me."

I busied my hands with the bottle, the glass, anything to avoid looking at her too long. My chest still buzzed from the performance, a mix of adrenaline and something else I hadn't quite named.

Casey giggled. "You were electric up there."

I forced a polite nod, but my eyes were already drifting. Whitney stood nearby, arms folded across her chest, mouth tight. She wasn't saying a word, but her silence cut deeper than anything Casey could throw at me.

This was going to blow up. I could feel it.

"What are you doing when you get off?" Casey asked, her voice all syrup and suggestion.

"I, uh…" I cleared my throat, still not meeting her eyes. "Heading home."

She leaned in. "You could come to my place. We could have a drink there…"

Before I could form a reply, a glass slammed down on the bar between us.

"Sorry, lady," Whitney said, her voice cool and sharp. "He's busy tonight. Rain check?"

Casey blinked, caught off guard. She slid off the stool with a huff and a toss of her hair. "I'll call you."

Whitney didn't respond. She just reached for the whiskey she'd poured, neat, and downed it in one hard swallow.

My eyebrows shot up. I'd never seen her drink. Not once.

"Whitney…" I reached out, fingers brushing her elbow.

She didn't look at me. Just rinsed the glass like it meant nothing. But it did. I knew it did.

"I'm fine," she muttered, shaking me off.

"You sure? That your first one in a while?"

She didn't answer right away, just rinsed the glass and set it aside like it didn't matter. But it did. I knew it did.

"I said I'm fine," she muttered, shaking off my hand.

She wasn't spiraling. Not even close. But something in her eyes looked tired. Not defeated, but defensive. Like she'd just crossed a line she'd drawn in the sand and didn't want to explain why.

And maybe she didn't have to.

I stepped back, letting her be, even though every part of me wanted to press.

When I turned back to the bar, a fresh line of women waited, smiling, batting lashes, leaning low. The same girls who'd never spared me a glance were now hanging on every movement, every word. All because I stood on a stage for five minutes.

And not one of them saw me the way Whitney did.

When we got home, Whitney didn't say a word. She walked straight past me, down the hall, and into Jackson's room. The door clicked shut behind her.

I stood there a beat, the guitar still in my hand, its weight suddenly too much. I set it gently on the couch, then followed her, the floorboards creaking beneath my bare feet.

"Whitney," I said, knocking softly. "Can we talk?"

There was a long pause. Then, a muffled, choked, "Go away, Grady."

I pressed my forehead against the door. "Not until you talk to me. Until I know you're okay."

"I don't want to talk."

I closed my eyes, letting the words sink in. Her voice didn't sound angry, just worn out. Like all her edges had frayed at once.

"Fine," I whispered. "Then at least come to bed."

The silence that followed was thicker than before. Then, soft. A dull thump, like her back hitting the other side of the door. I took it as my answer.

I lingered there for a moment longer, then let out a quiet sigh and turned away.

Some fights were worth pushing. Some lines you didn't cross.

This wasn't about being right.

It was about giving her space.

I stripped off my shirt as I walked down the hall to the bathroom, my footsteps slower now, the adrenaline from the night finally draining out of me. When I caught my reflection in the mirror, I almost didn't recognize myself.

Same too-long curls, still damp from sweat. Same faint scar above my upper lip. Same frame, too lean from skipped meals and sleepless nights. But my eyes... God, my eyes looked different. Alive, for once. There was light behind them I hadn't seen in years.

I stepped into the shower, letting the water run hot as I washed off the night. The music still echoed in my head. The stage. The applause. Whitney's face, beaming in the crowd.

It was, without a doubt, one of the best nights of my life.

If only she'd let me share it with her.

When I got back to my room, the bed was still empty, just the way I'd left it. No pillow indents. No whispered goodnights.

I stared at it for a long moment, then slipped under the covers.

The sheets felt colder than usual, like they hadn't retained any of my warmth. I rolled onto my back, staring up at the ceiling, trying not to think about Whitney's closed door. About the look on her face after confronting Casey at the bar.

I'd played tonight. I'd done it. And for a little while, I'd felt invincible.

So why did I feel so damn hollow now?

I shut my eyes, willing the storm to quiet inside my chest. But the stillness only made the noise louder.

My limbs grew heavy. My thoughts drifted...

...and then came the cold.

Not the kind from the bedroom, but a sterile, unnatural chill. One I hadn't felt in years but still remembered with painful precision.

The choir room.

A shiver rolled through me. They always kept the air on high, as though a little bit of heat was a gateway to Hell... *At least the cold made it harder for Miss Becky to get what she wanted from me.*

"Now, Grady. You listen to Miss Becky. She'll have you hitting those high notes again in no time."

My mom cupped my cheek and kissed my forehead, no doubt leaving a lipstick stain behind.

"Yes ma'am." I didn't know how to tell her about what I had learned, that puberty changed things. My voice was deepening, and when I could hit the high notes, they almost always cracked.

I tried talking to my dad about it, but he insisted I was too young.

The youth pastor called me a late bloomer. My voice changing at thirteen had him concerned, but not enough to say anything to my parents.

"Come on," Miss Becky said, her long fingers brushing over my shoulder as she turned me toward the back hallway. I hesitated, glancing over my shoulder one last time. My mom was already heading out, deep in conversation with the pastor. Probably trying to get me back into the tenor choir.

The door to the practice room creaked open. Just the lamp by the piano was on, casting everything in a low, golden haze. I stepped inside, the soles of my shoes echoing too loudly on the tile. My stomach twisted.

Miss Becky didn't sit at the piano.

She came up behind me instead, her presence pressing close, too close. I stiffened as her hands slid over my back and shoulders like she had every right to touch me.

I flinched and she laughed. "Relax," she whispered, her breath warm against my ear.

I shivered, but not from the cold this time.

"Wha-what song are we starting with?" I asked, my voice barely above a whisper.

"All business today, huh?" she murmured.

There was a flicker of something low in my stomach, something I didn't understand and didn't want. My whole body went still. I squeezed my eyes shut, willing everything to stop, willing her to go sit at the piano, willing myself to disappear.

"Ye-yes ma'am," I managed, though the words barely made it out.

"You know..." Her voice slithered past my ear, too close, too familiar. "The only way you're going to sing in the tenor choir again is if I give you a little help."

I froze. The room shrank around me.

"Please," I whispered, but I didn't know what I was begging for. For her to stop? For my mom to come back? For someone, anyone, to see?

My throat tightened, and I squeezed my eyes shut, heart hammering like it was trying to outrun my own skin.

She didn't stop.

The air felt thick, poisoned. My lungs burned as her voice sank deeper, coated in sugar and threat.

"Nobody takes care of you like I do."

It was always the same words. Always the same lie.

I shook my head. "No," I croaked. "We can't. It's a sin."

But the room kept closing in.

I couldn't move. I couldn't speak. I could only feel the shame, hot and sticky and clinging to every part of me.

I tried to disappear.

"No," I said again, louder this time. "No. No! Please, no!"

"Grady! Grady!"

"No! No! Please, no!" I jerked upright, heart slamming against my ribs. My chest heaved until I felt warm hands cradle my face.

"Shh," Whitney whispered, her breath a balm against my skin - soft, steady, real. "It was just a dream. You're safe now."

I blinked through the haze of fear, my pulse still thundering. Her eyes met mine, honeyed light in the dark, holding no judgment, only quiet understanding. She was here. Not Miss Becky. Not the cold.

Just Whitney.

I reached for her face, needing to feel her, to anchor myself to something that wasn't the past. Our lips met, tentative at first; an apology, a thank-you, a plea. But then she climbed into my lap, straddling me, and everything shifted.

I deepened the kiss, tracing the seam of her lips with my tongue until she opened for me. Our mouths moved together like we'd done this a hundred times, like our bodies already knew the steps.

Her hips began a slow grind, and I groaned, my hands finding her waist, gripping tight. Not to restrain her - God, no, but to hold on.

She moaned against my mouth, and the sound sent a jolt straight through me. Her touch was fire and forgiveness, want and wonder. I wanted more. All of her. To taste her skin, lose myself in the heat of her.

But even as my hands slid up her sides, skimming the curve of her back, something tugged at me. Not guilt, but clarity.

My fingers paused on her upper arms. I broke the kiss, resting my forehead to hers, catching my breath.

"Fuck, Whitney," I whispered. "You're perfect."

Color bloomed in her cheeks, like my words hit deeper than my touch ever could.

"You're not so bad yourself," she teased, rolling her hips again, slow and deliberate.

I groaned, head falling back against the pillow. "Oh, god. Don't do that."

She gave me a wicked grin and did it again. "But you feel so damn good."

I caught her hips, stilling them; not because I didn't want her, but because I did. Too much, maybe.

"So do you," I said, voice rough. "But I think..." She moved again, and I let out a helpless grunt. "I think we should talk."

Her breath caught, her hands stilling on my chest. For a heartbeat, we just breathed, tangled in heat and hesitation.

Chapter 29

Whitney

"I think we should talk."

The warmth drained from my body like I'd been doused in ice water. That soft, humming glow we'd created was gone, snuffed out in a single breath. I climbed off him, panic rising in my throat.

"I... I should go."

Grady caught my arm, gentle but firm. "Stay. Please."

"But..."

"Don't misunderstand me." He nodded toward the space between us. "I want this. I want you. But I think there are a few things we need to talk about. Before this goes any further."

I hesitated, then looked back and nearly crumbled. His eyes weren't full of regret or second thoughts. Just sincerity. Maybe something dangerously close to hope.

"Okay," I whispered.

Grady smiled, and God help me, my heart skipped. Things had shifted between us, when, I couldn't say. Maybe it was tonight, watching him light up onstage. Or that flare of jealousy when Casey put her claws on him. Maybe it was the sound of his laugh at mini golf. The songs he played, just for me. Or maybe it was always coming to this.

I sat on the edge of the bed, waiting.

"Come here," he said softly, reaching out.

I slid closer. He took my hand, threading our fingers together, then lifted it and pressed a kiss to my knuckles.

"First," he said, voice low, "thank you for tonight. I wouldn't have gotten on that stage without you."

"You looked like you belonged there," I said. "Like you were born for it."

He exhaled a shaky breath. "I really like you, Whitney. More than I've ever liked anyone. And that scares the shit out of me."

"Why?" I searched his face. "You're not afraid of Jackson, are you?"

He laughed, shaking his head. "No. Besides... your brother already gave us his blessing."

"He what?!" I shot upright, indignant. "He doesn't get a say in what, or who, I do."

Grady grinned. "I didn't exactly ask his permission."

"Good. And for the record," I said, sliding closer again, "I like you too. In case that wasn't painfully obvious."

He nodded, eyes softening. "There's still a lot you don't know about me."

"So?" I shrugged. "There's a lot you don't know about me, either."

"That's fair." He kissed my hand again. "So, tell me something. Something I don't know. Something *real*."

I closed my eyes, searching for something safe. Most of my life was an open book, at least the parts that didn't leave scars. Eric knew all the dark corners; he was there for a lot of it. Grady didn't need my demons; he had plenty of his own.

"I don't like snakes."

He chuckled. "Not quite what I meant, but I'll take it."

His gaze drifted downward. "I have a hard time letting people in."

I reached up and traced his jaw. "But you let me in."

"You're different," he rasped, curling his hand around mine.

"How?"

He searched my face like the answer might be written there. Then he cupped the back of my neck, pulling me gently toward him. "I don't know," he murmured. "But I want to find out."

That was all the invitation I needed.

I kissed him. Slow at first, tender. But heat surged through me like wildfire. My fingers roamed over his chest, the light dusting of hair, the solid muscle beneath my palms. He pulled me into his lap as our kiss deepened, our bodies moving in rhythm, like they already knew the choreography.

He tugged my shirt up and over my head, and my breath caught when his hands cupped my breasts, teasing my nipples until they peaked beneath his touch. His mouth followed, lips hot and greedy, tugging and teasing until I was gasping.

"God, Grady. Don't stop," I breathed, hips grinding down to find friction. I was soaked, aching, and he hadn't even touched me there.

I tangled my fingers in his hair, holding him close as I moved against him, chasing that edge. No one had ever made me feel this wild, this wanted. Not even Eric. Especially not Eric.

Oh God, Eric. My body begged for more, but my conscience twisted like a knife

"I need you," I panted, burying those thoughts beneath the heat. I kissed him again, tasting mint and desperation, a craving I couldn't name.

"Whitney," he groaned, hips lifting to meet mine. "Whitney... wait."

I froze, still straddling him, heart pounding.

"I need to know," he said, breathless. "Where do things stand with you and your boyfriend?"

A flicker of guilt coiled in my gut. "We... we have an open relationship," I said, avoiding his eyes. I didn't mention the rule about discussing new partners first.

"But you're still together?"

I nodded. "Yes."

He dropped his head to my shoulder, exhaling hard. I stroked my fingers through his hair, our heavy breathing the only sound in the room.

"What is it?"

"I can't," he whispered, lifting his head. "I can't be the other man. Even in an open relationship. I just... can't."

His voice cracked at the edges, and suddenly, I wasn't frustrated. I was gutted. Not because he said no, but because he said it with so much care.

"I understand," I said softly, even though part of me ached. I climbed off his lap and reached for my shirt, instantly missing his warmth.

"Sleep?" I asked, uncertain.

He pulled back the covers and gave a small nod. "Sleep."

And that was enough.

Chapter 30

Grady

Everything about her was perfect, the shape of her mouth, the feel of her bare skin against mine, the way she cried my name. I grinned and buried my face in her wild hair, breathing her in like oxygen.

Yeah. Whitney was perfect.

But more than that, I couldn't believe she was here. With me. Wanting me. Even if we couldn't be together, the fact that she chose me, even for a night, made my heart sing.

Still, damn. I wanted her. I wanted to hold her again, touch her, kiss her. I wanted to taste the sweetness of her skin, to lose myself in every soft sound she made.

But it wasn't just sex I craved.

It was her.

Her soul. Her fire. Her broken edges, smart mouth, and the way she looked at me like I mattered. I wanted to know her in ways words could never reach.

But for now, with her sleeping in my arms, I could pretend. I could close my eyes and believe this moment was real.

Whitney stirred against me, a quiet breath slipping past her lips. Her eyelashes fluttered before she blinked up at me, her face still warm from sleep. God, she was beautiful like this, unguarded and delicate, the morning light catching the edges of her hair.

"Good morning," she whispered, voice raspy with sleep.

"Morning, beautiful," I murmured, brushing a kiss across her forehead.

A blush crept into her cheeks, and I grinned. I didn't care how temporary this was. Right now, she was in my arms, and for just a little longer, I could pretend she might stay.

Her fingers traced the shape of my jaw, slow and thoughtful. "Grady?"

"Yeah?"

"Where do we go from here?"

The question hit me like a crack in the glass. Small. Dangerous. I exhaled slowly, holding her a little tighter as I stared up at the ceiling. "I'm not sure," I admitted.

She pulled back slightly, eyes searching mine. "Can't we just...?"

She looked up at me with eyes full of mischief and longing, her fingers tracing light patterns over my chest. The temptation in her voice was enough to weaken every part of me that still wanted to do the right thing.

One of her hands slid lower, teasing over the waistband of my boxers. She found me already hard and gave an easy smile like she'd won something.

"Whitney..." I groaned, unable to stop my hips from pressing into her palm.

"Yes?" she asked, her tone a blend of innocence and sin.

"We can't," I said, even as I closed my eyes and fought not to thrust into her hand.

"Why though?" She pushed herself up, straddling me now, her strokes feather-light but torturously steady. "I don't understand."

"Because you have a boyfriend," I said flatly, each word a nail I had to hammer down to keep myself in check.

"So?" she shrugged, brushing her hair back. "He's in Utah. I'm here. You're here." She studied me for a beat. "Do you want me to break up with him?"

I sat up, untangling myself from her and the covers. I couldn't think straight with her so close. "I won't tell you what to do."

She followed me with her gaze, but didn't move. "Can't we just have a good time while I'm here?"

Her words hit harder than I expected. Just a good time. A fling. Something she'd walk away from.

"So, you're going back," I said, my voice quieter now. "You're going back to him."

She tilted her head, like she didn't understand the question. "Well, yeah. Eventually. I have a job, a life to get back to."

"You have a life here. A job..." I said, grasping for something that would make her stay.

"Pouring drinks isn't exactly a future, Grady."

I let out a humorless laugh. "Ouch."

She winced. "That's not what I meant."

"Maybe not," I muttered, "but it's what you said."

Her expression softened, and she shifted to the edge of the bed. "There's Eric, too."

I didn't want to talk about him. I didn't want to think about him. He wasn't here. Not when she needed him. Not now.

"What if you could get a job here?" I asked, turning to face her fully. "One that you really loved. Would you stay then?"

"Grady…" she breathed, hesitant. "What are you asking?"

My heart pounded as I stepped toward her. "I want you to stay. Stay here. With me. Make a life with me."

The second the words left my mouth, I wanted to take them back. Not because I didn't mean them; God, I meant every word, but because putting them out there felt like handing her my heart, raw and trembling, and asking her not to drop it.

Her mouth opened like she wanted to speak, but no sound came. She looked at me, wide-eyed, and I could see the wheels turning, the reality settling in. I'd done it. I'd crossed that line.

"I know it's not perfect," I continued, my voice cracking around the edges. "I know I'm not perfect. And I get it, your life is in Utah, your friends, your job, your…" I couldn't bring myself to say his name. "But this, what we have, it's real. And I've never had anything like it."

I laughed, but it was empty. "Hell, maybe I'm crazy. Maybe I'm just the guy who wants something too good to be true. But for the first time in my life, I don't want to run. I want to fight for something."

I looked down, swallowing hard. "I want to fight for you. You're the first person who's ever made me feel like I wasn't broken. Like I could be more than my past."

Her mouth opened and closed, like she wanted to say something, but couldn't find the words. I swallowed, giving her time to process, while my mind ran away with all the possibilities.

"Grady, I…" Whitney reached out for me, then dropped her hands.

I nodded, unable to speak past the boulder that wedged itself in my throat. My chest felt tight, and I had to force air into my lungs.

She doesn't want me.

The thought shouldn't have felt so foreign. My own parents didn't even want me, biological or adoptive. Why would this incredible woman be any different?

She stood up and took my hand. "Come back to bed. Let's enjoy each other while we can."

All I could do was follow her lead, unable to put my feelings into words. I crawled back onto the bed beside her, waiting to see what she would do next.

Whitney crawled onto my lap, her fingers brushing my hair from my face with a tenderness that stole my breath. "What do you want?" she whispered, her voice barely audible.

I closed my eyes, inhaling her intoxicating scent - sweet, familiar, and dizzying.

What did I want?

The answer was both terrifying and simple.

"*You.*"

Her gaze flicked to my mouth, then down to where our bodies met. She exhaled, shaky but sure.

"Then take me," she whispered. "For as long as I'm here, I'm yours."

I froze; her words echoed through me like a prayer I didn't dare believe in. I shoved down the fear, the doubts, the aching knowledge that this moment wouldn't last. For once, I let go. The future could wait, because right here, right now, was everything.

Our kiss was anything but gentle - hungry, aching, desperate. I cupped her cheek with one hand while the other slipped around her waist, pulling her close until there was no space left between us.

Whitney melted into me, her fingers tangling in my hair, clinging to me as though she'd fall without me. I kissed her deeper, not just out of want, but out of fear; fear that this would be the last time I'd feel her like this. The last time I could pretend she was mine.

I trailed my hands down her sides, fingers skimming the smooth curve of her waist until they caught on the hem of her t-shirt. In one fluid motion, I pulled it over her head and tossed it aside. My mouth found her breasts instantly, lips closing around a nipple, savoring the feel of her skin, the sweet ache of her between my teeth. I bit down gently, just enough to draw a gasp from her lips before switching to the other, devouring her like a man starved.

She gripped my hair tighter, anchoring me to her chest, holding me like she never wanted to let go. And if I had anything to say about it, I never would.

A low groan rumbled from my throat as she rolled her hips, grinding against my growing hardness.

"Yes... fuck, yes," she moaned, and the sound shot through me like a lightning strike, straight to my dick.

In one swift motion, I flipped us, laying her down beneath me. She was bare now, except for those soft blue cotton panties, ones I knew came with a matching bra since I bought them. Seeing her in them, knowing how much she loved to tease me, made my pulse throb.

I kissed my way down her body, slow and reverent, drinking in every inch of her skin. When I reached the delicate juncture of her thighs, she instinctively tried to close them, but I held them open, kissing the inside of one, then the other - gentle, teasing, claiming.

"Grady," she whispered, voice unsteady. "Wh-what are you doing?"

I slipped a finger beneath the edge of her panties, brushing through the slick heat waiting for me. My mouth pressed to the damp fabric as I inhaled, the scent of her intoxicating.

"Fuck, you smell like heaven," I murmured.

Hooking my fingers in the waistband, I eased the panties aside, revealing smooth skin and silky folds glistening with want.

"You're so fucking beautiful," I breathed, parting her with my thumbs. "All of you." I ran my knuckles slowly up and down her slit, relishing the way she trembled beneath me.

And then, finally, I dipped my head, my tongue replacing my hand, tasting her like she was the only thing I'd ever craved.

Her breath hitched the moment my tongue slid between her folds - soft, slow, deliberate.

She jolted, her thighs tensing around my head. "Grady, wait," she gasped, her hand pressing against my shoulder. "I've never... no one's ever..." Her voice trailed off, embarrassed and uncertain.

I lifted my head just enough to meet her eyes. "No one's ever gone down on you?" I asked, voice low.

She shook her head; cheeks flushed with something between shame and vulnerability.

My heart ached for her, this woman who deserved the whole world. "Whitney," I whispered, brushing my lips against her inner thigh. "Let me. Let me show you how much you deserve to be worshipped."

Her lips parted, trembling, torn between instinct and surrender. I held her gaze, waiting, not demanding, not taking, just offering.

With a slow nod, her hand slowly slid from my shoulder into my hair. "Okay," she whispered.

I eased her thighs wider and dipped my head again, this time more tenderly. My tongue moved with patient devotion, learning her rhythm, her taste, the way her breath caught when I circled her clit just right. I felt her begin to melt beneath me, the tension in her muscles giving way to a quivering need. Her fingers clutched my hair tighter, pulling me closer instead of pushing me away.

"God... Grady," she whimpered. "It's too much."

"No," I murmured against her, lips brushing her slick heat, "it's exactly enough."

Her moans turned breathless, urgent, soft edges giving way to something rawer. When I slipped a single finger inside her, slow, careful, her hips lifted to meet me. She was so tight, so warm, I had to grit my teeth to stay in control. I kept my pace slow, letting her climb toward that breaking point, and when she finally cried out, shattering under my tongue, it was the most beautiful sound I'd ever heard.

I kissed my way back up her body, lingering on her hips, her belly, and finally, her lips.

She crashed her mouth against mine, tasting herself and moaning into it. Her legs wrapped around my waist, anchoring me to her. "Please," she breathed, eyes glassy. "I want to feel you."

I shoved down my sweats and boxer-briefs, kicking them off the foot of the bed. I lined myself up against her entrance, teasing her slick folds with the tip of my cock. I cupped her cheek, stilling. "Are you sure?" I asked, heart pounding louder than my words.

She nodded, pulling me down into a kiss. "I'm sure," she murmured. "Don't think. Just... be here with me."

I pushed into her slowly, every inch a battle not to fall deeper. She gasped, fingers digging into my back as I filled her completely. I stilled to let her adjust, brushing my lips over her cheek, her temple. Nothing had ever felt so good, so right. "You feel like home," I whispered, before I could stop myself.

Either she didn't hear me, or she didn't care.

Her body arched into mine, urging me forward. I moved in her, slow at first, savoring each sound that left her lips, each time her nails dragged across my skin. And still, beneath it all, something in my chest ached, because I knew what I wanted, and it wasn't just this.

I wanted more than now. More than she was willing to give.

I made love to her like I could change her mind, like maybe if I worshipped her enough, she'd stay.

Afterward, we lay tangled in the sheets, our sweat slicked bodies pressed together as our breaths slowed.

The silence wasn't uncomfortable, it never was with Whitney, yet it was heavier than it had ever been before. I traced lazy circles along her back, memorizing the feel of her while I still had the chance.

She rested her head on my chest, eyes closed, lips slightly parted. She looked peaceful, content. Perfect.

In my heart, I knew she belonged here with me. *Why couldn't she see it?*

I kissed the top of her head and whispered, "I don't want this to be over."

She didn't open her eyes, "Then don't think about the end."

God, I didn't want to. I wanted to stay wrapped in this lie a little longer, just until it didn't hurt so much.

And for a little while, I didn't.

Chapter 31

Whitney

When Grady took the stage, the bar fell into a hush, anticipation thick in the air. The moment he strummed that first chord, it was like the whole building held its breath. Then he sang and the room went wild.

He was made for this.

And I was just grateful to be the one who finally gave him the push.

After all, what was life if you weren't willing to take a few risks?

Grady's eyes skimmed the crowd, unreadable, until they found mine. And just like that, every woman in that bar vanished.

He winked and a flurry of butterflies burst in my stomach, dizzying and warm. I'd never felt this way before, like I was suited up and standing on the edge of the Empire State Building, wind at my back, ready to jump.

And I wasn't afraid. I'd jumped before with Eric, in every way a person could. But it never felt like *this*. Like the guy on the other side might actually catch me. Like he'd move mountains just to see me smile.

Was this what love felt like?

I shook the thought off, turning back to the glass I was currently washing. It was too soon to think about love when it came to Grady. Besides, I was still with Eric.

I *loved* Eric... *didn't I*? Then why did this feel like the first time I was seeing the world in color?

Grady strummed the final chords, and the room roared with applause. My jaw tightened as a cluster of women surged toward the stage, all bright smiles and reaching hands. I hated the way they touched him, casual, entitled, like they didn't even see me standing right here.

Sorry, ladies. He's mine.

It occurred to me then, that if Jackson ever wanted to take this place to the next level, he'd have to find a more secure way to get the artists on and off stage without the risk of being mauled.

"Get ready," Steven muttered, bumping my shoulder and nodding toward the incoming wave of thirsty admirers.

I sighed. I was thrilled by the reaction Grady was receiving, the crowd he had attracted. I just wished that crowd understood boundaries.

Grady slipped behind the bar, his hand grazing the small of my back as he passed, sending a bolt of electricity through me as he carried his guitar toward the office.

"Steven?" I asked. "Do you think..."

He smirked. "Go. Get your man before I do."

I kissed his cheek. "You're the best."

"Yeah, yeah," he grinned. "Hope you know I'm keeping your share of the tips."

"Fair trade."

I found Grady in the office just as he was locking the door, phone pressed to his ear. His lips curled up into a smile when he saw me and he ended the call, sliding the phone into his back pocket.

"Hey, beautiful." He pulled me into his arms and kissed me; soft, warm, and entirely his. "What're you up to?"

I wrapped my arms around his neck. "Can't a girl come see her man after he puts on a killer performance?"

"Mmm." He nuzzled into my neck, his tongue tasting the salt of my skin before trailing soft kisses up to my ear. "Killer, huh?"

"You know you're great." I swatted his chest, grinning.

"I don't care what anyone thinks but you."

"Oh yeah?"

"Mmhmm."

He kissed up my neck, across my jaw, and finally claimed my mouth in a kiss that left my knees weak.

"I want you," I whispered when we pulled apart.

"Soon," he murmured. "It's almost closing time."

I slid my hands down his torso, slipping them into his back pockets. "We could always christen the office..."

Grady groaned, thumping his head against the door. "Your brother would kill me."

"Not if he doesn't find out. Besides, he deserves it for not returning your calls."

He ran his hands up and down my arms, placing a kiss on my forehead. "I'm sure he has a good reason. Come on, we can't let Steven have all the fun."

We made it out there just in time to catch Steven belting a Sabrina Carpenter song like his life depended on it. The crowd was eating it up, clapping and singing along.

Grady didn't have to worry about Steven. He had this place in the palm of his hand.

The drive home was quiet, familiar. The kind of quiet that only Falcon Pointe could manage, peaceful whether it was two in the morning, or the middle of the afternoon. This town moved at its own pace, slow and steady.

"Will you take me somewhere?" I asked, breaking the silence.

Grady glanced over, his hand resting easy on the wheel. "Where do you wanna go?"

I shrugged, watching the trees blur past my window. "I don't know. Just somewhere... different, you know?"

Part of me wanted to go home and finish what we started in the office, but something about Grady made me want more than that. It wasn't just sex, not that it was like that with Eric either, at first. But with Eric, sex had become a huge part of our relationship. With Grady, it was starting to feel like we were just scratching the surface of something deeper.

Grady passed the turn for home without a word.

I leaned my head against the cool glass and watched the world fall away behind us. The night sky stretched endlessly above, littered with stars. It felt like we were driving into a dream.

He eventually turned onto a narrow dirt road, the truck rumbling softly as we bumped along. It ended at a wide, empty field under a velvet-black sky. He killed the engine and stepped out, circling around to open my door.

"Come on," he said, holding out his hand. "There's something I want to show you."

I took his hand and slid out and into his arms.

He led me through the tall grass until we reached an old fence shadowed by a small cluster of trees. He vaulted over easily, then turned and lifted me over like I weighed nothing.

"Where are we going?" I asked, breath catching in my throat.

"Just a little further."

My heart thudded, part excitement, part nerves. I had seen enough horror movies in my life to know that empty fields in the dead of night were an invitation for trouble.

At least it wasn't a corn field.

Grady stopped at the base of one particularly barren tree. Without hesitation he began to climb, like he had done it a hundred times. When he threw down a rope ladder I realized he probably had.

He perched on a wide branch, his legs kicking a steady rhythm on either side. "Can you make it up, or do you need some help?"

I rolled my eyes, then sighed. *Stupid cast.* Thank God it was coming off soon. "I think I can manage."

Jackson and I had climbed our fair share of rope ladders growing up. There was one on the school playground, and even one in Abby's backyard treehouse.

It took more effort than I liked to admit, but I finally reached the top. Grady pulled me up beside him, settling me between his legs, my back pressed to his chest.

His arms wrapped around me, and he pressed a kiss just beneath my ear, warm breath brushing over my skin. I shivered.

"I used to come up here all the time," he said, voice low, reverent.

The night wrapped around us, cool air, crickets singing, the faint rustle of leaves. The world felt suspended, quiet and sacred.

"It's beautiful," I murmured. "How did you find it?"

He was quiet and for a moment I thought he wasn't going to answer. Then he exhaled, long and slow.

"I never really liked taking the bus to or from school. Mrs. Bryant figured it out pretty quick. I'd drag my feet getting ready every morning. It was easier when Jackson was around, but you know Jackson. He's always got something going on. He couldn't always be there.

"I started walking home from school, preferring that to the jeers of my classmates. One day, I was walking when Jimmy Ramsey decided it would be fun to chase me down with his car. I ran like hell and managed to hop the fence."

He laughed softly, but there was something sharp underneath it.

He kissed the top of my head, taking a moment, like he was reliving that day all over again. "I heard the car doors slam, but I kept running until I saw this tree. I climbed so fast, probably higher than we are now. I held my breath until I thought my lungs would burst. Jimmy and his friends looked everywhere but up." He chuckled.

"I brought Jackson up here, after everything happened with Abby."

There was something different in his tone. Not just nostalgia, something heavier. A tenderness wrapped in pain.

I didn't press. But I could feel it in the way his arms tightened around me, in the way he looked out over the darkened field like he was seeing something I couldn't. This place meant something to him. And if he'd brought Jackson here when he was hurting...

He brought people here when they needed peace.

My heart squeezed in my chest, because I realized: he'd brought me here, too.

I smiled into the dark. "Let me guess... He provided the rope ladder?"

Grady chuckled, "How'd you know?"

I turned enough to press a kiss to his chin. "He never was very good at climbing trees. But he did manage to fashion a few good rope ladders back when we were kids."

"It's been a while, but I don't think he's gotten any better," Grady said with a grin, pressing a kiss to the top of my head.

We stayed like that for a while, held in each other's arms, high above the world, tangled in memory and moonlight. Up here, it was like the world couldn't touch us. No memories, no scars, just stars and second chances.

Chapter 32

Grady

Waking up with Whitney in my arms felt like heaven.

From her soft snores to the way her body molded perfectly against mine, I couldn't imagine wanting anything more. I was the second luckiest man alive, right behind her boyfriend, Eric.

I pulled her closer, inhaling the lingering scent of her shampoo and the faint trace of us. The thought of her leaving made my chest tighten. I knew she was going back to him, but a small part of me still held out hope that she'd wake up, see what we had, what we could be, and stay.

Jackson always said that the right woman would come along and change everything.

And God, was he right.

For the first time in my adult life, I was thinking about things I'd sworn off - marriage, a family. A future.

The kind of future guys like me had no business dreaming about.

I scoffed quietly to myself. With the shining example of my parents and a rotating door of foster homes, what the hell did I know about being anyone's husband or father?

Whitney stirred beside me.

"I can hear you thinking," she murmured, half-asleep. She rolled over and touched her fingers to my forehead, smoothing out the tension she found there.

I smiled, helpless when it came to her. Her thumb traced my cheek, steady and warm. "Morning, beautiful."

She leaned in and kissed me, slow and soft. "What's going on in that head of yours?"

I pushed a stray curl behind her ear - pointless, really, her hair had a mind of its own in the morning. I kissed her forehead and pulled her in tighter. "Just thinking."

She swatted my shoulder. "I *know* that. About what?"

I pulled back just enough to look into her honey-colored eyes. "You. Me. The future."

The shift in her expression was instant. She started to pull away, and I let her.

"Grady..." Her voice was gentle, but the words still hit like a slap. "I-I thought you understood. I'm going home."

The knot in my throat tightened. I nodded, swallowing hard. "Yeah. I know. I get it." I wanted to ask her not to go. Beg, even. But what was the point? You don't beg someone to love you. You don't plead your case like it's up for debate.

I climbed out of bed before she could say anything else. Knowing it was coming didn't make it easier to hear. I grabbed some sweats and a white t-shirt, trying to keep my voice steady. "You hungry?"

"Grady..."

"I'll make pancakes." My tone was too light. Too rehearsed.

I walked out of the room before she could stop me. Call it cowardice. I call it survival.

In the kitchen, I busied myself with mixing the batter, adding a hefty amount of chocolate chips, just the way she liked. Anything to keep my hands moving and my thoughts from collapsing in on themselves.

I felt it the second she left my room. I didn't have to hear her footsteps to know. I was tuned into her like a melody I couldn't stop humming.

The sound of the shower turning on allowed me the first real breath I'd taken all morning.

If only she could see it, the way we fit, the way I loved her without conditions or guilt. She deserved more than being the girl who waited around while her man fucked whoever struck his fancy.

Eric was trash. A man blind to gold even as it burned bright in his arms.

I rolled my neck from side to side in an attempt to release some of the tension. When that didn't work, I turned to plating the pancakes.

"That smells amazing."

I turned to find her stepping out of Jackson's room, a small smile on her face. She headed for the cabinets, grabbing plates like this was just another morning.

I forced a smile and followed her to the table, sliding the plate of pancakes in front of her. She needed comfort. I could give her that, even if I got nothing in return.

"Dig in."

She blinked in surprise. "Chocolate chip?"

I reached out and gently closed her mouth with two fingers under her chin. "Just the way you like them."

"About earlier..." She caught my hand before I could pull away, pressing a kiss to my palm, and holding on to me like she didn't want to let me go.

I couldn't think about that, couldn't hope for more when she already drew the line in the sand.

"Forget it," I said quickly. "I know the score. It's okay."

"But..."

I kissed the top of her head. I couldn't do this. Not without saying something I'd regret.

"I need to make a call. Eat up. I'll be right back."

Outside, I collapsed into a chair and pulled out my phone. There was only one person who could talk me off this ledge.

Jackson's voicemail picked up after a single ring.

"Hey, man. Call me when you get this," I said. "I need to talk... about the bar, but also... Whitney."

I hesitated, throat tightening. I almost told him I was falling. Almost said I was scared she'd walk away before I got the chance to say it. But the words stuck in my throat.

"She's... she's leaving soon."

The beep cut me off, but maybe that was for the best. Maybe I didn't need to say more.

I leaned forward, scrubbing a hand through my hair. Everything felt like it was slipping away - Jackson, Whitney. Like I was the only one standing still while everyone else moved on.

God, I missed my best friend. I just prayed he was having better luck with his girl than I was with his sister.

Jackson, where are you?

The ache in my chest sharpened into something darker. I rubbed at it with the heel of my hand. It didn't help.

I felt like a soda bottle that had been shaken too hard, pressure mounting, fizz clawing at the edges, ready to blow. I needed to let something out. Anything.

My shaving kit sat in the bathroom. I knew exactly where the blades were tucked inside.

They never ignored my calls. Never ran out of words.

They were always there.

The only thing holding me back was a promise I'd made. To Jackson. To myself.

I had just come home from work. A bouquet of red roses in one hand, a ring box burning a hole in my pocket. I'd spent months trying to talk myself into it, into proposing to Emily. It felt like the logical next step. The only step.

Then I heard it; wood knocking against the wall. A moan. A grunt.

I should've walked away. Should've turned and left. But I didn't. Something stronger than shame pulled me forward.

And there she was, Emily and a stranger in our bed. The bed we chose together. Her red nails clawing down his back while he fucked her like he owned her.

The flowers slipped from my hand. I don't even remember dropping them. I just ran.

I went back to the bar, to the office. I still had that box of blades meant for the box cutter. I grabbed a bottle of Jack and drank like it was air, the box in my other hand already half open.

If Jackson hadn't shown up...

The security alarm had gone off. I forgot to disarm it, and the company called him. He found me bleeding on the floor.

He saved my life.

I shook my head, dragging myself out of the memory. Back into the now.

I'd already broken my promise once this month. He didn't know, but that didn't make it less real.

And if he couldn't even call me back...

"Grady?"

Her voice pulled me back like a lifeline.

"Yeah. Hey." I stood quickly, wiping my hands on my pants like I could scrub away the shame.

"Did you get a hold of Jackson?"

I shook my head. "No. Left a voicemail. He'll call back when he can."

I held my breath as I brushed past her and stepped back inside. I didn't trust myself to say anything else.

The fire crackled as I added another log, its warmth chasing back the chill of a crisp September evening. It wasn't enough to keep the twins indoors, though. If my mom had offered me s'mores after dinner when I was their age, I'd have been right out there too.

"How are they doing?" I asked, absently picking at a lone graham cracker.

"Psh." Mrs. Bryant nudged my knee with hers, a familiar gesture that said I wasn't fooling her. "They're fine. What I want to know is, how are you?"

I gave her the surface-level answer first, the kind people expect. "The bar's doing great. Ever since we started open mic night, we've had full tables. Might have to hire some more help."

Even in the firelight, I caught the dramatic roll of her eyes. "Grady Allen Thomas, if I wanted a business update, I'd ask about the bar."

She took my hand and held it gently in her lap, her thumb brushing slow, steady circles on my skin. "How are *you*?"

I looked past her to the swing set, where Edward and Edie shrieked with joy. Whitney stood behind them, laughing, giving each swing a solid push. She fit here so easily. She belonged.

And she was leaving.

I dropped my gaze to my lap. "I don't understand."

Mrs. Bryant didn't rush me. She never did.

"She's in every part of my life now," I said. "The bar, my mornings, my thoughts. And she's just... okay with walking away. Like this, whatever *this* is, doesn't matter."

Mrs. Bryant squeezed my hand. "Have you told her how you feel?"

"Not exactly." My cheeks warmed. "But... how can she not see? I don't..." I waved a vague hand "with just anyone."

She tilted her head slightly. "You mean you've slept together?"

I nodded, cheeks burning even hotter. There was no judgment in her tone; there never was. But it still made something twist in my gut, my adoptive mother's voice threatening to come out.

"And you were okay? It was your choice?"

My mouth was dry. The words felt huge, like they could tip the scale one way or the other.

"Yeah," I said finally. "I was ready. With her, I felt... safe."

She placed a warm palm on my knee, grounding me. "Does she know about... everything?"

I shook my head. "It hasn't come up."

Only two people in the world knew the full story, Mrs. Bryant and Jackson. The past. The abuse. The way it rewired something inside me. I didn't share it. Not because I didn't trust Whitney. But because saying it out loud still made me feel broken.

"What makes her different, Grady?"

That was the million-dollar question.

"She quiets the voices in my head," I said. "She makes me feel seen, like I'm not just the sum of my damage. She pushes me. Not to be someone I'm not like Emily did, but to be better. For me."

I looked back out at the yard. Whitney had crouched in the grass now, helping Edie tie her shoelaces while Edward hung off her shoulders like a backpack.

"She's different," I whispered. "But maybe it's *because* she's leaving. Maybe I can only fall like this when I know it's temporary."

"You don't believe that," Mrs. Bryant said gently.

"I don't know what to believe," I admitted. "I just... I've never felt anything like this before. I've never *wanted* anything like this before."

She was quiet for a long moment.

Then, in that no-nonsense tone I'd come to associate with truth bombs, she said, "Don't you think she deserves to know that? Don't you think *you* deserve to say it?"

I opened my mouth, then shut it again. My chest ached, my throat dry.

"Yeah," I said eventually. "But would it even matter?"

She leaned in, pressing her forehead to mine like she used to when I was seventeen and lost. "You'll never know unless you open your mouth and speak, baby. And even if it doesn't change anything, at least she'll leave knowing she mattered to someone. And you'll stay knowing you were brave enough to love her out loud."

As I watched Whitney lift Edie into her arms, their laughter trailing through the night like wind chimes, something inside me cracked, just enough to let the light in.

The fire popped beside us, sending a spark spinning into the night.

Maybe Mrs. Bryant was right. Maybe the bravest thing wasn't holding on.

Maybe it was saying the words, and letting them fall where they may. I wasn't ready to say it. But maybe I was ready to try.

Chapter 33

Whitney

His mouth was nothing short of ecstasy.

Grady moved like he had all the time in the world, like every inch of me was sacred, something to be worshipped, not just touched. My back arched, a sharp gasp escaping my lips as he flicked his tongue again. Slow, sure, maddening. It wasn't just pleasure. It was everything.

My fingers tangled in his hair, and still, he didn't rush. He anchored me with his hands, firm on my thighs, grounding me even as I unraveled, piece by trembling piece.

The heat built low in my belly, curling and tightening, and my mind blurred beneath the wave of it, until all I could think, all I could feel, was *him*. The way he made me feel *wanted*. Cherished. *Known*.

It should have made me bolt. That kind of tenderness didn't belong to girls like me. But I stayed. God help me, I stayed.

I shattered on a sigh of his name.

When I opened my eyes, he was watching me. Still between my thighs, his cheeks flushed, his hair a wild mess from my grip. But his gaze… God, his gaze was what undid me. Not hunger. Not pride. Something else. Something deeper.

Love, maybe. Or the aching shadow of it. But that was ridiculous, Grady could never love someone like me. He was perfect, and I was… tainted.

He kissed my inner thigh like he couldn't help himself, then slid up beside me, wrapping me in his arms as if to hold the moment still.

I should have felt guilt. And maybe part of me did. But more than that, I felt *safe*. *Seen* in a way I never had with Eric. Never had with *anyone*.

And that terrified me.

I rested my head on Grady's chest, listening to the steady rhythm of his heart, my fingers trailing along the lines of his ribs. I'd never felt more at home, or more unsettled. Because I was still leaving. I had to. That was the plan. My *life* was back in Utah.

So why did it suddenly feel like everything I'd ever needed was lying right here beside me?

His fingers drew lazy circles against my hip. He kissed the top of my head, "Let me take you out," he murmured against my hair. "Someplace nice. Just us. I've got something I want to talk to you about."

I lifted my head. "Like at a restaurant?"

He smiled. "Yeah. There's this great little Italian place in WestEnd I want to show you."

"Like a date?"

His face was full of joy. "Yeah. A date."

I dropped my head back to his chest. I've been on dates before, years ago, before everything got complicated.

"I… I don't have anything to wear."

"You can wear whatever you like, you always look incredible. Besides, it's just a small family restaurant."

"Okay."

An hour later, Grady handed me a helmet and helped me onto the back of his motorcycle. I couldn't stop the thrill that ran through me, Grady had sworn he'd never take me for a ride.

Things had definitely changed.

He climbed on, and I wrapped my arms around him without hesitation. It had been years since I had been on a motorcycle. The last time with Eric, racing his Suzuki, hoping to get enough cash to pay the rent. Not only did he not win, but he had put his bike up as collateral.

That night was the first time I slept with someone for money. I didn't like to think of it as prostitution, just a necessary evil.

But I didn't do that anymore. Not since my arrest, since Jackson bailed me out.

I pressed my forehead to Grady's back. *Did he know? Had Jackson told him?*

We pulled out onto the open road and I raised one hand in the air, chasing the adrenaline that never failed to drown the darkness.

Thirty minutes later, we rolled into WestEnd, and to my surprise, right into the middle of a fall festival. I hadn't been to one of those since I was a kid, back before my parents died.

Grady parked easily. I hadn't even taken off my helmet before the smells hit me: funnel cakes, corn dogs, and even cotton candy. Music echoed from a live band on a makeshift stage in the middle of a nearby park. People milled everywhere, families with small children, teenagers running from one booth to the next, and even some couples sneaking kisses behind booths.

"Did you know this was happening?" I asked, still taking it all in.

Grady shook his head. "No. I had no idea."

"Can we stay for a bit?"

He pulled me in, one hand around my waist, the other brushing my cheek. "Whatever you want." He kissed me, soft and slow, and my heart flipped.

"What do you want to see first?" he asked.

I looked from one end of the street to the next, taking in the various booths and activities. I grabbed his hand, seeing the one I wanted to try out first. "Come on," I said, pulling him along behind me.

We stopped at a row of carnival games that reminded me of summers with my family. Jackson always played the game where you threw a ball to knock down the milk jugs. And he always gave his prize to Abby. Even before they were a couple. I always wanted someone to win something just for me.

"Can we try this one?"

"Of course," he gave my hand a little squeeze.

"Hey, there little lady. Care to give it a go?" The game man grinned as we stepped closer.

Grady handed him some cash, and the man set five softballs on the counter. "Knock down one tower, get a small prize. Two, medium. All three? Grand prize."

"Sounds easy enough." Or so I thought.

Three throws, a few bottles down, most totally missed. Two more and I managed to knock down a couple more.

Evidence that Jackson got all the athletic talent.

The man gave me a pitying smile. "Care to try again?"

I shook my head. "No, I think I've proven this is not the game for me."

Grady kissed me on the cheek. "Here, let me try." He handed the man another bill and once the towers were stacked back up, he set five balls on the counter.

He stepped up and I stepped back, half excited, half mortified.

He nailed the first tower with just one throw. The second with another. Two balls later and the last tower was down.

The man grinned. "What'll it be?" he asked, gesturing to the rows of stuffed toys across the back wall.

"You pick," Grady whispered.

I scanned the assortment of toys until a sad panda caught my eye. "That one."

Grady took the stuffed toy and handed it to me along with a kiss. "Good choice."

I stroked the panda's soft fur. My heart swooped. I was falling, hard. And if I wanted to keep him, I had a choice to make. Stay with Eric and the life I knew, or take a leap of faith into the unknown.

We wandered through the festival, pausing at various booths to see what goods were for sale, and even one where we got matching fake tattoos - monarch butterflies, on our wrists. It was silly, impulsive, and perfect.

Then I spotted the Ferris wheel.

"Wanna ride it with me?" I asked, tugging on his hand.

Grady looked up at the towering structure with a wary grin. "You trying to kill me?"

I smirked. "You survived the carnival game humiliation. Think you can handle the view from the top?"

He groaned playfully but followed me into line. When it was our turn, we climbed into one of the swaying gondolas. The attendant locked the bar in place, and the wheel jerked to life with a mechanical hum.

As we rose above the festival, the lights below looked like glitter scattered across velvet. Music and laughter drifted up in a hazy blur. I leaned into Grady, my head resting on his shoulder, and for a moment, everything felt weightless.

"It's beautiful," I murmured.

His arm wrapped around me. "So are you."

I laughed softly, nerves fluttering in my stomach. "You're full of it."

"I'm serious," he said, turning to me. "I could sit here all night."

The gondola rocked gently as we reached the top and paused, suspended in the night sky. I turned toward him, his face illuminated by the soft glow of the festival lights below. I kissed him, slow and sweet.

When we descended again, we strolled hand in hand to the food stalls. He bought us a funnel cake, and we shared it as powdered sugar dusted our fingers. He made a mess on purpose, just to lick it off mine.

He slung an arm around my shoulder as we wandered down the midway. Just ahead, tucked between a caricature artist and a booth selling candied pecans, sat an old-school photo booth, glowing red with neon letters.

"Wanna make it official?" Grady asked, tipping his head toward it.

I arched a brow. "Official?"

He grinned. "You, me, Sad Panda here. Memory preserved in all its awkward glory."

I laughed, hugging the panda to my chest. "Only if I get to pick the pose."

Grady opened the curtain like a gentleman and gestured for me to enter first. The inside smelled faintly of bubblegum and cheap plastic, and the seat creaked beneath us as we crammed in. He was warm and solid beside me, his arm brushing mine in the tight space.

I tapped the touchscreen and picked the four-photo option. "Okay. Serious face first."

Grady went solemn, brows furrowed like a Shakespearean hero.

"Cute," I said, as the shutter clicked.

"Now goofy." I stuck my tongue out and he crossed his eyes, and the flash went off mid-laugh.

"Okay, kiss me," I whispered, barely thinking.

He blinked once, but didn't hesitate. His lips met mine just as the next photo snapped, soft and sure.

The final flash caught me staring at him, lips swollen, heart in free fall.

When the strip printed, we both reached for it. Our fingers touched and lingered.

I tucked the photos into my pocket before I could overthink it. A keepsake. A souvenir of something I was starting to realize I didn't want to leave behind.

By the time we reached the music stage again, I felt high on sugar, adrenaline, and something dangerously close to love.

I closed my eyes and swayed, feeling free, alive.

I reached for Grady's hand without looking...

Nothing.

I turned, scanning the crowd, heart racing. "Grady?"

A second ago, he'd been right beside me. He wouldn't just leave, would he?

I pushed through the crowd, my stomach twisting tighter with every step. Five minutes passed. Then ten. Finally, I spotted him leaning against a tree on the edge of the lot, head tipped back like he was watching the stars. Or hiding from them.

"Grady?"

He startled at my voice, his expression distant before it softened.

"Hey. I thought I lost you," I said. What I wanted to say was, *Why did you disappear? Did I do something wrong?*

"I, uh..." He reached up, scratching the back of his head. "I just needed some air."

I'd think he wasn't big on crowds, but I saw him at the bar every night, he always seemed fine.

"Okay," I said, even though it wasn't.

"Ready to get out of here?" He asked.

"Sure."

He threaded our fingers together and led me down a quieter street, to a little restaurant with green awnings and white lights strung over the patio. *Bella's.*

I tried to smile, tried to hold onto the warmth from earlier. But it slipped, like water through my fingers.

Something in him had gone still. And I didn't know how to reach it.

The restaurant was quiet, too quiet after the laughter and noise of the festival. Bella's was charming in a quaint, old-world kind of way, with soft violin music playing overhead and flickering candles on every table. The glow should have been romantic. Instead, it felt heavy.

Grady sat across from me, staring at the unlit candle between us like he could will it to speak instead.

The waiter brought us water and breadsticks. I took one, mostly for something to do with my hands. Grady didn't move.

"Are you okay?" I asked, keeping my voice light, though my stomach was coiled tight.

He didn't look at me. "Just... I was just reminded of something I had forgotten."

"What was it?"

He shook his head. "It doesn't matter."

I wanted to push. God, I wanted to push. But something in his posture, shoulders hunched, gaze lowered, told me I wouldn't get far.

So instead, I nodded, like that was good enough. Like I didn't feel him pulling away inch by inch.

"Did you have a good time?" he asked finally, forcing a smile that didn't touch his eyes.

I thought about the Ferris wheel, the game, the kiss. The little booth tucked near the bandstand, where we'd laughed so hard over the ridiculous strip of photos, him sticking out his tongue, me trying to look sultry and failing, both of us cracking up on the last frame.

I reached into my pocket and pulled out the photo strip, smoothing it gently with my fingers.

"I did," I said softly. "Thank you."

"You said you wanted to talk to me about something?" I asked, desperate for any kind of bridge between us.

"I did?"

"Yeah. Before we left."

"Oh. Right." He rubbed the back of his neck. "I... I think we need to hire a new bartender."

I blinked. "You think we need to hire a new bartender."

"Yeah."

"That's... well, okay. Don't you think you should be talking to Jackson about this?"

He nodded, eyes back on his plate. "You're right."

"Is that all?"

"Yep."

Just like that, the door closed. Whatever he had been feeling earlier, whatever had cracked him open enough to let me in, was gone now, shuttered behind polite distance and meaningless conversation.

Grady was right in front of me, close enough to touch, and yet I'd never felt so far from him. I clutched the panda to my chest, its stitched eyes too honest, too knowing. This was more than a bad mood. Something inside him had shifted. And maybe something inside me had too. Because for the first time, I didn't want to walk away.

But I also didn't know how to stay.

Chapter 34

Grady

I parked in the garage and helped Whitney off the bike. The day had started out perfect, a ride on my bike, carnival games, music, her laughter in my ears. But perfect was an illusion.

In the house, silence greeted us. I didn't say a word, just grabbed my guitar and headed straight out the back door. I needed space.

Collapsing into a chair, I cradled the guitar in my lap; the strings greeted me like muscle memory, my fingers moving before my mind caught up. *Amazing Grace* flowed easily, my mother's favorite hymn. Ironic, really. I don't think she understood the meaning of grace. At least not the way Mrs. Bryant explained it.

I barely got through the first verse. My voice cracked on the word "wretch."

How sweet the sound.

Yeah, right.

I slammed my hand down across the strings, the sudden jangle of noise cutting through the quiet like a scream.

The song died in my hands. I curled my fingers into fists.

I had been ready to tell Whitney everything - all of it. But then that damned evangelical street preacher came out of nowhere. He grabbed my shoulder as we were heading to see the band. As he screamed scripture mere inches from my face, my pulse thundered in my ears. Whitney's hand slipped from mine, whether I let go or she pulled away, I didn't know. All I could hear was my mother's voice, braided into his like some unholy harmony.

"You're a sinner!" he shouted. "Repent now, for the wages of sin is death!"

I tried to shake him off, but he clung on, shouting scripture like bullets. "Depart from me, you cursed, into the eternal fire..."

The sour tang of his breath hit me like communion wine turned to vinegar... Suddenly I was thirteen again, back in my childhood bedroom, already condemned.

I wanted to yell, to tell him to shut up, but the words stuck in my throat.

By the time I shook him off, the damage was done.

I sat still on the porch, guitar silent in my lap, the hum of cicadas rising in the dark like static under my skin. The air was thick with the scent of pine and cooling earth. I focused on the rhythm of my breathing, the way the strings beneath my fingers still vibrated faintly from the last chord.

But even that peace, thin as it was, shattered beneath the weight of memory.

The preacher's voice had crawled inside my head like a parasite, wrapping around the parts of me I thought I'd buried. His voice blended with hers, my mother's, until I couldn't separate one from the other.

And just like that, I was thirteen again.

The scent of cut grass lingered in the air, but it didn't reach me. Not really. I wasn't on the porch anymore. I was thirteen again, trapped in that too-quiet bedroom, every second thick with shame.

I lay on my back, tossing a baseball at the ceiling, catching it, tossing it again - anything to keep the guilt from swallowing me whole.

The Bible sat on my nightstand, its leather spine cracked from years of use, its pages marked with highlighter and grief. I was supposed to be reading it. Repenting. But I knew every verse by heart, and none of them had saved me.

Miss Becky had touched me two weeks before. My body still remembered, even if I tried to forget.

And now it was happening again, my body betraying me. Pressure stirred beneath the waistband of my slacks, unbidden and burning with shame.

I hated that my body could still react. Still want. Like I hadn't already been ruined.

I clamped a hand over myself, breath catching. "No. No. No."

I shut my eyes and whispered the only defense I had:

"Create in me a clean heart, O God... and renew a right spirit within me..."

I didn't hear the door open until it slammed against the wall.

I shot upright. Too late.

My mother's gasp was worse than a scream.

"What is that?" she shrieked, pointing as if I'd grown horns.

"I... I wasn't... I didn't mean..."

She dropped to her knees, eyes wild. "This is the will of God, your sanctification," she shouted, hands outstretched like she could physically drag the sin from my skin. "That you abstain from sexual immorality!"

My father stood in the doorway, frozen. Then he stepped forward and placed a hand on her shoulder like a judge delivering a sentence.

"I think it's time."

She rose slowly, her face blotchy with tears.

"I'll start the car."

I didn't cry. I didn't scream. I just sat there, my heart pounding so hard I thought it might crack my ribs, waiting for the moment they'd stop looking at me like I was something that needed purging.

Later, she told the social worker I was defective. Unclean. Not what God intended.

She didn't want a defective son.

I rubbed my eyes with the heel of my hand. Twenty-nine years old, and I still couldn't forget the look on her face; that moment she saw me as something dirty. Diseased. Like I'd chosen this. Like I wanted to be broken.

That kind of rejection didn't fade - it festered, calcified.

I carried it in my bones.

"Grady?"

The sound of her voice twisted something sharp inside me. I blinked fast, but the porch light caught the wetness on my cheeks before I could hide it. Whitney stood barefoot in the doorway, concern written all over her.

I turned away, swiping at my face like none of it mattered.

"Is everything okay?" she asked softly.

"Yeah."

I stood too fast, slipping the guitar off my lap, eager for motion, any motion that might keep me from shattering.

"I need to run down to the bar. You okay here?"

"I could come with you."

I wanted to tell her.

About the preacher. About my mother. About how hard it was to breathe sometimes without choking on the past.

But if I opened that door, I didn't know if I'd be able to close it again.

So I smiled, a brittle thing, and lied.

"That's okay. Take the night off. You deserve it."

She reached for my hand, but I didn't stop.

Before she could respond, I grabbed my jacket and left.

The bar was dead quiet.

Invoices lay scattered across the desk, a haphazard mess Jackson wasn't here to deal with. I'd meant to organize them, or at least make a dent in the backlog, but the bottle on the desk had stolen my focus.

I poured another glass of whiskey. Tossed it back.

It burned going down, but not enough. Not yet.

My head already hummed. My mother would be so proud.

I stared at the bottle, jaw tight.

When I was little, I thought whiskey was a demon in a glass. A test of morality. Drink, and you fail. Drink, and you're lost. That's what my adoptive mother told me. That's what the church preached. Liquor led to lust. Lust led to sin. Sin led straight to hell.

And still... here I was.

"Whiskey dick," I muttered with a bitter laugh. "God's little mercy."

I drank to forget. Not Whitney - God, never her. I drank to forget the memory of her hands on my face, her voice saying my name like it meant something. Because I didn't deserve it. Didn't deserve her.

I knew better. Knew I was sliding back into the same pit that had almost swallowed me whole. But right now, the warmth spreading through my veins was easier to face than the cold truth creeping up my spine.

My mother's voice echoed, sharp and cruel: *You're weak. Broken. Full of sin.* I gritted my teeth and took another long pull from the bottle, straight from the neck this time.

It wasn't like I *wanted* to drink. I wanted to feel *worthy*. I wanted to forget Miss Becky. I wanted to unhear the hymns that told me I was beyond redemption.

But mostly, I wanted to quiet the ache.

The ache of knowing Whitney had seen me. Really *seen* me, and I'd pushed her away anyway.

You don't get to have good things, the voice whispered.

The thought made me angry. I stood up too fast, the desk chair scraping backward. The room tilted a little, not enough to lose control, but enough to notice.

I braced myself on the desk. The guilt hit hard, creeping in like a slow fog. It didn't scream, it whispered. *This is why she left. This is who you really are.*

The worst part? I didn't even like how it felt anymore.

I hated the taste.

Hated the warmth.

Hated the way my skin buzzed and my chest stayed cold anyway.

I wanted to throw the bottle against the wall, but I didn't. I just stared at it, my reflection warped in the amber glass.

Maybe the bar was a mistake. Maybe everything was. Owning this place, was it really about building something new? Or was I just proving my mother right?

I sank back into the chair and ran a hand down my face.

I was going to hell anyway, wasn't I? Might as well be drunk for it.

Another sip. Another numb inch between me and the truth.

Then...

A knock broke through the silence.

"Yeah?" I called, voice rough.

Steven peeked in. "Hey, sorry to bother you, but we've got a problem out here."

"I'm not a problem!" came a shriek from behind him.

I winced. Not tonight.

Steven's mouth flattened. "She won't leave until she talks to you."

I took another pull from the bottle. "Go away," I growled, too tired to yell.

Before he could step back, the door flew open.

"I said..."

"Get out of my way!" Emily screeched, shoving past him.

And there she was, five-foot-eight of bleach-blonde chaos, stuffed into a dress that looked like it lost a fight with a napkin.

God, no. Not tonight.

My stomach turned, already unsettled from the liquor. I gripped the edge of the desk to keep steady, willing the room to stop shifting.

Steven hesitated. "You got this?"

No.

Not even a little.

"Yeah," I lied, waving him off with a shaky hand. "I got it."

The door clicked shut behind him. Emily strutted inside like she owned the damn place. She sauntered over and perched on the desk like it was a stage, one leg crossed over the other, eyes lit with something that felt more like conquest than affection.

"Hey, baby," she purred.

I didn't move. "What do you want, Emily?"

"I came here for you..."

"We've had this conversation. We're done."

"You don't mean that," she said, leaning in, dragging one icy finger across my chest.

I flinched at the touch, not because it was cold, but because my skin *remembered* her. My body had muscle memory I hated, a traitor in every sense.

"I do mean it." I knocked her hand away, but she didn't flinch.

Instead, she slid between my knees, hips swaying like a siren's song. I tipped the bottle again, needing the burn to keep from shoving her back. *Needing* something to quiet the thunder in my head.

One second she was standing. The next, her dress hit the floor, and I was drowning in a past I didn't want.

Her skin was on mine.

Perfume and desperation.

Cheap vanilla and old ghosts.

My stomach flipped.

I didn't want this. God, I didn't want this.

The worst part? My body didn't either.

Good. Thank God.

I used to think this meant love. Or at least safety. It didn't. It never had. But back then, I'd been too broken to tell the difference.

My head fell back against the chair, too heavy to hold upright.

"Why don't you go fuck Jimmy. Or Frank. Or Brad. Or whoever."

She leaned in, lips at my ear. "I only want to fuck you."

Her tongue flicked against my skin and I flinched again. Not from lust. From nausea.

"Well, I don't want to fuck you."

She ground her hips against me, and I nearly laughed at how limp my body stayed.

Her face shifted, confusion tightening her mouth. "What the hell..."

"Go home, Emily." My voice was flat. Final.

She pulled back just enough to reach for her phone, holding it up like a threat.

Let her take the photo. Let her twist it.

I didn't have the fight left in me to stop her. I barely had the will to breathe.

I stared at the bottle on the desk. My reflection warped and fractured in the glass - eyes glassy, mouth slack, posture defeated. Just another sinner in a borrowed room.

"This is pathetic," she muttered, tugging her dress back over her head.

She didn't even slam the door when she left.

And somehow that was worse.

I sat there for a long time after she was gone. The fan hummed above me. My skin itched where hers had touched mine. I stared at the crack in the wood grain on the edge of the desk, trying not to think about anything, especially not Whitney.

Especially not how she looked at me last night. Like I was worth something.

I curled forward, elbows on my knees, head in my hands. I was too sick to cry. Too far gone to pray.

But somewhere inside me, under the liquor and the shame, there was this hollow, echoing truth:

I think I just ruined everything.

Chapter 35

Whitney

I heard them before I saw them. The uneven shuffle of footsteps, the scrape of boots on hardwood, the low murmur of Steven's voice trying to steady him.

Then Grady appeared.

His arm was slung around Steven's shoulders, head drooped, feet dragging. His jacket hung open, his shirt half untucked, and I could smell the whiskey from the hallway.

He was drunk. Not tipsy. Not buzzed. Gone.

I stood in the doorway of Jackson's bedroom, frozen.

He left me. Just left me. So he could do *this*?

Steven didn't notice me at first. He was too busy trying to keep Grady upright as they staggered past. But then his gaze lifted, and he paused.

Our eyes met.

"Whitney," he said quietly, his voice lined with fatigue and something gentler. Sympathy maybe. Or warning.

I didn't speak. Couldn't. I just looked at Grady, at the man I'd trusted enough to give all of myself to, barely able to stand, eyes glassy and unfocused.

He mumbled something unintelligible and let out a breathy, humorless laugh as Steven guided him down the hall and to his bed. Grady collapsed face-down without protest.

Steven adjusted the pillow under his head, then turned back to me, rubbing a hand down his face.

"Hey, girl." he said.

I still didn't move. My arms were folded tight across my chest, holding in everything I didn't want to spill out. "I..." I shook my head. "I don't understand. We had a great day. Things were going so well."

Steven hesitated, then took a step closer.

"Grady is..." He sighed. "You should talk to your brother."

That caught me off guard. "What? Why? Did something happen?"

He nodded toward Grady. "About *him*. About what he's been through. About why he... Does what he does."

Confusion tightened my throat. "Why would Jackson...?"

"Just talk to him," Steven said gently. "He'll help you understand."

And then, without waiting for a reply, he left.

The front door clicked shut behind him, leaving me alone with a passed-out Grady and a thousand questions clawing at my chest.

The silence after Steven left was deafening.

I stood there for a long time, watching Grady's back rise and fall with each shallow breath. His hair was a mess. His face was flushed. He hadn't even taken off his boots.

So this was what he needed tonight, instead of me.

I wanted to be angry. I wanted to scream, to shake him awake and demand to know why he'd run from me, from *us*, just to drown himself in whiskey and whatever else he thought might numb the truth.

But all I felt was hollow.

The kind of hollow that echoes.

I turned off the hallway light and went back to Jackson's room. There was no way I was sleeping with Grady tonight, even if it meant the nightmares came back. The sheets were still warm from when I'd been lying there earlier, waiting for him to come home. Hoping.

I sat on the edge of the bed, pulled my knees up to my chest, and stared at the phone on my nightstand.

Steven's words clung to me like smoke.

You should talk to your brother… He'll help you understand.

Understand what?

Grady's silences? The way he shut down without warning? The pain behind his eyes that he never let me close enough to touch?

I didn't want to need Jackson for this. I wanted Grady to *tell me*. To trust me. But clearly, we weren't there yet.

Maybe we never would be.

I picked up my phone, thumb hovering over the screen for a long moment before I finally opened our old thread.

> **Me:** Hey. Can we talk sometime soon? It's about Grady.

I hit send before I could second-guess it.

Then I turned off the lamp, crawled under the blanket, and lay there in the dark, listening for nothing, hoping for something.

The steady ringing of my phone pulled me from my dream.

I blinked against the morning light seeping through the blinds, disoriented for a moment. My phone rang again on the nightstand. I reached for it with one sluggish hand.

Jackson.

I cleared my throat, trying to shake off the fog. "Hello?"

"Hey," my brother said. "Sorry for calling so early."

"It's okay." My voice came out rough. "I didn't think you'd call so soon."

"Your text... Is he okay?"

I sat up slowly, the blanket falling around my waist. My eyes drifted to the hallway. The door to Grady's room was still closed. No sound from inside.

"I don't know," I admitted.

Jackson exhaled on the other end. "What happened?"

I hesitated, not sure how much to tell him. "He got drunk last night. *Really* drunk. Steven had to bring him home. I don't even know why he left. We were fine, and then... he just disappeared."

"Fuck," Jackson muttered.

"Steven said you could help me understand."

There was a pause. Long enough that I thought maybe he wouldn't say anything at all.

"I don't know where to start," he finally said. "But if you're serious about him, Whit... you need to know that he's not just moody or guarded. He's scarred. Deep."

My chest tightened. "I've figured that much out."

"I don't know what you endured during your time in the foster system, but for him, it goes back, even before that."

My breath caught in my chest. "What do you mean?"

"Grady was adopted when he was a baby. His adoptive parents were..." he paused, as if looking for the right words. "Very religious."

"He mentioned that."

"Right. Well. There was this choir teacher, Miss Becky. Has he ever said anything about her?"

I thought back to all our conversations and shook my head. "No, I don't think so."

He went quiet for a moment, and I let the silence settle, my stomach turning.

"He never told anyone for a long time," Jackson said. "But she molested him. When he was a kid."

I covered my mouth with my hand, nausea curling hot in my throat.

"He didn't understand what was happening. He thought he was the one doing something wrong.

"And when he was thirteen, his mom walked in on him... just being a normal teenage boy. But she saw it as proof. That he was broken. That he was... tainted."

A tear slipped down my cheek, and I didn't bother wiping it away.

"She blamed him," Jackson said. "Told him he was a sinner. That he needed to pray for forgiveness. She called a social worker. Said she didn't want a defective son."

His voice cracked on the word.

I couldn't speak. Could barely breathe.

"He never said anything, but I always knew something was wrong. He'd go silent for days, flinch when people touched him. I just didn't know what it was."

Jackson sniffled on the other end, like saying it out loud hurt.

"Nobody protected him, Whitney. Not when it counted. So now he protects himself, by shutting down. By running. And yeah, sometimes by drinking until he can't feel anything."

I sank back against the headboard, one hand pressed to my heart like that might slow it down.

Jackson's voice softened. "But he's not defective. He's not broken. He just doesn't know how to believe that yet."

I nodded, even though he couldn't see me.

"Please," he said. "Be patient with him. He's worth it."

"When are you coming home?"

"I... I'm not sure yet. Soon."

A muffled noise from the hallway made me turn. Then the creak of a floorboard. Movement.

Grady was up.

"I have to go," I whispered.

"Call me later, okay?"

"I will."

I ended the call and stared at the bedroom door.

Everything felt different now.

He wasn't just hurting.

He'd been hurt, in ways I hadn't even imagined.

And now... I had to decide what to do with that truth.

***

Grady looked like hell and my heart ached for him.

He stood in the kitchen doorway, one hand braced on the frame, the other rubbing the back of his neck. His eyes were puffy, bloodshot. The kind of tired that doesn't come from sleep.

"Morning," he mumbled, his voice low and hoarse.

"Morning," I replied, not moving from my place at the table.

He walked past me without meeting my gaze, heading straight for the fridge and pulling out a bottle of water. He twisted the cap and downed half of it before leaning against the counter.

"I... I owe you an apology."

I waited, curious about what he would say. If he would give me anything deeper than surface level guilt.

"I shouldn't have left like that. I just... I needed space."

I closed my eyes, only mildly disappointed. "Instead, you got drunk."

He winced, nodding. "Yeah. I did."

A pause stretched between us like a bridge neither of us wanted to step onto.

"I don't know what you're going through," I said quietly. "You don't let me in. But if you want this to work, Grady... you can't shut me out every time it gets hard."

His eyes flicked up to mine, guilt sharp on his face.

"I know."

Silence settled over us again, heavy but not angry. Just... full.

I got up and made him a cup of coffee. "Here. You look like you need it."

"Thank you."

I squeezed his shoulder and kissed his cheek. "We don't have to be at the bar for a while," I said after a moment. "We could have a quiet morning in. You could play me something."

He blinked. "Really?"

I smiled. "Yeah. I know you've been working on some new songs. I wanna hear them before you share them with the world."

His brow furrowed, like that wasn't the reaction he expected, then slowly he nodded. "Okay."

I made my way to the living room and got comfy on the couch.

He disappeared for a minute, then returned with his guitar, settling into the armchair across from me. His fingers moved slowly at first, testing the strings. Then came a few chords, soft and familiar.

He started to play - slow, soulful. I didn't listen to a lot of country music, but I knew the second he opened his mouth, "Holding On" by Bailey Zimmerman.

I didn't wait for an invitation. I joined in on the second verse, our voices blending rough and unpracticed, but something about it worked. Honest. Unpolished. Real.

We sang like that for a while, until the tension in the room softened into something that almost felt like peace.

***

The bar was busier than usual, but nothing we couldn't handle. Steven had the night off, so it was just the two of us. I couldn't help but smile at the ease in Grady's movements - shoulders relaxed, lips tilted in that faint, effortless grin. He stood behind the counter, tossing a towel over his shoulder as he poured a drink for Ray, who looked ornery as ever.

It felt like a normal night. Almost.

I turned back to wiping down tables, but a flutter of unease settled low in my stomach.

When I finally made it behind the counter again, Grady nudged my shoulder. "Hey, have you heard from Jackson lately?"

"I... uh," I hesitated. I didn't want to lie, but I didn't want him to know I'd already talked to my brother about him. "Yeah, he called me this morning."

He frowned. "He still hasn't returned any of my calls or texts."

I glanced up. "Really?" That didn't sound right. Jackson had called me first thing. He wouldn't ghost Grady like that, especially after our conversation.

"Yeah. I don't know…" His shoulders sagged. "I'm starting to feel like…" He let the words hang, then turned away to help another customer.

"Can I see your phone? Maybe something got corrupted?" I asked.

Without hesitation, he pulled it out and handed it to me. "Here."

His trust made my chest ache.

I opened his messages, scrolling to Jackson's name. And that's when I saw it.

A new message notification. From Emily.

My thumb hovered. Maybe it was nothing. Maybe she was just stirring shit, like always. Maybe…

I tapped it.

> **Emily:** Thanks for last night. You're exactly what I needed.

The words hit me like a slap. My mouth went dry.

A second later, the photo came through.

Her. Bare. Straddling him.

I stopped breathing.

It had to be old. *Please let it be old.*

But then I saw his wrist.

The monarch butterfly.

I still had mine.

My fingers curled reflexively over it, nausea rolling through me like surf in a storm. I wanted to claw the damn thing off. Erase every trace of him from my skin.

I set the phone down, screen face-down on the bar, my hand trembling.

Grady turned back around, smiling faintly. "Did he say anything?"

I didn't trust my voice. Didn't trust the way my heart was cracking open in my chest. So, I forced a smile. A lie on my lips. "No. Not yet."

I turned and walked away before the truth leaked out.

In the back room, I pulled out my phone. Steven answered on the third ring.

"Hey," I said, my voice already unraveling. "Can I crash at your place tonight?"

"Well, hello to you too. Everything okay? Does this have anything to do with last night?"

"I'll fill you in later," I murmured. "I... I just need a girls night."

He didn't push. "Say no more. I'll make cocktails and popcorn."

"Perfect."

I headed back out to the bar.

Grady reached for my hand as I passed him, but I stepped around him like he wasn't even there.

"I'm going to Steven's tonight," I said, not meeting his eyes.

He frowned. "Everything okay?"

"Yeah," I lied. "Just felt like having a girls night."

And before he could ask anything else, I walked away, heart pounding, throat tight, like if I didn't get out of there soon, I'd shatter right there on the bar floor.

Steven was a godsend.

He picked me up before Grady even had the chance to ask any more questions. I climbed into the passenger seat, relieved when he didn't press me for answers. He just drove, one hand on the wheel, the other reaching over to squeeze mine every so often.

His apartment was in the middle of town, cozy and modern, everything carefully placed and warmly lit. So very Steven.

The second we stepped inside, I made a beeline for the kitchen.

I cranked the faucet to full heat and grabbed the dish soap, lathering my wrist as I scrubbed hard at the fake tattoo.

It didn't budge.

Hot tears burned in my eyes as I scrubbed harder, thumb working in frantic circles, like I could erase the memory itself.

"Whoa, whoa, whoa." Steven reached around me, turning off the faucet. "What are you doing?"

He gently took my wrist, brows furrowing when he saw my face. I couldn't even see him through the blur of tears, but I felt his hands steadying mine.

"I need it gone," I choked out.

"Whitney," he said softly. "Talk to me. What happened?"

I shook my head, "I... I can't. I can't do this anymore. I need to go home."

"To Utah?" he asked gently.

I nodded, lip trembling.

"Is this about Grady?"

Steven didn't wait for an answer. He wrapped an arm around me and led me to the couch, guiding me like I might fall apart if he didn't.

"Start from the beginning," he said. "Just spill it."

So I did.

I told him everything.

About the way things with Grady had slowly shifted, from tension to tenderness, from guarded glances to falling asleep in his arms. What it felt like to *make love* to someone for the first time, not just have sex. How safe I'd felt, like something inside me had finally exhaled. Like maybe I didn't need to run anymore. Like maybe I could heal.

I told him my nightmares were gone. The toxic cravings too.

"I thought I was getting better," I whispered. "Because of him."

Then I told him about the text.

The photo.

Emily, naked on Grady's lap in the office.

The fake tattoo that suddenly felt like a brand I didn't ask for.

"Why would he cheat on me?" My voice cracked as I dissolved again. "What the hell did I do wrong?"

Steven pulled me against his chest, rubbing my back in slow, steady circles. "Oh, honey... Grady would never cheat on you."

I let out a short, bitter laugh. "Yeah, because we're not even really together."

"You don't believe that."

"I do." I pulled away, scrubbing my sleeve across my face. "And it's my fault. I let myself believe he actually wanted me. That he was different."

"Whit..."

"I was going to break up with Eric for him," I whispered. "I was ready to give up everything just to stay."

Steven didn't try to stop me from crying. He didn't offer advice or try to talk me down. He just sat there and let me fall apart.

At some point he got up to use the bathroom.

That's when I pulled out my phone.

My hands shook as I typed.

I stared at the screen. My thumb hovered over "Send."

Once I pressed it, there'd be no going back.

I pressed it anyway.

Chapter 36

Grady

I lay awake in bed, eyes fixed on the ceiling fan. I'd barely slept. Every time I closed my eyes, I saw Whitney walking away, her hand slipping out of mine.

I rolled over, pressing my face into the pillow she used to sleep on. It still smelled like her, sweet and soft and maddening. I used to find comfort there. Now it just reminded me of what I stood to lose.

The old voice crept in.

You're a sinner. You brought this on yourself.

God, I missed her.

She said she was having a girls' night with Steven, but the longer the silence stretched, the more that lie curled inward. Not that I could blame her. Not after everything.

I grabbed my phone, blinking against the glare. 6:08 a.m. I hadn't slept at all. I opened the gallery, scrolling back through the photos we'd taken at the festival, the one where she's sticking out her tongue and

I'm looking at her like she hung the damn stars. Because she did. At least in my world.

I needed to talk to Jackson. *Why the hell hasn't he called me back?*

I rolled out of bed and wandered into the kitchen. The air felt thick, heavier than usual. I poured a cup of coffee, black, because I couldn't stand the taste of anything sweet right now. That creamer she loved was still sitting in the fridge door. I stared at it a moment longer than I should have, then shut the door.

I took the coffee and my guitar to the armchair, sinking into it like it might hold me together.

I started strumming, low and slow. "Holding On." It was the only thing that made sense anymore. Her voice had wrapped around mine so seamlessly yesterday. I could still feel the shape of it, still hear her singing even though the house was empty.

The song cracked me open.

I'd been clinging to the belief that I didn't deserve good things. That if I let myself have her, if I reached too far, I'd ruin it, ruin *her*. But what if that belief was the real poison? What if the sin wasn't wanting her... but walking away?

I thought about the bottle in my office. The way it had numbed me just long enough to let the past take the wheel. It wasn't just the alcohol that haunted me, it was what it represented. My old life. The one I was supposed to have buried.

I thought I was stronger than that. I thought I was past needing to drink to quiet the ghosts. But when Whitney looked at me with so much tenderness after the festival, after the song, after all of it... I panicked. And I ran. Just like I always did.

But something was different this time. I didn't *want* to run anymore.

I was tired of letting fear drive every decision. Tired of letting guilt rob me of every good thing.

I looked at the door, hoping, *aching,* for her to walk through it. Maybe with messy hair and sleep in her eyes, one of my T-shirts hanging off her shoulder, asking if I'd made coffee.

But the hallway stayed empty.

I stared down at my hands, calloused fingers wrapped around the neck of my guitar. These hands had held her. Comforted her. Pushed her away.

They'd held a bottle, too.

I set the guitar aside and buried my face in my hands.

You don't have to be clean to be loved.

Mrs. Bryant's voice rang in my memory. That's what she said. But maybe the truth was deeper than that.

Maybe love was the only thing that could *make* me clean.

I reached for my phone again, fingers shaking. Opened Whitney's contact, thumb hovered.

Me: Hope you're having fun. Miss you.

I sent it before I could second-guess it.

Then I sat in the silence and let the weight of what I wanted finally settle.

I wanted *her.*

And for the first time in my life, I didn't just want to be better; I believed I *could* be.

The bar was busy with the usual afternoon crowd, the low hum of conversation and clinking glasses a welcome distraction from the silence that had haunted the house all morning. I welcomed the noise. Needed it. Anything to drown out the voice in my head whispering that something wasn't right.

Ray tapped his knuckles on the bar, sharp against the wood. "Hey, where's my girl at?"

I raised an eyebrow. "*Your* girl?"

He grinned, unfazed. "Okay, your girl. Where's Whitney?"

I poured him a beer and slid it across the counter. "She went out with Steven last night. She'll be in later."

"Steven, huh?" He took a sip, nodding. "You better be careful, son. Let a girl like that slip away, and you'll regret it the rest of your life."

I forced a smile. Didn't I know it.

The afternoon wore on in slow, anxious minutes. I tried to focus on the rhythm of bar work; refilling the ice well, restocking shelves that didn't need restocking, wiping the already-clean counter until the wood shone. I even let Ray ramble about his days in the Navy and flirt with the waitress just for something, anything, to focus on.

But my phone kept pulling my eyes like a magnet. No new messages.

I told myself not to spiral. She needed space. That's all.

Still, a pit had settled in my stomach, heavy and cold.

I brewed another cup of coffee, maybe my fifth of the day, maybe sixth. I'd lost count. I leaned against the bar, the warmth of the mug in my hands doing nothing to cut the chill crawling up my spine.

She'll be here, I told myself again.

But the silence was starting to scream.

I pulled out my phone, thumb hovering over our last text thread. *Hope you're having fun. Miss you.* Simple. Casual. Maybe too casual. Was it enough? Too much?

I sighed and closed it, about to check on my unanswered messages to Jackson when I saw a message I hadn't noticed earlier.

Emily.

My blood went cold.

I tapped it, heart in my throat.

> **Emily:** Thanks for last night. You're exactly what I needed.

Then came the photo - her, naked, straddling my lap, that smug smile on her face like she'd won.

I stared at it, breath frozen in my chest.

No. No, no, no.

My eyes dropped to the timestamp. Sent last night. Read not long after.

When I'd handed Whitney my phone.

I felt like I was going to be sick. My stomach pitched, my hand trembling as I gripped the edge of the bar for balance.

She'd seen this.

Of course she had. And she hadn't said a word.

I tapped her contact and hit *Call*. Straight to voicemail.

"Whit, please... please call me back," I said, my voice rough with panic. "I haven't heard from you today, and I'm worried. Just... please."

I ended the call and set the phone on the counter, staring down at it like it might change its mind and ring after all. My heart was racing, but my limbs felt leaden, numb.

I needed to do something - *move, breathe, focus* - anything but stare at that fucking message. I busied myself with wiping glasses I didn't need, restocking things that didn't matter, rearranging bottles that were already perfectly lined up. But it didn't help. Not this time.

The weight of it pressed in from all sides. The silence from her. The photo. The guilt.

Somewhere deep down, I knew something irreversible had just happened.

And this time, I wasn't sure I could fix it.

Just then, the front door slammed open, hard enough to rattle the pictures on the wall.

"Is she here?"

I froze, the mug of coffee halfway to my lips.

Jackson.

Hat pulled low, eyes wild with panic, he stormed in like a soldier on a mission. I hadn't seen him in over a month. Hadn't heard from him, either, not a single call or text returned in weeks.

And now here he was, tearing through the front door like a bomb had gone off.

"Jackson?" My stomach dropped. If he was here like this, something was wrong. Really fucking wrong.

He stalked across the bar, fists clenched at his sides. "Where is she?"

"What?" I asked, still trying to catch up. I set the mug down, stepping out from behind the bar.

"Whitney," he barked. "Where is she?"

I swallowed hard, dread curling through my chest like smoke. *What did you do, baby?*

"She... she stayed at Steven's last night. Said she needed a girl's night." The words felt weak, even as I said them. An excuse, not an explanation. And we both knew it.

Jackson shook his head, jaw locked tight. He pulled his phone from his pocket and set it on the bar. One tap, and Whitney's voice filled the space between us.

"Hey, Jackson. I wanted to wait till you got back, but I can't do this anymore. I love you."

The bottom dropped out of my world.

"What the hell happened, Grady?" Jackson's voice was tight, barely restrained. But it wasn't the voice of a man looking for a fight. It was the voice of someone who'd just had the ground ripped out from under him.

He sank onto a barstool, elbows on the counter, head in his hands.

My knees buckled. I grabbed the edge of the bar to stay upright. "I-I don't understand," I managed. "She said she just wanted a girl's night."

But I'd known. Deep down, I'd known something was wrong the second she walked away from me.

"She wouldn't just leave," I said, my voice rising in desperation. "Not without saying goodbye. Not without telling me why."

Jackson shook his head, rubbing the back of his neck like he was trying to ground himself. "She's not answering my calls. I drove straight here the second I got her message."

I opened my mouth, closed it. Then the truth tumbled out.

"There was a message on my phone... from Emily. A picture." I hesitated. "Naked. On my lap. It's from a couple nights ago, when she just showed up at the bar. But I was already drunk. I didn't even see the message until a little while ago. It had already been read."

Jackson's eyes snapped to mine. "She saw it."

"I think so."

"What the fuck were you doing with Emily?" His voice was low, dangerous. But underneath it, I could hear the hurt - for me, not just for Whitney.

"Nothing. I swear. She forced her way into the office, tried to pull her usual shit, but I told her no. I didn't touch her, Jackson. Sh-she took a photo. I didn't really think about it after I kicked her out."

"Goddamn it, Grady." Jackson stood up and shoved the barstool away with a scrape and a clatter. "You let her get close enough to do this?"

I hung my head, shame and fury burning through me.

"Why haven't you been returning my calls?" I finally asked.

Jackson's brow furrowed. "What?"

I pulled out my phone and handed it to him, showing the string of unanswered calls and messages. "I tried, man. I thought you were ghosting me."

He took the phone, scrolling with a frown. "Grady... I've replied to every single one. I swear."

Then he stopped. His jaw locked tight. He turned the screen toward me.

"I'm blocked."

My chest clenched. I took the phone back, staring at the screen. BLOCKED.

"How the hell..."

Jackson's eyes narrowed. "When was the last time Emily had your phone?"

"Never..." I started, then froze. That last day at her apartment. I'd gone to clean up. Left my phone on the nightstand.

"Fuck."

Jackson swore, dragging a hand over his face as he began pacing. "That fucking bitch."

I nodded slowly, throat too tight to speak.

Of course she did this. Of course she needed one final blow. And I let her.

I thought I was done with her. Thought I'd clawed my way out. But somehow, she still found a way to get her claws in, twist the knife when I wasn't looking.

I trusted her with nothing, and still, it was too much.

And Whitney paid the price.

The silence that followed was brutal. Heavy. I stared down at the wood grain of the bar, willing it to offer answers that weren't coming. Something in me fractured. Not all at once, but in slow, splintering cracks that had been forming for years.

"Do you think she's okay?" I asked, barely above a whisper.

"I don't know, man," Jackson said, voice softer now. "I wish I did. But if she's going back to Utah, back to that asshole Eric, I don't know if we'll ever see her again."

A knife twisted in my gut.

"I thought I'd already lost everything once in my life," I murmured, my voice hollow.

"I know," Jackson said. "Me too."

We stood there in the dim bar, two men shaped by pain and pasts we didn't choose, both gutted by the same woman who'd somehow become the center of our world.

Chapter 37

Whitney

T he tires hummed against the pavement like a lullaby I couldn't fall asleep to.

Eric's window was cracked, smoke curling out like lazy fingers into the cold morning air. The acrid scent of weed clung to everything - his hoodie, the seats, my hair. He passed me the joint without looking. I waved it off.

"You sure?" he asked, a soft smile on his lips. "It might take the edge off."

"I'm fine," I murmured, turning my head to watch the landscape blur by. Miles and miles of empty road, the kind that made you feel like you weren't going anywhere even when you were.

He didn't push, just nodded and took another hit. "Let me know if you change your mind."

"Cold," by Jessie Murph played on the radio, I wrapped my arms around my middle, heart pounding in the quiet as I let the words flow through me. I felt sick. My chest ached like something inside me had been cracked open and left raw.

I missed him.

God, I missed him.

Why did I miss him?

I closed my eyes and pictured Grady's face - his tired eyes, the way he held his guitar like it was a lifeline, the way he looked at me like I was something worth saving. And more than that, like I was saving *him*. My throat tightened.

But he still had Emily.

He still let her get close. Drunk or not, that was a choice.

And maybe it wasn't cheating. Technically, he hadn't done anything wrong. After all, I was with Eric. But the hypocrisy burned. Even if he didn't say it, I knew he wanted me to break up with him, to leave this life behind. He wanted me to choose him. But how could he ask for that when he hadn't chosen me, not really, anyway.

I bit the inside of my cheek until I tasted blood.

A twinge of guilt stuttered through me for leaving Steven the way I did. I didn't even say goodbye, just snuck out as soon as he was asleep and had Eric pick me up at a gas station at the edge of town.

Steven deserved better than me. They all did.

I shifted in my seat as Eric droned on next to me, oblivious to my inner turmoil, or maybe just pretending to be. "So, anyway, I managed to work out a deal with Marco's guys. If I help collect, he'll start knocking down my debt. It's not the worst deal, and..." he rubbed the back of his neck. "It's keeping me from gambling."

I said nothing.

He kept talking, like he was nervous. "I'm serious about quitting this time, baby. I never want to put you in danger again." He reached over and squeezed my thigh. "I... I thought you were dead."

I wanted to scream, *"You let them rape me! Beat me unconscious! Break my bones!"* But what was the point?

Mostly, I wanted to cry.

By the time we pulled into the apartment complex, the ache in my chest had gone numb. I stared blankly out the windshield as Eric put the car in park and climbed out.

"We're home," he smiled, tossing his keys in the air and catching them with a grin.

He took my hand, leading the way up the stairs and down the hall. The moment he opened the apartment door, the smell hit me, stale beer, old pizza, sweat, and cheap perfume. Like the place had been sealed shut for weeks.

The place was a disaster.

Beer cans lined the coffee table and couch cushions like trophies. A few open pizza boxes sat on the floor, hardened cheese curling at the edges. On the coffee table, bold and unashamed, sat three thin white lines of cocaine, a rolled-up dollar next to them like an invitation.

I froze in the doorway. At least the blood was gone.

Eric walked in, looking sheepish. "Sorry. I meant to clean up before you got here. I…" He shrugged, rubbing the back of his neck. "Honestly, I wasn't sure if you were coming back."

I didn't answer. I couldn't.

"I'll clean it up, babe. Just give me a minute." He grabbed a garbage bag and started shoving trash into it, like that would erase everything.

I drifted toward the bedroom. My footsteps felt too light, like I wasn't really there.

The door creaked open.

If anything, it was worse.

Dirty laundry spilled from a tipped-over basket. The bed sat unmade, a lump of tangled sheets and old regrets. A half-eaten burger in a greasy paper bag rotted on the nightstand. The trash smelled like sour milk and something I couldn't place, something rotting underneath the surface.

This was my life now.

This was what I came back to.

I sat down on the edge of the bed. The mattress dipped beneath me, too soft, too familiar.

That's when I saw them.

Two used condoms on the floor, nestled like dead things between a pair of jeans and a crumpled receipt.

I stared at them, hollow.

My breath caught, but I didn't move. Didn't cry.

I just buried my face in my hands, the silence pressing in from all sides.

This wasn't like the quiet in Grady's house, where peace lived in the corners and love softened the silence. No. This quiet was loud. Smothering. The kind of quiet that made you feel like you were drowning inside your own skin.

I wanted to scream.

But if I started, I wasn't sure I'd stop.

That's when I felt it, a familiar weight pressing against the side of my backpack. I reached for it absently, my fingers brushing the fabric, and then, without even thinking, I pulled it open.

Inside, crumpled but still intact, was the photo strip of Grady and me from the festival, from the photo booth that night. A time when everything was simple. When we laughed, when we *were* happy, before the world turned upside down.

I stared at the photos, and for a second, it was like I could still feel his warmth, the way his arm had fit so perfectly around me. We were happy, so happy. I could almost hear his laugh, see the way he looked at me like I was the only person in the world. And then the memory of that night came crashing back - the way he left me, got drunk and lost in someone else. I couldn't understand how the man in those photos became the man who'd hurt me. How could he do that to me? To us?"

I let out a shaky breath, the weight of those memories hitting me all over again. What happened to us? What made him do it?

What did *she* have that I didn't?

I wanted to smile, to remember the joy of that night, but it was too hard to ignore the pain that came with the memories. It felt like another lifetime ago, like someone else's story. And yet, here I was, still holding onto these photos like they were the only part of me that was still *real*.

"I tucked the photo strip back into my bag, pressing it deep into the fabric like I could bury all those memories with it. But even as I closed the zipper, I could still feel them - those moments between us. The love. The hurt. It was like trying to shut out a part of myself. But I had to. I couldn't face it, not yet.

But I couldn't keep running either. Not from the past, not from him.

I sat back against the wall, staring at the backpack, and for the first time, I realized that hiding the photos wasn't the same as burying the past. It was just a moment of silence, a pause. One day, I'd be ready to face it, to understand why everything changed. But for now, all I could do was wait.

Our footsteps echoed down the wide hallway. The hospital smelled like bleach and too many bad memories. Nurses offered polite smiles as we passed, but I couldn't return them. I felt like if I cracked a smile, the rest of me would crack too, and I was having a hard enough time holding it all together.

I sat on the edge of the exam table, fingers nervously tapping against the hard plastic surface while Eric paced near the door, arms folded, avoiding eye contact.

"You nervous?" he asked, glancing at me through a curtain of dark hair that had grown too long.

"About getting my cast off?" I shrugged. "Nah. I'm ready."

He nodded but stayed quiet for a beat. Then, softly, "Was it... how bad was it? That night?"

I looked up, surprised.

He was staring at the floor, jaw clenched. "I mean, I saw you there on the floor. I know how bad it looked. I mean, I called 911, but... I just... shit, Whit. I didn't know it was that bad. I didn't know they were gonna... do that."

I exhaled slowly. "Does it matter?"

His shoulders slumped. "Yeah. To me, it does. I never want anything bad to happen to you. Especially because of me. I'm so sorry. I can't tell you enough."

Before I could answer, the doctor walked in, a woman in her early fifties with kind eyes and a no-nonsense demeanor.

"Whitney Taylor? Let's see how that arm of yours is doing."

She logged into the computer and pulled up the X-rays. "You're healing beautifully," she said. "Let's get that cast off."

The saw buzzed, loud and jarring, but I didn't flinch. I watched the pieces fall away like dead weight, like skin I'd outgrown. When she peeled it back, my arm felt foreign. lighter but tender. Vulnerable.

She gave me instructions for stretching and rebuilding strength, and then we were on our way.

"Mind if we stop by Everest?" I asked as we walked through the parking lot. "I want to see if I can get my job back."

Eric looked a little surprised, but nodded. "Of course."

The rock climbing gym sat nestled in a weathered strip mall, the kind of place that looked unimpressive from the outside but had always felt like a sanctuary inside. I hadn't been back since everything happened, but stepping through the door felt weirdly comforting. Like muscle memory.

Ashley looked up from behind the counter and did a double take.

"Whitney?" she said, stepping out. "Wow. Look at you. You look great!"

"Thank you." I lifted my arm, flexing gently. "Cast came off today. I'm still a little weak, but I'm ready to get back into it."

Ashley grinned. "You sure you're up for it?"

"Completely."

She gave me a soft smile. "I'd love to have you back, but... I'm gonna need you to take a drug test first."

I nodded. "I understand. No problem."

She looked surprised, which sent a bolt of sadness, and oddly enough, pride, through me.

"Great. Well, we need someone to lead Saturday's family hike. You think you'll be good to go by then?"

"Definitely," I said, relief rushing through me like a second wind.

As we walked back to the car, my phone buzzed in my pocket. Again.

Jackson - missed call

Then, a second later, Grady's face lit up the screen.

Eric glanced down. "You want me to answer that?"

"No." I silenced it.

"You could block them, you know. If you really didn't want to hear from them."

I hesitated. "Yeah," I said with a shrug. "Maybe."

But the truth was, I didn't want them gone. I liked knowing they were still thinking about me. Still reaching out.

Even if I wasn't ready to pick up.

Saturday came with blue skies and bird song, the kind of morning that made it easier to breathe.

I hiked with a group of seven: two couples, a pair of sisters, and a teenage boy who was clearly trying to impress one of the girls by not complaining. I'd missed this, the trail dust under my boots, the scent of pine and sun-warmed stone, the way the world got quiet when you climbed just high enough to leave the noise behind.

"And over here," I said, pointing to a cluster of sagebrush blooming along the trail, "you've got a whole community of native pollinators - bees, butterflies, even hummingbirds sometimes. The sage gives off a strong, earthy smell that deters predators, but the flowers still attract what they need."

The group nodded, snapping pictures, asking questions. I felt useful.

Alive.

Strong.

I hadn't talked about Utah like this before. Back then, it was just something I did between climbs, something to keep the adrenaline at bay. A cage I lived in while I waited for my next high. But now, every pine needle and hawk overhead felt like a choice.

I'm here because I want to be.

Because I need to be.

Still, my thoughts kept drifting east.

To Falcon Pointe.

To Grady.

I could still see his hands cradling his guitar, the way his voice dropped when he spoke only to me. I missed the way he looked at me like I was more than my past. Like I was worth staying for. Worth saving.

Maybe that's what love is. Or maybe it was just the closest thing I'd ever felt to home.

But maybe love, if that's what it was, wasn't enough when you were both still learning how to breathe.

I pressed a hand to my chest, took a breath, and kept walking.

The mountain waited ahead.

And I had people to lead.

Chapter 38

Grady

T he thunderous chorus of "Grady! Grady! Grady!" made my head throb. I could use a drink or several. There was no way I was getting up on that stage. Not now, not ever again.

"Come on, man. You have to play," Jackson squeezed my shoulder, his face full of understanding.

After all, he was home, without his girl too.

Just one more thing I felt guilty about.

It had been weeks since I had seen Whitney, heard her laugh, smelled her perfume, which wasn't even perfume at all - it was just... her. Something soft and warm and unmistakably her. I'd give anything to bury my face in her neck, to feel her breath against my skin.

But she was gone.

She left without a goodbye, and I was left standing in the wreckage like a fool who didn't even see the storm coming.

"She's not answering my calls either," Jackson said, almost like he could read my thoughts. "I'm giving her time, but I figured she'd at least text by now."

"Maybe she has you blocked," I muttered. That wasn't Whitney's style.

"She's punishing me," I added quietly. "She saw Emily's photo and thought the worst." Lord knows I would have.

Jackson hesitated, then rubbed the back of his neck, his jaw tightening. "Yeah, well, I can't blame her. The timing was shitty, man."

I didn't argue. I couldn't.

But what stung most was that she hadn't even asked.

"I can't go up there," I said again, more to myself than to him.

Jackson jerked his head toward the back hallway, where our new hire was moving inventory with one hand. "Xander can't cover this time. Smashed his damn hand trying to fix his car. Or so he says."

I leaned forward and squinted down the hallway. Xander moved like a man who'd been in more than one fight - coiled and casual, like he was always ready to throw a punch or walk away from one. He was tall, broad-shouldered, with dark hair that curled just past his ears and a jaw that looked like it had taken a few hits and given twice as many back.

"You believe him?" I asked.

Jackson snorted. "Not even a little. Knuckles are split. Looks like whoever he hit got a few licks in too."

I watched him for another moment. "He ever say why he came to Falcon Pointe?"

Jackson gave a shrug that said everything and nothing. "Said he needed a change. Place to lie low."

"Lie low from what?"

"That's the part he didn't say."

I kept my eyes on Xander as he dropped the box and shook out his hand with a wince. There was a flash of something behind his expression - pain, anger, maybe fear, but it was gone just as fast. He caught me looking and nodded once, respectful, detached.

"He's running from something," I muttered.

"Probably," Jackson said. "But he's a hard worker. Keeps to himself. Doesn't start shit, just seems to find it."

"Sounds familiar," I murmured.

Jackson didn't respond, but his silence said enough. He was thinking it too. We'd both worn that edge once.

I turned back toward the bar, exhaling hard. "So... you're saying I'm the only one left to cover?"

Jackson gave me a pointed look. "Unless you want me up there singing country covers from the early 2000s, yeah. You're it."

I groaned. "I can't go up there, man. Not tonight."

"You can. You just don't want to."

I glared at him, but he didn't flinch. That was Jackson for you, never asked me for anything unless it mattered.

"They're not here for me, Grady," he added quietly. "They're here for you."

I looked over at the stage. My guitar already sat on its stand under the lights, waiting like it knew something I didn't. My throat tightened.

"She wouldn't want me to keep hiding," I said aloud, mostly to myself.

Jackson clapped my shoulder. "Exactly."

I nodded, heart pounding like I was walking into a fight instead of singing a damn song.

"Fine," I muttered. "But I'm not smiling."

Jackson grinned. "Wouldn't expect you to."

I walked to the mic like a man walking to his own execution, the crowd cheering louder with every step. I looked back at the crowd. I could *feel* their eyes on me, waiting. Expecting. Part of me wanted to give them the middle finger and walk straight out the back door. But I could almost hear Whitney's voice - low, teasing. "Coward." And maybe I was. But I was also tired of being afraid.

I sat on the stool, adjusted the guitar on my lap, and let my fingers find their place on the strings.

I didn't say a word.

I just started playing.

I went with a crowd favorite, something I didn't have to think about.

A few cheers broke out, but the room settled into a hush as I began to sing. "Thinking Out Loud" wasn't mine, but it may as well have been. Every damn lyric hit like a bruise, reminding me of the way Whitney laughed, the way she looked at me when she thought I wasn't paying attention.

The crowd started singing along, off-key, off-tempo, but God, they loved it. That just made the ache in my chest worse. I was surrounded by people but felt like I was singing into a void.

When I strummed the final chord, I held it out, eyes still closed. The room erupted, and I nodded, forcing a small smile as a few people shouted requests. I ignored them. I wasn't here to take requests.

I needed to play, to *feel*. To let go.

One song became two. Then three. A little Matt Hanson, some Weathers. I lost myself in the rhythm, in the sting of the strings beneath my fingers.

The crowd blurred into a haze of noise and light - cheering, clapping, raising glasses - but none of it reached me. I kept my head down, letting the lyrics bleed out like open wounds.

I didn't feel better.

But I felt *something*.

When my fingers finally stilled, the applause rose up again. A few women at the front shouted for more. One of them even blew me a kiss.

I nodded, but didn't smile.

None of them were her.

As I stood to leave the stage, I caught Jackson watching me from the corner. He raised his drink in a silent toast, pride and concern both written in the lines of his face. He should've been back in Kansas by now, chasing down his girl. But he stayed here, for Whitney. For me.

I never asked him to stay. I don't think he'd have left even if I had. That's just who Jackson is; ride or die, even when he's barely hanging on himself.

I set my guitar down gently, like it might break, and headed toward the bar. Maybe this was what starting over looked like, playing songs I didn't want to play in a town that remembered every version of me I was trying to outgrow.

But it was something.

And for tonight, something had to be enough.

Chapter 39

Whitney

Eric's hands gripped my hips, rough and possessive, dragging me back with each deep thrust. He took me from behind, breath hot and ragged in my ear. The mattress creaked under us, the sheets twisted and damp beneath my palms.

I closed my eyes and tried to feel something. Anything.

"Slower," I whispered, bracing myself. "Can we... take it a little slower?"

He grunted, hesitating. Then pulled out almost completely before pushing back in with less force. His hand skimmed my side, almost gentle, but it was awkward, disconnected. Like someone trying to dance to a song they didn't really like.

Afterward, he collapsed beside me with a heavy breath, already reaching for the joint he'd left half-smoked on the windowsill.

I stared at the ceiling, feeling more alone now than before we'd touched. I could feel the slow trickle of his come between my legs, and for some reason, it made me think of the twins - Edward and Edie. About the night I pushed them on the swings until they couldn't get any higher. About Edie's tight hugs and Edward's laugh when I tickled him. About the way they looked at Grady, with so much adoration and love.

Something tugged at me, unexpected and quiet. "Do you ever think about kids?" I asked quietly, my voice thin in the dark.

He exhaled a plume of smoke. "Where'd that come from?"

I shrugged. "Just wondering."

But really, I wasn't. I never wanted kids before, but something about them, about *that* life, had changed something in me.

"I mean, no, not really," Eric said, scratching his chest. "With the childhood you had, I didn't think you wanted kids."

"Yeah, you're right," I nodded. "Forget it," I said, rolling away from him.

I faced the wall and pulled the blanket higher over my chest, pretending not to care, pretending it didn't burn in the hollow part of me he could never reach.

A tear slid onto the pillow beneath me, warm against my cheek.

***

Sunlight cut through the blinds like a slap - sharp, unwelcome, too bright for how I felt. I blinked against it and sat up slowly, wrapping the sheet around me as I padded toward the bathroom. My body ached in familiar ways. Not all of them good.

The mirror was cracked down the side, a jagged reminder of wild nights long past. I avoided my reflection as I brushed my teeth, tying my hair up into a messy bun and pulling on one of his too-big hoodies.

When I made it to the kitchen, I found Eric at the stove shirtless, flipping eggs. He hummed something tuneless under his breath, glancing up when I walked in.

"Want some?" he asked, holding the pan up.

"Sure." I grabbed two mugs from the cabinet and filled them with coffee.

He slid a plate across the counter toward me, then leaned on his elbows, watching me as I ate. I felt it before he spoke, his eyes on me, an unspoken question hanging in the air.

"What do you think about Vegas?" he finally asked, casually.

I blinked, my fork pausing halfway to my mouth. "Like... the city?"

He smirked. "No, the concept." Then he shrugged. "Yeah, the city."

I chewed slowly, buying time. "I dunno. I've never really thought about it. Why?"

Eric looked down at his eggs, pushing them around with the edge of his fork. "Just thinking." He swallowed, his Adam's apple bobbing with the motion.

My pulse ticked up. He never just asked questions like that.

There was always a reason.

A knot twisted low in my stomach. I took a sip of coffee instead of answering.

He didn't push it, and I didn't ask. But it hung there between us anyway, another unspoken thing. One more added to the pile.

***

Logan Canyon spread out before us, jagged edges softened by long, golden shadows as we crested the final stretch of the climb, sweat trailing down my spine, breath steady, sure. Behind me, the group of climbers cheered as they reached the top, dropping their packs and pulling out water bottles, laughing and clapping each other on the backs.

The air was crisp with the bite of late October. This would be the final climb of the season; snow could hit any day now, and the rocks would soon be too slick, too dangerous.

But I couldn't have asked for a more perfect day to end the season.

I gave them space to celebrate and stepped away toward the overlook. The wind tugged at my braid as I looked out across the sprawling valley below, filled with fire-colored trees, an incredible blend of burnt orange, deep red, and fading yellow, while the last of the leaves danced lazily in the breeze. Roads like ribbons cut through the land, and then there were the peaks in the distance, dusted with the first traces of snow.

It was beautiful. Just like I remembered.

But so much had changed.

A few months ago, I woke up in a hospital bed, a detective hovering in the doorway. Then Jackson showed up out of nowhere and dragged me home with him, back to Colorado. I found myself in a strange new place, trying to figure out who I was without the typical chaos of my life.

I used to crave the rush of danger; climbing too fast, running too close to the edge, living hard and reckless. It felt like the only thing I could control. But my time in that small, Podunk town had softened something in me. Maybe it was the stillness. Maybe it was the people. *Maybe it was Grady.*

God, Grady.

I shut my eyes for a second as his face flashed in my memory. The way his voice sounded when he said my name, like it was precious, like

I was precious. The way his guitar filled a room. The way he looked at me like I was the only thing keeping him breathing.

It's been weeks now. Weeks without hearing his voice or seeing Jackson's name pop up on my screen. And still, every time my phone buzzed, I hoped, but I never answered. I couldn't.

I closed my eyes and inhaled deeply. My nightmares were back. Most nights I jolted awake drenched in sweat, the sound of wind roaring in my ears, the distant wailing of the tornado siren. I was eleven all over again, watching the tornado rip through my neighborhood, consuming everything in its path while I just stood there, frozen in the distance. And every time, I woke up gasping, only to find Eric beside me, rubbing my back, murmuring, *"It's okay, babe. I got you."*

He meant it. And God, he was trying. But even in his arms, the fear never really left me.

He hadn't gambled once since I came home, and even though I hated the work he was doing, he was keeping us afloat. And if that wasn't evidence enough of his love, he even stopped sleeping around, admitting the open relationship wasn't helping anything.

He missed *me*.

We weren't perfect. Hell, some days we were barely okay. But it was something. A rhythm I could manage.

I glanced over my shoulder and back at the group. They were re-hydrated, chatting, stretching sore limbs. As much as I would love to stay up here forever, it was time to head down.

I clipped back in, anchored the ropes, and smiled as I leaned into the harness. I was *still an adrenaline junkie,* I thought as I lowered myself over the edge. But I moved slower now. More careful. More grounded. Falcon Pointe had changed me. Grady had changed me. Even if he didn't know it.

Even if I never saw him again.

The door clicked shut with a dull finality, and immediately I knew something was off.

Not the peace-and-quiet kind. The before-a-storm kind. I paused in the entryway, letting my hiking pack slip from my shoulders and fall to the floor with a soft thud. My shoes followed, toeing them off as I called out.

"Eric?"

No answer. Just hushed, muffled voices.

I moved toward the kitchen, each step heavy with dread. The scent of weed hung in the air, sharp and cloying, mixed with the tang of sweat and something darker. My heart rate picked up as I rounded the corner.

And froze.

Eric sat slouched in a kitchen chair, head tipped back and eyes closed. His jeans were unzipped, sitting low on his hips, a woman I didn't recognize on her knees in front of him. Her mouth wrapped around him like she'd done it a hundred times, her dark hair wrapped around his fist as she slurped and gagged.

My stomach dropped.

Three men sat at the kitchen table, beer bottles in hand, cigarettes smoldering in a cracked ashtray, like this was just another casual Tuesday afternoon.

All four of them looked up at once.

Eric jumped like he'd been electrocuted. "Whit - shit! I didn't think you'd be back so soon." He shoved the woman's head away with one hand, fumbling with his zipper. "It's not… Fuck, it's not what it looks like."

I didn't move. Couldn't breathe.

"What the hell is going on?" My voice came out low and deadly, tight with disbelief.

The woman stood slowly, wiped her mouth with the back of her hand, and barely spared me a glance as she stumbled to the side, tugging her shirt down.

One of the men leaned back in his chair, grinning at me with a leer that turned my blood to ice. I knew that face.

"Forget her," he said, nodding toward the girl Eric had just pushed aside. "I'd rather have another go at you, sweetheart."

My breath caught. My vision tunneled.

I knew that voice. That sneer. I looked from one face to the next, all three of them. They were the same men who'd come to collect months ago and nearly destroyed me.

Eric sprang to his feet. "Don't talk to her like that," he snapped.

"Sit down," one of the men growled, pulling a handgun from his waistband and pointing it at him.

Eric froze, both hands lifted, palms up, pleading with his eyes for me to let him explain.

One of the others stood and crossed the kitchen with slow, deliberate steps. "Come on, sweetheart," he murmured, placing a hand on my shoulder. "Let's have a little chat."

I couldn't move. Couldn't think. But my body responded on autopilot. I let him guide me to the living room, knees buckling as he shoved me gently onto the couch. He plopped down on the coffee table across from me, resting his elbows on his knees like we were just two friends catching up.

Behind him, I could hear the men talking to Eric again.

"So what's the plan for Vegas, pretty boy?"

"I... I...," he stammered, and suddenly I knew where his question from this morning had come from.

"Marco's a patient man, but you're pushing it."

Their voices blurred together, twisted and sharp. My ears rang. My skin crawled. I couldn't tell if I was shaking or just so still I felt like I wasn't there at all.

Eric mumbled something in response, voice hoarse, terrified.

I blinked back hot tears, staring at the man across from me. He watched me with a smirk, his gun still visible beneath his jacket.

Then my stomach dropped. The shape of his sneer, the scent of cheap cologne and cigarette smoke.

And then...

The scar.

It curved just under his jaw, jagged, like a reminder carved into flesh. The one I left him with when he forced me to my knees in this very apartment just a few months ago.

The memory hit me like a fist - my nails, his blood, his laugh.

I didn't cry out. Didn't scream. Just let the tears slide down my face silently as the last bit of my world crumbled into ash.

Eric had lied to me about how deep he was in. Lied about everything.

A crash split the air followed by raised voices and a chair scraping against the tile.

I flinched, heart slamming into my ribs with each grunt and thud. The man on the coffee table stood suddenly, muttering a curse under his breath as he stalked toward the kitchen. Minutes later, he returned, followed by the other two, one of them holding a leash. When I followed it to the other end, I found it latched around the woman's neck, as she stumbled past me, pulled along like their pet.

"You've got a pretty mouth, sweetheart," one of them called to me with a crooked grin as they made their way toward the front door. "Maybe next time you'll join in."

I didn't move.

The last man chuckled as he stepped outside. "Tell your boyfriend to get his shit together. The clock is ticking."

Then the door slammed.

For a beat, the silence rang louder than the chaos. Then I was up, racing to the door, throwing every lock, deadbolt, and chain I could find into place. My fingers trembled with urgency.

"Eric?" I called out as I ran toward the kitchen. "Eric!"

He was crumpled on the floor beside the table, blood dripping from his lip, one eye already swelling shut. His arms were wrapped around his ribs, breath coming in shallow pants.

"Oh my God... Eric!" I dropped to my knees beside him, trying to touch his face, but he recoiled slightly. "What happened? What the hell is going on?"

He winced. "They... they didn't like what I had to say."

"What did you say?" I demanded.

"I told them I'm not going to Vegas."

I blinked, stunned. "Vegas? You never said..."

"I didn't think you were coming back," he whispered, eyes clouded with shame. "You were gone, and you stopped answering my calls. I was in deep, baby. So fucking deep. I needed a way out, and Marco offered me one. A steady gig, good pay... just working collections on the Strip. He made it sound easy."

I sat back, stunned.

Eric coughed, then pushed up, leaning against the cabinet, his hand pressing against his side. "And then you called me, You came home. I was so fucking happy, Whit. I thought…. I thought maybe it's not too late. I told Marco I changed my mind, but that only pissed him off."

I swallowed hard, my mind spinning. "And today? The girl?"

"They brought her with them. Said I had to prove to them I was still loyal. That I still belonged to Marco. I didn't want to, but…" his voice cracked. "They made it clear what would happen if I said no."

I stared at him, heart heavy and splintering.

"I didn't want to hurt you," he said, finally meeting my eyes. "Please… I didn't know what else to do. I fucked up. Bad! But I never stopped loving you."

The words landed hollow.

I looked at him, this man who had once made me feel invincible, and now looked so small, so broken. A part of me still ached for him, still saw the version of him that saved me. The man who held me through my nightmares and kissed the bruises life left behind. But the rest of me… didn't know what to feel.

"I forgive you," I said quietly, even though the words felt strange in my mouth.

His eyes widened, hopeful. "You do?"

"But," I shook my head. "I need time." I rose to my feet slowly. "To think. To figure out what I want… who I am… because I'm not the same girl I was when I left."

Eric nodded, wincing as he tried to sit up straighter. "Okay. Take whatever time you need."

I turned and walked into the bedroom, closing the door gently behind me. And for the first time in weeks, I let myself cry. Not for Eric, not even for Grady. I wasn't crying because I lost him. I was crying because, somewhere deep down, I knew I was never going to come back.

I cried for me.

Chapter 40

Grady

The scent of pot roast hit me the second Jackson and I stepped through the front door. It wrapped around me like a memory - warm, familiar, safe. A smell that made it easy to forget everything falling apart outside these walls. Mrs. Bryant didn't do anything halfway. Not food, not love, not raising kids who weren't hers by blood, but still called this place home.

Mr. Bryant looked up from his recliner in the living room, a football game humming from the TV. "There they are," he said, smiling behind a pair of thick glasses. "Don't let the roast get cold."

A flash of guilt washed over me, I hadn't even realized he was back yet.

"Go wash up," Mrs. Bryant called from the kitchen.

Jackson groaned like a ten-year-old. "We're not kids anymore."

Mr. Bryant gave him a mock stern look, shaking his head with a grin. "Go on and do as you're told."

Jackson rolled his eyes but obeyed with a smile.

I helped get the twins situated at their table, their plates already set with cut up pieces of roast and a large helping of macaroni and cheese with carrots. When Jackson came in, he leaned down, whispering something in Edward's ear. He broke out in a fit of giggles, while the rest of us took our places at the main table, where Mrs. Bryant was dishing out slices of roast and mashed potatoes.

We all dug in while Mr. Bryant launched into a story about his latest business trip, this time to Ohio. Jackson asked questions and laughed at all the right places, tossing in the occasional sarcastic comment that Mrs. Bryant swatted him for, but my thoughts kept drifting.

I remembered sitting at this very table just a couple months ago, Whitney's laughter ringing through the kitchen, her hands covered in bubbles as she helped with the dishes. She'd slipped into this place like she'd always belonged.

I pushed my food around my plate, appetite gone. It was like watching someone else's life through glass. Jackson belonged here. I didn't know where I belonged anymore.

After dinner, Mr. Bryant retreated back to his recliner, cracking open a beer and settling in for the second half of the game. The Broncos were currently ahead, their new quarterback was incredible - or at least that's what Jackson said.

With their plates cleared, the twins settled in with a puzzle, an ocean scene full of different sea creatures. I was just about to take my seat at the table, when Mrs. Bryant gave Jackson a scrutinizing stare. As much as I wanted to be there for my best friend, I wasn't ready to hear what happened while he was gone. It was because of Whitney that he came back before he was ready, and the guilt ate at me. So, like the coward I was, I took a seat at the kids table, watching the scene play out from the corner of my eye.

"Alright," she said, leaning back in her chair with her arms folded. "You've been back for about a month now. I've given you time to come clean on your own, but since you haven't, care to tell me where you disappeared to?"

Jackson let out a slow breath and scratched at the fresh stubble on his cheek, like he was stalling for time. "I was... chasing a ghost," he said finally.

Mrs. Bryant's brows arched. "This ghost have a name?"

He nodded. "Abby. After all these years, I finally found her. I had to go, I had to see..."

"And did you find out what you needed? Were you able to get closure?"

He rested both his arms on the table and leaned forward, like what he had to say was so important, he couldn't risk her not hearing.

I focused my attention on the twins, not ready to hear about his heartbreak, or whatever plan he was cooking up next. I couldn't take it, I was drowning in my own pool of misery.

I forced a smile, "How's the puzzle coming?"

"It's the ocean!" Edie beamed.

"I can see that," I picked up a piece and carefully fit it in, completing the head of the blue whale that skimmed the edge of the puzzle.

Edward leaned his head on his hand, "When's Whitney coming back?"

I smiled sadly and rubbed his shoulder. "I'm not sure. Soon, I hope." I couldn't tell him she was never coming back. He was too young to feel this sort of pain, especially with how recently they lost their parents.

Thankfully he let it go, fitting a piece of the dolphin into place while Edie practiced making dolphin sounds. God, I loved these kids. They made me wish I could be a dad one day, take my own son and daughter to the aquarium, the zoo, hell, even a football game.

A few puzzle pieces later, Jackson's phone buzzed on the table.

He didn't rush to check it. Just glanced down, and froze.

I knew. I *knew*.

He picked it up, thumbed the screen, and said her name like a prayer he didn't believe in.

"Whitney?"

The blood drained from my face. My hands went still, the puzzle piece I'd been holding slipping from my fingers and hitting the floor with a soft click.

I couldn't hear her, but I could see the way his whole body tensed, the lines forming between his brows, the hand that gripped the edge of the table like he needed something to anchor him.

"Whoa, whoa. Slow down," he said, leaning forward. "What happened? I came home as soon as I got your message..."

I was already standing, though I didn't remember moving. My pulse roared in my ears, drowning out the rest of the room.

"Vegas?" Jackson echoed, voice sharp. "Why Vegas?"

His expression shifted - softening, then breaking. "No... not really. I think you should talk to him."

He didn't pass the phone.

I took a slow step forward, stomach twisting into knots, but he turned slightly away, like shielding me from whatever she was saying.

"Are you sure that's what you want?" he asked, voice low. "You can come back, Whit. You'll always have a home here."

A beat.

Then, softer, "I love you, too."

He hung up.

I didn't need him to say it.

"She's not coming back, is she?"

My voice didn't shake, but it felt like something inside me splintered as I said it.

Jackson didn't answer. He didn't need to. The silence said everything.

I stepped back. Once. Twice. My lungs burned like I couldn't get enough air.

Then I turned and walked out of the house.

The door slammed behind me, rattling the frame, but I didn't stop.

Cold air slapped my face as I hit the porch, my boots thudding against the pavement in a blur of motion. I didn't care where I was going. I just needed to move. To get out.

Rage surged in my chest - hot, aimless. Not at her. Never at her. At myself. For not being enough. For not chasing her. For letting her believe Emily meant something.

The trees blurred past as I hit the path, my feet pounding the dirt with a desperation I couldn't contain.

By the time I reached the clearing, I could barely see straight. My hands fumbled for the rope ladder, trembling with the weight of everything I hadn't said, everything I'd lost.

The tree had been my first escape, the one place that didn't ask anything of me. No judgment. No pain. Just branches strong enough to hold the weight of a broken kid. Or a broken man, apparently. When the world got too loud, too painful, too much, I climbed. So that's what I did now. My boots gripped the wide rungs of the rope ladder, and I pulled myself up onto the thick branch that never failed to hold me through the worst times.

I hauled myself up onto the thick branch and sat, legs shaking, chest heaving like I'd run a marathon.

The silence up here was louder than any scream.

And then I did scream. I curled my knees to my chest as best as I could and wrapped my arms tight around them, as I fought to keep myself from falling apart. But it was no use. My vision blurred. I pressed my forehead to my knees and let it all out, the grief coming in waves - thick, suffocating, relentless.

She was gone. Really gone.

And I didn't know how to be without her anymore.

Every second of missing her.

Every bit of guilt for not being enough.

Every scream I'd never said out loud.

The leaves rustled below, and then I heard the soft creak of the ladder again.

Jackson.

He climbed up and settled across from me like he used to, no words, just presence. Like gravity. Like a brother.

We sat in silence until it cracked open.

"She's not happy," he said.

I didn't answer. Couldn't.

"I could hear it in her voice. She's trying to convince herself that going back was the right thing. But it's not. You know it. I know it. Hell, deep down, she knows it too."

The wind rustled through the branches above us, brittle and dry.

"But even if she never comes back, I need you here, man. I need you breathing, okay? I already lost Abby. I can't lose you too."

His words hit like a bruise I didn't know I was carrying.

He nudged my knee. "One day at a time, yeah?"

I kept my gaze on the horizon. It was a blur of orange and gray, like dusk couldn't decide what it wanted to be.

"One day at a time," I whispered.

Even if it tore me apart. Even if she never came back. I'd still be here.

One breath. One step. One damn day at a time.

Because, for whatever reason, Jackson still needed me.

I took my place in the center of the makeshift stage. Fear still coiled in my belly, but it didn't paralyze me this time. Things were different.

I was different.

And it was all because of her.

Whitney.

I used to let the fear of being laughed at, or worse, pitied, keep me in the shadows. I convinced myself I didn't need the stage, didn't need an audience. But she... she saw right through me. She heard something in my music worth sharing and never let me forget it.

So what was I afraid of now? I was afraid of letting her down, of her never knowing how I truly felt, and I had no way of letting her know. Not without the risk of hurting her further, and I refused to do that. If she was moving on, then I would too, in the only way I knew how.

"Good evening, everyone," I said, voice rough as I rubbed the back of my neck. "I know I never do this," I added, gesturing vaguely between myself and the mic, "but tonight I wanted to try something a little different."

I glanced toward the bar, toward her spot. The place where she'd stand, arms crossed, that half-smile tugging at her lips as she waited for me to start. But when my eyes landed there tonight, they met Jackson's instead. He tilted his head slightly, an unspoken question in his gaze: *You sure about this?*

I wasn't.

But I closed my eyes anyway.

I strummed the first chord. "This is a song I wrote for a girl who came into my life like a wildfire."

And then my hands were forming the chords I knew better than my own name.

Whitney's song.

The one that had started as a few notes and a melody I couldn't shake. One that grew and became more in the quiet of that morning after we first made love. When she was still asleep beside me, her bare shoulder bathed in light from the window. The one that said all the things I'd never been able to.

The bar went still.

I didn't say anything more, just started picking out the melody. My voice was softer now, raw around the edges.

> Told myself I wouldn't feel a thing
> You walked in, and I broke that rule again
> Your laugh hits harder than a heartbreak song
> Now I'm caught, and it's been way too long
> I swore I'd never play the fool
> But here I am, breaking every rule
> You're in my veins like gasoline
> And I light the match - yeah, that's on me

The bar was silent.

Not politely quiet - *hushed*. Reverent.

But I didn't notice any of them. All I saw was *her*. Whitney. The way she danced barefoot across the living room. The way she sang off-key in the car. The way she held my face when she thought I might fall apart.

I sang the chorus like a confession. Like a prayer I knew would go unanswered.

I'm addicted, and I hate it

Tried to run but I can't shake it

You're a habit I don't wanna break

Every hit, another heartquake

Tried to numb it, but I feel it

Every look, I start to need it

You're the fire, I'm the flame

Burning up but I can't escape -

I'm addicted

When the final chord rang out, it felt like the room held its breath.

And for a second, I almost believed it mattered.

Then the applause broke - loud, euphoric.

But it didn't touch me.

Because the only person I'd written that song for...

Wasn't here.

Wouldn't hear it.

Might never come back.

So I nodded. I packed up my guitar. I walked off the stage.

And the ache in my chest stayed right where it was.

Chapter 41

Whitney

The car was packed to the brim. Duffel bags stuffed with clothes, boxes of gear, a worn-out toaster wedged beside a plastic bin of tangled chargers. It wasn't much. But it was everything we had.

Salt Lake City disappeared in the rearview mirror, its skyline blurred by distance and haze. Ahead, the endless stretch of desert unrolled like a dare neither of us were ready for.

Eric drummed his fingers on the steering wheel, eyes on the road, lips set in a hard line. He hadn't said much since we left and I didn't press. He was one of the strongest people I had ever met - but even strength had its limits. I knew Vegas wasn't his dream. It wasn't mine either. And yet here we were, forging a path forward, not talking about the hard stuff because if we were honest, we were both carrying too much.

I flipped through the rock climbing guide I picked up last-minute at a used bookstore. *Climbers' Guide to Southern Nevada*. It was serendipity, despite being worn at the edges like it had already been read a hundred times by someone else. My thumb hovered over a page about *patina rock*, all sun baked and rust colored. It looked beautiful. Unforgiving, but beautiful.

I swallowed thickly, I wasn't sure I was ready for it.

Climbing was my adrenaline, my therapy. But the more I read, the more I wondered if I was in over my head. Patina rock was nothing like the limestone routes in Logan Canyon. *Maybe it's time to stop chasing danger and start building something real.*

But what did that even look like?

"What are you reading?" Eric asked, pulling me out of my thoughts.

"Climbing guide," I said, holding it up. "Nevada's got some wild stuff."

He nodded, eyes still forward. "Is that what you want to do down there? Keep climbing?"

I shrugged. "Maybe. I don't know. I'm worried that I'm getting too old to keep starting over, you know?"

There was a beat of silence before he said, "You could always do something different. Safer. You're smart, babe. The possibilities are endless."

I wasn't sure if that was a compliment or a quiet push to give up the things that made me feel alive. Eric loved me, there was no question about that. He understood my need to push boundaries, but it was no secret that he wasn't as eager to feel that rush, that high. He preferred his in a pretty package, while in the safety of our home.

I glanced over at him. He looked... tired. Not road-trip tired, but *something's-wrong* tired. His jaw was tight, and his hands gripped the wheel like it might fly away if he didn't hold on tight enough.

"You okay?" I asked, already knowing the answer.

"I'm good," he said too quickly, then forced a smile. "Just thinking."

"About Vegas?"

"Yeah."

I didn't believe him. Not really. I didn't know if his silence was fear or guilt. Maybe both. Maybe neither. I didn't trust my instincts anymore, not when it came to Eric.

I turned the dial on the radio and scrolled through stations until something familiar cut through the static. I grinned as one of my favorite songs by Friday Pilots Club filled the air waves. Eric took me to see them a year ago, back when things felt easier. We stood close to the stage, so close I could see the sweat rolling down their faces. It used to be one of my favorite memories.

Until the day Grady played that very song for me.

The way his fingers moved so effortlessly across the strings. The way his voice filled the room, soft and aching. I closed my eyes, letting the melody crawl under my skin like a memory I didn't want to let go of.

I started singing along, loud and intentionally off-key.

Eric laughed softly. "You're such a dork."

"You love it."

He didn't say anything.

The next track was by The Band Camino, and this one hurt a little more. I could see Grady again, barefoot on the couch, humming the harmony while I twirled in the kitchen.

"You know," Eric said after a moment, "you ever think about actually doing that?"

"Doing what?"

"Being a singer. Like... start in a club. Vegas is the place, right? Lounge singers get picked up all the time."

I snorted. "That's a long shot."

He looked at me then, something almost sad in his eyes. "But it was your dream once. You used to say that all the time when we first started dating."

"I also used to say I wanted to join Cirque du Soleil when I was little."

"You're still bendy," he teased.

I shoved his shoulder, laughing despite myself.

But when I looked out the window again, the laughter faded. The desert stretched wide and sun-bleached, an endless canvas of beginnings. But it didn't feel like a fresh start. It felt like surrender.

Vegas was glinting somewhere far ahead, a mirage of neon and noise.

And Grady... Grady was somewhere behind me, writing some of the most beautiful music I had ever heard, in a town I was too afraid to stay. Would he ever play his own music on stage? Would he ever show the rest of the world how amazing he is?

Will he dedicate his songs to *her?*

I pressed my forehead to the cool glass.

I knew what starting over looked like. Eric and I seemed to start over every couple of years or so. Usually, I welcomed it, but this time, something was different.

This time it didn't feel like freedom.

It felt like leaving pieces of myself behind, hoping whatever was left knew how to survive.

By the time we hit the edge of the city, the sun was sinking behind a haze of brownish-orange smog. Vegas didn't sparkle like I imagined. It just glowed, dim and distant, like a city trying to convince itself it hadn't lost its shine.

The apartment was on the outskirts, sandwiched between a shuttered laundromat and a vape shop that never seemed to close. Beige stucco walls, rusted railing, and a crooked sign that read The Residence at Warm Springs in flaking gold paint.

Two men were waiting in front of the building when we pulled up.

I knew them now as Marco's men.

I didn't know their names; I didn't want to. They looked the same as they had the last time I saw them, smug faces, tight black shirts that didn't hide the fact that they were armed beneath them.

"Right on time," one of them muttered as Eric cut the engine.

I sat still in the passenger seat, backpack clutched tight, watching like they might disappear if I didn't blink. But they didn't. One handed Eric a key like it was a collar.

"The place is furnished," the taller one said. "Marco's paying for the first two months. After that, you better have your shit together."

Eric nodded stiffly.

"No excuses this time," the shorter one added, flicking his cigarette into the gutter. "Marco was generous. Don't make him regret it."

I could feel their eyes on me as we stepped out of the car. I kept my shoulders back and my face neutral, but my insides were coiled tight.

They didn't leave until we walked through the gate. A black SUV waited for them just down the street. They got in like shadows disappearing into smog.

I let out a breath I hadn't realized I was holding. "Friendly."

Eric didn't answer.

The apartment was on the third floor. No elevator. Good thing I didn't mind the stairs.

When we pushed open the door, a wave of musty, cool, conditioned air hit my face. The place was already set up - couch, TV, basic kitchen with new appliances, even a little glass coffee table. It was nicer than I expected.

But it didn't feel like home.

It felt like someone else's idea of what our life should look like.

I dropped my bag on the floor and walked through the space - bedroom, bathroom, closet just big enough for two people who owned next to nothing. No pictures, no curtains, no books on the shelf. Even the towels in the bathroom were still crisp and unused.

"It's clean," I said finally, just to fill the silence.

Eric ran a hand through his hair. "Better than the old place, I guess."

"Yeah."

He didn't look at me. He just wandered to the kitchen and opened the fridge. It was empty aside from a few bottles of water and some off-brand soda.

I sat down on the edge of the bed. The mattress was firm, like hotel beds always were. I bounced once, then leaned back, staring at the ceiling.

So this was it.

New city. New apartment. New life.

But I didn't feel new.

I felt like a girl carrying too many ghosts in a suitcase that couldn't quite close.

Eric came back and stood in the doorway of the bedroom. "We'll get groceries tomorrow. I'll talk to Marco's guy, see where they want me posted."

I nodded.

"Wanna order something?"

"Maybe later." I didn't want to tell him I had lost my appetite.

He scratched the back of his neck like he wanted to say more. But instead, he disappeared into the bathroom and shut the door.

I curled onto my side, pulling a pillow under my head. The room was too quiet. The bed too stiff. The air too cold.

I found myself once again missing the smell of Grady's sheets. The faint scratch of his stubble when he kissed me goodnight. The quiet way he said my name like it was a promise.

I squeezed my eyes shut and willed myself not to cry.

I chose this, *didn't I?* I just didn't know what it would cost.

Soft lips brushed my forehead, and for one fragile moment, I thought my dream had followed me into the morning. Then I heard Eric's voice, low and familiar.

"Back later," he whispered.

I mumbled something that might have been *okay*, but I wasn't really awake. Just drifting in that warm, heavy space between dreams and disappointment.

When I finally pried myself out of bed and into the shower, the bathroom felt too small. Too bright. The hot water helped chase off some of the stiffness, but my chest stayed tight. Even when I dressed and stepped outside, the desert heat felt oppressive, like it had been waiting for me.

The streets near our complex were a wasteland of strip malls and sun-bleached signs. I kept my head down as I walked past a gas station, a nail salon, and a laundromat that smelled like bleach and burnt fabric, my hands stuffed into my pockets as if I could hide from my own thoughts.

Eventually I ended up in front of a little shop with a peeling vinyl sign that read OUTDOOR ADVENTURE TOURS. The window was streaked with dust. Inside, the air was dry and tired, a few racks of climbing gear scattered like afterthoughts, and a topographic map of Red Rock Canyon yellowing on the wall.

A guy in his mid-thirties glanced up from behind the counter. "Can I help you?"

I hesitated, then asked about work.

He offered me a sympathetic shrug. "Not hiring right now. And even if we were, we'd need CPR and Wilderness First Aid certs. Back-country permits too."

"I've got experience," I tried, hoping my voice didn't sound as tired as I felt.

"Yeah? From where?"

"Utah. Logan Canyon mostly. I led climbs every weekend," I added, stretching the truth like an old shirt.

He studied me for a long beat. Almost impressed. Almost.

"Sorry," he finally said. "Rules are rules."

I nodded, too tired to argue, and left as the bell over the door jingled behind me like it was laughing.

That ache in my chest spread as I kept walking.

A couple of lounges appeared up the block, neon signs buzzing faintly under the afternoon glare. I pushed my way into one after another, hoping maybe there was some work, some outlet, anything.

But the air inside was stale and harsh with cigarette smoke. A woman in a sequined bra belted a tired pop song on a tiny stage while the manager scrolled on his phone. When I finally spoke up, his gaze skimmed me like merchandise.

"You got anything to show?" he drawled, lips curling.

"I can sing," I said simply.

That was when he actually looked up. His gaze traveled down my body before settling on my face. "You got anything better to wear? Skimpy dresses? Lingerie? Anything that's not..." he waved at my jeans and blouse like they offended him.

I didn't need to hear the rest. I already knew the look, the one that said what he wanted had nothing to do with my voice.

There was a time when that would've felt like an invitation. When I would have played the part, leaned into the attention because it was easier than saying no.

But not anymore.

I walked out without a word.

By the time I made it home, my feet throbbed and my heart felt heavier than when I'd left. The apartment was stuffy, the kind of dark that settles into the walls. I dropped onto the couch, picking at a chipped nail, and stared at the blank TV screen.

When Eric finally came home, the sky was deep indigo and the apartment darker still.

"Hey," he said, lifting a brown paper bag. "Sandwiches. Some shop off Charleston. Pretty good."

"Thanks," I murmured as he kissed my temple and handed me one.

He kicked off his shoes, plopped down in front of the TV, and unwrapped his food without saying more.

I wanted to ask about his day, but the set of his shoulders told me not to. Instead, I leaned into his side, hoping the warmth would drive away the hollow ache that had taken up residence in my chest. It didn't.

And even as I closed my eyes and breathed him in, my thoughts kept circling back to someone else.

* * *

The weeks passed in a blur of restless sleep and long, empty days. October slid into November, and the promise of holidays only deepened the ache. Fake snow in store windows. Twinkling lights strung across cracked fences. It all felt like someone else's joy, like a world I was watching from the outside.

I tried. God, I tried.

Applied at gyms, tour companies, a couple of coffee shops. Nobody called back. No one even looked twice. Maybe I'd forgotten how to sell myself. Or maybe I just didn't care enough anymore to lie in interviews about how passionate I was about smoothies and early mornings.

Eric was slipping away. Not in some dramatic, yelling kind of way. In the slow, quiet kind. Like steam fading from a mirror. He came home later and later, dragging the scent of weed and exhaustion behind him. Sometimes he reeked of cheap cologne and someone else's perfume. I didn't ask. I didn't want to know.

But deep down, I knew.

He wasn't cheating on me. This just wasn't the life he wanted. The life he had always envisioned for himself. But I didn't know how to help him; he dug his grave when he got involved with Marco. When he couldn't stop himself from joining those underground card games.

It felt like the things that made us, *us*, were slipping away. When it became clear he was tired of talking, I tried to reach him the only way I knew how. I curled close in bed, tried to press my body into his like old times. Kissed his neck. Touched his stomach beneath his shirt. Whispered promises I didn't even believe.

He shook his head. Something about stress. Work. A headache.

I rolled away and stared at the ceiling, blinking fast against the burn in my throat.

Tonight, I couldn't sleep. Again.

So I reached for my phone, craving something brainless. TikTok - stupid dances, absurd hacks, people pretending life was easy and curated. A million voices talking all at once, none of them the one I wanted to hear.

Until... it was.

I almost scrolled past it.

A slow pan over a mountain lake; still water, red and gold leaves. Gorgeous, nostalgic. The kind of video that made you ache without knowing why. And then...

That voice.

Rough. Low. Beautiful in a way that felt unfair.

Grady.

I sat up so fast I nearly dropped the phone, thumb scrambling to pause, rewind, play again. His voice filled the small, lifeless apartment, and suddenly everything felt full.

He was singing.

The lyrics were new, but I knew the song. I'd heard pieces of it in his humming, in the chords he strummed half-asleep. He'd never had the words before. Just the melody. Just the ache.

Addicted, the screen read.

My breath hitched.

That was *our* song. The one that had played between kisses and almosts. The one I used to tease him about, begging for a full verse. He always said he wasn't ready. That it wasn't finished.

But he had finished it.

I tapped the username, chasing every repost and snippet until I found it - the original clip. Grainy footage. A crowd packed tight in The Hideaway. Him onstage, hunched over his guitar, eyes closed, like the weight of the song might break him if he opened them.

And he sang like he meant every word.

Like he was still singing *to me.*

I covered my mouth. Then my heart. Then the phone. As if holding it close would bring him closer.

But all it brought was the truth.

I'd left Falcon Pointe.

I'd left *him*.

And still, somehow, he was here. Haunting the internet. Haunting *me*. Threading his voice through an algorithm like a ghost I'd never outrun.

My vision blurred as I pressed the phone to my chest.

And I cried.

Not just for what I'd lost.

But for what I still wanted.

What I was terrified I didn't deserve.

Chapter 42

Grady

The bar smelled like furniture polish and whiskey, a strange combination, unless you focused on the man wiping down each table like his life depended on it.

Xander may not always look like it, but he was a good guy. The tall, dark and handsome type, with busted knuckles and the occasional bruise marring his otherwise pretty-boy face. He had some weird quirks, like his obsessive cleaning habits, but then again, it could be worse.

I shook my head, emptying another box of mixers while Jackson sat on the other side of the counter, hand in a bowl of peanuts while he watched the CU Buffaloes get their asses handed to them by Oregon.

"Swear to God," Jackson muttered, tipping back his beer. "If they don't figure out how to run a damn defense…"

I snorted. "Whatever happened to Coach Prime being a god?"

He rolled his eyes. "Whatever."

I started to laugh, but the phone rang again. It had been ringing off the hook for days.

I didn't move to answer it.

Jackson shot me a look. "You gonna get that?"

"Nope." I knew what it was, and I was done fielding questions.

The phone rang on, like it had something to prove.

He raised an eyebrow. "You gonna tell me what's going on, or do I have to start guessing?"

I sighed, rubbing the back of my neck. "People heard the song."

"'Addicted'?"

"Yeah."

Jackson blinked, a beat of disbelief. "Wait, you mean *really* heard it?"

I nodded. "Someone recorded it that night and posted it on Tik-Tok. Apparently, it blew up."

He sat back, his eyebrows shooting up. "*Blew up?*"

"It's got a couple hundred thousand views. Last I checked, anyway."

Jackson let out a low whistle. "Damn, man."

The phone rang again, like it was trying to prove a point.

"I don't even know how they got the bar's number," I muttered, moving a bottle of bourbon to the front of the shelf. "They want to know when it's going on Spotify, when I'm playing next, if I've got more."

"Do you?"

I glanced at him, cocking an eyebrow.

"You've got more," he said, grinning. "I hear you play when you think no one's listening."

Yeah, I had more. I had a lot more. But it wasn't about that.

"Hey," Xander interrupted, grabbing a box of limes from the counter. "If it's that big a deal, why don't you just record it and be done with it? Put it out there. You could make some extra cash."

"It's not about the money," I said, not looking at him.

"Then do it to shut people up."

Jackson laughed at that, sipping his beer.

I wiped my hands on a bar towel, leaning against the counter. "I'll think about it."

Which was the best I could do for now.

A couple hours later, the lights dimmed and the crowd began to buzz with excitement. It was Open Mic Night at The Hideaway, and people expected a show. Lately, it felt more like the Grady Thomas Show...

I took my place on the small stage, guitar slung across my shoulder, adjusting the mic stand just so. I kicked off with a couple of my favorites, some Zach Hood, then a heartfelt song by Gavn! Nothing fancy, just enough to keep the room buzzing.

And then I felt it. The moment when the music becomes the only thing that matters. And everything else, every doubt, every fear, every part of me that wanted to run away, fades into the background.

The crowd had begun chanting. It was almost playful at first, teasing, but I could feel the weight behind it.

"Grady! Grady! Addicted! Addicted!"

I let out a shaky breath. It wasn't just the crowd's enthusiasm; it was *me*. I was standing at the edge of something, and I couldn't tell if I was about to fly or fall.

"All right," I said into the mic, my voice a little rough, trying to steady myself. "You asked for it."

I could feel the weight of every pair of eyes on me and a nervous sweat gathered on the back of my neck. My fingers hesitated over the strings for a brief moment, longer than I cared to admit, but then I strummed the opening chords. The sound was familiar, but tonight, it felt heavier. It felt real.

As the first verse spilled out, my mind tried to pull me back, tried to remind me of the rawness that *Addicted* carried, the truth it exposed. But this time, there was something different. The ache, the bitterness that had clung to the song for so long, it didn't feel as sharp. It was still there, but it wasn't all-consuming.

Whitney's face flickered in my mind, that haunting smile, the memory of her presence. She was everywhere in the lyrics. Yet, in this moment, it wasn't about her anymore. It wasn't about the past. It was about *me*, finding a way to move forward, even with the weight of it all still clinging to my bones.

Each note felt like a slow exhale, releasing the pain, letting the crowd bear witness to the song that had kept me together when everything else felt like it was falling apart. I let the words spill out, raw and unfiltered. I didn't try to hide anything. Not the cracks, not the hurt.

The room seemed to fall away, the only thing that mattered was the connection - between the song, my voice, and the people who were listening.

When the last note rang out, I let it linger in the air, trying to hold on to the peace I hadn't felt in ages. The cheers from the crowd felt like they came from a distance, muffled somehow, like I was in my own world for just a moment. I let out a slow breath and closed my eyes for a second. Just a second. Long enough to feel the relief.

Because, for the first time in weeks... maybe even months... I didn't feel broken.

———

The bar quieted after my last note. The crowd still hummed with excitement, but I felt the buzzing under my skin fade away. I was lost in it, caught in the music, until the last chord slowly drifted off into the air. A brief silence lingered before the crowd erupted in applause, but for a moment, it was just me. Just the music.

Addicted had always been a part of me - raw, painful, but mine. Whitney's face flashed in my mind, her smile, the way her eyes used to light up when she laughed. I wanted to hold onto that, to keep her with me in the music, but it wasn't just about her anymore.

I missed her. More than I cared to admit. The way she made me feel seen, even when I was a mess. The way I felt when we were together, like I was part of something bigger than myself. But more than anything, I wanted her to be safe, to find the happiness that she deserved. If I could do that, if I could accept that we weren't meant to be together, then maybe I could finally move on.

I want you to be happy, Whitney.

It was the only way I could move forward. And if that meant letting go of the past, of what we could've been, then maybe I was ready.

But the ache, the yearning, still lingered, soft and persistent, like the echo of the song I'd just played.

I stood there for a moment, letting the relief of the performance wash over me, but also feeling the weight of it. I didn't feel broken anymore, not in the same way. But I wasn't whole either. Not yet.

Then Jackson's hand on my elbow pulled me back to reality.

"Hey. These guys want to talk."

I turned to see two men standing by the jukebox, well-dressed in a way that screamed "we belong here." They had that polished *L.A. confidence*, the kind that suggested they were used to getting what they wanted. It made my gut tighten.

The taller one stepped forward, flashing a smile that felt too rehearsed.

"Grady," he said, extending a hand. "I'm Matt. This is Kyle. We're with a label out of Denver. We came to hear you play."

I took his hand, my grip firm but guarded. "You drove all the way out here just to hear me?"

Matt nodded, his smile never faltering. "We've been keeping an eye on some local talent. Heard you had something special, so we figured we'd make the trip."

Something about the way he said it rubbed me the wrong way, like he was trying to sell me something I wasn't sure I wanted.

Kyle, the other rep, spoke up, his voice smooth and persuasive.

"You're a hell of a songwriter. That voice? Raw. Real. People are hungry for it."

I swallowed hard. "I wrote *Addicted* because I needed to. It wasn't meant for anyone else, just..." My voice faltered, and I immediately tried to cover it up with a forced smile. "But I get it. It's real. People like it. I just... didn't think it would blow up like this."

Kyle leaned forward, like he could sense my hesitation. "It's not just about blowing up, Grady. It's about giving people something they can feel. And *Addicted* - that song? It's something special. We'd love to get you into a studio."

I felt the pressure of his words, the weight of the future they were selling. My heart started to race. *What would Whitney do?*

I glanced at Jackson, trying to get a read on him. He leaned back, watching, but his eyes were encouraging. I couldn't tell if he was giving me permission or just letting me figure it out on my own.

"I don't know," I said, my voice cracking a little. "It's not about the money. It's... just a song. *My* song."

Matt's smile didn't falter, but there was something in his eyes, an edge, like he wasn't used to getting hesitation. "You know the music business, Grady. People get hungry for real talent. It's not just about the song anymore. It's about making sure people hear it. *Really* hear it. And we can make that happen."

I shook my head a little, trying to get my bearings. I wanted to say no. I wanted to shut it down and walk away from this whole thing. But there was a part of me, the part that had been holding back for so long, that wanted to know what it would feel like to *not* keep hiding.

I cleared my throat, my voice low. "I don't know if I'm ready for all that. It's just... it's *Addicted*, you know? It's not just a song. It's... I don't know what happens to me if I let it go. If I give it away, will it still be mine? Will it still mean the same thing?"

Kyle's gaze softened, "That's part of what we do, Grady. We'll help you figure out those details."

I took their card, sliding it into my back pocket, feeling the weight of it like a promise. Or maybe a chain.

"I'll think about it," I said, this time with a little more conviction.

When they walked away, I stood there, staring at the spot where they'd been. Jackson didn't say anything for a moment, letting the silence stretch.

"You going to call them?" he asked, his voice quiet.

I stared at the empty space where they'd been standing. "I don't know. Part of me wants to, and another part..." I shook my head, not sure how to finish that thought. "Part of me wants to keep it all to myself."

"Yeah, well," Jackson said, half-smiling, "there's a lot of pressure in doing that. But whatever you decide, man, you've got a hell of a gift."

I looked at the card again, feeling the weight of my decision hang in the air. *What would Whitney do?*

Chapter 43

Whitney

The air conditioner rattled in the window, doing its best to cool down the tiny living room, but it was still hot. Too hot for November. It was Thanksgiving week, and there wasn't a single snowflake in sight.

I hated that I missed the snow. The way it blanketed the mountains back in Utah, how it softened the world just enough to make it feel quiet, safe. Everything here felt sharp, too bright. I never liked the cold, but now I would've given anything for the peace it brought, for a moment where things felt right.

Instead, I was stuck on a peeling leather couch in a stifling Vegas apartment, watching Eric flip through the channels with glazed eyes and one hand buried in a bag of chips.

I knew he was doing drugs again. All the signs were there. I could see it in the way his hand shook when he reached for the chips, the way he avoided my eyes when I looked too long. I didn't ask. Didn't want to know. But I could feel it, like I felt the heat pressing in from the broken air conditioner.

And, honestly, I couldn't even blame him. He didn't talk about where he spent all his time, what he was doing, but I knew without asking, that it weighed on him heavily.

"You wanna watch a movie?" he asked, not looking at me.

"Sure," I said, even though I didn't mean it. What I wanted was to go snowboarding. Skiing. Sledding. Build a fucking snowman.

He flipped past an old rom-com, a rerun of *Friends*, a commercial for something cheesy, and then…

"Wait." I leaned forward. "Go back."

He hesitated, flipping back a few channels. And there he was.

Grady.

Not a video, not a voice drifting through TikTok or someone's Instagram story. This was a news show, one of those national ones, complete with fake smiles and pre-scripted jokes. But Grady was real. He sat center stage, a guitar in his lap, the soft lights casting warm shadows over his face.

He looked older somehow. Not physically, though his hair was longer, brushing his shoulders. But it was like the weight of everything he'd been carrying showed more now. In the set of his shoulders. In his eyes.

He strummed the opening chords of *Addicted*, and I moved to the edge of the couch like I could get closer, like if I reached out, I could touch him again. One last time.

His voice filled the apartment; raw, aching, like the sound of someone who'd felt every inch of what he sang.

You kiss me like a dare I lost

And I take it, no matter the cost

You're in my lungs, I breathe you in

It hurts so good beneath my skin

I'm addicted, and I hate it
Tried to run but I can't shake it
You're a habit I don't wanna break
Every hit, another heartquake
Tried to numb it, but I feel it
Every look, I start to need it
You're the fire, I'm the flame
Burning up but I can't escape-
I'm addicted

Call me crazy, call me weak
But I still fall every time you speak
You've got that high I crave at night
I lost the fight, and that's all right

(Whoa-oh-oh)
You're the poison that I choose
(Whoa-oh-oh)
And I don't wanna lose
This twisted kind of truth-
I'm addicted to you

Eric said nothing, his thumb frozen on the remote.

When the song ended, the host leaned forward. "That's *Addicted*, the viral sensation written and performed by Grady Thomas. Grady, thank you for sharing that with us."

Grady smiled, modest and a little shy. "Thanks for having me."

"Did you ever imagine this song, *any* of your songs, would go viral like this?"

He shook his head. "Not even a little. I mean, I've always loved music. I sang in the choir when I was a kid, and then when I was seventeen, my foster mom, Mrs. Bryant, taught me to play the guitar. Music was always just... something I did to stay grounded."

The host nodded. "It's clearly personal. Especially *Addicted*. Is it about someone special?"

Grady didn't answer right away.

And when he did, his voice was softer. Lower.

"Yeah," he said. "It's about a woman who changed my life. She came into it like a storm, and I didn't stand a chance. She showed me how to live, how to love. How to stop being afraid."

The host's eyes lit up. "Are you still together?"

Grady looked up, right into the camera. Like he knew I was watching.

He shook his head. "No ma'am. She's the one who got away."

The words hit me harder than I expected. *The one who got away.* That's what he thought of me now? Just someone who slipped through his fingers? I couldn't breathe. His voice, the way he spoke about her... it was like I was being dragged back into everything I'd tried to outrun. The love we had, the mess we made of it, and now... hearing him talk like this, I couldn't ignore it anymore. I couldn't ignore how much I missed him.

He looked wrecked, even as he smiled through it.

"I didn't even know I could love someone like that. And I didn't know how to keep her when I had the chance."

The host said something else, something about whether he thought she'd hear this interview, but I wasn't listening anymore.

My fingers curled into the edge of the couch cushion, my chest suddenly felt too tight, like I'd been holding my breath for days and only just realized it.

Eric's voice broke through the fog of my thoughts. "You okay?"

His words were casual, but I could hear the hollow ring in them. I didn't answer. I couldn't. Not because I didn't hear him, but because I didn't know what to say. Not when I was still stuck on Grady's words, on the ache in my chest that hadn't gone away.

I didn't answer, I couldn't.

Because I wasn't, not really.

Because hearing Grady's voice, seeing him like that, knowing *I* was the one he was singing to... It unraveled something I'd been trying so hard to hold together.

And for the first time since I left Falcon Pointe, I let myself ask the one question I'd buried too deep to face:

What if I made the wrong choice? What if I'd been too scared to even try? The thought gnawed at me, something I'd kept at bay for so long. The thought of everything I lost in the chaos of my escape. It wasn't just about the snow. It was about Grady, about us, and the way we never got the chance to see what we could have been.

I wanted it to feel like home.

I really tried.

The small dining table was set with mismatched plates and cloth napkins I picked up from a thrift store. I borrowed a casserole dish from the elderly neighbor next door and somehow managed the rest. The turkey sat proudly in the center of the table, not perfect by any stretch, a little too brown on one side, but it was the first turkey I'd ever cooked, and most importantly, it was cooked through, or so the red button said when it popped. The rest of the table held mashed potatoes with gravy, stuffing, green bean casserole, cranberry sauce - from the can, and yams topped with marshmallows, just like my mom used to make.

It smelled like Thanksgiving. It looked like it too.

I even lit a candle that smelled like fall.

Eric didn't say much, just sat across from me, offering a faint smile that didn't quite reach his eyes. He looked tired. We both did.

I hated the distance that was growing between us, what Vegas was doing to us. I still couldn't find work, and he was stuck, working for Marco.

Maybe we should run away. Go somewhere he couldn't find us.

I tried broaching the subject before, but Eric always shut me down before I could say too much.

The silence stretched and swelled, thick and uncomfortable. I tried to break it with light talk - Christmas decorations, maybe putting up lights next week, possibly finding a fake tree. He nodded but didn't say much. His eyes kept drifting toward his plate like it held answers.

Halfway through dinner, he set down his fork, wiped his hands on the napkin, and looked up at me.

"Whit," he said, voice low, steady. "I don't think this is working."

I blinked. "What?"

"I love you," he said quickly, like it might cushion the blow. "I love you more than anything. But... I think we both know this isn't the life you want."

The words hit like a bucket of cold water.

"Eric," I said, trying to keep my voice from shaking, "what are you talking about? Of course I..."

"It's not what I want for you either," he cut in, gentle but firm. "I've been thinking about it for a while. Since before we left Utah."

I sat back, stunned. "Then why the hell did we come here?"

"Because I thought I could fix it. Thought I could fix *me.*" He let out a shaky breath. "But I can't. Marco's got his claws in deeper than I realized. And it's only getting worse."

I stared at him, my appetite gone.

He rubbed a hand over his face, avoiding my gaze. "You've been scared every day since we got here. I see it. You jump every time the door creaks. You check the locks twice before bed. I hate that. I hate what this life has done to you."

"I chose this," I said, maybe a little too sharply. "I chose *you.*"

"I know," he said. "But I wish you hadn't had to."

The silence that followed felt unbearable.

Then, quieter: "You looked at the TV the other night like your soul left your body."

My heart stalled.

He looked up, and for once, there was no edge to his voice. Just sadness. Understanding.

"Tell me about him."

I swallowed, hard, the words lodged in my throat like a stone. He didn't deserve this. He deserved the truth, but the truth felt like it would tear everything apart.

"His name's Grady. He's my brother's best friend. He left me with him in Falcon Pointe when he had to take care of something. He took care of me. He... he saw me. We got close."

Eric didn't flinch. He just nodded, like he already knew.

"Do you love him?"

I blinked, my pulse quickening. The question hit harder than I expected. A part of me wanted to deny it, to lie and say that no, I didn't love him. But I couldn't.

I wanted to tell Eric everything. I wanted to scream that it was *him*, that he was the one I was supposed to be with. But there was that pull in my chest, the undeniable truth of what I felt for Grady.

I swallowed again, the words scraping my throat. "I... I love you," I blurted, desperate, almost frantic. "I love *you*, Eric. I never wanted anything more than this, than us."

But the truth was, I couldn't lie about Grady. I felt it deep in my bones, and it ached.

"I love you," I repeated, but this time it felt hollow, like I was begging myself to believe it.

Eric's expression softened. He reached out to gently take my hand, his fingers trembling just slightly as he squeezed it. There was no anger in his gaze, only quiet understanding.

"I know," he whispered. "But you're not in love with me anymore. Not the way you used to be. And I can see it, Whit. You deserve more than this... than us."

I shook my head, refusing to let go of the hope that maybe, just maybe, he was wrong. "I don't deserve more. I..."

But he cut me off, his voice low but firm. "Yes, you do. Ever since we were kids, I wanted to give you the world, Whit," he whispered. "But I don't have a world left to give. Not anymore. And you... you should be free. You deserve a life that doesn't come with warnings and escape routes." He swallowed, glancing away for a moment. "I want that for you. More than anything."

I felt a lump rise in my throat. The words hit harder now, the truth sinking in deeper. But I couldn't stop myself. Not yet. Not when the pull between us was still so strong.

"I'm sorry," he whispered, his eyes brimming with unshed tears. "But I'm not the one for you anymore, Whit. You need to let go. For both of us."

I opened my mouth, but no words came out. I couldn't, because a part of me knew he was right. I had known it all along, even if I hadn't been ready to face it.

He stood slowly, and for the first time, I felt the finality in the way he looked at me. He walked around the table to me, knelt in front of me, and took my hands gently in his. His lips brushed softly over my knuckles, a tender kiss that felt like the end of everything we had been.

When he stood, he pressed a soft kiss to the top of my head, the kind of goodbye I had been dreading, but I hadn't known how much I needed.

"Thank you," he said quietly, his voice warm but broken. "Thank you for loving me. Even when I didn't deserve it."

And just like that, my heart broke again. Not the same way it did when I thought Grady betrayed me - when I thought he had let me down - but deep and quiet, like a goodbye I knew was coming long before it happened.

Chapter 44

Grady

It's been a week since *Good Morning Denver*.

A week since my face and my voice got broadcast into every living room in the Mountain West and half the damn country via rebroadcast on one of those national shows.

People don't just recognize me now, they *know* me. They know my story, or at least the curated version of it. The version where I'm the guy who grew up in foster homes and learned guitar from the woman who raised me like her own. The guy who fell in love with someone he couldn't keep. The guy who wrote a song about her and sang it like his whole soul depended on it.

And now they want more.

I finally gave in. Called Matt and Kyle with Redline Records. They were ecstatic when I said I'd do it, that I'd drive down to Denver and record "Addicted," maybe a couple of the others I've been working on in the quiet, late hours of the night.

The problem is, they want me there today, and they can't tell me how long it's gonna take.

I picked up my phone and dialed the one guy, besides Jackson, who I could always count on to help me out of a bind.

It only rang once before Steven answered, "Hey, what's up?

"I could really use a favor," I started. "The guys with Redline Records asked me to come down and record today. I could really use your help at the bar."

"Sorry man, no can do," he said, sounding distracted. "I've got plans."

"...Plans?" I shook my head. Steven was always down for an extra shift. He lived for the social scene at the bar, especially here lately with all the new faces that have been coming by to see the heartbreaker with a guitar. He's charming in that effortless, *I-wasn't-even-trying* kind of way, and I know he's scored more than a few dates since this all started.

But today?

"Yeah. Sorry, maybe Xander can help."

That's all he said before hanging up. I scratched the back of my head. Steven *never* turned down hours. Something about it made me feel like I missed a memo.

I called Xander next. He's been absolutely amazing, a real godsend at the bar. But he's also worked the past five nights in a row. He groaned as soon as he picked up, but when I told him why I needed his help, he changed his tune.

"Recording studio? Hell yeah, man. Go get it. I'll hold down the fort."

I could almost see the shit-eating grin on his face.

The studio was both intimidating and familiar, like walking into someone else's home and realizing it smelled like your own.

My guitar was slung across my back, the same one I'd played since I was seventeen, a gift from Mrs. Bryant.

Matt and Kyle greeted me with warm handshakes, then walked me through the sound booths, the mics, the process. It was more technical than I ever imagined, but when I sat down to play, the nerves faded.

I strummed a few bars of *Addicted*, slow and unpolished, just to get my bearings. The guitar felt foreign in my hands, like it didn't belong. This wasn't just a song anymore. This was *her*, this was *us*, and every note felt like it weighed a ton. I wanted to nail it; to prove I could do this. But when the lyrics came pouring out, they didn't feel like a performance. They felt like I was peeling back a part of myself I wasn't sure I wanted to share with anyone, let alone the world.

I played like she was right there in front of me, listening. Like she was hearing the words for the first time the way they were meant to be heard; not as a performance, but as a confession.

If she saw the interview, if she heard me... I hope she knows. I hope she *feels* it. I never betrayed her. I never stopped loving her.

When it was over, Matt and Kyle were grinning from ear to ear.

"Man, that was incredible," Matt said. "You got more like that?"

I shrugged, wiping my palms down the sides of my jeans. "I write when I feel something. Don't really do it on command."

They nodded like they understood, but I knew they didn't, not really.

They wanted hits.

I just wanted her.

The sun was already down when I got back to the bar. The place was busy but not slammed, the kind of night where the music hummed low and people leaned close across their drinks.

I pushed open the door, head down, already thinking about what needed to be done once I let Xander go. But then, I saw her. Whitney. It stopped me cold. For a second, I thought my mind was playing tricks on me. I almost wished it was. But there she was, really there, behind the counter like she belonged.

My heart kicked so hard I actually had to glance away, thinking it was a trick of the light. That maybe I conjured her up in my mind one too many times and it finally caught up with me.

But when I looked back... she was still there.

And god, was she beautiful.

The air felt thin. My pulse rushed like wind in my ears. The room felt smaller, tighter, as I moved toward her, afraid that if I blinked, she'd vanish. She didn't move, didn't look away. She just watched me, and for a moment, it was like the whole world fell away. It was just me and her. And everything we never stopped feeling. The ache, the desire, the *want* that had never really left.

Chapter 45

Whitney

I didn't think it would hurt this much.

Maybe I had fooled myself into thinking leaving would be easier. Maybe I thought the pull of the future would outweigh the weight of the past. But standing here, in front of Eric, with my heart breaking, it felt impossible to walk away. But I had to. I had to save myself. I just wished I didn't feel like I was leaving everything behind.

My bag was packed. Everything I owned stuffed into one worn-out backpack, the same one I'd carried from Utah to Vegas like it would carry me into a new life.

Eric stood beside me, hands shoved deep in his pockets, trying to be brave for both of us. "Are you sure about this?" he asked, his voice rough, eyes red-rimmed. "You can still change your mind. Tell me I'm being an idiot."

I shook my head, even as the ache in my chest screamed for me to stay. "I have to go."

He nodded once, then swallowed hard. "You were never meant for this life, Whit."

I leaned in, wrapping my arms around him and breathing in the smell of his jacket one last time. The comfort, the familiarity, the safety of what we had gone in an instant. I pressed my face into his neck, needing to feel him one last time, to feel what we once had before it was over.

"Neither were you," I whispered. "You were my first love, my best friend, my forever." The words felt heavy, like I was drowning in them. "Thank you. For loving me when I didn't love myself. For saving me."

He pulled back, tears in his eyes. "Go find the life you deserve."

I stepped onto the bus like my legs didn't belong to me, like I had left a part of myself behind. My heart splintered into a thousand little pieces, scattered across the floor, and I couldn't reach them. The seat felt too small, too far away from everything that had been my life. I curled into the corner, pulling Eric's hoodie over my head - the one thing I allowed myself to take from him, and let the tears come.

They weren't the kind of tears I was used to, the kind that came when I felt abandoned or unloved. These were different. These were slow, silent, and devastating. They came from somewhere deeper, somewhere I couldn't reach.

I cried for him. For us. For the man I left behind. For the man I might never get back. I cried for the version of me I no longer recognized, the girl who had loved him with everything she had and thought that love could keep them together, no matter the distance.

I had to leave. I knew I did. But why did it feel like I was breaking my own heart in the process?

The weight of everything settled on me in the stillness of the bus, and I realized, for the first time, that the woman who had clung to him, to this life, had to be left behind. I had to make space for the woman I was becoming. But what if that meant losing everything I used to be?

Eventually, sleep took me.

I woke to the rumble of the road and the soft murmur of strangers around me. My phone buzzed in my pocket. I pulled it out with trembling fingers and stared at the screen.

Eric: Let me know when you get there. That you're safe. I love you

Eric's message blinked back at me, its simplicity almost more painful than the words themselves. *I love you.* The same words he'd said so many times. They felt like a weight pressing down on my chest, making it harder to breathe. I wanted to call him, to hear his voice, but I didn't. I couldn't. Not when everything in me was telling me that this was the end.

Then I tapped on Steven's name.

I stared at the screen for a moment longer before I pressed the call button. My hand was shaking, and I wasn't sure if it was from the tears or the weight of what I'd just done. When Steven's voice cracked on the other end, it was like a lifeline thrown to me. It wasn't a solution, but it was something familiar. Someone who wouldn't ask too many questions. "Can you pick me up?" I asked, my voice barely above a whisper. "I'm at the bus station."

"I'll be right there."

The moment I saw him, the tears started again.

Steven opened his arms and I crashed into them like I hadn't just disappeared in the middle of the night months ago. Like I hadn't broken his heart too.

"I'm sorry," I sobbed. "I should've said goodbye. I should've explained."

He tightened his arms around me. "You're here now. That's all that matters."

I pulled back, swiping at my face. "God, I must look horrible," I laughed, tugging at the frayed edges of Eric's hoodie.

Steven grinned. "You look beautiful. Puffy eyes and all."

We walked out to his car, and as we drove, I asked about the bar, how business had been, if Jackson had gotten any less annoying... I *wanted* to ask about Grady, but I couldn't.

I was scared.

What if he hated me?

What if... what if...

Steven didn't bring him up and while part of me was grateful, another part of me wanted to scream.

Back at his apartment, I showered, washing Vegas from my skin. When I stepped out and looked in the mirror, I almost didn't recognize the girl staring back at me. She looked older. Braver. More certain of what she wanted.

Steven drove me to the bar just before the dinner crowd rolled in. My stomach was a mess of nerves, my palms sweaty as we pulled into the parking lot.

But the second I stepped through those doors, I knew I was home.

Jackson saw me first.

"Holy shit," he said, jaw dropping. "Are you...?"

I slapped his arm before he could say another word. "Don't make me cry or I'll ruin my makeup."

He laughed, pulling me into a hug. "You don't need it. You're perfect."

That *did* make me cry.

Then came some guy I didn't know. He eyed me like he could see everything I'd been through without me saying a word. He nodded, like something he'd been waiting on finally made sense.

"That's Xander, don't mind him," Jackson said, shaking his head.

I ducked into the bathroom, fixed my makeup the best I could, then stepped back out into the bar.

I wasn't there for more than five minutes when the door opened behind me.

And my whole world stopped.

I wasn't ready for this. My stomach twisted, my palms went clammy, and I realized just how much I'd been holding back. I hadn't thought about what this moment would feel like, standing here, facing him after everything. After all the time and all the distance, how could it still feel like this? I froze, not sure if I should run toward him or run away.

But then, I saw him.

Grady.

When our eyes met, it was like time stopped. It was like nothing had changed, and everything had changed. His chest was rising and falling in quick, shallow breaths, and his eyes, those eyes, were wide with disbelief. He stopped just a few feet away, like he wasn't sure if he should come closer or not. But then, as if the universe couldn't wait any longer, he closed the gap between us, his hands reaching for me like he was starved for something he hadn't been able to get. I didn't pull away.

And then... God. He kissed me. Hard, fast, like he was starving for it. For me. His lips crashed into mine, desperate and unrestrained. I melted into him, my hands fisting in his shirt, my body pressing against his as if I could collapse into him and never leave. His arms wrapped tight around my waist, grounding me in the reality of his touch. It was a kiss of hunger and healing. A kiss that felt like coming home.

When he finally pulled back, both our cheeks were flushed, our lips swollen, and the bar?

Cheering.

I wanted to laugh, to cry, to say something that made sense, but the only thing I could do was bury my face in his chest and hold onto him like I'd never let go.

"Hi," I whispered, my voice shaky, still trying to catch my breath.

"Hi," he said, breathless. "You came back."

And for the first time in what felt like forever, I let myself believe it was true. That we could actually be here. That this was real. But deep down, the same question still haunted me: Would I ever be able to have everything I wanted without losing myself in the process?

"I never really left," I murmured. "Not where it matters."

The applause slowly faded, but the feeling stayed, like the whole universe had conspired to pull us back together. I held tight to Grady, heart pounding like it was trying to memorize the rhythm of his breath, his presence.

He pulled back just enough to see my face, brushing his fingers over my cheek like he couldn't believe I was real.

"Everyone missed you," he whispered, and then with a playful smirk, added, "But not as much as me."

I smiled, cheeks still burning. Around us, the energy was electric. Familiar faces gathered close; Jackson clapped me on the back like a proud older brother, Steven hugged me again, and even Xander lifted his glass in a silent toast.

Grady laced his fingers through mine and tugged me toward the stage. "C'mon," he said with a glint in his eye. "They've been asking for an encore for weeks. Let's give 'em something good."

My stomach flipped. "What? No... Grady..."

But he was already pulling me up the steps, his guitar slung over one shoulder, dragging me into the spotlight.

He strummed a familiar intro, then turned to me, eyes sparkling.

"Holding On," he said. "Like old times."

My breath caught. That song...

He started first, his voice low and steady, the lyrics weighted with meaning. I joined in a beat later, my voice shaky at first, then strong, twining with his in a harmony that felt like coming home.

The crowd melted away. The noise disappeared. It was just him and me, two hearts finally back in sync.

The last note echoed through the bar like a promise. And when it faded, the room erupted.

Grady pulled me close again, forehead against mine, breathing hard. "That song doesn't sound right without you."

I swallowed, blinking back tears. "Neither does my life."

***

The ride to the house was wrapped in silence, but it wasn't empty. It was charged, thick with everything unspoken between us. His hand found mine across the console and didn't let go. I could feel the tremble in his fingers, the way he was holding himself together with every ounce of control he had left. The silence wasn't awkward, it was full of questions, of words we couldn't yet say.

When we walked inside, it felt like no time had passed at all, and yet, like everything had changed. He shut the door behind us, and we just stood there, looking at each other. I wanted to say something, anything to break the tension, but no words felt big enough.

His chest rose and fell with shallow breaths. I could feel the weight of every moment we'd spent apart pressing down on him, on both of us.

"I don't know how to do this," he said. His voice was tight, strained with the rawness of everything he was feeling. "I don't know how to be near you and not want every single part of you."

The words hit me harder than I expected, like they were pulling the breath right out of me. But I wasn't scared. Not anymore. I stepped in close, so close our bodies brushed, the contact sending a shock through me. "Then don't hold back."

That was all it took.

Grady's mouth was on mine before I could breathe, devouring me like he'd starved for months. And maybe he had. Maybe we both had. I kissed him back with everything I had, fingers threading into his hair, pulling him closer, needing to feel him, all of him, against me. His hands were everywhere - urgent, desperate, like he needed proof I was real.

We didn't fumble. We didn't hesitate.

Clothes disappeared in frantic, fevered movements. Tugged, dropped, forgotten. His hands roamed every inch of me like he was learning my body all over again, like he needed to remember every detail. Each touch, each kiss, was a promise, a vow that we weren't just reconnecting physically, but emotionally, too.

He walked me backwards to the bed, his lips tracing fire down my throat, across my collarbone, over the tops of my breasts. I gasped as we tumbled down together, skin to skin, breath to breath. The heat between us felt like it could burn us alive, but it was the kind of fire I needed.

When he settled over me, we paused for the barest second, our eyes locked, foreheads pressed together, hearts racing in sync.

"I thought I'd lost you," he whispered, his voice cracking with the weight of everything he was feeling.

"You didn't." I ran my fingers down his back, nails grazing the skin there, memorizing the feel of him. "I was lost... but I found my way back. To you."

He slid into me with a groan, slow and deep and devastating. My back arched, and my fingers dug into his shoulders. It wasn't just physical, it was soul-shaking. Like our bodies were speaking all the things our mouths couldn't.

Every thrust was a promise. Every kiss, a plea. He moved with raw need, like touching me could somehow undo the distance and time we'd spent apart. And God, I wanted it too. I wanted to erase every lonely night, every ache, every moment I'd doubted this love.

I held him close, legs wrapped around him, pulling him deeper. "I love you," I said, barely more than a breath, my voice shaking as the weight of it all finally hit me.

He stilled for just a second, then crushed his mouth to mine. "I love you. I never stopped."

Tears blurred my vision, falling as fast as my heart had when I thought we'd never find each other again. His lips found my cheeks, kissing them away like he couldn't stand seeing me cry. "You're everything," he murmured. "You're it. You always were."

Our rhythm shifted, slower but more intense. I could feel him everywhere - inside me, around me, under my skin. It was more than sex. It was surrender.

When release finally broke over me, it felt like falling apart and coming home at once. I clung to him, my name breaking on his lips as he followed me over the edge, trembling in my arms.

He didn't let go.

Even after, when we were tangled in the sheets, bodies slick with sweat, hearts still pounding, he held me like I was the most fragile thing he'd ever touched.

"I'm not going anywhere this time," I whispered, pressing a kiss to his chest.

His arms tightened around me, his voice a raw whisper against my hair. "Good. Because I couldn't survive losing you again."

I lay there, my body still humming from the electricity of him, of us. The air in the room had shifted, warmed by more than just the press of skin or the friction of need. Grady's fingers traced lazy circles on my back, his other arm cradling my head like he never wanted to let me go.

Neither of us spoke for a long time. We didn't need to. The silence between us was full, heavy with everything we hadn't said and everything we didn't have to. I closed my eyes, pressing my cheek to his chest, where his heartbeat thudded beneath my ear, steady and alive and real.

His lips brushed my forehead. "God, I missed you."

I felt it, the ache in his voice. The way it trembled just enough to make my throat tighten. I tilted my face to look at him. His eyes were soft, glassy even, the hard lines around them relaxed in a way I hadn't seen before.

"I thought about you every day," I whispered. "Even when I tried not to."

His hand cupped my cheek, and I leaned into it instinctively. "I kept looking for you in the crowd," he said. "Every time I sang that song, I hoped you'd somehow hear it."

"I did." My voice broke. "And it wrecked me."

His thumb brushed the tears away, his touch reverent. "You never ruined me, Whitney. You woke me up."

My breath caught. "I was so scared, Grady. I thought I'd lost you. I thought I didn't deserve you."

"Don't say that." He shifted, pulling me fully on top of him. His hands slid into my hair, holding me like I might vanish if he didn't. "You've always deserved everything good. Every single thing."

I kissed him again, slower this time. A kiss that was more than longing or lust. It was a vow. A question. A prayer.

He rolled us gently, his weight comforting as he kissed every freckle on my shoulder, every scar like it mattered. Like it meant something.

"I don't want to run anymore," I whispered into the dark.

"Then don't," he said, his breath dusting against my collarbone. "Stay with me. Let's figure it out. One day at a time."

And I knew, as he pulled the covers around us and held me tight to his chest, that I already had.

I was home.

The first thing I noticed was the light - soft and golden, spilling through the bedroom window in hazy ribbons. The second was the weight of Grady's arm, draped protectively across my waist, anchoring me to him, to this moment.

For a while, I didn't move. Just listened. His breathing was slow and even, his chest rising and falling against my back. I'd never felt safer, never felt surer that I was exactly where I was supposed to be.

My phone buzzed on the nightstand, a quiet vibration that pulled me gently from the haze of sleep. I turned, careful not to disturb him, and reached for it. One missed call. A text from Eric.

> **Eric:** You okay? Just want to know you made it

My chest ached as I stared at Eric's message. Guilt gnawed at me, but I knew I had to let go of the past. I had to stop living in the shadows of the choices I'd made and start looking toward the future. The past would always be a part of me, but it couldn't define me anymore. I typed back slowly, my fingers hovering over the keys before I finally hit send. And in that moment, something inside me clicked. I was finally letting go.

> **Me:** I'm safe. I'm okay. I promise. Thank you for everything. I hope you find peace, Eric. You deserve it

I stared at the message a long time before hitting send. When I finally set the phone down, I felt the bed shift behind me. Grady's arm tightened around my waist, and his voice was low, still rough with sleep.

"Everything okay?"

I nodded before turning to face him. "I just needed to let Eric know I'm safe."

Grady propped himself up on one elbow, his brows pulling together. "You don't have to explain. I get it."

I studied him - his tousled hair, the warmth in his tired eyes. I reached up and traced the line of his jaw, needing to say something I hadn't yet found the words for.

"I never stopped loving you, Grady."

He exhaled sharply, like those words had been locked inside him too. "Whit..." He brushed his knuckles along my cheek. "There's something I need to say. About Emily."

I stiffened slightly but didn't pull away.

"She showed up at the bar that night. I was drunk. Stupid drunk, and she climbed into my lap. I didn't even realize what was happening until I saw her text after you were gone." His jaw tensed as he spoke, like the words were ripping something open inside him. "I never wanted her, Whitney. I swear to you. I didn't even realize what was happening until it was too late. But nothing happened. I wanted you. I've *always* wanted you." His eyes were pleading with me, searching for some kind of reassurance I wasn't sure I could give. But when I looked at him, I saw the truth. The vulnerability in his eyes. The ache of everything we'd been through together.

And all the pain I'd been holding onto began to melt away.

"I believe you," I said softly. "I think I knew, deep down. I just... didn't know how to handle everything."

He nodded, swallowing hard. "Neither did I."

For a long moment, we just held each other. No past, no pain. Just presence.

I leaned in, the space between us vanishing in a heartbeat. Our lips met softly, without urgency, without heat. Just love. Just the kind of love that speaks without words. The kind that says everything we hadn't said yet, the forgiveness, the trust, the healing. It wasn't just a kiss. It was a promise that everything was going to be okay.

When we finally pulled apart, Grady tucked a strand of hair behind my ear. "So... what now?"

I smiled. "Now? We start over. We live. We heal. Together."

He grinned, that crooked smile that always made my heart flutter. "I like the sound of that."

Outside, a new day stretched wide and waiting. But inside this little room, with Grady beside me, with our hearts beating in sync, I knew we already had everything we needed. We had each other. And that was more than enough to begin again.

Epilogue

Grady

One Year later

If someone had told me a year ago that I'd be here, hand in hand with the love of my life, about to record a duet with her and waiting on our baby any day now, I'd have laughed them out of the bar.

And yet here I am. And I've never felt more like myself.

Whitney's fingers are laced with mine as we walk into the studio, her free hand cradling the curve of her belly. She's all glow and grit, her hair pulled up in a loose knot, a soft smile on her face even as she waddles just a little from the weight of nearly nine months.

"You good?" I ask, pushing open the studio door for her.

She smirks. "Grady, I'm pregnant, not fragile."

"Right, but if you go into labor while we're tracking vocals, I'm not above delivering this baby myself on a pile of soundproof foam."

She rolls her eyes, but she's laughing, and God, I'll never get tired of that sound.

Inside, Matt and Kyle greet us like old friends. They've been helping me piece together what's slowly becoming a full album. I never thought I'd say those words out loud. A full album. My name on it. Our story in every chord.

The funny thing is, the more I've shared with the world, the more I've found pieces of myself I thought I'd lost.

Music was always therapy, but now, it's more than that. It's *ours*. Whitney and I sing together in the evenings sometimes, even when it's just her and me and the quiet hum of the dishwasher back home. It's like the best parts of us were made to harmonize.

Today's track is the last one we need to finish before the album is ready. It's a duet, something intimate and raw, about second chances, and showing up when it matters most.

We take our places, headphones on, her voice warm and low in my ears as we rehearse a few lines. I watch her sing; how she closes her eyes, how her hand rests on her belly like she's already introducing the baby to music.

And in that moment, I'm floored.

By her.

By this life.

By how damn lucky I am.

As I watch her, I can't help but think about how far we've come, from the fear of losing each other, to finding our way back. This song we're about to record, this new life we're building together, they're both proof that the road we've walked was worth every step.

After we wrap the session and pack up, I help her into the truck and steal a quick kiss before we head back to Falcon Pointe. She leans into me like it's the most natural thing in the world, because it is.

The Hideaway is waiting for us. Jackson's been texting updates nonstop about the stage extension. With Whitney's help, we've been slowly transforming it from a local watering hole into something bigger, a place where people can really feel the music. We've got plans to book full bands, maybe even bring in a few tour stops from Denver. It's still our bar, but now it's something more. Something that feels like home for more than just us.

As we pull into town, the sun dipping behind the foothills, Whitney grabs my hand again.

"You realize everything's about to change, right?"

I glance over, grinning. "Yeah. But for the first time... it doesn't scare me."

She squeezes my hand. "Me neither."

I don't know what the future holds, not exactly. But I know this: with her by my side, a guitar in my hand, and a baby on the way... I've already got everything I need.

And as the stars scatter like confetti across the Falcon Pointe sky, Whitney leans her head on my shoulder.

This life - the noise and the quiet, the love and the ache, the baby kicking between us and the future we're building brick by brick, it's nothing like I imagined.

It's better.

Because no matter how far we fell, how lost we got, how hard we fought to let go... we always came back.

To the song.

To each other.

To the kind of love you don't just feel. You crave.

Maybe it's not perfect.

But it's real.

And I'm not just in love with her.

I'm addicted.

Addicted

[Verse 1]
Told myself I wouldn't feel a thing
You walked in, and I broke that rule again
Your laugh hits harder than a heartbreak song
Now I'm caught, and it's been way too long

[Pre-Chorus]
I swore I'd never play the fool
But here I am, breaking every rule
You're in my veins like gasoline
And I light the match - yeah, that's on me

[Chorus]
I'm addicted, and I hate it
Tried to run but I can't shake it
You're a habit I don't wanna break
Every hit, another heartquake
Tried to numb it, but I feel it
Every look, I start to need it
You're the fire, I'm the flame
Burning up but I can't escape-

I'm addicted

[Verse 2]
You're chaos dressed up in control
Every word digs deeper in my soul
Told my friends I'm good, I'm fine
But they see the wreck behind my smile in time

[Pre-Chorus]
You kiss me like a dare I lost
And I take it, no matter the cost
You're in my lungs, I breathe you in
It hurts so good beneath my skin

[Chorus]
I'm addicted, and I hate it
Tried to run but I can't shake it
You're a habit I don't wanna break
Every hit, another heartquake
Tried to numb it, but I feel it
Every look, I start to need it
You're the fire, I'm the flame
Burning up but I can't escape-
I'm addicted

[Bridge]
Call me crazy, call me weak
But I still fall every time you speak
You've got that high I crave at night
I lost the fight, and that's all right

[Breakdown]
(Whoa-oh-oh)
You're the poison that I choose
(Whoa-oh-oh)
And I don't wanna lose
This twisted kind of truth-
I'm addicted to you

[Final Chorus]
I'm addicted, and I hate it
But you're the drug and I can't fake it
You're a storm I'll never tame
But I'd still dance in all your rain
Tried to run but I'm not leaving
You're the scar I keep believing
You're the fire, I'm the flame
Burning up and I won't escape-
I'm addicted

Foster Care & Ways to Help

Foster care is a critical system designed to protect children, but the reality is that many kids in the system face significant challenges. Here are just a few:

- In 2020, more than 400,000 children were in foster care in the United States.

- On average, children in foster care are moved between 3 or more foster homes. This instability can lead to trauma, attachment issues, and difficulty forming lasting relationships.

- Only 50% of foster youth graduate from high school, and even fewer pursue higher education. Many foster children experience disruptions in their schooling, making it harder to keep up academically and emotionally.

- Foster children often experience emotional and psychological distress, due to the trauma of abuse, neglect, and instability. These children are at higher risk for mental health issues such as anxiety, depression, and PTSD.

- Many children in foster care have limited access to mental health services, tutoring, and extracurricular activities. The lack of these resources can make it harder for them to heal, grow, and thrive.

- Unfortunately, children in foster care are at greater risk of experiencing further abuse or neglect due to the instability of their placements. This can result in long-term psychological and emotional damage.

- Every year, 20,000+ children in foster care "age out" at 18 without a permanent family. These youth often face significant challenges in securing housing, education, and employment, and are at increased risk for homelessness.

How You Can Help

There are many ways to make a difference in the lives of children in foster care. Here are just a few ideas to get you started:

- Become a Foster Parent:
  Foster parents provide a safe and loving home for children in need. By offering a stable environment, you can help change the trajectory of a child's life. To learn more about becoming a foster parent, visit The National Foster Parent Association.

- Mentor a Foster Youth:
  Many organizations offer programs to mentor children and youth in foster care. Big Brothers Big Sisters and CASA (Court Appointed Special Advocates) are two organizations that provide mentorship programs for foster children, helping them succeed academically and emotionally.
  Visit CASA or Big Brothers Big Sisters to find local mentoring opportunities.

- Volunteer at Foster Care Organizations:

  Foster care agencies need volunteers to assist with various tasks such as tutoring, organizing events, and providing emotional support. Volunteer your time to help make a difference in a child's life.

  Consider volunteering with organizations like Foster Care to Success or your local foster care programs.

- Donate to Foster Care Charities:

  Many foster care organizations rely on donations to provide essential resources like clothing, school supplies, and holiday gifts for children in care. Donations can also go toward programs that support the emotional and mental health of foster children.

  You can donate to organizations like The Dave Thomas Foundation for Adoption or Foster Care to Success.

- Advocate for Foster Care Reform:

  Advocate for better support systems for children in foster care. Contact your state representatives to push for reforms that focus on mental health services, educational support, and reducing the instability that children face while in care.

- Support Foster Youth Aging Out:

  Children who age out of the foster care system at 18 often face overwhelming challenges. You can help by supporting programs that assist with housing, job placement, and higher education for these young adults.

  Consider donating or volunteering with organizations that support youth aging out of foster care, like Foster Youth in Action.

Resources

- National Foster Parent Association (NFPA): https://nfpaonline.org

- Foster Care to Success: https://www.fostercare2success.org

- Court Appointed Special Advocates (CASA): https://www.casaforchildren.org

- Big Brothers Big Sisters: https://www.bbbs.org

- The Dave Thomas Foundation for Adoption: https://www.davethomasfoundation.org

- Foster Youth in Action: https://www.fosteryouthaction.org

Final Words:

Every child in the foster care system deserves a chance to thrive, whether through a stable home, mentorship, or just knowing they have someone in their corner. If Grady and Whitney's story touched you, and if you believe in the power of second chances, I encourage you to get involved and help make a real difference. You can be the person who changes the future for a child who needs it most.

Thank you for caring. Together, we can create lasting change.

Acknowledgements

First and foremost, I want to thank you, the reader, for picking up this book and taking the time to dive into Grady and Whitney's journey. Your support means the world to me, and I hope their story resonated with you in some meaningful way.

To the friends I grew up with in the foster care system, your strength, resilience, and unbreakable spirit are a constant source of inspiration. Your experiences and the lessons we learned together are deeply woven into the fabric of this book. Thank you for showing me the power of survival, connection, and the possibility of healing.

To my friends and family, thank you for your unwavering support and encouragement. Whether you believed in me from the beginning or gave me a push when I needed it most, your love and faith have been a constant source of strength. This book wouldn't have been possible without you.

A special thank you to pastors Jim Burgen and Scott Nickel, whose teachings have profoundly shaped my understanding of Christianity and what it should be. Your wisdom, kindness, and commitment to living authentically have inspired me in more ways than I can express.

This book is a reflection of all of you. Thank you for being a part of this journey.

With gratitude,

Jennifer Harrison

About the Author

What happens when your inner child "forgets" to choose a career? Suddenly, the princess, doctor, lawyer, and mechanic all come looking for their piece. Without a cloning machine, what's a girl to do?

Write.

As a writer, I live vicariously through the characters I create and the stories they tell. Every day is an adventure to be had, and if I can't do it myself, I'm going to put my daydreams to work.

9 7989 9 1 1 3 1 5 3 7